DARK
WATERS

Mary-Jane Riley is a former BBC talk show presenter and journalist. She has covered many life-affirming stories, but also some of the darkest events of the last two decades. Mary-Jane is married with three children and two dogs and lives in rural Suffolk. *Dark Waters* is her third novel set in East Anglia and featuring journalist Alex Devlin.

Also by Mary-Jane Riley

The Bad Things
After She Fell

DARK WATERS

MARY-JANE RILEY

KILLER READS

KillerReads
an imprint of HarperCollins*Publishers* Ltd
1 London Bridge Street
London SE1 9GF

www.harpercollins.co.uk

This paperback edition 2018

First published in Great Britain in ebook format by HarperCollins*Publishers* 2018

A catalogue record for this book
is available from the British Library

ISBN: 978-0-00-828511-1

Set in Minion by
Palimpsest Book Production Limited, Falkirk, Stirlingshire

Printed and bound by CPI Group (UK) Ltd, Croydon, CR0 4YY

MIX
Paper from
responsible sources
FSC™ C007454

This book is produced from independently certified FSC™ paper
to ensure responsible forest management.

For more information visit: www.harpercollins.co.uk/green

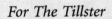

For The Tillster

The Norfolk Broads – a haven of peace and tranquility simply waiting to be discovered and explored. And a boating holiday on the Broads opens up a world of beauty, cruising through reed marshes, woodland and meadow. Find hidden waterways teeming with wildlife. Moor close to welcoming riverside pubs, quaint villages, and market towns. Choose a Harper's Holidays cruiser and start unwinding today!

Three Weeks Earlier

Decomposition sets in.

First, both hearts stop beating and the cells and tissues are starved of oxygen. The brain cells are the first to die – all that 'being' ended.

Blood drains from the capillaries, pooling in lower-lying parts of the body, staining the skin black. Rigor mortis has been and gone by now, the muscles becoming stiff three hours after death, but within seventy-two hours rigor mortis has subsided. The bodies are cool. They are pliable again.

As the cells die, bacteria begins to break them down. Enzymes in the pancreas cause each organ in each of the bodies to digest itself. Large blisters appear all over the bodies. Green slime oozes from decomposing tissue, and methane and hydrogen sulphide fill the air. Bloody froth trickles from the mouths and noses.

And all this time the insects are enjoying themselves. One fly can lay three hundred eggs on one corpse, and they will hatch within twenty-four hours. The hatching maggots use hooks in their mouths to scoop up any liquid seeping from the bodies. They are efficient, these maggots. Their breathing mechanism is located on the opposite end to their mouths so they can breathe and eat at the same time.

Within a day the maggots reach the second stage of their lives and burrow into the putrefying flesh.

The pleasure cruiser has been tied to the wooden mooring post on Poppy Island for at least three days. There has been no movement. The curtains are drawn. The doors and windows are closed. Somebody will find them soon.

1

Gary Lodge and his wife, Ronnie, both noticed the boat as they motored past the island on the second day of their holiday. It looked brand new, its white paintwork gleaming in the sunshine. Although it was the middle of the day, the curtains were closed. They didn't remark on it to each other, though – Gary thought the people on board had probably been on the razz the night before (though when he thought about it later he realized there was no pub on the island and no way off it except by boat). Ronnie thought it was a case of daytime nookie; though, if it had been her, she would have left the curtains open.

Three days later, the Lodges, after lazy days of boating, drinking and sweaty sex, travelled back down the Broads.

'Isn't that the same boat?' said Gary.

'As what?' Ronnie was enjoying the cool breeze on her face.

'You know. As when we came by the other day. It had its curtains closed then. Still does.'

Ronnie smiled, put her arms around Gary and nuzzled into the crook of his neck. 'Probably, babes. I don't know. We've had a good time though, haven't we?' She didn't want to think about other people, she wanted to keep hold of this loving feeling she had towards Gary – all too rare during their mundane everyday life that seemed to be filled with work and just getting by.

But Gary didn't react to Ronnie's amorous advances. He started to turn the wheel of the boat.

She looked up. 'What are you doing now?'

'Just want to have a look,' he said, guiding the boat across the water and behind the other cruiser. 'Tie her up, will you?'

Ronnie frowned. The loving feeling evaporating into thin air. She wanted to tell him to jump off the boat and tie the frigging thing up himself. He'd thought himself some sort of Captain Birdseye, but without the beard, the whole bloody holiday. But she didn't say anything. She swallowed her irritation, sighed, grabbed the rope and jumped out onto the bank. That was one thing she wouldn't miss: all this jumping on and off.

'Okay,' she called when she was done.

'Done the right knot?'

Same question every time. 'Yep.'

Gary stepped on to the bank, then hesitated.

'What now?' said Ronnie, hands on hips, scowling.

Gary rubbed his hand around his mouth. 'I dunno.'

'They've probably left it and gone somewhere. Done a runner or something. Come on, let's get back on our boat. We've gotta get it back to the yard. I don't want to be caught up with loads of traffic on the A12.' She turned away from him and began fiddling with the rope.

'It doesn't …' Gary hesitated. 'It doesn't feel right.' He sniffed the air. 'It smells funny.'

Ronnie sniffed too. 'That's just the countryside, isn't it?'

Gary put a foot on the other boat and knocked on the sliding canopy. 'Hello? Anybody there?' He glanced at Ronnie, then tried the door. It was stuck.

He knocked again, and frowned. 'I'm just gonna—'

'Gary. I think you should leave it.' He was bound to make a mess of things and then they'd be in trouble. And she wanted to get out of there. Pronto.

Too late. Gary tugged at the door. It slid open. He stuck his head inside.

'Ronnie, it smells minging in here.'

His voice, thought Ronnie, was wavering, as if he was scared, and all at once she was worried. 'Perhaps you shouldn't go in, Gary.' She shivered and looked around. Goosebumps. Why had she got goosebumps? There was nothing but water and sky and flowers and green stuff. Too much green; she preferred the concrete blocks of home. 'Gary, come on, let's go. We'll tell that lot at the boatyard when we get back. Let them come out and deal with it.'

But Gary had already stepped inside.

Twenty seconds later he stumbled out, fell off the boat, and threw up in the grass.

2

Afterwards, Alex Devlin would associate the music of Wagner with the time her relatively settled life began to slip from her control.

The day hadn't started well, beginning with a disjointed conversation with her parents, just as she wrote the last sentence of her most recent article for *The Post*.

'Your father would like to see you, Alex,' her mother said, her tone mildly censorious.

Guilt immediately corkscrewed through her. 'I know, Mum, I will come.'

'When though? You always say you're going to visit and then you don't. Here's your father. Talk to him.'

There was the muffled sound of the phone being handed over.

'Who is this?' Her father's once mellow voice now reedy.

Alex clutched her phone tightly. 'Alex. Your daughter.'

'Oh yes, Alex.' He paused, and Alex could almost hear the effort he was making to form the right words. 'When are you coming? Your mother says you haven't been.' Another pause. 'For a long time,' he finished.

'I'm—'

'You like balloon animals.'

She closed her eyes, hearing the note of anxiety in his voice. The making of animals out of balloons had been one of those things that they had done together when she was young, just her and him. It used to make her laugh.

'I'll make some for when you come round.'

Alex's throat was blocked. The time for her father to make balloon animals had passed long ago.

'The weather's been nice.' It was her mother again.

'I'll come over,' said Alex, knowing she must.

'Can you make it later? This afternoon some time?'

'Of course.' She looked out of her study window, and could just about see the sun glinting on the water of Sole Bay.

'Thank you.' Her mother put the phone down.

Her plan had been to spend the rest of the morning and the afternoon on the beach after having been immersed in the world of extreme couponing for the last few days. (Spend hours scouring the Internet! Browse newspapers and magazines and cut out vouchers! Organize your vouchers in folders and ring binders! Keep your vouchers handy in your purse!) Not exactly stretching the brain but it did at least help pay the bills. And gave her tips on how to save money at the supermarket, which was particularly appropriate as she was going to have to fill the fridge with food for Gus who was coming to stay with her in Suffolk. How was it that she spent a fortune in the supermarket (vouchers or no vouchers) and the food she bought was all gone in an instant as soon as her son turned up? Locusts could learn a lot from him, she thought. Still, it was going to be lovely to see him. It had been a long time. And thank God she'd finished that wretched article, and had sent it away with the press of a button. Couponing. Channel 4's Cathy Newman she was not.

She sighed. It had to be done. No, she wanted to do it. God knew life had been hard enough for her mum and dad, what with having to cope with her sister, Sasha, as a troubled teenager – unsuitable boyfriends, self-harming, all spit and fire. Alex had done as much as she could, although she hadn't been a model daughter either.

But it was so hard to see her once gentle father slowly turning into someone else. Early-onset dementia, they called it. A miserable twist of fate, she called it. And because she had found it hard, she had not given her mum as much support as she should have done. Her excuses had been her work, visiting Sasha in the mental health unit – anything, really. But it wasn't good enough.

She looked out of the window of her study. The sun and the promise of the kiss of warm early summer air on her skin beckoned. An hour? Maybe half? To recharge her batteries, that was all. Then she would go and see her parents. She pushed back her chair and went to fetch a towel.

Alex settled on the sand, finding a comfortable spot where there weren't any pebbles sticking into her skin. She was sheltered from the worst of the sharp sea breeze by the dunes.

The sun was warm on her face. She closed her eyes, feeling drowsy. A few more minutes she thought, though it was becoming more difficult to ignore the creeping guilt.

In the background, she heard the sea dragging on the shingle at the shoreline, mingling with the insistent barking of a dog, and children playing a game of volleyball on the beach.

'It's my serve,' said a girl.

'No, it's not, it's mine.' A boy's voice, younger. Brother perhaps? A sigh. 'Go on then.'

Thwack! The sound of the ball being hit.

'Yesss!'

'Oh.' This from the girl. 'Shall we call it a draw?' she said.

'No, you lost,' said the boy.

Alex smiled. Kids arguing. Fine when they weren't your own. She sat up and then leaned back on her elbows. A few hardy souls were trying to swim in the North Sea, their screams testament to how cold it was. A dragon kite was flying high above her. She was trying to clear her head – be mindful, as some yoga teacher had once told her – trying to think of nothing.

'Ride of the Valkyries' boomed out from her bag. Her phone.

For a brief moment she considered not answering it. But it could be anything – Gus finally telling her what time he was arriving (what was it about children that they didn't realize you had a life, too, and to be able to organize it was helpful?), or (please God, no) something more to do with her sister, or maybe someone offering her work.

She sighed and rolled across to her bag, fishing inside until her fingers made contact with the hard case. She squinted at the screen, but the sun was reflecting off the sand and she couldn't see a thing.

'Hello?'

'Alex Devlin?'

She didn't recognize the voice, but all sorts of people had her number – it was how she often got commissions. 'Yes, hello.' She had her friendly I-can-do-work-for-you voice on.

'I was wondering if you could help me.' The voice was smooth.

'I'll try.' She kept a smile in her voice.

'It's about your sister, Sasha Clements.'

Alex froze. 'Who is this please?'

'My name's Penny, and I wondered what your reaction was to her being released from Leacher's House?'

'None of your bloody business.' She stabbed at the screen and thrust the phone back in her bag.

She lay back on the sand, a knot of irritation tying itself up inside her stomach. And so it starts, she thought, all over again. Of course journos would want the story, want to rake over the events surrounding the killings for which her sister had been responsible.

And now Sasha was returning to society and Alex was to look after her. It was a chance to do more for her sister.

She was dreading it. And trying not to think about an email

she'd received that morning about Sasha. It had to be a mistake, though, surely? Push it out of your mind, she told herself. Don't worry about it now. Deal with it later.

'Ride of the Valkyries' again. She snatched up the phone, any pleasure leaching out of the day. 'Go away, I don't want to speak to you.'

'Is that you, Alex?' Uncertainty clouded her mother's voice.

Alex suppressed a sigh and forced a smile onto her face. 'Mum. Sorry. I thought it was a … never mind.' Any mention of journalists or newspapers would send her mother into a right state. 'I'll be leaving soon,' she said.

'I was wondering if you could you go via Great Yarmouth and go to that Greek shop? I thought your dad might like some of the Greek tagliatelle he loves. And a pound of those special smoked sausages.'

Alex's heart twisted. Her mother was trying so hard, but her father wouldn't be in the least bit bothered what pasta or sausage he ate, not these days. And Great Yarmouth was hardly on the way to her parents – more like a bloody great detour. Still, her mum didn't ask for much.

'Of course I will,' she said.

3

The road out of Great Yarmouth was slow, and Alex tuned her radio to the local station in time for the news on the top of the hour as she drove.

'Two bodies have been found on a boat on Dillingham Broad in Norfolk, police have said,' intoned the newsreader. 'We'll bring you more news as we get it.'

Her ears pricked up. Two bodies on a boat. Who? Why? 'Come on, give us some more,' she muttered, her journalistic instincts cutting in. She turned up the volume, as if that would entice the newsreader to give her some more interesting facts. Instead all she got was a story about a leisure centre being built on the edge of a Norfolk village and how Anglo-Saxon finds had been made at a wind farm site in Suffolk.

Only the bare facts then. Not even 'Police are treating the deaths as unexplained'. Hmm. But then Norfolk Police were known for being cautious – only a few years before a couple had been found battered to death in their home but local coppers refused to say it was murder until all the 'i's had been dotted and all the 't's crossed. Caution was probably a good thing, but it could go too far.

She glanced at her watch. Her mother wasn't expecting her at any particular time, and a little detour to Dillingham wouldn't take her that long. The story might be something and nothing. Or it could be interesting.

There was only one way to find out.

The countryside became ever more flat as she neared the Broads. The rivers and lakes of the Norfolk and Suffolk Broads had been formed by the flooding of medieval peat excavations that had provided fuel to Norwich and Great Yarmouth. She'd learned that somewhere. School, maybe? Or perhaps she had read it in a Sunday supplement. Today the watery landscape was home to a myriad of boats and yachts and old wherries and was a magnet for tourists wanting a relaxing holiday. The two on the boat, whoever they were, had certainly found relaxation – permanently.

She turned down the road that led to Dillingham Broad. It was lined with trees and very comfortable-looking houses with gardens that no doubt went down to the water. What sort of price they would go for she couldn't imagine. Nothing she could afford, that was for sure. A few minutes later she reached the end of the road and pulled up on the staithe.

A small knot of people was gathered on the concrete apron looking into the distance. She recognized a couple of bored-looking journalists from the local papers and gave them a nod. A lone fisherman sat on his collapsible chair under a large green umbrella at the edge of the water, a rucksack on the ground next to him. He appeared unperturbed about the goings on around him. Alex shooed away the ducks and geese that came waddling towards her in the hope of food and, shielding her eyes with her hand, peered across the water to a line of trees that were almost in full leaf, and to the two boats moored up against the bank on Poppy Island. Figures in white suits and masks were looking busy around the boats. Forensic officers, she thought. Probably the pathologist was there too. She wondered how long the bodies had been on board and what state they were in now.

'The poor sod that found 'em won't forget his holiday in a hurry.'

Alex turned towards the voice with its distinctive Norfolk lilt. 'Oh?'

The man had the tanned and weathered face of someone who'd worked on the water all his life and was probably younger than his leathery skin implied. He wore jeans that were slightly too tight for his stomach and a tee shirt designed to show off his biceps. A cigarette dangled from the corner of his mouth.

He shook his head. 'One of my boats, wasn't it? Firefly Lady. And one of my customers who stopped to see what was what. Found the bodies. Or what was left of them. Then he came to tell me. I asked him why he hadn't called the police and all he could do was look at me, couldn't say anything. Shaking he were.' He pinched the cigarette between his thumb and forefinger and drew the smoke deep into his lungs. 'So I called 'em. Gave the poor sod some brandy.' He nodded towards the police boat. 'Now they're all over there, aren't they? Coastguard, fire, police. Overkill, if you ask me.'

'Where is the "poor sod" now?' asked Alex.

'Jim here said he's being given hot tea. So's his wife. Bloody tea. I ask you, what use is that? And he's being kept away from everybody.'

'Aye.' This from Jim. 'A bad business.'

A satellite truck rolled up, and a reporter looking like an eager young puppy jumped out.

'Vultures,' said the boat man.

'Aye,' said Jim, nodding before he spat a blob of green phlegm onto the ground. The ducks and geese waddled over again, looking eager.

'Not nice for you being involved in all this,' said Alex, trying not to look at the green slime near her feet. 'My name's Alex, by the way.'

'Colin,' said the boat man. 'Colin Harper. Of Harper's Holidays.'

He gestured towards Jim. 'And that's Jim. And it's a bad business and bad for business.' He shook his head before drawing on his cigarette.

'I gather there were two people on board. That's what the radio said. A man and his wife, wasn't it?' asked Alex nonchalantly fishing for information, still looking over the water.

Colin shook his head and threw the stub of his cigarette onto the ground, grinding it under his heel. 'They might be a couple but it ain't a man and his wife.' He chuckled. 'One of them was someone from London, young Eddie told me.'

'Eddie?'

'Copper. I've known him since he was knee-high to a grass-hopper. Little sod. Said the stink was like nothing he'd ever smelt. Them bodies had been there for at least three days. Humming, it must have been.'

Alex winced. It had been unseasonably warm over the last few days. 'Three days.' She whistled. 'Wow.'

'Yup. That's when I hired the boat out. They didn't get very far, did they?'

'And the other one?' she asked.

'Other one what?'

Alex damped down her impatience. 'Body. The other body. You said one was from London. What about the other one? Was it a man or a woman?'

Colin turned slowly and looked at her. 'Why you so interested then?'

Alex shrugged. 'I'm from round here.' *Almost.* 'Like to know what's going on in my back yard.'

'Well the coppers said I wasn't to talk to anybody until I'd given a proper statement.' He puffed out his chest. 'So I shouldn't be talking to you.'

'Fair enough,' said Alex. She stared out over the water again. The silence didn't last long.

'It were two men,' said Colin. 'Dead on my boat. The one from

15

London was supposed to be someone well known. I didn't recognize the name. Probably some reality show type. I dunno. The other from over the border. Suffolk,' he added, as if Alex wouldn't understand what he meant.

A well-known man found dead on a boat. That could be some story. 'So,' said Alex, knowing she had to tread carefully, 'what was the name? Of the man from London?'

'Who wants to know?'

'Only wondering.'

More silence, though this time Colin obviously didn't feel inclined to fill it.

'Now you've got to clean the boat up,' Alex added eventually, in a sympathetic tone.

'Too right. Clean it up meself. I can't ask the staff; there'd be a mass walk-out if I did.' He gave a mock shudder. 'Won't be pleasant. Can you imagine the stink?'

No, she couldn't. And she wouldn't want to be the next holidaymaker to hire it. Colin would probably be best to change its name. Though there would be some ghoulish enough to want to holiday on the actual boat where people had died.

'Which one of them hired the boat?'

Colin frowned. 'Coppers want me to check that. I think it was done, you know, online. I don't have a lot to do with that side of the business. I'm more hands-on.' He sighed as he pulled a crumpled packet of cigarettes out of his pocket and peered into it. 'Bugger.' He screwed up the packet and shoved it back in his pocket.

'Here.' Alex pulled a packet out of her bag and offered him one.

'Ta, love,' he said, brushing her fingers as he took one, then lit it.

Alex put the packet back in her bag, glad she kept some cigarettes for times like these. 'Can you remember a name or names? You know, who was booked on the boat?'

'Nah, not offhand.' He looked at her suspiciously. 'You ask a lot of questions.'

Alex shrugged. 'You've got to ask or you never find out.'

Colin grinned. 'Too right, gel.' He blew out a stream of smoke. Shook his head. 'But I can't rightly remember. I leave it up to the girls in the office to do the paperwork. Me, I like messing about with the boats when I can. Less trouble than people.' He shrugged. 'They're back in the office anyhow. Names, I mean.' He looked her up and down, a sly grin appearing on his face. 'Come and have a look some time if you like.'

Alex smiled sweetly. 'I might just do that. What about your "poor sod"?'

'You mean the one who found the bodies? What about him?'

'What was his name, do you know? He's going to be famous soon. So are you. More people wanting to hire your boats.' She knew she'd pushed the right buttons when she saw the gleam in his eye.

'No reason why I shouldn't tell you, is there? Gary. Gary Lodge. And his wife's name is Ronnie.'

They both turned back to look at the boats across the water. Alex shivered as she tried not to think of the state of the cabin interior.

'You reckon it could do me a bit of good?' Colin didn't look at her as he spoke.

'I reckon.'

'Daley. That was the name of the man who hired the boat. Least that's what the girls in the office told me. Derek Daley. Is he a reality star?'

'No.' Alex's heart began to beat furiously. 'He's not a reality star. Or anything like it. He owns a magazine.'

'Is that all? Still, I suppose if it was someone really famous the publicity could follow me round like a bad smell.' He laughed. 'If you pardon the joke.'

Derek Daley. Magazine proprietor. Wealthy. Influential.

17

Climbed the ladder not caring who he stepped on as he made his way up.

Interesting.

4

More locals were arriving by the minute, and the staithe on the edge of Dillingham Broad was becoming crowded.

Colin Harper shook his head. 'I've had enough of this. I'm off.' He looked across at Alex. 'Don't you forget what I said. My door's always open.' He gave her a knowing wink.

Alex tried not to roll her eyes. 'Thanks, Colin. Nice to have met you.'

She looked around. She couldn't see any likely stringers for the nationals yet, and it was too soon for journos from London to come calling. Then she spotted a police officer and hurried over to him.

'Alex Devlin from *The Post*,' she said, with what she hoped was a winning smile, while holding out her NUJ card as identification.

The officer, whose paunch more than filled his hi-vis vest, didn't crack a smile, merely lifted a tufty eyebrow.

She wasn't going to be intimidated. 'And you are—?'

'Police Constable Lockwood.'

'Well, Police Constable Lockwood, I understand the deaths are thought to be suicide?' She carried on smiling, hoping she didn't look too manic.

Nothing.

'And one of the people found on board was a—', she pretended to consult her notebook, 'Derek Daley, from London? The other man was from Suffolk?'

'My, you have been busy.'

'Are you able to confirm those facts for me, please?' Now her cheeks were aching.

'No.'

'Right. Any chance you can give me a bit of a steer? Would I be wrong in thinking one of the people on the boat is called Derek Daley?'

He narrowed his eyes. 'I couldn't say.'

'Suicide or an accident?'

'Strange accident, if you ask me. Now, if you would let me do my job—' He moved away.

Yesss, thought Alex, wanting to punch the air. No denial. Still not confirmed, but almost there. She moved away from the crowd and onto the rough grass lining the Broad, taking out her phone. There was a fluttering in her chest, a gnawing in her stomach. They were feelings she hadn't had for a long time. She was excited, invigorated, chasing the story.

'Yes.' A gruff voice answered. A voice that said *I am very busy so this had better be important*. A voice that had the capacity to make even the most hardened hack turn pale if they didn't know him. Bud Evans, the news editor of *The Post* and her previous boss. But he had been more than a boss. He had picked her up more than once when her life was falling apart, had been her mentor, had given her work and who had introduced her to the features editor of *The Post* when she had announced she wanted to return to live in Sole Bay. She owed him.

'Bud, it's me, Alex Devlin.'

'Ah, Alex.' His voice was slightly friendlier, about as friendly as it would get. And, of course, no small talk.

'I won't waste time—'

'Good.' She heard him vape.

20

'I'm at Dillingham Broad, in Norfolk—'

'Back of beyond. Godforsaken.'

'Maybe, but listen. Two bodies have been found on a boat.'

'And?' He sounded almost bored.

'It may have been suicide or an accident, but the point is one of the people who died is Derek Daley.' She almost felt him sit up and begin to listen to her.

'Daley, dead.' Interest in his voice. 'Sod's definitely got what he deserved.'

'Bud.'

'What? Don't speak ill of the dead?' He laughed. 'Come on, he was a rival. And a nasty piece of work. Are you sure it's him?'

Alex wasn't surprised at the careless way Bud was taking the death of someone in the industry. It was well known within *The Post* that Bud had little or no time for Derek Daley. Although Bud was known and admired as news editor of the paper, he was more than that – he actually owned The Lewes Press Group, of which *The Post* was a part. But he didn't flaunt his success like Daley. He didn't go to media parties, didn't have fluffy magazine articles written about him, and if someone tried to take a photo of him, he would turn the other way. He gave money to children's homes, but that was as far as he went. No, Bud Evans was an old-fashioned newspaper man with a flair for business, and that's where it stopped.

'Not totally confirmed yet, but there's enough to get a flash ready for the website and something for the morning. I could even do you a colour piece if you want.' She held her breath, realizing she really wanted this.

'No, don't worry about that. I'll get someone onto it ASAP. Send someone to confirm and pick up any other strands.'

'Oh.' Alex was deflated. 'Bud—'

'Yes?'

'I'd really like to do this.'

'Why?'

21

'Why not? I can write a story, you know that. I'm here, on the spot. Surely it would be a good idea if I at least got it started?'

More vaping.

'Get some colour. We'll prepare the flash here. Has PA arrived?'

Alex looked around to see if she could see Jon Welch from the Press Association, but there was no sign of him. He was probably in court somewhere. 'No, I can't see him yet.'

'Right. Do me a one par story that can go when you get final confirmation, and then write me a colour piece. Email ASAP. I don't want to see it on the wires. I want it in *The Post* first. And let me know when the press conference happens. If we hear about it first, I'll let you know.'

Alex sat down on the grass, first making sure she wasn't about to get duck droppings over her skirt. It was a bit damp, but what the hell. She was fizzing. She opened up a new email on her phone and began to type.

The one paragraph stating the bare facts was easy, and she had it written and sent over in a matter of minutes. The colour piece was more challenging. How to convey what was going on around her without sounding over the top and sensationalist.

'Dillingham Broad,' she wrote, 'is at once peaceful and beautiful.'

Rubbish.

'The peace of a beautiful part of Norfolk has been shattered by—'

Hmm. Not great, but she could build on it.

Ten minutes and one throbbing finger later and she had two hundred and fifty words that she hoped captured the essence of what was happening across the water. She checked the signal and pressed send.

As she stood and stretched her legs she saw a familiar face with a cloud of auburn hair standing by a Mini at the edge of the parking area. It was her friend, Lin Meadows.

'Lin!' she called, hurrying over to her. 'How great to see you.'

Lin looked up, the frown on her face dissolving when she saw Alex. 'What are you doing here?'

Alex grinned. 'Doing a bit of old-fashioned reporting for my old-fashioned news editor.'

Lin looked at her, obviously puzzled.

'A couple of men have been found dead on a boat out there, on the other side of the water. Look. You can see forensics walking around.'

'Ah, that's what's going on.' She pulled a face. 'Gross. So what's with the reporting?'

'I heard about the bodies on the radio, and I was nearby, so I thought I'd come and see what was going on. Then I rang Bud – I worked for him when I lived in London and he gave me my first job – and he wanted me to look into it—' She stopped. Lin was laughing at her. 'What is it?'

Lin gave her a hug. 'For a start, Bud? Sounds like someone from an American B movie. And for another thing, I don't think I've ever seen you this energized.'

Alex drew back. 'Really?'

'No, you look as though you're enjoying yourself.'

'I suppose I am,' said Alex, realizing she meant it. 'But I'm only doing it until the reporter from London turns up.'

'What?' Lin looked indignant on Alex's behalf. 'You don't mind being someone else's bitch?'

She shrugged. 'No.' That's the way it worked sometimes.

Lin wrinkled her nose. 'Right.' She shrugged. 'I'm not sure I understand, but, hey, what do I know? Lovely to see you, though.'

'And you. It seems ages.'

Alex really was delighted. She had met Lin shortly after she'd moved back to Sole Bay. Lin was renting a house next door to her and had stopped to chat to Alex on her way to buy some food for her evening meal just after she'd moved in. Alex was weeding the little patch of earth that passed for a front garden, and Lin had stopped to admire the one good thing in that garden

– a beautiful palm tree – saying she had a similar one in her garden in London. Her smile had been wide and her body language so open and friendly that Alex had to ask her what she was doing renting a house in Sole Bay. Hoping to find inspiration, had been Lin's answer. She was an artist and wanted to live by the sea for a year and see where that took her in her work, she'd said. Sole Bay was such a beautiful place. Inspirational. She also wanted to find a local gallery to display and sell her paintings and collages. Perhaps, she had asked hesitantly, Alex knew which galleries might be receptive to her? Alex had invited her in, of course, and over coffee and cake gave her the names of some of the more friendly gallery owners. Then they fell into chatting about this and that and found they had a lot in common – both loved to be by the sea, both had hated school and both were single and in no hurry to go down the relationship route again.

'Who was the man in your life, then?' Lin had asked, after Alex had told her how someone she thought was "the one" who was going to share her life had buggered off without so much as a goodbye. 'Gus's father, or?'

'The "or",' Alex had said with a wry smile. 'Done and dusted and best forgotten.'

Lin had nodded, and Alex had appreciated the fact she didn't pry any further. And so began what was, for Alex, an easy friendship. Usually wary about becoming close to people, Alex made an exception for Lin who was relaxed and undemanding as a friend. And if Lin had heard from one of the many gossips around town about Sasha, she didn't bring it up. Another reason, Alex felt, to like Lin.

'Where have you been?' Alex said now. 'Why haven't you been round?'

'I've been in London on an art course. I told you about it – remember?'

Alex frowned, then shook her head. 'I'm sure you did but my brain is like a sieve. So what are you doing here?'

'I was taking some pictures', she pointed to the digital camera hanging from around her neck, 'for my next project, you know? Boats and ducks and so on, and came across this commotion.' She shivered dramatically. 'How did they die?'

'I don't know yet, that's what I'm hoping to find out.'

'What have you got so far?' Lin looked at her, wide-eyed.

'Not a great a deal – I've sent off a colour piece and a one par breaking news story that'll go on the website when I can confirm it: that's it so far.'

Lin nudged her. 'Get you. Colour piece. Breaking news. Hope you get a whatsit, a byline. And get paid.'

'Ha! Haven't broached the idea of money yet. Depends how much more I do.'

'Anyway.' Lin looked at her watch. 'I must go.' She jumped in the Mini and put the window down. 'Come round for supper later, let me know how you've got on.' And with that she drove away.

Alex shook her head, smiling. That was a hasty departure.

Lin was right about the money, though. She'd been so eager to get something more worthwhile than celebrity news or how to collect coupons into *The Post* that she hadn't mentioned money to Bud. How naive. And how – she struggled to find the word – how parochial. She'd never had any ambitions to be a foreign correspondent or an anchor on a TV show. She wanted to make a living doing something she enjoyed. So how had she ended up in Sole Bay writing features for *The Post*?

Her choice.

She had given it a go in London; Bud had given her work, but it was mainly fillers for the paper, hardly ground-breaking stories. Sole Bay was where her heart was, so she'd compromised and come home, and generally she was content. But on days like these, when something half decent came along, she had the adrenaline rush, the tightness in her belly, the fizz in her head.

'Excuse me.'

Alex turned towards the voice. It was PC Lockwood.

'I thought you'd like to know', he said without any preamble, 'that there's going to be a press conference at six. About the deaths on the boat.'

'Thank you,' said Alex, surprised. 'It was good of you to—'

'It's my job to tell you. It'll be at the station in the town. Nobody's saying anything until then.' He nodded behind her. 'Your mates have caught up with the story.'

Alex turned. Sure enough, a couple of likely-looking reporters were scribbling in notebooks. She recognized one of them, from the local TV, setting up his own camera before turning and facing it and doing a piece to camera.

She sent a text to Bud.

Press conference at six.

She got an immediate reply.

Go. Reporter will meet you there and liaise.

'And thank you for all your hard work, Alex,' she muttered. 'You've done really well, Alex. Liked the colour piece, Alex.'

What else had she expected?

Suddenly the crowd on the staithe fell silent.

The police boat was pulling the cruiser across the water towards land.

5

Cambridge 1975

The silence was terrifying as my dad and I heaved the battered school trunk we'd found in a junk shop through a small doorway at the side of the old stone building and up Staircase C. As it bumped up each tread, worn smooth by the shoes of generations of students, my heart sank lower and lower. What was I doing here? An ordinary boy from an ordinary town who did as he was told, stayed on an extra six months at the local grammar, passed exams, a three-day interview and was now at Cambridge.

When Dad left, exhorting me to enjoy myself and meet people (subtext: a nice girl from a nice family – and thank Christ Mum hadn't come: she would have been unbearably fussy), I sat on my narrow single bed staring at the beige carpet and nursing a glass of the Blue Nun I'd brought with me ('to share with other students', my mum had said hopefully), trying to ignore the slight smell of drains and praying nobody would knock on my door. Soon I would Blu-Tack posters of Bowie and college events to the wall and unpack my record player and books, but for now I was looking at bare magnolia walls, empty bookshelves, and a basin in the corner with an annoying dripping tap. And I kept glancing over to my desk nervously, looking at the array of invitations I had picked up from my pigeonhole in the porter's lodge on my way through. I wasn't sure I would have the courage to accept any of them. I had the sense that at any point I could be found out, that I didn't deserve to be here, not really.

Then, unexpectedly, I felt a surge of happiness. I was here. I'd made it. Cambridge. Bright, glittering. I could be whoever I wanted to be. I could reinvent myself. I could be exciting, intriguing, interesting. No longer dull. There would be people to fascinate me. I might fall in love. I would no longer be ordinary.

I didn't know then that I would soon be craving an ordinary life.

The first person I met was Stu.

He knocked on my door that night while I was nursing my Blue Nun.

'Hi,' he said, hopping from one foot to another, pushing his glasses back onto the bridge of his nose. 'I'm Stu.' He held out his hand. I took it and he gave me a firm handshake. His hair was receding, and he wore jeans that had been ironed. His accent was pure Birmingham. Coming from the Midlands I recognized it instantly.

'I saw your dad helping you earlier. I thought—' His glasses had slipped again; he pushed them back. 'I heard your dad, and I thought you were probably from somewhere near Birmingham—'

'Somewhere near,' I said.

'I'm not sure whether I should be here—' He trailed off, looking around nervously.

'Where? On this staircase?'

'No. Here. In Cambridge.' His smile was hesitant.

I smiled back, warming to him. 'I know what you mean.'

'Do you?' he said. 'Do you really?' He came in and sat on my armchair. 'Perhaps we can pal up. Go to things together. I'm reading Philosophy.'

'So am I,' I said.

So for the rest of the week Stu and I stuck together. It helped me because Fresher's Week was an endurance, even though I guess that's where it all began. It was a week packed with filling out forms, going to dusty rooms where professors lurked with warm sherry, and trying to avoid the jolly red-faced students trying to get us to sign up to their societies. But the old fear of being found out once again got in my way, so the only society I joined was the Philosophy Society. I felt that's what you did at places like Cambridge.

Stu joined the Philosophy Society with me. He eschewed the same societies as I did. He talked to the same people as I did. He was good to have around, if a little dull, and I wondered if I'd still be friends with him at the end of our three years.

Then came the end of the week party at the college. I got ready carefully, putting on new jeans (unironed) and a tee shirt with some sort of logo on it, washed my hair and splashed out on aftershave that smelled vaguely spicy. The party took place in a dark hall – the Junior Common Room – with music from the Sex Pistols making the walls and floor vibrate. No food – that wasn't the point – and the evening dissolved into a blur of cigarettes and alcohol and a joint or a spliff; I wasn't even sure what to call it I was that naive, but I smoked as though I knew what I was doing.

Shamefully, I tried to shake off Stu, telling him I was going to get a drink, but I had no intention of finding him in the crowd again. I wanted some of that elusive excitement, and I thought Stu would cramp my style. Then I went back to someone's room to carry on the party and started talking to a student who looked as though he had just stepped out of an Evelyn Waugh novel, complete with pullover, casually worn scarf (even at a party, and he told me later it was cashmere) and a cigarette in a holder. A mix of secrecy, amusement and decadence radiated off him. He told me his name was Willem. 'Though I'd rather be Seb. After

Sebastian Flyte,' he explained, pinning me with his ice-blue eyes. 'You can call me Seb, if you like.'

'I don't think so,' I said, suddenly giddy with the idea of standing up to someone with his air of entitlement.

The time for my reinvention had arrived.

6

The Harper's Holidays building was by the side of the River Ant next to Lowdham Bridge, some six miles from Wrexfield. Alex had driven past it many times, but had never had occasion to stop.

Now she navigated the car across a yard full of boats of all different shapes and sizes, some covered with tarpaulins, others dilapidated and listing to one side, all of them looking out of place on dry land. Any number of bodies could be hidden around here, thought Alex. On the river she could see three sleek cruisers moored – presumably ones for hire. No sign of Firefly Lady – that particular crime scene would be with the coppers for some time to come.

Alex parked next to a building by the water's edge that appeared to be a large shed with a corrugated iron roof. She went through the door marked 'Harper's Holidays Reception' thinking to find something akin to a tyre and exhaust workshop – a little grubby, a bit seedy, populated by men who were unused to office work. And with one of those coffee machines in the corner that dispensed execrable drinks. Instead she found a bright, clean office with three smart women working away at their computers. She should never think in stereotypes – she should have learned that by now.

One of the women looked up and smiled a red lipstick smile. 'Can I help you?'

'Is – Colin here?' As Alex asked the question she realized she didn't know what she would do if he wasn't in his office. He might have gone home after the events of the morning. Or be in the pub she'd noticed over the road, nursing a pint or two.

'Is he expecting you?'

'Not really. Though he did say to drop by.' Alex gave her what she hoped was her best smile.

'Is it to do with a booking?'

'In a manner of speaking.'

The woman's smile slipped slightly.

'If it is to do with a booking I'm sure I can help. Though we tend not to do hen parties. Or stag parties. Too much trouble. Was it a particular boat you wanted? Two or four? Or we do have boats that sleep up to ten. And when were you thinking? We are quite booked up from now until September, but we might be able to find—'

'No, no, it's not about a holiday.' Alex wanted to stop her before the hard sell really began. At least she hadn't said Colin wasn't about.

The woman's eyes narrowed. 'Are you press?'

'Yes, but—'

The woman stood up, red lipstick glistening, her smile a gash in her face. 'I think you should leave now, Miss—?'

'Devlin. Alex Devlin.'

'Well, Miss Devlin, we have been asked not to talk to the press about the – ah – incident. And, as you can imagine, it's all been rather upsetting.'

Alex stood her ground. 'Colin said to call in.'

'I don't think Mr Harper meant you to call in now. While all this is going on. He's only just got back from the police station himself.' Her mouth made a moue of distaste.

'It's all right, Kerry, I'll take it from here.' Colin appeared from a door at the back of the office and winked at Alex. 'Nice to see you again. Come on through.'

Alex walked past the woman with the lipstick and followed Colin through a door into a back office.

This office was more what she had expected: a jumble of papers, magazines, dirty coffee cups and a calendar with a picture of a boat tacked on the wall. There were a couple of spanners and an oily rag on the desk too. The air smelled of cheap cigarettes. The front office was for show: this was where the real business took place.

Colin was still in his too-tight jeans and too-tight tee shirt. He gestured for Alex to sit. He took the chair on the other side of the desk and swept four mugs to one side with a clatter.

'I'm sorry to come so soon after this morning—'

Colin grimaced. 'No worries. Had to come back to the office. There might be a couple of stiffs on my boat but the wheels of commerce still turn. At least, I hope the wheels haven't come off the wagon. A living's got to be made. Now.' He leaned back in his chair. 'I'm guessing you're not here to book a holiday on one of my boats?'

Alex smiled. 'You guess right.' She looked around at the tottering piles of paper. 'Looks like you're really busy.'

Colin nodded. 'Yep. Lots of people want a Harper's Holiday. That's me. Colin Harper. Rent the boat, have a holiday of a lifetime.' He grinned. 'Unless you're Derek Daley and his mate.' He shook his head. 'Still don't know how I'm going to clear up the mess on that boat.' He grimaced.

'You could get professional cleaners in. You know, ones who clear up after unusual deaths.'

He looked interested. 'Didn't know there was those sort of people.'

'I'm sure the police would put you in touch with someone.'

He gave a short laugh. 'Those damn coppers don't know their arses from their elbows. Running round like headless chickens, told me they didn't know when I could have me boat back. Impounded it, they said. Evidence, they said. I told them it was costing me every day it wasn't cruising down the river with some knobhead from London on board. I mean, what are they doin'? They'll have scraped the bodies off it by now. Surely they've taken all the photos that are needed as well?' He shook his head. 'They don't seem to care about a man's livelihood. Or reputation. No one will want to hire a bloody boat from me at this rate. My granddad started this business with one small boat. Now we've got a fleet.' He tapped his pockets and brought out his battered cigarette packet, this time full of cigarettes, which he offered to Alex.

She shook her head with a smile.

He shrugged, took a squashed cigarette out and lit it, ignoring the 'No Smoking' sign stuck to the wall.

'So. Didn't expect to see you so soon.' He grinned. 'Or mebbe I did. You're one of them journalists, aren't you?'

'Can't deny it.'

'Knew it. And you want to know who else was booked on Firefly Lady, don't you?'

'Yes. And confirm it was Derek Daley on that boat.'

'See it with your own eyes, like?'

'You've got it.'

He smiled at her. 'Jim said you'd be likely to pay me for information.'

At least he didn't beat about the bush. She nodded. 'We can give you a bit of money. For your time, you know.'

'Expenses like?'

'Exactly.'

'How much?'

Alex thought back to the conversation she'd had with Bud on the way to the boatyard when she told him what she was doing and how she hoped to confirm absolutely who had hired the boat. *Give him what he wants, Devlin,* he'd said. A pause. *Within reason, of course. Of course,* she'd replied, wondering what 'within reason' meant. How much Bud, usually tight-fisted with the cash, was willing to pay for information about a magazine editor who had been his rival in business.

She named a figure. Colin looked disappointed, made to get up out of his chair. She stifled a sigh. Named another figure. Colin grinned.

'Cash, of course.'

Alex raised an eyebrow before delving into her bag and pulling out an envelope, thankful she'd had the foresight to stop off at a cashpoint on the way. She slid the envelope across the desk. Colin made to take it. She kept her hand on it. 'One other thing.'

Colin cocked his head to one side. 'Go on.'

'Have you got a boat here that's like Firefly Lady?'

'You mean, the same inside and that?'

'Exactly.'

He looked at her, then at the envelope. 'I reckon that's worth a bit more.'

'All or nothing.' She held his gaze.

Finally he nodded. 'Okay.' He put his hand over the envelope and pulled it towards him. 'Feels fat enough.'

'So?' asked Alex.

'We'll show you round one of the boats.' He slid the envelope into a drawer. 'And I'll tell you another thing. For free.'

'Oh?' Alex could see he was bursting to tell her something.

'Barbecue.' Colin Harper leaned back in his dilapidated office chair, hands folded behind his head.

'Pardon?'

'Barbecue. That's what killed 'em. So Eddie said.' Eddie, the loose-mouthed police officer. 'They'd had a barbecue the night before and then brought it inside the boat. Strictly forbidden, of course. Stupid arses. If they're going to have a barbecue they have to have it outside. There's a perfectly good cooker inside. Eddie said they died of carbon monoxide poisoning. All the windows were tight shut. So was the door. Probably an accident, Eddie said.'

Alex was puzzled. 'Why would they want to bring the barbecue inside, though? It wasn't cold – far from it.' She wasn't buying the accident line.

'You'd be surprised what some of them folk from London do. I've had all sorts to clear up on these boats. Not so bad since we banned hen and stag dos – dirty buggers they all were.' He smirked. 'Shisha pipes, blow-up dolls, party pills, all sorts of paraphernalia I wouldn't want to talk about in front of a lady.'

Alex suppressed a smile. She got the distinct impression Colin would happily talk about anything in front of anybody, the more prurient the better.

'Once I had to throw away several pairs of knickers. You know, underwear.' He raised his eyebrows.

'I think I do know, yes.'

'See what I mean? You should never be surprised what folk do.'

'Especially if they're from London.'

He sat back in his chair, satisfied. 'I knew you'd know what I was on about.'

Alex thought it would be best not to pursue the barbecue line at the moment. 'Did your friend Eddie say whether the police think they knew each other?'

'Looking into it, he said.'

'Okay. Now, about the name of the other person who'd been booked on the boat?'

He shook his head. 'Can't give you that. Confidential. Data protection.'

'What? But—' Damn. That was the whole point of the bloody money. Her charm obviously wasn't working.

He held up his finger. 'But, say, if I was to go and get us a cup of coffee leaving my computer on, then—?' He winked at her. 'How do you take it?'

She winked back, relieved. 'White, no sugar.'

'Right you are.'

After he had left the room, Alex waited a few seconds, then went round to the other side of the desk. Although she knew this was what Colin meant for her to do, her palms were still sweaty and her heart pounding. Taking a deep breath she tapped the space bar on the keyboard, and the computer sprang to life.

And there it was. Details of the booking for a four-berth cruiser for a Mr Derek Daley and a Mr Roger Fleet. Booked – she peered at the date. Six weeks ago. Really? They'd been planning this for six weeks? Name of the person who booked it – Mr Derek Daley. She scrolled down, hoping to see addresses for Daley and Fleet. Sure enough, there they were. Derek Daley's address was for a house in Hackney, Roger Fleet for one in Lapford in Suffolk. All she had to do was to give Daley's address to the news desk and they could make sure it was that of the magazine editor and there it would be, confirmation. Enough for *The Post*, anyway. She frowned. So why did Derek Daley hire a boat for himself and Roger Fleet? A man from London and a man from Suffolk. What was the connection?

Suddenly she heard footsteps and the sound of someone whistling – Colin? Must be. She whipped out her phone and took a picture of the screen before going back to her seat.

'All right, gel?' Colin said, rubbing his hands together. 'Didn't bring you that coffee, thought you might want a look round that boat now?'

'Please. It'll give me a sense of where they were when—'

'They weren't on board long. Alive, that is. Bloody waste of money if you ask me. Took the boat out in the morning and were dead by the evening. That's what the police reckoned anyway.'

'The police being Eddie?'

He grinned in answer.

They went outside into the boatyard.

'He's a good lad is Eddie. His father was an eel catcher, you know. Dying out now. Eel catchers in the Fens. What a life, eh? The wildlife, the peace and quiet, the slow pace. No chasing to an office or anything like that. They used willow for the traps and set them in the evening and hopefully have a good catch by the next morning. Then it was local people what bought them. Or they went to market or whatever—'

'Colin.' Alex spoke firmly, hoping to stop him from reminiscing. 'I'm sure it was a great job, but—'

'Delicious.'

'Delicious?'

'Eels. To eat.'

'I'm sure they are,' said Alex, not convinced. She needed to get him back on track. 'Do you need a deposit?'

'From you?' He looked surprised.

'No. I mean, when you hire the boat, do you have to pay a deposit?'

'You think I was born yesterday? Lady, just because I'm not some jumped-up fancy pants from London doesn't mean to say I came down in last week's shower. Of course we ask them for a deposit. They have to pay it to secure the boat, see? Like any good business.' He shook his head. 'As if I was born yesterday.'

'I'm sorry, I didn't mean—'

'It was booked by Daley, so it was Daley who paid. Simple.'

Alex felt stupid. She tried again. 'Who showed Daley and Fleet to the boat? Gave them their lesson? I presume they had a lesson in how to steer and where things were and all that sort of thing?'

'Well I'm not going to let them traverse the Broads of Norfolk and Suffolk without letting them know what's what, am I now? That's Mickey's job. He's around here somewhere – ah, talk of the Devil.' He put two fingers between his lips and gave a piercing whistle. Alex had always wanted to be able to whistle like that but had never mastered the art and was always in awe of people who could. 'Mickey, come on over here. I've got a young lady what wants to talk to you.'

Mickey strode over. He, too, had the look of someone who worked outdoors, with a tanned face and furrows of lines around his mouth and deep crow's feet by his eyes. Black curly hair. A tattoo of a spider's web on each elbow. Late forties, Alex guessed. He had a friendly smile.

'Colin?'

'Mickey, I would like you to show this young lady around a boat, please.'

'Sure. Ms—?'

'Alex,' said Alex. 'Alex Devlin.'

He nodded. 'Nice to meet you, Alex.'

'Mickey's just started with us. Been here about – what?' Colin pursed his lips.

'Couple of months, actually.' Mickey's smile was easy. 'Have I missed something? Which boat are you hiring today?' He looked from one to the other.

'No, you're all right, Mickey, Alex wants to take a look around a boat because—'

'I might want to hire one out with a couple of girlfriends sometime,' she interrupted smoothly. She wanted Mickey to show her around not thinking of her as a journalist but as an ordinary punter.

'Yeah. Course.' Colin nodded vigorously. 'That's right. Can you do the honours, Mickey? And Mickey,' he pointed at him, 'tell the lady anything she wants to know, okay?'

'Sure. Come on. This way.'

'She wants to see Firefly Sister, I think, lad. Four berths, isn't that right?'

'Yes,' said Alex, thrusting a business card into Colin's hand before hurrying after Mickey. 'Give us a call if you think of anything else,' she said over her shoulder. 'And thanks, Colin. For everything.'

'Anytime. You know where I am.' He gave the inevitable wink again.

Four white and gleaming boats were moored side by side along the river. They stopped by the second one along.

'This one here is Firefly Sister. If you want to hop aboard?'

Alex didn't think 'hop' was quite the right word. She'd never been one for boats, and despite living near the Broads for most of her life, had never sailed on one. She stepped gingerly onto the cruiser and peered through the open doors into the cabin.

'This is the rear cabin, with one double and a single,' said Mickey. 'Go on through.'

Bending her head, Alex stepped inside the cabin.

The double bed looked comfortable enough, with its flowery duvet cover, white pillows, and neatly folded towels on the end. A mirror was fixed to the wall of a cupboard. The single bed was shaped like a coffin, and the bottom half of it disappeared underneath a cupboard. She didn't fancy sleeping in that bed. There was a small chest of drawers.

'If you go through, you'll find the galley and the toilet and shower as well.'

She saw the small bathroom on her right, then a compact kitchen, another single bed, and the steering wheel. The whole boat did feel light and airy. 'Oh,' she said, 'I didn't realize there would be an ordinary steering wheel. And inside, too.'

'It's called the helm.' Mickey sounded bored.

'Right. Helm.'

She stood for a minute, thinking about Derek Daley and Roger Fleet coming on board a boat just like this a few short days ago. Who had the double bed? Which of them was consigned to the coffin bed? Or, more likely, the single bed in the living area. Did they have a cup of tea or any food before they died? What were they thinking about on that short trip up the river to Dillingham Broad and then to Poppy Island?

'Is this like the boat where they – you know?'

Mickey frowned. 'What do you mean?'

She relaxed her shoulders, wanting to sound casual. She stooped, peering through the window onto the towpath. 'I heard they found a couple of dead people on a boat today. Was it a boat like this?'

A short silence.

'What do you want to know for?'

Alex jumped, his breath was in her ear, his body close to hers, the smell of oil and the outdoors swirling around her. She turned around slowly, and he took a step back.

He smiled, but it didn't reach his eyes. 'I mean, it's a funny thing to ask about, if you're thinking of having a boating holiday yourself.'

'I just heard about it and—'

Mickey stepped away from her and leaned against the worktop, crossing his arms. 'Well, yes, it was a boat just like this. One on the double bed, the other on the single. I heard that Mr Harper is going to have to get new mattresses because they were soaked through with bodily fluids and slime and stuff. It was the warm weather and the flies. The stench was overpowering, I heard. A couple of the coppers threw up. Is that the sort of thing you wanted to know?' He wasn't smiling now.

'Er—' Alex didn't know what to say.

'So. Who are you? You're not really wanting to hire a boat, are you? But you don't strike me as a rubbernecker, either.'

So much for being an ordinary punter. She lifted her hands in surrender. 'Busted,' she said, lightly, wanting to get him back onside. 'I'm a journalist.'

Mickey raised an eyebrow. 'We're not supposed to talk to any journalists.'

'I appreciate that, Mickey, but Colin—'

'Colin, is it? You want to watch him.'

'I know what you mean.' God, this was becoming more and more awkward. 'But he's been helpful. Seems to think you might be, too.'

'Give him cash, did you?'

Alex looked at Mickey. She had no more readies to give him.

He shrugged, pushed himself away from the little kitchen worktop. 'What the hell. What else do you want to know?'

'These boats don't have barbecues on board as a matter of course?'

'No, though people do bring them. I mean, we have all the mod cons like you see – fridge, cooker, hob, but on balmy days people like to cook outside, don't they? Can be dangerous if you take them inside before they're fully burnt out. Or at all, really, because you can never tell.'

'And I gather that's what seems to have happened here.'

Mickey stared at her. 'Fumes? From the barbecue?'

'That's one theory.' She sat down on the bench running alongside the table. It was pretty comfortable. 'What were they like?'

'The two guys?'

'Yes. I mean, did they seem like really good friends? Did they talk to each other when you were showing them the boat? Were they nervous?'

Mickey hesitated. 'How much should I be telling you? Only, I don't want to lose my job. Good money for doing eff all really, just showing people who should know better how to behave on one of these boats and how to respect the water.'

'Where are you from?' Alex was curious to know what a man like Mickey was doing in Suffolk. He had a distinctive accent.

'London. Lost my job.' He shrugged. 'Gambling. House went, and my family. Drifted around, came up this way, you know, for a bit of sea air, and found Colin one day. He was looking for someone to help him over the summer; I used to do some sailing and engineering and stuff in a former life, so he hired me. There might be some winter work, too. In the office as well as showing people the boats. If I stay here that long.'

'You might move on?'

'Maybe. Depends what happens. You know.'

'You won't lose your job because of me. You heard Colin – you can talk to me.'

'Trust me I'm a journalist?'

Alex couldn't help but laugh. 'Something like that, yes.'

'I wouldn't want it to get out that I'd been talking to you, though. I've started to get together a good life here. I've got some mates. I feel as though I'm starting to turn things around.'

'There won't be any comeback on you, I promise. I'm not like that. Really,' she emphasized, seeing his look of scepticism. 'I know you've got to live round here. I'm fairly local too, so it's not going to help anyone if I get their backs up, is it?'

'Maybe.' He still seemed wary.

'So? The two men on Firefly Lady? How friendly were they?'

'Not that friendly, not gay friendly, you know. I could tell that. They didn't talk much.'

'What sort of things did they say?'

'The usual.'

'Which is?' This was getting to be hard work.

'You know – would they be able to steer it okay, would they crash into the bank, what should they do if they did. Standard stuff.' He looked off into the distance. 'One of them was talking about his animals and then he said to me he hated leaving them. I said something like "I hope you've got someone to look after them or the RSPCA will be after you, ha ha." And he sort of smiled. I remember him smiling. The other bloke, he looked a bit pale and I remember thinking the fresh air would do him good. I was wrong about that, wasn't I?'

'Just a bit.'

They shared a rueful smile.

'I hope you're going to tell Colin how helpful I've been. Perhaps he'll give me a bonus.' He winked.

Alex stood. 'I'll let you get on.' She stepped off the boat and onto dry land, with Mickey following, just a little too close.

'Ah, coppers. I think I'll make myself scarce.' She felt Mickey step back onto the boat.

Turning, she saw a man and a woman in pain clothes walking purposefully along the towpath. In their shiny suits they looked out of place among the holidaymakers in shorts. The man was completely bald, tall, lanky even, sporting a stubbly beard flecked with grey; the woman petite, her hair scraped back in a ponytail.

'We're looking for Mickey Grainger,' the man said, flashing a warrant card at her. 'Detective Inspector Berry,' he said. 'And this is Detective Sergeant Logan.'

Alex tried not to smile. Logan and Berry? You had to be kidding.

'Yes, yes,' Berry said, testily. 'I know. Loganberry. Don't think we haven't heard it. So. Have you seen Mr Grainger? Colin Harper said we would find him here.'

'Well—' said Alex, not sure what to say. Mickey hadn't seemed keen to meet Berry and Logan and she didn't want to drop him in it.

Berry narrowed his eyes. 'And you are?'

There was no point in pretending, she thought. 'Alex Devlin. Reporter from *The Post*.'

'Ah, yes. PC Lockwood said you were nosing about.' He glared at her.

'Can you confirm the identities of the bodies?' She might as well give it a try.

'No.'

DS Logan stared straight ahead.

'Are they Derek Daley from London and Roger Fleet from Suffolk?'

'Wait for the press conference. Six o'clock. This Grainger's boat?' He began to step aboard Firefly Sister.

'Not his boat exactly,' said Alex.

DI Berry frowned. 'How "not exactly"?'

'It belongs to Harper's Holidays. Mickey works for Colin.'

'I see. Mickey works for Colin. I think I did realize that.' Sarcasm

44

dripped from his lips. He stepped on board the boat. 'Mr Grainger,' he called. 'I'm Detective Inspector Berry and I would like to have a word with you please.'

There was silence for a few seconds, only the sound of distant voices and the phut phut of engines and then Mickey emerged from the other end of the boat, looking as though he wanted to be anywhere else but here, on this boat, with these police officers.

DI Berry smiled, but, to Alex, it wasn't a particularly reassuring smile. DS Logan's face hadn't moved, and Alex wondered if she was frightened of her boss, or if she was naturally like that.

'Mr Grainger. At last.' DI Berry looked at Alex, his thin lips in a parody of a smile. 'Thank you, Miss Devlin, for your help.'

She was dismissed.

7

Alex shifted about on one of the uncomfortable wooden chairs that had been laid out in rows for the press. The room was stuffy and impersonal with high windows and almost bare walls. There were three tables in a row at one end of the room, with the logo of Norfolk Constabulary behind it. It also had a strange smell of school about it, that heady mix of sweat, feet and boiled mince.

Her mind wandered back to the visit she had just made to her mum and dad. They lived in a small village several miles outside Sole Bay – they couldn't bear to stay in the town after the death of Sasha's twins – in a neat house down a country lane. It was identical to the one they had left behind in Sole Bay. It had a fitted kitchen, a white bathroom suite, a three piece suite in the sitting room and a hardly used mahogany table and six chairs in the dining room. The garden was a well-tended lawn both at the back and the front, and flowers that were ranked in straight borders varying with the seasons. It was as if her parents wanted to underline their stability, the fact they lived very ordinary lives. Good lives. Despite Sasha.

'Thank you for coming,' said her mother as she'd ushered her in, making Alex feel guilty immediately. It was the beaten tone in her mum's voice that did it.

Alex had handed over the pasta and the smoked sausages. 'Here, Mum. I hope Dad enjoys them.'

Her mother had smiled gratefully.

'Hello darling,' her dad had said. 'I'm just making a cup of tea for us.'

Darling. It had only been in recent weeks he had begun to call Alex 'darling'. She rather liked it, even if it was a product of his dementia. And tea. He never made tea; he loved his coffee. He had looked around with a new vagueness, as if he wasn't at all sure where he was or what he was supposed to be doing.

The tea never materialized. Her dad forgot he was making it and wandered off into the sitting room to watch goodness knows what on the television. So her mum had taken over and made it without a word.

'Have you seen the specialist recently?'

Her mum had shaken her head. 'No. Not for another six months. Then there'll be more tests to see if he's got any worse. I'm not sure I can bear it. To watch him struggling in that horrible hospital room while he tries to copy a picture or spell something backwards. I can't do it, Alex, I can't.' She'd buried her face in her hands.

Alex had put her arms around her, noticing how thin and frail she had become over the last months. 'I'll do what I can, Mum. And I'll come with you next time.'

Her mother had stood up straight. 'I'm sorry. Sometimes—'

'Look, I know it all gets a bit much for you. You must let me help more.'

'We'll be all right. Don't worry. Most of the time I'm perfectly fine. Sometimes, though, I want to scream at the unfairness of it all.'

Alex could understand that. After all, her parents weren't old – they were only in their early sixties. It wasn't a time for her dad to start losing his mind and for her mum to have aged years in months. They'd had her and Sasha when they were young, and so should have had years of child-free time together. But what had happened with Sasha had aged them prematurely, Alex realized that. And on bad days, really bad days, she blamed her sister for making that happen. And now with her father's illness, well, it really was taking its toll on them both.

'Don't let it be so long before you visit again, will you?' Her eyes had swum with tears and she'd worked her mouth in an effort to stop them falling. With a flash of understanding Alex had realized her mother was frightened and that her dad had been the person her mum had leaned on for years. They had always been a self-contained couple, a private family, which was why all that business with Sasha had hit them so hard. Now her mother was having to cope on her own. Alex knew she had to do more.

Impulsively she'd hugged her mother. 'I'll be back soon. I promise.'

'Please.'

'Here.' Her dad had appeared holding something in his hands. It was a long, yellow balloon. 'This is for you. I blew it up, but I couldn't think what to do next. But I did blow it up.'

The growing chatter in the police station conference room brought Alex back to the present. The bank of microphones looking like furry caterpillars on the table was growing. Alex scanned the room, looking for someone from *The Post*. She was bound to recognize them, wasn't she?

No one.

She brought up the newspaper's website on her phone – surely Bud would have run what she'd written by now? He wasn't one for hanging around before he published. Normally, he took a chance. 'Not wrong for long,' he used to say.

But there was nothing there. No breaking news, no colour piece from her. Perhaps he was having to play it safe this time for one reason or another.

She refreshed her phone again. Nothing.

Someone slipped into the seat beside her. A lemony fragrance wafted over.

'You've been keeping my seat warm, then?'

Alex shook her head. Bloody hell. Not him. 'Hello, Heath,' she said.

Heath Maitland grinned at her, all white teeth and Hollywood smile, floppy fringe half over his eyes. Designer jacket. Handmade shoes. Claimed to be late thirties but more likely early forties. Money; not courtesy of *The Post*, but of his family, so the rumour mill had it. His name courtesy of his mother who was an authority on the works of the Brontës. Heath – he had dropped the 'cliffe' bit pretty early on in life – had the reputation of being able to get any woman into bed. Not her, she wasn't that stupid. But he never ceased trying.

'When Bud said you were looking at the story, I couldn't believe it. Long time no see and all that,' he said. 'Christ, these chairs are hard. Don't they give you cushions or something?'

'If he'd told me he was sending you, I wouldn't have bothered,' she replied, tartly. 'And no. No cushions. This is a police station, remember?'

'Come on, Alex, you know you're pleased to see me really.' He nudged her arm.

She felt her lips twitching. 'No, I really am not.' But, in truth, Heath Maitland was impossible not to like. Irritating. Pushy. Arrogant. Lazy. A dilettante. But fun to have around – mostly.

'You win some you lose some.' That megawatt smile again. He turned it onto a journalist a few rows away. To Alex's annoyance, the woman returned it. 'Last I heard,' Heath continued, 'you were hanging around with some dodgy character.'

Alex stiffened. 'I don't know who you mean.'

'Yes, you do. Some bloke who fancied himself—'

She snorted. 'And you don't?'

'You know me better than that.' He glanced sideways at her. 'Malone. Wasn't that his name?'

It was. Malone who had run out on her twice now. Malone

49

who she thought would stay the course this time despite the fact that his life was a mess. Malone who'd helped her son find his father, told her she was beautiful, wanted to make a go of things. And then he'd fucked off. That Malone.

'Yep. But we're not together any more.' She hated articulating it out loud, but she couldn't go on hoping he'd come back, or even get in contact with her. He'd been out of her life for seven months and three days now and she knew she had to move on. But that would not be with Heath Maitland.

'Really?' He raised an eyebrow.

'Yes, really.'

'Doesn't know what he's missing.'

Oh, that smile.

'No. And nor do you,' she replied tartly. 'Now, do you want to know what's going on here or not?'

He yawned and glanced at what looked to be a very expensive watch on his wrist. 'Two stiffs on a boat, that's what I know. Are they going to be long?'

'How should I know?' she snapped, and immediately regretted her petulance.

'Chillax,' he said.

That made her laugh. '"Chillax"? Who did you learn that one from?'

He looked indignant. 'My godson, if you must know.'

'Hah. He was pulling your leg.'

'I don't think so.' Heath looked around. 'Took me hours to get here. No decent roads.'

'What do you mean? They've only recently dualled the A11.'

He laughed. 'Maybe, but bloody hell, they still allow tractors on it.'

Alex laughed. 'We don't want people like you discovering Norfolk and Suffolk. We like to keep it to ourselves.'

'Some of the countryside I drove through was lovely,' he admitted.

Alex liked him for saying that. She was so used to the wide open skies that went on forever and the special soft light that shimmered and the air that was fresh and clean, she sometimes forgot how special a place it was. It wasn't that she didn't appreciate it – two years in London breathing in fumes and dust that was other people's skin made sure of that – but she occasionally needed to step back and look at it anew. She thought about ripples on water, trees that were green and lush, ducks and geese on the commons, and the Broads that welcomed every new visitor, and the cerulean blue sky. She smelt the tang of brine when she was by the sea, and the scents of early summer flowers when she went walking. 'I love it here,' she said.

'And did you leave London in such a hurry because you were dying to get back to sticksville or because of Malone?'

She glanced sideways at him. 'I didn't think anyone had noticed I'd left.'

He didn't look at her. 'Oh, they did. Well, I did.'

'Don't be daft. I was in a completely different department to you.'

'Only the other side of the desk.'

'Features versus news, hey? Soft bubbles versus proper journalism?' Now she nudged him with her elbow. 'Anyway, I wasn't there often.'

'Often enough.' He looked at her with those blue, blue eyes. Flirting as ever.

For a brief moment Alex was flattered. Then she remembered his reputation and thought she had better get on with the business in hand. She cleared her throat, leaned forward and whispered: 'Right. Two men dead on the boat, one from London. I'm reliably informed it is Derek Daley. And—'

He stared at her for a moment. 'That's confirmed, is it?'

'Well, I've confirmed it and I've sent a piece to Bud, but there's nothing up on the website. Don't you think that's strange?' She tried to sound offhand about it.

51

Heath shrugged. 'Not necessarily. Perhaps he wanted to keep it for the paper. Exclusive. Not bother with the website – you know what a Luddite he is. I mean, if it really is Derek Daley—'

'Sssh, not so loud.' Alex glanced around to see if anyone had heard. It didn't look like it. 'And it is.'

'Then it should make great headlines. And the other?'

'A man from Suffolk. Roger Fleet. Don't know any more than that at the moment.'

'And how did you get this information?'

She smiled. 'I've got an "in" with the owner of the boat hiring company.'

'Really?' A smile tugged at the corners of his mouth.

'Not that sort of "in".'

'Right. Okay. So Derek, and Roger from Suffolk. I've never heard anything on the grapevine about Del Boy being gay.'

'Perhaps they were just friends. You know, maybe they were hanging out together? I do believe it can happen.'

'Hardly likely, is it? The smooth as silk Daley with a yokel?'

'Watch it, you.'

'Natural death? Murder? Suicide?'

Alex shook her head. 'I'm not sure yet. It's unlikely to be natural deaths though, don't you think? Not two of them?'

'Never assume, Alex, you know that. It makes an ass out of you and me, remember? Could be natural causes. Could be an accident, it has been known.'

'Colin Harper seemed to think it was suicide. He said they had taken a disposable barbecue inside and the fumes got them.'

Heath twisted round to look at her. 'Really? Anything else?'

Alex shook her head. 'No, nothing. Tell me, Heath, why is Bud so interested in this story? I mean, it's a tragedy and I can imagine him running a piece with some Press Association copy and pics, but first letting me loose on the story and then paying your expenses up here … It's not like him, is it?' She had been thinking about this. 'But then he hasn't published anything yet.'

'By all accounts Daley and Bud go back a long way; though, as you know Bud never liked him: he always said there was something unsavoury about our Del. And maybe he's right, we'll have to see. Maybe he's covering his arse. I mean, if there is something dodgy going on, he'd look stupid if *The Post* missed it, wouldn't he?'

At that moment, two police officers paraded onto the stage. DI Berry and DS Logan. No family. So no 'emotional' appeal. Not yet, anyway. Or perhaps it wouldn't be necessary.

'Hang on, what do you mean, "something unsavoury"?' asked Alex.

A look flashed across Heath's face that she couldn't identify. 'I don't know what he meant; but you never know, if he did top himself, then there must have been a reason.'

'Could he have been depressed?'

Heath snorted. 'What, with his lifestyle?'

'Don't knock it. You know damn well money isn't everything.'

'No, but it bloody well helps. Believe me, that I do know.'

Alex looked at him. There was more to Heath Maitland than a pretty face and a flirty manner, that was for sure, but she had yet to find out what.

Berry and Logan had sat down. Logan was making sure her papers were in order, neatening them with her hands. Nervous, Alex guessed. Berry gazed around the room. His stare alighted on Alex and she began to feel uncomfortable.

Heath leaned into her. 'Whatever did you do to him?' he whispered. 'He's giving you the evil eye and more.'

'I met him earlier.' Alex spoke from behind her hand. 'We didn't seem to hit it off.' She made the effort and smiled and nodded at Berry. The police officer glared back.

'Evidently.' Heath began jiggling his knee. 'When are they going to get on with it?'

'Patience. You're not in London now.' She refreshed *The Post*'s website on her phone once more. Nothing.

DI Berry cleared his throat. DS Logan folded her hands in front of her. Berry leaned into the bank of microphones. 'Good evening, ladies and gentlemen,' he began, 'and thank you for coming this evening. Earlier today two bodies were found on the boat Firefly Lady moored off Poppy Island on Dillingham Broad. They have been identified as Derek Daley, aged sixty-two, a magazine proprietor from London, and Roger Fleet, also aged sixty-two and a farmer from Suffolk.' He stopped and surveyed the room. There was a low murmur as the various journalists took in the information. Those who knew who Derek Daley was would realize immediately it was a pretty big story. Alex texted Bud.

Names confirmed by the cops.

'Their deaths are being treated as unexplained. At the moment, we are not seeking anyone else in connection with the enquiry. That's all I have for you at this time, but if anyone saw anything suspicious around the time the boat was hired three days ago, or motored past the boat in the last three days, please get in touch.' Berry held up his hand. 'I'm not taking questions, thank you.'

He marched off the stage, Logan in tow.

'He likes talking to the press, doesn't he?' said Heath, standing up.

'We need more. Especially if Bud is being cautious.'

'Mmm. Berry didn't even give out the fumes from the barbecue line. I wonder why not?' He grinned. 'I think you should ask your Detective Inspector Berry – get a bit more colour.'

'More colour? Two bodies turning to liquid on a boat not enough for you? And he's not *my* Detective Inspector Berry, thank you.'

'He could be. We need a handle on how they died.'

'You ask him.'

'You're prettier.'

'You're sexist.'

'I know. Go on, I'll buy you dinner.'

Alex laughed. 'You mean *The Post*'s expenses will buy me dinner. Anyway, no thanks, I'm out tonight.'

He raised an eyebrow.

'Nothing like that,' she said. 'A friend. A girlfriend.' Why did she feel the need to explain?

'Tomorrow then?'

'Are you expecting to be here tomorrow?'

'We still need to know how they died. And Bud will want a backgrounder.'

'I could do some digging for you.' The words were out of her mouth before she'd hardly thought them. Where did that come from? Was she really offering to do Heath's work for him? But then, she had felt alive these last few hours, in a way that she hadn't felt for a long time. And she was involved in the story; she wanted to find out more about Daley and Fleet and how a man from London and a man from Suffolk ended up on a boat together on the Broads.

Heath seized eagerly onto her words. 'I wouldn't mind that. I'll get home quicker then. I'll square it with Bud. I think more than two nights in The Travelling Inn would just about do me in.'

'I know that place, it's outside the town here, isn't it?'

He shuddered. 'Yes. I think I'm the only person staying there. Or everyone else has died and are lying undiscovered in their lumpy beds. Look. I mean it. About dinner. Perhaps you could do some asking around tomorrow and then we could reconvene at a restaurant of your choice.' He frowned. 'There are decent restaurants around here, aren't there?'

'Yes,' Alex replied, affronted. 'We even have chefs who can cook, you know. The Fox and Goose in Sole Bay is excellent. And is probably better than your Chiltern Firehouse or Soho Farmhouse or wherever you like to hang out.'

'I'm sure the Fox and Goose will be fine.' He grinned. 'That's a date then.'

'No, it is not,' she retorted crossly. 'It's a business meeting.'

'Shame. Now, you talk to the friendliest policeman in town and let me know how it goes.'

Alex looked at him. Patronizing git. 'As a matter of interest, Heath, what are you going to do tomorrow?'

'Have a look around, get the lie of the land, that sort of thing.'

'Don't work too hard, will you?'

'I'll try not to.'

'I was being sarcastic.'

'I know.' He grinned. 'Don't worry, I've got a couple of people to talk to.' He tapped the side of his nose. 'I'll let you know how it goes.' And with that, he stuck his hands in his pockets and sauntered off. Whistling.

How irritating was he?

She would have to stay one step ahead.

8

'So how are things going?' Lin refilled Alex's wine glass. 'You seem tired.'

Alex leaned back in her chair, running the tip of her finger around the rim of the glass. 'Not too bad. It's been an interesting day.' She yawned, trying not to think of Heath Maitland and how annoying he was. And trying not to think of DI Berry who had merely glared at her and walked off when she'd tried to ask him a question. What a rude man. Listen to her – what an old woman she was turning into. 'That was a lovely meal, thanks, Lin.'

They were sitting in Lin's kitchen, the folding glass doors open, the air soft and still. There was a faint smell of the sea and the odd sounds from the road were of people talking, footsteps, a dog barking, rather than actual traffic. The scent of honeysuckle drifted in. Alex was full and sleepy. Must be relaxed, she thought. Even the kitchen, which was peaceful with its off-white and duck-egg blue décor and a couple of Lin's oil paintings on the wall, was neat and ordered as though no cooking had gone on there, despite the ravioli in pesto sauce topped with mozzarella cheese and accompanied by a side salad Lin had made.

Lin put down her glass and seemed to steady herself. 'Look. I didn't tell you the whole truth about where I'd been for the last few days.' She chewed her bottom lip.

'What do you mean?' She had never seen Lin look so vulnerable.

'I did go on a course like I said, but I also went to visit my brother. My younger brother. In Craighill. It's a unit for people with mental health problems. He has schizophrenia and hasn't been taking his medication properly so …' The words came out all in a rush. Her eyes glistened with unshed tears.

Alex sat up, her tiredness gone. 'Lin—'

Lin held up her hand. 'I don't want your pity.'

'I'm not—'

'It's difficult to tell people, you see. I don't normally do it. People don't understand. It's not like having a broken arm or something that you can see and that you know will be mended in a few short weeks. But I thought we were becoming good friends and it's a relief to say it. I can't keep it bottled up any longer, not from you.' She gave a little hiccup. 'I used to tell people and they would drop me as their friend, as if it was contagious or something like chickenpox or herpes.' She looked at Alex. They both giggled. 'You know what I mean.'

Alex reached for her hand and squeezed it. 'What's his name?'

'Name?'

'Your brother.'

'Bobby.' She sniffed. 'There. Now you feel sorry for me. I can't have that.' Her smile was wobbly.

'I don't feel sorry for you.'

'Yes, you do.'

Alex looked at Lin. If her friend had heard any gossip about her then she was keeping a pretty good poker face about it. Normally Alex didn't like talking about what Sasha had done to her family – her whole family – and, deliberately, she didn't easily invite confidences, but Lin was watching her with pain in her eyes and Alex wanted to reach out to her. Could she do it, though?

Could she really expose herself and her life to a relative stranger? But Lin was her friend, and you should trust friends, right? She took a deep breath. 'I don't feel sorry for you because I know what it's like to have someone close to you who has mental health problems.'

'A bit batty, you mean?'

Alex smiled. 'Something like that. My sister, Sasha, has been very ill over the past few years.'

'How so?'

'She suffers – suffered – from severe post-natal depression. These days it would be called post-partum psychosis because she … um …' Alex's throat filled up with tears. She swallowed hard. 'She killed her children. They were twins. Four years old. And she's been getting treatment in a mental health unit. The judge was very kind to her. During the trial.' She waited for the gasp of shock and horror from Lin, but none came.

'That must be so hard for you.' The hand she had reached out to Lin was now being squeezed, and Lin's careful tone pulled Alex back from the brink. She was able to tell Lin the story of how Sasha had drowned her twins in the North Sea more than fifteen years earlier, how two people were jailed in connection with their murder. How neither of those two people lived to see Sasha tell the truth. The truth that had only come out two years ago.

'Was there ever a part of you that over the years thought Sasha had killed her babies?'

Alex didn't know how to answer that. It was something she had asked herself over and over again. Had she turned a blind eye to what Sasha could be capable of? Had she been lying to herself for years? Alex couldn't fully answer those questions, which was why the guilt still haunted her however much she told herself she had dealt with it.

'Look, it was unfair of me to ask you that,' said Lin.

'No, it's perfectly fair but I don't know the answer. And I feel guilty about that. That and the fact the children were taken from my garden while I was in bed with a man.'

Lin gave a low whistle. 'Right.'

'A man who was arrested for their murder but died in prison.'

'God, woman, it sounds like something off Jeremy Kyle.' Her friend was obviously trying to lift the atmosphere and Alex liked her for that. Lin stood up. 'I know what you need.'

'My bed?' said Alex, hopefully. All this confessional stuff was exhausting. Yet liberating too. She felt as though some of what she called her cloak of doom had been peeled away from her shoulders.

'A bit of fresh air. Come on, let's go to the beach.'

'Really?'

'Yes. I want to know all about what you were doing today and also what else is on your mind.'

'What else?'

'Yep. What else. And my guess is that it's something to do with that troublesome sister of yours. Either that or a man.'

Alex laughed. 'What are you? A mind reader?'

'So it's a man?'

'No.' But talking about Sasha had brought her to the forefront of her mind. A problem she had to solve. She didn't want to think about it now.

'Come on.' Lin grabbed the wine bottle and two clean glasses from the cupboard. 'Let's go and blast the cobwebs away.'

'Hardly blasting,' grumbled Alex, standing. 'There's no wind and it's quite warm.'

'All the better, then,' said Lin. 'Come on.'

The walk to the prom and down onto the beach took them less than ten minutes. There were still plenty of people around enjoying the unseasonably warm evening. Lin settled down with her back up against the wood of a groyne and pushed the glasses and bottle into the sand. Gulls still wheeled and screamed above them, and the sea whispered on the shingle at the shoreline.

Alex sat. 'I love the sea. Because it's always there, coming in, going out. It's dependable.'

'Dependable?'

'You know what I mean. The tide going in and out has been happening for millions of years, and it'll go on happening. Long after human beings have become extinct. Puts things in perspective somehow.' She picked up the wine Lin had just poured and took a sip. She looked around in the fading light. It wasn't far from here that Sasha had waded into the sea with her two babies and just let them – drown. She shivered.

'Cold?'

'I'm fine,' said Alex, putting the memory back in its box.

'So?' Lin raised her eyebrows.

Alex picked up a handful of sand and let it trickle through her fingers. 'So?'

'Tell me about today first of all. You said it had been interesting?'

'There's not much to tell. As I said when I saw you, my old news editor, Bud, asked me to keep an eye on what was happening with the boat where the bodies were found.'

'Oh yes, keeping the seat warm for some hotshot to come and take all the credit for your hard work.'

Alex laughed. 'Hardly, Lin. But—'

'But you quite enjoyed the thrill of the chase and now you want to stay on it?'

'Something like that.' Alex paused, trying to marshal her thoughts. 'I came alive again today. Felt I was doing something, not just writing about, I don't know, the Aldeburgh Festival or the price of beach huts in Sole Bay. Or even extreme couponing.'

'Extreme what?'

Alex waved her hand. 'Never mind. It's too dull to go into.'

'Okay. But I thought you liked doing those features?'

'I do. Though—' She frowned.

'Today was more exciting.'

'I think that's what it is, yes.'

'So don't let Heath Maitland take all the glory. Get in there.'

'Maybe.' She thought about the tingle of excitement she'd had when she'd spoken to Colin Harper. How she had felt she belonged when she sat at the presser.

'No "maybe" about it. It's your story.'

That's what she liked about Lin – that she was so loyal, so behind her. She looked at her friend and grinned. 'You seem awfully keen to keep me on this story. You'll have to talk to Bud.' A thought suddenly struck her. 'Heath Maitland. How did you know it was him who came up from London?'

Lin poured them both some more wine. 'You told me.'

'Did I?'

Lin nudged her gently. 'Yes, you did. Over dinner.' She looked at Alex over the rim of her glass. 'So tell me how far you've got. With your investigating. Sounds so grown-up.'

'Ha! Not really. And I haven't got very far at all. I managed to get the addresses of Derek Daley and Roger Fleet. Mind you, I expect Bud knows Daley's address anyway – and I had a tour around a boat similar to the one Daley and Fleet hired.'

'Is that it?'

'Yep. Why, did you think I should have unmasked the killer by now?'

'Of course,' Lin laughed. 'I have every faith in your abilities.'

'And what were you doing there this morning?'

'Where?'

'Down at the staithe?'

'I told you, heard there was something going on and I wanted to find out what it was. Plus I needed some pictures for my artwork. You know, of all those ducks and geese. And the fisherman for that matter.'

'And the bird shit?'

'That too.'

Alex smiled. They looked out over the grey sea.

'So. What's on your mind, Alex? I know there's something.'

Alex sighed deeply and shut her eyes. She knew she was going to have to face this sooner or later. Sooner was probably better. 'You're right. It is about Sasha.'

'Okay. And now you've told me all about her, you can tell me what the latest is.' She leaned across and kissed Alex softly on the cheek. 'That's what friends are for.'

Alex opened her eyes. 'She's been released from the mental health unit.'

'Right.'

'I had an email this morning asking me how she was getting on now she'd been with me for two days. I didn't know how to reply; well, I haven't replied, because she's not with me. She left the unit and could be anywhere.'

Lin sat back. 'Not with you? You must be frantic. Where could she be?'

'That's just it, I know I should be worried, chasing around and I am, but …' She hugged her knees.

'You have made some calls?'

'Yes. But she hasn't got many friends.'

'Police?'

Alex shook her head. 'I haven't gone down that road yet.'

'But she's a vulnerable person—'

'I know.' Alex managed to stop herself shouting. She took a deep breath, steadied herself. 'I've tried her phone, left a message.'

'You need to do more than that.'

Alex felt the tears prick at the back of her eyes. 'I will. I will. I keep thinking she'll phone me. Or that she's gone to stay with someone she met in the unit. That she wanted to have a bit of time to herself. That if I don't hear anything I will go to the police tomorrow.'

'Right.' Lin sounded doubtful.

Alex sighed. She had to go on, tell Lin the truth. She took a deep breath. 'The thing is, I've been dreading having her with me.'

And that dread was why she had pushed the problem of Sasha to the back of her mind. And that in itself was unusual for her. All her life she had been the one caring about her sister, trying to do right by her, shielding her as much as she could. Not that it had done any good in the end. But now she had had several months with Sasha not being her responsibility, and, though she hated to admit it to herself, had enjoyed the freedom that had brought.

'Okay,' said Lin, slowly. 'But you want to have your sister back home with you, don't you? So you can look after her?'

'Yes. But—'

'But what? She's your sister, Alex. And you need to know where she is.'

Alex blinked at the harshness in Lin's voice.

'I'm sorry, I'm sorry,' said Lin, shaking her head. 'What am I like? I should know better, what with my brother and his problems.'

'No, you're right. But – I don't know if I'll be able to cope,' she whispered. It wasn't just that. Alex thought she might let Sasha down again. Not be able to look after her properly. Or was it something else entirely – something Alex couldn't bring herself to think about: that she didn't want her troubled sister with her?

'Of course you'll cope,' Lin said. 'She's your family. If you think you can't manage, what about your parents?'

Alex shook her head. 'No. Mum's got enough to do with Dad and everything, and anyway, Sash says she's caused them enough grief.' She laughed, but it was hollow. 'As if she hasn't caused me any over the years, sabotaging my life, my relationships.'

'Your relationships?'

Alex wished she hadn't said anything. 'You know.'

'No?'

'Well, she married my boyfriend, Jez.'

'What? She nicked him off you? More fodder for Jeremy Kyle.' Alex couldn't help but smile. 'Not exactly. We had finished with each other. And they did fall in love. Married young. Had the twins shortly after. And that's when the depression and the self-harming got worse. After the two children died, Sasha needed even more looking after, until it came out she had killed the children herself.'

'Shitstorm.'

'You could say that.' Alex leaned back. 'You know, you really are easy to talk to. I hardly ever, well, never really, tell people about Sasha. Not all about her. You're the first person in a long while.' Only Malone knew this much about her. Only Malone knew the depth of her guilt. But he wasn't here now.

'Should be a counsellor, me. Well,' Lin went on, 'she's your sister. Family. You've got no other ties, have you? Apart from Gus, I mean.'

Alex briefly thought again of Malone, wondered where he was, what he was doing, then shook her head. 'No. No other ties.'

Gus. She groaned.

'Now what?'

'I haven't done the shopping. Gus is due home sometime soon and I haven't got anything in for him. Or Sasha for that matter if she does deign to come to my house.' She smacked the palm of her hand against her forehead. 'Oh, I'm such a bad person.'

'No, you're not. You can do the supermarket run tomorrow. And you can shop for Sasha while you're at it. Spoil her a bit.'

Alex nodded. 'I suppose I could.'

'And you must find out where she is and get her home. To your home.'

'Yes. I know.'

They sat in silence, sipping their wine, watching the sky turn gold and then red as the sun began to set.

'Have you ever been married?' asked Lin, suddenly.

'Me?'

'Yes you,' she laughed, sweeping her arm around. 'There's no one else in hearing distance, is there?'

'No. Never married.'

'I never liked to ask you before. You seem so – contained.'

'Do I?' Alex was surprised. She'd never thought of herself as 'contained'. Perhaps that's what happened when you lived on your own. Or when you lost someone you thought would be around forever. Someone she'd fallen in love with. Who had taken a phone call and walked out of her life again. One phone call, that's all it had taken. 'I've had boyfriends – is that what you call them? I feel a bit old saying that, though. Most of them mistakes.'

'Even Gus's father?'

'Especially Gus's father. One-night stand in Ibiza. Too much drink, a bit of E and there I was, pregnant. But it's all worked out. Gus finally met his father and is working with him at the moment.'

'Whereabouts is that?'

'Ibiza. It's good for him,' she said firmly. 'To get to know his dad. I denied him that for too many years.' Alex looked at her. 'What about you? Relationships, I mean?'

'Who me?' She shook her head. 'No. Me and relationships are a no-no. Toxic.'

'Come on, Lin.'

'Truly. Anyway, I don't want to talk about me—'

'And I don't want to talk about me any more.' Alex jumped up. 'I'm too boring for words.' She yawned widely. 'And I must get back and get some sleep.'

Lin pouted. 'Spoilsport. Just when I thought you were going to tell me about the men in your life.'

'Nothing to tell.' Alex brushed sand and small pebbles off the back of her jeans. 'Come on, race you to the prom.'

Lin struggled up, clutching the empty wine bottle. 'Cheater.'

Alex laughed.

9

The early morning air was crisp and fresh and the hedgerows were covered in frilly cow parsley as Alex drove to Lapford. She reached the home of the late Roger Fleet in little under an hour. She wanted to see where he had lived, to get a feel for the man from the depths of Suffolk who had chosen to end his life with a magazine owner from London. She hoped if she got there early enough she would beat Heath Maitland to it – he'd never made an early start in all the years she had known him – and also, with any luck, there wouldn't be anyone around to question her as to why she was there.

The satnav took her through the actual village of Lapford itself, past a high school, a crinkle-crackle wall, and along a high street that could have come out of the Middle Ages, all beamed houses and cottage gardens. Some had notices outside advertising free-range eggs or garden vegetables. One enterprising householder sold jam and pickles at his gate. Alex wondered how long it would take the health and safety police to get to that one. There was even a little duck pond in the centre of a green, complete with duck house in the middle and a wooden bench on the edge. And actual ducks too. The only people she saw were an old boy on a bike in his wellingtons, probably going to work at a local farm, and two dog walkers.

She turned left opposite the primary school with three distinctive arches at its entrance and a couple of cars parked on the bit of grass next to it, past a newsagent, a butcher's shop, a deli and an imposing church with a tall tower, and on to the road out of town.

After a few more twists and turns Alex drew up outside a five-bar metal gate. A wooden board at the side of the gate proclaimed it to be Hillside Farm. Excellent, she thought, as she parked up on the grass verge.

The soothing sound of a harp made her look at her phone. It was a text message from Gus, at last.

Hi Ma, it said, *planning to get a flight from Ibiza to Stansted in the next day or so. Will try and let you know tomorrow what time and when. I'll make my own way to Sole Bay, just get the food in, I'm Hank Marvin!*

Alex smiled. She was looking forward to seeing her son again – it was many months since he'd gone to Ibiza to meet his father for the first time. Gus had slotted into his father's family of Argentinian wife and three children as if he'd known them all his life. Which was a good thing. A really good thing. And it was good that he got on with his dad. It was the right thing to happen.

So why did she always feel that twist of jealousy when she spoke to him over FaceTime and he waxed lyrical about what fabulous people they all were and how he was enjoying working for his father and how he couldn't believe he'd waited so long to find him? Alex nodded and made encouraging noises, all the while feeling the envy and the slight resentment (slight? really?) that he should have this much enthusiasm for a man she'd had a one-night stand with and who hadn't wanted to know her the next morning.

Stop it, she told herself. Just stop it. Gus was happy and that was all that mattered.

Great, she typed. *So looking forward to seeing you.*

Texts, she thought, were lifesavers. She could stop worrying about Gus, and she'd had one from Sasha earlier that morning telling her not to worry, that she was with a friend. Right then, she wouldn't worry. Much.

She jumped out of the car and pushed open the gate, shutting it behind her. Then she took a picture of the pebble-dashed bungalow in the distance with her phone, and a close-up of the veg garden.

Walking up the drive she marvelled at the rows of young vegetables growing either side of the gravel. If she was a proper gardener she would have known what was there; as it was, she could only identify some curly lettuces, the beginning of frondy carrot tops and wigwams made out of canes ready for runner bean plants to curl around. As she got closer to the house she sniffed the air. The sweet, earthy smell told her there were pigs in the vicinity, and she heard the triumphant crowing of at least one hen that had just laid an egg.

Police tape had been fixed across the front door of the bungalow. They must have come yesterday, maybe looked for clues to – what? – to see why he killed himself? She frowned. So, the house was still the subject of a forensic investigation.

She walked around the back and found a number of fenced-off areas with chickens, pigs, and sheep. There was also a goat tethered in one corner underneath an apple tree. When she got closer she saw large plastic buckets of feed and water. So the animals were being cared for.

'What do you want?'

Alex turned and saw a woman whose age could have been anything from thirty-five to sixty with a sharp, ferrety face. She was carrying a bucket and a shovel and was wearing wellington boots together with a muddy-coloured skirt (or perhaps it was muddy) and a faded pink tee shirt, partly covered by a flowery cardigan. So much for nobody else being about this early. She hadn't thought about someone coming along to feed the animals.

The woman put the bucket and shovel down. 'I said, what do you want?' There was no friendliness in her voice.

'I was worried,' said Alex, thinking quickly, 'about the animals.'

'Why would you be worried?'

'Because—' Alex floundered.

'RSPCA, are you?'

'No.'

'DEFRA?'

'No.' Did she look like someone from a government department then? She would have to take more careful note of what she wore.

'So what business is it of yours?'

'None really, but—'

'Well, bugger off then. Go on. Roger doesn't like visitors. Never has. Never will.'

With a sinking feeling Alex realized the woman probably didn't know about the death of Roger Fleet on the boat.

'I'm sorry, but—'

'Did you not hear me?' She raised her voice. 'I'll call the police if you don't leave. Now.'

Alex had to try again. 'Are you Mr Fleet's wife?' Unlikely, she knew, as a wife would have been told by now of Fleet's death, but she thought talking to this woman could be useful.

The woman laughed. 'Wife? That's a fine one. Best I've heard yet. No, Roger hasn't got a wife. Never had, never will, I shouldn't think. Likes his own company. Anyway, what's it to you? And why should you be worried about the animals? He loves them and always asks me to look after them when he goes away. He'll be back later today or tomorrow at the latest. Not that it's any of your business.'

'You haven't seen police here?'

She shook her head. 'Why should they come out here?'

So she hadn't seen the police tape at the front door. 'Mrs—?'

'Archer.'

There was nothing else for it. She stepped forward. 'Mrs Archer, perhaps we could go somewhere and sit down.' She took her elbow.

'"Sit down"?' Mrs Archer shook off Alex's hand. 'What do I want to do that for? I've got animals to feed.'

Alex took a deep breath. 'Look, I'm really sorry to be the one to tell you this, but I'm afraid I've got some very bad news. Roger Fleet has passed away.' She flinched inwardly as she used that phrase – she had always thought it mealy-mouthed – and she wanted to go and put her arms around the woman, but she didn't think it would be welcomed. Instead, she watched as the colour drained from Mrs Archer's face and her whole body sagged.

'"Passed away"? Died, you mean? Oh my.' Mrs Archer put her hand to her throat. 'What was it? Heart attack? He never looked after himself properly, all the years I've known him.'

'I don't know how he died, I'm afraid.' That much was true.

'Where did it happen? In Penstone?'

'Penstone?'

'The Priory.'

'The Priory?' Alex frowned. 'I'm sorry, I didn't realize Mr Fleet had problems?'

'Problems?' Mrs Archer sighed. 'He certainly had problems. No love, not that fancy place that's always on the news with some celebrity or other falling through its doors. This priory is the Catholic place in Penstone. He was on a retreat.'

'A retreat?'

'Bugger me, girl, do you always repeat everything? He was praying and that. Searching his soul. That's what he told me. He went ten days ago. Load of old nonsense, if you ask me. I was surprised, though, because I know he didn't have a lot to do with religion.'

'Did he say why he was going at this particular time?'

'Said he needed to make his peace with God.' She frowned. 'And now he's dead. Poor sod. What's going to happen to his animals? I can't look after them all the time. What's going to happen, tell me that?'

'I don't know, Mrs Archer. Perhaps the RSPCA could help. Did he have any family?'

'A sister. In London.' She frowned as she thought. 'Uptight piece she is. Treated me like I was the home help when I met her. I don't think they got on. Not much love lost, if you know what I mean.'

'Do you know his sister's name?'

'Margaret. Margaret Winwood. Lives in Twickenham. I remember that because of the rugby. You know, the stadium. I want to go to a match one day. Love watching it. All those well-built men in shorts running around barging into one another. Do you like rugby?'

Alex tried to keep a straight face – she was having a hard time reconciling Mrs Archer with a love of rugby players. 'I quite enjoy watching it sometimes.'

'Anyway, why do you want to know about his sister?'

'I—'

'Because I can't stand here chatting all day otherwise the poor buggers'll die of hunger and thirst.' Mrs Archer picked up the bucket and shovel. Her lip wobbled slightly. 'Roger wouldn't want his animals to go without.' She shook her head. 'It's a bad business. He was quite a troubled soul, I think.'

'Oh?' Alex wanted to keep her talking.

'Something had gone on in his life that had made him sad. He never would tell me, well, I wouldn't have expected him to, but he was a kind man. He would invite me in for a cuppa of a morning and we would sit and put the world to rights, though he would never say anything bad about anybody. Such a gentle soul. Educated too. "Mrs Archer", he'd say, "things might not have always gone right, but I do have my animals and my land". That's what he'd say. And he loved his dogs, Bramble and Cotton. Two brown labs they are.' She put her free hand over her mouth.

'What's going to happen to them? They're with me for the moment, but I can't keep them. Pigs and sheep and hens are one thing, but those lovely dogs. Oh my word.'

'I'm sure arrangements will be made.' Alex felt helpless.

'"Arrangements". Poor bugger. I suppose they'll let me know when the funeral is.'

'I'm sure they will.' Though Alex did wonder who 'they' were.

'Anyway,' went on Mrs Archer, who seemed to have found that once she started speaking she couldn't stop, 'you haven't told me how it happened. Roger dying, I mean.'

'It was on a boat. On the Broads.'

'On a boat?' Mrs Archer looked disbelieving. 'Roger wouldn't go on a boat, not for all the tea in China. He hated boats. And he was on a retreat.'

Alex filed that away. 'I'm sorry, Mrs Archer, it seems after his retreat he went on the Broads. On a boat. I daresay the police will be able to fill you in, even if you're not next of kin.'

'I might not be next of kin, but I'm the one who knew him best these past years. What was it, an accident?'

'The police aren't totally sure,' Alex answered. There was no way she was going to add to this woman's distress.

'I see. And who are you exactly?' Mrs Archer suddenly eyed Alex suspiciously.

'I'm—'

'You one of them reporters, aren't you?'

'I am, yes.'

'Guessed as much.' She pulled her cardigan tight around herself. 'Now bugger off, I need to get on.'

'I'm so sorry, Mrs Archer. About Mr Fleet, I mean.'

'Yes. Well.' Mrs Archer shrugged and walked away, her body stiff, her head held high.

Alex watched her go, then hurried back to her car where she opened Google on her phone. Thank goodness 4G had reached even rural Suffolk; this part of it anyway. Penstone Priory was about an hour away. According to its website, it offered a 'tranquil environment' for people who wanted a 'break from the trials and tribulations of everyday life'. It was run by Augustinian monks, who would doubtless keep their counsel and not breathe a word about what was troubling Roger Fleet even if they knew. Hmm. Maybe she'd keep that on the back burner.

Now for Margaret Winwood in Twickenham. Her address. Surely it wouldn't be as easy as – yes it was. BT Phonebook, thank you very much. Only one Winwood in Twickenham, and that was an 'M Winwood'. Had to be her, surely? Unless Roger Fleet's sister was ex-directory of course. She could ring, but— She looked at her watch. Thanks to her early start she had more than enough time to get down to London and be back in time to meet Heath at the Fox and Goose. Much better to talk to Mrs Winwood face-to-face.

As she turned the key in the ignition there was a sharp knock on her window. Startled, she looked up to see the glowering face of Detective Inspector Berry. She glanced in her rear-view mirror. Bloody hell. She'd been so intent on looking up Penstone Priory and Margaret Winwood that she hadn't noticed the car parked across the road from her.

She pressed the button to lower the window, a smile fixed on to her face. 'DI Berry. How lovely to see you.' Be polite to police officers. That was always her mantra. Where possible.

He leaned down towards her. 'Fancy seeing you here, Ms Devlin.' No smile.

Ah. Not good when they remember your name.

'And what are you doing here, may I ask?'

'DI Berry,' she said with great patience, 'I'm a journalist. I needed some background, some colour on Roger Fleet. I wanted to see where he lived, that's all.'

'You're trespassing.'

'I—'

'Was trespassing. There are laws against that, you know.'

'I've been speaking to Mrs Archer.'

'Ah. The lady who feeds the animals. Yes. We are about to speak to her ourselves.'

'Right.' Alex couldn't think of what to say.

'Ms Devlin, please don't interfere with our investigation.'

'So it is an investigation?'

DI Berry sighed and raised his eyes to heaven. Probably to find inspiration, she thought. 'Until we have established the exact cause of death then it is an investigation. We are very thorough.' His fingers tapped the top of the window. 'A word of advice.'

'Yes?'

'Leave well alone. Let us get on with our job. It's hard enough without people like you running around like headless chickens.'

Alex made sure her smile didn't slip. 'Of course, DI Berry. I won't interfere.'

'Thank you. That's the right answer. We wouldn't want to have to haul you in for impeding an investigation now, would we?' He straightened up. 'On your way.' And he gave an irritating two bangs on the car roof.

Alex drove away. Sedately. Giving a small wave to a boot-faced DS Logan who was climbing out of the parked car.

She thought for a minute. Had he just threatened her?

10

Willem Major was the beginning of my reinvention. He was glamorous, exciting, fascinating. He took me under his wing. I completely abandoned Stu for Willem, who liked to baffle me with Wagner and Strauss, with Anouilh and Brecht, with any number of subjects I knew nothing about. I learned he had landed at the university three weeks early – 'Parents didn't want me hanging around,' he said. But I was surprised he was only a first year like me; he seemed so confident around the university and the city, and he also greeted everyone he met as though he knew them. 'Puts them on the back foot, darling,' he said. 'They think they should know you, but of course they don't. It leaves them racking their brains for when they met you first. Great stuff.' Then he would quote Chaucer or some obscure poet at me for no particular reason.

Always playing a part was Willem.

Those early autumn days were sharp and sunny, and Willem and I bought bikes that just about fulfilled the brief and we gloried in freewheeling down the hill in the sunshine and under plane trees with their golden leaves, and then we would go on to

76

lectures or to sit in book-lined rooms in front of spitting log fires.

We drank weak tea and ate cornflakes in the tiny kitchen shared by all on my staircase until he rousted me out and took me to drink weak coffee in backstreet cafés. Eventually Willem deigned to take me to Fitzbillies ('What, have you never heard of it? You are so parochial!') to gorge on proper tea and Chelsea buns. This is what I had dreamed about all those years in my dull Midlands town, what I had been reaching for. And no one questioned who I was or what I was. I made other friends, acquaintances; I even saw Stu from time to time, but Willem was the one who interested me, fascinated me, even.

He introduced me to uppers and downers and everything in between. I was ripe for new experiences.

Then I met Rachel.

Rachel was small and slim, with fine white-blonde hair that hung straight to her shoulders. She was studying English, and I met her in a café one day when I was, for once, without Willem. We got talking and found we had so much in common – books, music, bands. Her shyness, her delicate bones and porcelain skin, made me feel protective. I wanted to spend more time with Rachel and less with Willem. But Willem kept bombarding me with his company.

'What do you see in her?' he asked me. 'I don't understand it.'

'She's … sweet,' I said.

'Sweet? What does that even mean?' And then he said: 'Have you slept with her?'

The colour that rose in my face told him what he wanted to know. 'And I'll bet it was the first time for both of you?' he jeered.

'Leave it, Willem,' I said. 'I like her, and I won't let you spoil it.'

One day I was working at my desk in two thick jumpers and a long woolly scarf, trying to get to grips with philosophical logic and failing completely, when Willem breezed in.

'There's a party going on at a house in Hills Road,' he said.

The nights were well and truly drawing in and I wanted to get to the bottom of this bloody branch of philosophy that seemed to involve a great deal of impenetrable maths and then have a drink in the bar and relax. Maybe play some pinball. Rachel was round at her friend's house for the evening. I didn't want to have to find my coat and shoes and go traipsing across the city in the dark and cold to some sleazy digs.

'Come on,' he said. 'We haven't been out together for simply ages.'

As usual Willem got his way.

The hallway of the party house was packed, as were the two rooms off it. Willem and I elbowed our way to the kitchen where we put down our bottles of cheap wine. Well, mine was cheap. I suspected Willem's had been carefully chosen, even if it was only going to be necked by some student low-life.

Willem spied the punch, at least he said that was what the crimson liquid in a large plastic bucket with three or four bits of fruit floating on the top was meant to be, and ladled generous quantities into thick wine glasses. 'Drink it,' he told me. 'Relax.' I sniffed it, searching for the remains of disinfectant that was probably the last liquid to have been in the bucket.

Then Willem dug into his pocket and brought out a couple of pills. Fluff was stuck to one of them. He swallowed one, handed me the fluff-covered pill. 'Here. Take it.' He grinned and pushed the hair away from his forehead. 'Come on.'

I took the pill and followed him out and into what I presume was the lounge – Willem liked to call these front rooms 'drawing rooms', I thought he was being pretentious – where the light came from candles and the furniture had been pushed back against the walls to give room for dancing. The air was redolent with sweat and weed and a musky scent. Every inch of floor space was taken up by bodies – couples intertwined, shuffling to the beat, single men, women, all pretending they were having a great time on their own. I saw the odd student from my college, but most I didn't know at all. I smiled at everyone and no one.

Willem pushed through the bodies. 'Let me introduce you to the host.'

Our host, so-called, I presumed, only because he was one of the people who rented the house, was sprawled on a sofa with his arms draped along its back, a girl one side of him, a boy the other, a cigarette dangling down from between his fleshy lips, a camera hanging round his neck. Louche was the word that came to mind.

'This is Derek,' Willem said to me, pushing me forward so I almost fell into the boy's lap.

'Hello, Derek,' I said, watching Willem as he disappeared out of the room. Where was he going? I didn't know anyone else.

'Hi.' He nodded towards his companions. 'This is Jen, that's Rog.'

Jen and Rog nodded. Then Jen smiled at me and her face lit up, making her pretty. She had long, straight black hair and olive skin. She was wearing some sort of cotton shirt and a skirt of purple and yellow and black. Her lips were full. I smiled back.

'So you're Willem's latest pet?'

Derek's breath was hot in my ear. I jerked my head away.

'No,' I said. 'I'm Willem's friend.'

'Willem doesn't have friends. He's a collector. He collects people and shapes them in his own image.'

'I'm not shaped in anyone's image,' I said, sharply.

'That's what you think.' Derek threw his cigarette down on the floor and ground it under his heel. The suburban bit of me hoped it hadn't marked the carpet. It probably had. 'He monopolizes you, doesn't he? Takes you out, teaches you things. Drugs, sex—'

'Not sex.'

Derek raised an eyebrow. 'Really?'

'I've got a girlfriend.'

'Really?'

'Yes, really.' I peered around the room, hoping to see someone I knew. I was getting tired of Derek already.

'And what does Willem think of that?'

'I don't care what Willem thinks about it.'

'He won't like it.' This was from the girl, Jen.

'No, he really won't,' said Derek.

'It's nothing to do with him,' I said.

'Where is he now?' asked Derek. Kindly, I thought, which was odd.

'Dunno,' I said.

Derek stood up and offered me his hand. 'Come on.'

Tentatively, I took it. It was warm and fleshy.

He led me out of the room, along the hall and up the stairs where the carpet had worn through on the treads. I heard groaning and someone puking from behind one door. The bathroom, I surmised. Derek opened another door.

This room was dimly lit by a lamp in the corner, a red scarf or maybe a bit of material flung over the shade to give an eerie glow. Like a brothel.

Willem was lying face up upon the bed, arms flung out either side of him, naked from the waist down, his trousers round his ankles. A girl was sitting astride him, skirt hitched up around her hips, another was sitting on the edge of the bed, naked, with a cigarette in her mouth. She looked at us and smiled. 'Come on in,' she said.

I stood frozen in the doorway. The girl on top of Willem turned her head towards me.

Rachel. Her mouth was a round 'o'.

'Well?' Derek said in my ear. He was smiling, and in the half-light I couldn't make out whether it was with triumph or sorrow. Perhaps it was a bit of both. He took the camera from round his neck and snapped a picture of the tableau on the bed, the flash lighting the room for a second. 'There you go, Willem, got you for posterity.'

'Fuck off, Daley,' said Willem with a languid wave of his hand.

I shook my head, feeling sick and gullible and provincial. I didn't know who I hated more – Willem, Rachel or myself.

Willem came with a groan and a shudder. His eyes never left mine.

I fled.

11

The trouble with moving out of London, thought Alex as she tried to manoeuvre her Peugeot 206 into a parking space only big enough for one of those tiny Smart cars, was you forgot pretty quickly how noisy, how dirty and how impossible it all was. At least she'd managed to find somewhere to park: that was a miracle in itself.

She was taking a bit of a chance by not phoning ahead, she knew that. Apart from wanting to talk to her in person, she didn't want Roger Fleet's sister to tell her not to bother to come, that she didn't want to see her. No, she was relying on human nature here – that Margaret Winwood would want to talk about her brother, about the sort of person he had been. If she could get her onside then it would really round out any sort of background colour story she did. Even so, Alex was nervous. Door-knocking someone who had been recently bereaved didn't come easily to her.

Roger Fleet's sister lived in an unassuming terrace house on a road not too far from the station. Probably not too far from the rugby ground, either, and Alex wondered what the town was like on match days. Then she thought about Mrs Archer and tried to imagine her in the crowd at a match. But she couldn't.

She found the right number, opened the little gate, walked the two steps to the front door and knocked. It opened quickly, almost as if someone had been watching out for her.

A tall woman with severe grey hair and a ramrod-straight back looked at her. 'I saw you coming. If you're a journalist, I've got nothing to say. All that was in the past anyway. I'm mourning my brother, so please leave me alone. And if you're not a journalist, my brother has just died and I don't want to speak to you.' Margaret Winwood – for that must be who it was – made to close the door.

'Please, just a minute.'

There must have been enough pleading in her voice because Margaret Winwood didn't slam the door in her face. Alex took a deep breath. 'You're right, about what you said earlier. I am a journalist and I live in Suffolk, not far from your brother—'

'Did you know him?'

Alex shook her head. 'No, but—'

'So why are you here, then? Which paper did you say you were with?'

She hadn't said. '*The Post.*'

'And are you trying to rake up some muck about Roger?'

'No, not at all. I'm trying to piece together what happened. The man who Mr Fleet – Roger – was with when he died was a friend of a friend, and that friend wants to know what went on. Why they died.' She spoke quickly, wanting to gain the woman's confidence. 'I'm hoping to put together something for the paper. Talk about Roger's life. Make him a real person, not merely a statistic.'

Margaret Winwood pursed her lips. 'You're honest, I'll give you that. You'd better come in, then.'

A minute later and Alex was perching on a hard chair in what she took to be the main living room. She looked around. The room was oppressive, despite there being a large picture window looking out onto the street. Alex put it down to the grey décor, and the brooding pictures on the wall. One was of Christ with his crown of thorns, blood dripping down his forehead, a hand held out beseechingly. The other, what looked like a snowy mountain scene; but the colours were a dirty yellow and grey and the picture would make anyone gloomy looking at it.

Margaret Winwood came into the room carrying a tray with two cups of coffee and a plate of digestive biscuits.

'They said Roger killed himself.' She put the tray down on a round table with spindly legs.

'I know.'

'They also said he had contacted the other man on the Internet and they had agreed to kill themselves together. Apparently it's easier that way. Give each other strength. I hope the coffee's not too strong.' She handed Alex a cup. Her hand shook imperceptibly.

Alex sat motionless. Met on the Internet. A forum, presumably. Interesting. It was the first she had heard of that. Was that the only connection between the two men? It seemed an odd thing for two men in their sixties to do. Or maybe not. She kept quiet, wanting the other woman to fill the silence.

'They said ...' Margaret Winwood paused, her cup halfway towards her lips. 'They said they didn't know each other. That they had met on this Internet thing and had decided to die together.' She shook her head disbelievingly. 'Have you ever heard of such a thing? Talking to someone over the Internet and then meeting up to die? They said it was all on his computer. Well, have you heard of that?' She stared hard at Alex.

'As a matter of fact, I have.' She remembered reading about a couple who had mixed a lethal cocktail of chemicals and sealed themselves in a car parked down a country lane. They had met on an Internet suicide forum. They'd only been in their twenties.

'They said they lit a barbecue and then when it was smouldering brought it inside. They closed all the doors and windows tight, then lay on their beds to die. I suppose they didn't feel anything.'

Alex didn't know what to say to the other woman's obvious pain.

'I find it hard to believe that Roger would take his own life,' Margaret Winwood went on. 'It's against his religion. We're Roman Catholic,' she explained. 'And yes, the Church's position has softened over the years by giving people the benefit of the doubt, but I'm sure Roger – no, I absolutely know – he wouldn't do it.' Her eyes were bright, though whether with unshed tears or fervour, Alex wasn't sure. 'He wouldn't do it, in spite of ...' She stopped, rubbing her throat.

'In spite of what?' Alex asked, gently.

Margaret Winwood shook her head, visibly upset now.

Alex decided to change tack. 'Did you see much of your brother?' She sipped her coffee. It was surprisingly good and full of flavour.

Margaret Winwood shook her head. 'No. We had become estranged; I think that's the word for it. He lived his life in Suffolk, and I lived mine here. I'm a widow, you see. No children. But I do have the Church. Father Michael is very supportive.'

'Of course,' murmured Alex. So much for a detailed family backgrounder. 'So your brother was religious?'

The woman worked her mouth, as if she was chewing something unpleasant. 'That's just it,' she said. 'He lost his faith.'

'Oh?'

'But once a Catholic, always a Catholic. That's why he wouldn't kill himself.' She shook her head and stood, taking Alex's cup out of her hand. 'I really need to ask you to go now. I have to get on. You must understand, I have arrangements to make. Even though they haven't yet released his ...' she hesitated, 'mortal remains, there are things I must do. Paperwork to sort.'

'Of course.'

As Alex stood up, a framed photograph caught her eye. It had been taken in a garden. It must have been summer because there were pink roses in bloom, as well as geraniums and begonias in a flower bed. A man in a dark suit and a dog collar was in the centre of the photograph, his head thrown back, laughing. She picked it up to have a closer look.

'That's Roger.' Margaret Winwood's voice came from behind her. 'In the good days.' her voice was bitter.

'He was a priest?'

'He was for some years. I told you, he lost his faith. That's when he decided to bury himself in East Anglia. Where no one knew him.'

'He looks happy here.'

Margaret Winwood smiled – a genuine, relaxed smile. 'He was happy then, for quite a few years. We thought he was settled, had found his vocation. We didn't know the turmoil he was in.'

'Was there a reason? For him losing his faith, I mean?' She put the photograph back.

'There's always a reason,' said Margaret Winwood bitterly. 'But he chose not to share it with me. He took himself off to Suffolk and only communicated with me once in a blue moon, and never with our mother. You wouldn't believe that we had been quite close as children. Still. It happens. I think he knew I wanted him to seek help.'

'When he was a priest, did he have his own parish?'

'No. After he was ordained in the mid-eighties, he went to Rome to the university there for some years. He came back to England in the mid-nineties, I think it was, and taught at a college in London, where that photograph was taken. Parish life would not have suited him – he was more of an intellectual. He didn't get on in the community or with people as a whole. Sometimes he would become very withdrawn, not want to speak to anyone, and that's no good if you're supposed to be their shepherd in a parish, is it? That's when it was suggested he go into teaching, and for a while that worked. As you can see, he was happy. But then ...' Her shoulders slumped. 'Who knows? I'm just glad our father wasn't alive when he decided to leave the priesthood. It would have killed him.' She must have noticed the doubt on Alex's face. 'You don't believe me? I tell you, it's a big thing to have a priest in the family, even these days. Perhaps especially these days. Anyway, I won't keep you any longer.'

'One thing I don't understand.' Alex spoke carefully. 'Roger said he was going on a retreat to the Catholic priory in Penstone. I think he might have been there before he went on the boat. If he had lost his faith, why do you think he'd do that? Go on a retreat?'

Margaret Winwood stared at her. 'A retreat? Roger?' She shrugged. 'Perhaps he was finding his path back to the Lord. Perhaps his guilt at the harm he'd done to his family was becoming overwhelming. Catholics are very good at guilt. I hope that's the case. It would make his death easier to bear if I thought he was close to God again.'

Alex fleetingly thought she would have made a good Catholic. 'Anyway—'

'Yes, of course,' said Alex. 'Thank you for seeing me, Mrs Winwood. And if you need to talk to me anymore about Roger—'

'Why should I want to do that?' Her astonishment was genuine.

'Because it can help,' she said gently. 'To talk about your loved one. Here, take my card.'

Margaret Winwood didn't look at the business card Alex had put in her hand. 'Thank you. But I won't be needing it.'

'Mrs Winwood, the college where Roger was teaching – what was it called?'

'It doesn't matter. There's no need for you to go poking around there.' And before Alex could say anything else, she closed the door. Firmly.

Why, Alex mused as she walked away from the sad little house, did Roger Fleet leave the priesthood? And, if he'd lost his faith, why had he gone on a retreat?

She looked at her watch. Just about enough time to go and visit Goldhay College where Roger Fleet had once been a teacher. Luckily she had seen the name of the college on the back of the photograph frame, and it wouldn't take much to find the number.

12

Alex couldn't be sure, but she thought she saw DI Berry's car as she drove away from Margaret Winwood's house. If so, he was bound to find out about Goldhay College, so she wanted to get there first. Once a copper had told someone not to talk to the press, they usually didn't, so she probably wouldn't get much more out of Fleet's sister. Mrs Archer, on the other hand, was not likely to be intimidated by the likes of DI Berry. She smiled at the thought of Mrs Archer in conversation with Berry and Logan. That would be something to witness.

Goldhay College was an ugly Victorian building on the outskirts of Buckhurst Hill in Essex. Alex knew it was a college of the University of London specializing in Theology and Philosophy. The principal was Father Paul Hayes, and she had phoned ahead for an appointment.

Her footsteps crunched on gravel as she made her way round to the door marked 'Reception', where she was greeted by a friendly looking woman who directed her into the college gardens.

'Father Paul likes to be in the gardens when he can; he treats it as his second office,' she told Alex with a smile. 'Says he feels relaxed there, says it's less intimidating than the mahogany and leather of his room. Follow the corridor down to the bottom, go through the double doors, turn left then right and that will bring you to the gardens.'

'I'll try to remember that,' said Alex, not at all sure she would.

But she found the gardens at first try – lawns and hedges and mature trees, some borders coming to colourful life under the sun – and looked around for Father Paul. There was more than one man in a dog collar, and three in the whole flowing robes ensemble. She thought their offices must be a bit miserable if they were all out here. There were some younger people, too; students perhaps.

A priest sitting on a bench put down the weighty book he was reading and beckoned her over.

'Sit here, my dear.' He patted the bench beside him. 'Alex Devlin, I presume?'

'Yes,' replied Alex, already warming to this avuncular man with his ready smile and laughter lines. He looked so ordinary, it was hard to believe he had written a number of books on subjects like the theology of Jewish-Christian relationships, and spirituality and imagination. She could hardly understand the titles, never mind what they might be about. 'Father Paul Hayes?'

'Indeed. I understand you're working on a piece for your newspaper about the deaths of those two men on the Broads in Norfolk, God rest their souls?'

'That's right. And thank you for seeing me.'

'I have a niece who is studying journalism at university and I know she will be asking for work experience favours eventually. I like to help where I can.'

Alex rooted around in her pocket and handed a business card to Father Paul. 'When the time comes, tell her to get in touch with me. I might not be able to help, but I could point her in the right direction.'

'Oh, I didn't mean—'

'I know you didn't, Father. But tell her.'

'Thank you, I will. That's very kind of you. Now. I don't know how I can help you. I mean, we're a long way from the Broads here.' His smile was calm.

'One of the men who died was a Roger Fleet.' She watched, hoping to see recognition dawn on his face, but there was nothing. 'He taught here, some years ago. In the mid- to late nineties.'

'Ah.' Father Paul shook his head. 'I'm afraid I can't help you there. I didn't arrive at the college until 2004.'

Alex slumped back on the bench. A dead end.

'Tell me, my dear, what sort of information were you after? And what makes the sad deaths of those two men newsworthy? According to the BBC website, it is most probably suicide.'

'I know, Father. But one of the men is Derek Daley, a prominent businessman. He owns a successful magazine. And the other was Roger Fleet, a former priest who, as I said, taught here. There doesn't seem to be any connection between them. Apparently they met on the Internet on a suicide forum.'

Father Paul winced. 'What troubled souls they must have been.'

'I know. So I want to do a piece about these forums, how much they encourage people to take their own lives. I believe they should be shut down, though I know the Internet is hard to police. I also want to look at what sort of people Derek Daley and Roger Fleet were.'

'Hmm.'

'It's not sensationalist. If anything, I want to look at the dangers, maybe even get a debate going about it.' Alex was warming to her theme. This was exactly what she wanted to do. Campaigning journalism, doing something that would make a difference.

As long as she could get Heath out of the way, or to agree to her doing part of the story. But where should she go now?

'Anyway, Father, thank you for your time.' She began to get up off the bench.

'I'm sorry I can't help you, but Father Vincent might be able to.'

'Father Vincent?'

'Yes. He lives in the presbytery by the church. He's being looked after by the parish priest, Father David.' Father Paul laughed. 'I can see by your face that all these Fathers are confusing you.'

'A little,' Alex admitted.' There must be a collective noun for you all, surely?'

'A prayer of priests?'

'Not bad.' Alex grinned. 'In fact, I rather like that one.'

'So it shall be.' He inclined his head with a twinkly smile. 'So. Father Vincent was at Goldhay for years. He taught here about the same time as your Roger Fleet, and he might be able to help more than I can. Now he's not in the best of health and can be a bit curmudgeonly. I'm afraid I can't give you anything about Roger Fleet from our records as they are confidential, but that's not what you want anyway, is it?'

'No, I'm after the person. Though facts do provide the scaffolding.'

Father Paul looked at his watch, picked up his book and stood. 'I'm afraid I have a class to teach, but I will email you over what I can, and I will phone the presbytery now and warn them you are coming. It's at the Church of Our Lady of Perpetual Succour, and it's only five minutes from here. As I say, Father Vincent can be bad-tempered and doesn't like journalists much.'

'Is that a warning?'

Father Paul laughed. 'I suppose it is.'

Fifteen minutes later Alex was knocking on the door of the presbytery. It was a small bungalow built in the grounds of the church, which was a very modern building in the shape of a cross, constructed of light wood and glass with gardens and a car park wrapped around it.

'Welcome, welcome.' A young man in a black suit and a dog collar answered the door. 'I'm Father David. Father Paul let us know you were coming. Father Vincent is in his study.'

Father Vincent was like a children's storybook version of a priest. He was large and round, with a thatch of wild white hair. He wore a black cassock and a large wooden cross around his neck. A red plaid rug was tucked around his legs. 'Forgive me if I don't stand up,' he said. 'My knees are bad today.'

'His knees are bad every day,' said Father David. 'I'll get you both some tea. Sit down, Ms Devlin.'

Alex looked around the study. It was a bright and airy room, with bookcases along two walls, and a desk in the large window that looked across to the church.

'So?' said Father Vincent. The priest may have been large and round and kindly looking, but his eyes didn't twinkle and he had no smile on his face. 'I don't see what I can help you with. If I'd known earlier that Father Paul was sending you here I would have told you not to bother.'

Curmudgeonly was being too kind. Alex plastered her very best professional smile on her face. 'I am looking into the death of Roger Fleet. He died on a boat on the Broads.'

'I'm aware of that,' the old priest said, testily. 'Father Paul told me. Suicide. What's it got to do with you?'

Alex tried not to be knocked off course in the face of the hostility that was coming off Father Vincent in waves.

'I haven't anything to say. Especially not to journalists who twist words and meanings.'

Alex tried again. 'It's thought that Mr Fleet met Derek Daley – the other man who died – on an Internet forum. I want to raise awareness of—'

'"Raise awareness". What a terrible, empty phrase that means nothing.'

'I'm sorry you feel that way.'

'I do. So if you'll excuse me …' he waved his hand over his desk, 'I have work to do.'

'I really want to do my best by Mr Fleet.'

'Do you? Well, you'll have to do it without any help from me, I'm afraid. Roger Fleet was a very private man with a troubled soul and it doesn't need me to be adding fuel to the fire.' His eyes bored into her. 'That's all, Miss Devlin.'

At that moment the door opened, and Father David came in with a tray of tea and biscuits.

'We won't be needing those,' said Father Vincent. 'The young lady was just leaving. Weren't you?'

Alex knew when she was beaten. 'I was. But thank you for your help.' Again she gave him a wide smile. She always liked to be overly polite to those who were rude to her.

'Er ... right ... I'll see you out.' Father David put the tray down next to the other priest. 'You may as well have your coffee anyway, Father.'

The younger priest showed Alex to the front door. 'I'm sorry you caught Father Vincent on a bad day.'

'You mean he has good days?' said Alex, wryly.

Father David laughed. 'Not often, no. But ...' he looked over his shoulder, then turned back to Alex. 'He has spoken to me of Roger. He said they didn't try hard enough to help him here at the college. That's all I know.'

Alex nodded. 'Thank you.'

The door closed behind her, and Alex let out the breath she had been holding. And she thought priests were supposed to be gentle and polite and, well, nice.

Father Vincent was obviously deficient in the milk of human kindness.

13

The restaurant terrace overlooking the beach was packed. The sound of the sea mingled with the clinking of glasses and the chatter of diners. Alex spied Heath sitting at a corner table and waved, making her way over to him, swerving to avoid a waiter balancing an enormous platter on the palm of his hand loaded up with lobster, mussels, crab, oysters, langoustines, winkles and whelks all over crushed ice and decorated with seaweed.

'Good choice,' said Heath, as Alex slid into the seat opposite him. 'And popular. How did you get a table?'

Alex smiled. 'The owner is an old friend of my mother's. He can usually squeeze me in however busy it is.' She picked up the menu. 'And one of the chefs trained with Marcus Wareing. I thought it would suit your sophisticated London taste buds.'

'It certainly looks good. I've ordered a bottle of rosé.'

Alex raised an eyebrow.

'I hope that's okay?'

He looked worried, so she decided to let him off the hook. 'Yes, perfect for the start of summer. Thank you. And I could do with some alcohol, it's been a long day. Lots of driving.' She stifled a yawn.

'Worth it?'

'I'll tell you when I've had something to drink. And some food.'

Heath nodded, then frowned. 'Am I that boring?'

'What do you mean?'

He nodded towards Alex's phone that she had placed prominently on the table.

She blushed. 'Sorry, I know it's a bit rude, but I'm waiting to hear from Gus.'

'Even worse,' he said in mock horror. 'Out for dinner with one man while waiting to talk to another. Now you are making me feel really special.'

Alex's lips twitched. 'Gus. My son. I *have* told you about him?'

'Phew.' He pretended to clutch his heart. 'Not a rival then?'

She raised her eyebrows. 'A mother's son is always a rival, Heath. But not in your case. Because you and I don't have that sort of relationship.'

'Can't a man dream?'

'No. I'm waiting for a text from Gus telling me what plane he's going to be on. He's been abroad – long story – and now he's coming to be with me for a few weeks.' Or longer, she hoped. 'I'm looking forward to seeing him.'

'Of course you are.' Heath's eyes crinkled in a smile. 'I like that about you, Alex. The way you love your boy.'

Alex was irritated to feel herself blush. 'It's only natural, isn't it?'

'Not always.' He picked up the menu. 'Shall we order?'

After they had spoken to the waitress and the wine had arrived, Alex settled back in her chair, her fingers curled around the stem of her glass. 'So, what have you been doing today?'

'This and that.' He gazed around the restaurant. 'Your parents' friend must be making a mint.'

'Heath,' said Alex warningly, 'don't dissemble.'

'I'm not. I only—'

'Want to keep the story for yourself. Yeah, I get that. But I have helped you, stood around waiting to see what was going on, getting an "in" with the man from the boatyard. Giving you the addresses of Daley and Fleet.'

He waved his hand, dismissing her work. 'I could have got those quite easily. Anyway, I went to Roger Fleet's house today.'

Later than she had. She suppressed a smile.

'And?'

'Nothing there apart from a few animals. When I had a snoop around a woman who was obviously looking after them told me to "bugger off".'

Alex put her hand over her mouth. She must not smile. She must not. She was damned if she was going to say anything about her own eventful day interviewing Roger Fleet's friends and family. Not until Heath gave her something in return.

The waitress set down the plate of roasted cauliflower with feta and olives that they had agreed to share. Then the calves' liver with charred chicory for Heath, and the bavette steak with a spicy chocolate sauce for Alex.

'And a side salad,' said Heath, smiling at the waitress, who blushed, apologized, and hurried off to fetch it.

They ate without speaking for a few minutes, but soon Alex couldn't help herself. 'What about the Lodges? Gary and Ronnie? Did you talk to them?'

'I did.'

'And?'

'Not a lot. All they saw was the boat that looked closed – curtains shut and all that; Gary was worried, opened the door, and there they were. Derek Daley and Roger Fleet. Well, what was left of them anyway. Not pleasant by all accounts.'

He was being deliberately cagey.

'And have you come across the Logan and the Berry?'

'What?'

'DI Berry and DS Logan? The two officers who are on the case.'

Heath laughed, raised his glass to her. 'Are they really called that? Nope. I haven't had the pleasure.'

'Hmm. They appear to be following me around.'

'Who wouldn't?'

'Thank you, Heath. Enough of that,' she said, tartly. 'What do you think, though?'

'Think?'

'Is there a story here? I think there is. Not just about what happened, but about the people involved. Derek Daley is famous, for God's sake.'

'In some circles, yes.'

'And then there's the whole Internet suicide thing. That's incredible, something we could really expose.' How she wanted to do this.

Heath looked startled. 'Hang on a minute. Internet suicide? How did you find that one out? I thought it wasn't common knowledge?'

'But you knew too?'

'Well—'

'It's a good job I found out, then, isn't it? As you weren't going to tell me.' She was irritated.

Heath looked sheepish, then he put down his knife and fork. 'Look.' He poured them both some more wine. 'It was really great of you to find out the addresses and stuff, even though I could have done it myself, but it looks like it's an open-and-shut case of suicide – albeit an unusual suicide with the Internet connection. Worth a feature article, I guess.'

She didn't believe him. She speared a cauliflower floret and popped it into her mouth followed by a forkful of feta and black olives. 'Perfect combination,' she said, relishing the tangy, salty taste. 'Pull the other one.'

'What?'

'I don't believe this nonchalance from you about Daley and Fleet.' She leaned forward. 'Two men who don't know each other meet over the Internet and kill themselves. Come on, Heath. Okay, maybe they were gay, couldn't hack it any longer. Possible. But one was a well-known, mostly respected, magazine proprietor. The other was a farmer of sorts. Why would they want to die?' She waved her fork at him. 'Being gay in this day and age isn't a crime between two consenting adults. And why on a boat on the Norfolk Broads? Carbon monoxide poisoning is painless I'm told, but they could have been found sooner, the barbecue might not have given off enough fumes, or any at all. It's not a certain way to die, is it?'

'No—'

'Come on, you must have questions. You didn't win journalist of the year all those years ago for nothing.'

'Reporter of the Year.' He looked affronted.

Alex grinned. 'Whatever.' She waved her fork around before applying herself to cutting a piece of the steak. 'Wow, this sauce is fantastic.'

'Is everything all right for you?' The waitress set down the side salad and smiled.

'Perfect, thank you,' said Alex. 'The food is, anyway. Do you think the chef will give me the recipe for the sauce?'

'I'll ask her,' said the waitress, before moving away.

'Alex. Bud—'

'I told Bud about the damned story in the first place. I got the names and everything. Not that he ran much before anyone else.' She waved her fork again, this time with a piece of bloody meat on the end. 'I saw Mrs Archer too. Got a lot more out of her than you did. And I did a lot more digging.'

'Really?'

'Yes, really.' She felt triumphant.

'What sort of digging?'

'Don't think I'm bloody well going to tell you that. Not at the moment. So what about Bud anyway?'

He gave a deep sigh. 'Bud wants me to look around a bit more, put something together. There isn't room for two of us on this.'

'What?' Alex felt the hope drain away. She hadn't realized how much she was looking forward to getting her teeth into doing something, into exposing the danger, the sheer horror of Internet suicide forums.

'If you could give me anything else you've got?'

'Like?' No way. No way at all.

'Like you said you were exhausted, done a lot of driving today. Where have you been? Who have you seen?'

Alex shook her head. 'No. If Bud doesn't want it, I'll sell it somewhere else.'

Heath sighed and put down his knife and fork. 'Cards on the table?'

Alex nodded. 'Cards on the table.'

'So, you know there are cutbacks all across the board?'

She did know. It was proving harder and harder to get decently paid freelance work – it was only the fact she was well known in the industry that made editors come back for more. *The Post* took something from her most months, but she had heard that the paper was streamlining its operations, something to do with a sale in the offing.

'I fucked up last year,' said Heath. 'I won't go into the details. Let's just say I went too far to get a story and I'm not Bud's flavour of any month.'

'Oh, Heath.'

'I know, I know. That has put me at the top of the list for the push from the paper, and I can't afford it at the moment. You see …' He took a gulp of his wine. 'My girlfriend is going to have a baby and I want us to be together.'

Alex's mouth dropped open. Heath Maitland the serial shagger, the biggest flirt in the office was going to settle down and have babies? Well, there was a thing.

'All right, all right,' said Heath testily. 'I know how you feel. How all the girls are feeling right now.'

'How are "all the girls feeling"?' Her lips twitched.

'Devastated.'

Alex rolled her eyes.

He grinned. 'Just joking. But you see what I'm getting at.'

Since Heath was too wrapped up in what he was saying to pour Alex any more wine, she helped herself then leaned forward. 'Yes, I do. You think this could be a big story, a really big story.' She drank from her glass.

Heath leaned back in his chair.

Alex clicked her fingers. 'You're hoping this could make your career, maybe get you an award or two? Or, at the very least, make Bud sit up and realize how good you are.'

'Er … well … yes.'

'Yes. And you don't want me interfering and taking all the glory. Or any glory.'

'Something like that,' he mumbled, not looking at her.

'In fact, you know there's more to this than meets the eye. There's a reason why Bud was interested in this in the first place, isn't there? Not just because Daley was a big rival or that Bud never liked him as a person – if that was the case.'

Heath nodded. 'It was.'

'I think you have an idea what it's about.' She put down her knife and fork. 'You do, don't you? Did Daley have another life or something?' She saw a look in his eyes and leaned forward. 'I'm right, aren't I?'

Heath shook his head. 'Come on, Alex, you know I can't tell you.'

'Can't or won't?'

He smiled. 'Actually, I don't know anything. But I do know Bud's not sure the story will fly. Which is why—'

'He wants you to do it and not me. More experience.' Alex felt herself grow hot. Calm down, she told herself. She knew losing her temper wouldn't help. She took a few deep breaths.

Heath didn't reply.

Alex picked up her knife and fork again and chewed on some steak. Drank some more wine. Steadied herself.

101

'Alex. You look as though you're thinking. I can hear the cogs turning.'

'I could help you,' she said at last.

'But I've said—'

'I know what you've said. But I know the area. I'm in with Harper's Holidays, and as you've just said, I did a lot of driving today. And two heads are better than one.'

'Why should you want to help me?' His voice was full of suspicion.

'Because for the first time in a long time I feel alive, Heath. I feel I could be part of something good. Do something good. Something worthwhile. I mean, how many of these suicide forums are there? One's too many. Let me help you. I haven't got a lot on over the next few days.' She leaned forward and pointed her knife at him. 'I want to make a difference.'

'Tell me what you've got.'

She shook her head. 'Don't think I'm telling you anything until I have your agreement that we'll work on this together. You carry on writing the everyday news copy, when there's something to write about, while I do some real digging. What do you say?'

He leaned back in his chair. 'There's something else, isn't there?'

There was something else. A thought that had been growing, taking hold, over the day.

'Yes,' she said. 'Do you remember you asked me about Malone? The other day?'

'The undercover police officer you've been seeing, right?'

She nodded, then stopped. 'How did you know he was undercover?'

'I read the article you wrote about some undercover policeman's shadowy exploits some time ago – that was him, I guess?'

'Yes, it was, but—'

'Good old office gossip.'

'Really?' Alex was surprised.

'Come on, you haven't been away that long. Nothing stays private in the offices of *The Post*.'

'What else do you know about me and Malone?' Alex was curious. 'I mean, no one is supposed to know who he is. That's the whole point of being undercover.'

Heath smiled. 'I usually make it my job to know about the other halves of beautiful women.'

Much to her annoyance, Alex again felt a blush beginning across her collarbone. 'Shut up you arse.'

Heath smiled again. 'I don't know that much,' he admitted. 'And I won't put him at risk, don't worry. I know he helped you out up in north Norfolk.'

'Saved my life,' said Alex.

'But you're definitely not together any more?'

Alex shook her head. 'No. He did his usual disappearing act. Went outside to take a phone call and never came back.'

'And that was it? No text? Nothing?'

'Nothing.' She surprised herself with the nonchalance in her voice when her gut was all twisted.

'Wanker. You're well rid of him.'

That was the trouble, though. Alex wasn't rid of him. He was constantly in her thoughts. They had been through a lot together, and she felt he was part of her. And she couldn't understand why he had gone without a word, without looking back. Even here, in this lovely restaurant, with the chatter of happy diners as background she felt a longing for him. They had come here more than once. And it was here he had told her he loved her. Her heart twisted at the memory. 'I want to find him.' She wanted to find him so she could be the one to tell him to fuck off. To be in control.

'These undercover officers, many of them had wives, you know, that they married to get information. They aren't the most scrupulous of people to know.' Heath looked worried.

Alex almost smiled. Scrupulous. No, you couldn't accuse

Malone of that. He certainly did have a wife, Gillian, who he sent to prison, and a daughter, who would be what, about eight now? But, despite all that, she'd trusted him. Perhaps it was because her life hadn't exactly been straightforward that she felt he understood her. He'd been on her side, done things for her without question. Nothing was black and white in life, nothing was certain. They both knew that and that's what had bonded them. Or so she had thought.

'I know. I want to know why …' She bit down on her lip. Damn these sudden tides of emotion.

'Why what?'

'Why he left when I thought he'd stay.' Then she'd tell him to fuck off.

'Isn't that the refrain of all jilted lovers?' Heath smiled to take the sting out of his words.

'Maybe. But humour me. Use some of those investigative skills and the resources I don't have any more since I left the paper in London to see if you can get any idea of where he is. You know I can't log into those websites that find addresses or other information on my computer at home. There are people in the office that'll help you, not me. Contacts I know you've got. Helpful contacts. Please. And I can use my local knowledge and my contacts to help you. Quid pro quo as they say.'

'Who says?'

Alex laughed. 'No idea. Some philosopher at a guess.'

'Any dessert for you?' The waitress was back.

They gave their orders and then sat in silence. Alex looked out across the beach. It was almost completely dark now, and the stars were coming out in the inky sky.

'Okay,' said Heath, just as their chocolate brûlées with white chocolate panna cotta and a chocolate brownie arrived.

Alex cracked the sugar covering on her brûlée. 'You'll help?' She didn't look at him as a tide of emotion swept over her.

'Sure, why not. It'll be fun.'

'And you should get your scoop.'

'And you don't want any credit?'

She felt him examining her, as though she was about to tell a monstrous lie. 'I've told you, no. If you help me, I'll help you. Though—'

'Here it comes,' said Heath, biting into his brownie. 'I knew it was too good to be true.'

'No, nothing much but maybe an "additional reporting by". Would that be too much to ask?'

Heath sighed. 'I guess not.'

'So, deal?'

He grinned. 'Tell me what you found out today.'

Thrust and parry.

Alex considered him. He looked roguish in the candlelight of the restaurant, his eyes twinkling. No. Not twinkling, glinting. Hungry. She put a spoonful of the panna cotta into her mouth. It was deliciously rich and creamy. 'I found out that Roger Fleet used to be a Catholic priest, but he lost his faith and left the Church,' she said.

Heath snorted. 'Is that shorthand for saying he abused little choirboys and it got hushed up?'

Alex shook her head. 'No, I don't think so. And I think his faith was coming back. According to the aforementioned Mrs Archer, he was on retreat for a few days before he died.'

'Retreat?'

'You go to a monastery or convent and retreat from the world.'

'And get your shit together, yes, I know about those. Okay. What else?'

'Before Fleet lost his faith and after he'd become a priest he taught at a Catholic college, but he left under a bit of a cloud, though I'm not sure what it was. Not abuse,' she said as Heath opened his mouth. 'I told you that. But I might pay his sister—'

'Sister?'

'His sister,' she emphasized, pleased to have his undivided attention, 'another visit.'

Heath smiled slowly at her. 'Good work, Devlin. We have a deal.'

It was later than she thought when they left the restaurant, though the night was still warm. She said goodbye to Heath, and went for a walk along the prom to clear her head, which was foggy from drink and cluttered with thoughts. Thoughts about Malone, about her sister, about Heath, about her longing to do something that mattered.

There were still a few people around as she walked along the path above the beach. It was one of Alex's favourite times to be in Sole Bay – the dreary days of winter had gone and the air was becoming warmer; the season was on the cusp of summer. On one side the moon glinted off the sea as the water undulated lazily beneath the starry sky. On the other side lights were on behind curtains, people living their lives in their own houses. She often wondered who they were, what sort of life they had.

Was she being stupid asking Heath to help her look for Malone? She stopped and leaned on the railing, looking out to sea and to the empty horizon.

No, another voice said to her. She needed to lay his ghost. Anyway, she'd set it in motion now. Heath had been intrigued by Malone after she'd told him the few things she knew about him. And it wasn't until she talked to Heath that she realized how little that was. How much he had kept private. How much he had kept from her.

She heard voices down below her on the beach. A couple, entwined, only having eyes for each other.

Heath had eventually told her what Gary and Ronnie had said when he went to see them. They were still shaken up about finding the bodies. Gary had described the smell as catching in his throat, staying in his mouth for hours after. A meaty, sweet smell that clung to his clothes. He'd only been trying to do a good turn, he told Heath. And what had it got him? The sight of bloated and blackened decomposing bodies he would never forget, a smell that wouldn't leave him and several hours of questioning by the cops. Ronnie had one interesting snippet of information: that when she had seen a picture of the two men on television later that night she had recognized Roger Fleet. She was almost sure she had seen him the morning they'd hired their boat, arguing with a girl or a woman in Lowdham village. She'd noticed them because their body language had been so angry, was how she put it. Alex told Heath that she would go to the village and have a poke about.

The couple below her moved away, still in their own world. Alex sighed. Why was she such a disaster at relationships? A one-night stand that resulted in pregnancy, an affair with a man who was eventually accused of murder and a fling with someone who walked in and out of her life every so often. Not a great track record. It wasn't that she was desperate to be involved with someone, it was that it was good to be able to share things with another person – the good and the bad. That was the point of being together, wasn't it? And she got so lonely.

And even if Heath found Malone, really, what was she going to do then? Run after him? Hit him? Fuck it, she'd cross that bridge if she came to it.

She turned away from the sea and started to walk briskly down a now deserted street towards home.

All at once she became aware of footsteps behind her, mirroring her own. She paused, the hairs on the back of her neck prickling as she pretended to look into a shop window. The footsteps stopped. Ridiculous really, she told herself, the bloody window was dark. Her heart was hammering, and her mouth was dry. She began walking again even more quickly, and the footsteps kept pace with hers.

She stopped, turned around suddenly, saw a figure dart into an alleyway. Part of her wanted to run after the figure, demand to know what they were doing following her. She waited, but no one appeared. Overactive imagination. There was no one following her at all, just someone going home for the night. Her breathing steadied. Then 'Ride of the Valkyries' burst onto the air. God, she must change that ringtone.

Withheld number.

Breathing on the other end.

'Who is this?' Alex tried to push the fear away.

There was a sniff. 'Alex? When are you coming home? I'm waiting here for you.'

'Sasha?'

'I'm here.' Her sister's voice was plaintive.

'Where?'

'At home. Your home.'

Alex felt relief flood through her bones, closely followed by anger. 'Where have you been?'

'Why? Have you been worried about me?'

'Don't be stupid, of course I have. You were supposed to be in Sole Bay two days ago.'

'I'm here now.'

'But – never mind. Hang on, I'll be there in two minutes.' She put the phone back in her bag. Sasha. What on earth was she doing?

Alex hurried down the road to her house, so intent on getting back that she failed to see the shadowy figure following her every step.

14

'Have some breakfast, Sasha,' Alex said, putting two pieces of bread in the toaster. 'I've got honey or lemon curd.'

She tried not to yawn, but it was difficult. She'd lain awake until the small hours, turning things over and over in her mind, thinking about the boat, the dead men, why they were there, why Derek Daley felt the need to kill himself, why Sasha had appeared seemingly out of the blue, why she was feeling so bloody lonely. And had she made a mistake asking Heath Maitland to try and find out something – anything – about Malone? Had she come across as hopelessly needy?

At about four o'clock, after she'd tried reading, listening to the radio and counting white woolly sheep, she'd decided she would take a sleeping pill. She had been resisting them ever since being prescribed them some months ago. But perhaps now was the time to stop resisting. On the other hand, she didn't want to wake up and have a foggy head for the rest of the day.

She'd compromised and had half a pill.

At least the fog in her head was more like an autumn mist, though she did have a throbbing behind her eyes.

Sasha sat down at the table, pulling the frayed sleeves of her jumper down over her hands. 'That would be great,' she said, smiling. 'Sorry about last night. You know, just turning up like that and not wanting to talk or anything.'

'No problem.' The toast popped up and Alex put it in front of her, together with butter and honey and the lemon curd.

'Mmm, great. One of each I think,' said Sasha, beginning to butter the warm toast. 'Any coffee?'

'Are you ready to talk now?'

'There's nothing much to talk about. They said they'd emailed you to tell you I was coming, but I guess they didn't say when.'

'Sash ...' Alex didn't know what to say. The email that told her Sasha had been released and would be living with her. As agreed. Guilt reared its ugly head. 'You came out, what, two days ago? You haven't been in touch; I've had no idea where you've been even. According to the social worker, you should have been here, with me. It could have been awkward. I mean, what if your social worker had decided to pay us a visit?'

'Well, she didn't, did she? Do you really want me around?' She began to hum.

'Sasha, of course I do,' Alex said, gently. 'And Gus will be so pleased to see you.'

She stopped humming. 'Okay. And if you're not going to make coffee, I'll just have to do it.' Sasha shook her head and was smiling as she filled the kettle. 'Where's the cafetière?'

'Top right cupboard,' said Alex, not sure what to make of this new, energized Sasha. It hadn't been that long ago that she was sitting in a chair in a room not saying a word. Now she was chatting away and doing stuff as if, well, as if she was normal.

'And talking about Gus, I'm looking forward to seeing him, too,' said Sasha, pouring boiling water on the coffee grounds. 'He gets on with his dad?'

'Really well. He's been working for him.'

'In the bar?'

'That, and some odd building jobs.'

'And that's what you want for your son, is it?' asked Sasha, mildly. 'Here's your coffee. Any more toast?'

Alex's head was beginning to swim. What was Sasha up to now? Taking an interest in Gus. Going from normal to nasty and back to normal again. She couldn't keep up.

'If that's what he wants to do, then yes, I'm happy.'

'Okay.' Sasha studied the toaster.

'What do you mean "okay"?'

'It seems to me you should have more ambition for Gus. He's a bright boy, could go to university or do anything. When he was growing up—'

'What, Sasha?' Alex tried to breathe steadily, the throbbing behind her eyes increasing in intensity. 'What about when he was growing up?' When you weren't there for him.

'He was quite clever in school, wasn't he?' She pinched the toast between thumb and forefinger before throwing it on to the plate. 'Ouch. That was hot.' She sat down again.

What was going on here? 'I'm proud of Gus,' she said, eventually. 'He had a difficult time when he was young. And he is now doing what he wants and is happy doing it. That's all I want for him, Sasha. To be happy.'

Her sister looked at her over the rim of her cup.

'So. He's coming home. The good life getting him down?'

'No, don't be so shitty.' God, her sister could be irritating. 'I told you. He's coming to see me. I don't know what his plans are. He's his own person now.' Alex felt the pressure behind her eyes. She still hadn't had a text from him telling her when he was arriving. Perhaps he would tell her when he had landed. That was it. That's what he would do. 'Anyway. Enough of that. What about you?'

'Nothing wrong with me that a couple of years in a funny farm hasn't cured.'

'Oh, Sash.' Something like pity washed over Alex and she enveloped her sister in a hug.

'I know you don't really want me here.' Her shoulders were stiff beneath Alex's arms.

'Don't be daft.'

'I had nowhere else to go. Mum's got enough on her plate and I didn't want to go back to my house. Not yet. Not until I can redecorate it. It's so …' She sniffed. 'So sad in there. All those pictures stuck to the wall.'

Alex knew the pictures she meant. Pictures of the twins torn out of newspapers on the days following their disappearance. Blurry pictures of Sasha, crying on Jez's shoulder. Pictures of police officers fingertip searching the lay-by where Harry's body was found. Endless pictures. Endless photographs.

'No, and you shouldn't be on your own. I'm happy to have you.' She kissed the top of Sasha's head. 'I'm your sister.'

Sasha lifted one arm to rub Alex's shoulder. Alex tried not to look at the silvery traces of scars on her skin – memories of the time when Sasha was self-harming, when Alex had to bathe her wounds, bandage them, occasionally take her to hospital. Suddenly Alex's throat was thick with tears.

She swallowed the tears down. 'Where have you been since you were released?'

Sasha gave a crooked smile. 'Isn't the word discharged? Or is that only from a hospital? Anyway. Whatever. Where have I been? Nowhere. Stayed with a friend. Needed to get my head together, think about life, before I actually came and lived it.'

'A friend? Really?'

'What?' Her eyes flashed. 'You think I haven't got any friends, is that it? Do you think you were the only one visiting me in that godforsaken place where all they did was pump me full of drugs?'

Alex was taken aback by Sasha's vehemence. 'Okay. So you stayed with friends.'

Sasha jumped up out of her chair. 'How many times do I have to tell you? Yes, yes, yes. Now will you drop it?'

'I should have come to collect you.'

Sasha glared at her. 'You see, Alex, that's just it. You stifle me. You want me to be something I'm not. You want me to be good and docile and to do whatever you say. You always try to manipulate me. You always have.'

Alex didn't open her mouth. She had to think before she spoke or she might say something she would regret.

Sasha sat down again, pushed her plate away and took a packet of cigarettes out of her pocket. 'What?' she said to Alex, as she unwrapped the cellophane and pushed one out of the packet. 'I'm not allowed to smoke now?'

'It's up to you. I didn't know you smoked though.' She kept herself calm; she didn't want to be lashed by Sasha's tongue again.

'Not much else to do sitting in a chair all day.'

'You never did when I came to see you.'

Sasha shrugged. 'I do now. Besides, we weren't allowed to indoors.' She drew smoke deep into her lungs, as if to make a point.

'But when I took you outside you—'

'Leave it, Alex, will you.' She stubbed her hardly smoked cigarette out in the saucer Alex had put in front of her as an ashtray and immediately lit another. She poured some coffee for them both. 'Look. You want to know where I was. Why I didn't come to you straightaway. It was because I was worried some tabloid had got wind of the fact I was leaving Leacher's House and they would be camping out on your doorstep.' Her voice was soft. 'Have you heard from any journalists?'

'Just the one. Someone called Penny. Not sure where she was from, I didn't give her a chance to speak.'

'So what are you working on at the moment? The latest wedding fashions for celebrities? Or have you moved on to covering their actual weddings? I mean, you haven't done anything worthwhile for ages. That's what you told me in hospital.'

'What do you mean?'

Her sister waved her cigarette around. Ash floated to the floor.

113

'You used to talk to me about all sorts of things when I was incarcerated in that place. You went on about our childhood, about how much you loved me, how you wanted to help me. Blah blah blah. How sorry you were you hadn't helped me when I needed it. You told me how dissatisfied you were with what you were doing – that you wanted to do something useful, write stories that would make a difference.' She looked at Alex and laughed. 'What, you thought I wasn't listening to you?'

Alex blinked. That's exactly what she'd thought. She had been talking to a Sasha who sat mute in her chair looking out of the window most of the time.

'I took a lot in, you know. I liked to think about what you'd said when you'd gone. It made a change from my thoughts I can tell you.' She smoked quietly for a few minutes. Alex busied herself tidying things up that didn't need tidying.

'I'm sorry for what I said earlier. About Gus.' She spoke quietly.

'That's all right.'

'No, it's not, it was unfair. He's a good boy. Not so much of a boy now, though, I guess. All grown up.' She gave a harsh laugh. 'For what it's worth, I think you've done a good job with him.'

'Thank you.'

'I'm probably jealous.'

There was nothing Alex could say to that to make it better.

Sasha drank the rest of her coffee, then sprang out of the chair and prowled around the kitchen, taking cups out of the cupboard, putting them back again. Rearranging tins, moving the toaster to the left, the salt pig to the right. 'I'm going out,' she said suddenly.

'Where to?'

'Why do you want to know?' She looked defiant.

'Sasha. Please.'

'You're not my mother,' she said, as she flounced out of the kitchen, slamming the door behind her.

'No, but you're acting like a little kid,' muttered Alex, clearing

114

away plates and mugs. This was why she had been dreading Sasha coming to live with her: her mercurial moods, her vituperative tongue. Normal behaviour was resumed.

'Ride of the Valkyries' blasted out again. Heath.

'So,' he said without preamble, 'according to the post-mortem, Daley and Fleet had both drunk a glassful of barbiturates. That, according to my source, would have been enough to kill them without the old barbecue trick. They really went for belt and braces.' He sounded gloomy.

'So?'

'So I'm not sure this is going to be the explosive story I had hoped. But—'

'No sign of foul play then?'

'"Foul play". You sound like someone in an Agatha Christie novel. Hang on a minute.' There was a pause. Alex heard a clicking sound. He must be in a car on speakerphone. It explained the rather odd quality to his voice.

'Come on, you know what I mean.'

He laughed. 'No, no foul play. Evidence they'd been in touch through a suicide forum, but that's about it. Just two lonely old guys who didn't want to die alone, I guess.'

Alex frowned. 'No, Heath, I'm convinced there's more to it than that. I've got this feeling—'

'Journalist's intuition?'

'If you like. And you can keep that mocking tone out of your voice. Look at the bigger picture. We still don't know why they did it, so there's definitely a story in that. Magazine editor – possibly dodgy – a lapsed priest, come on, where's your journo nose?'

'Stuck up the business unit's arse.'

'What?'

'Alex, I may have to leave it with you for a while.'

'You're not bailing out on me already?' God, he was such a lightweight.

115

'Not exactly.'

'What then?'

'I'm on my way back to London now. Doing a stint on the business desk.'

'"The business desk"? But last night—'

'Things change. Redeployment.'

'Bloody quickly. What do you know about business?'

'Enough. I started as a business reporter, low level of course. I got out of it as soon as I could, but now the experience has come back to bite me in the arse.' He sounded gloomy. 'Dull as bloody ditchwater. Where talent goes to die. Unless you're Robert Peston, I suppose. Or Evan Davis.'

'Hang on, let's rewind here. Why are you going to the business desk at all?'

'In a word: Bud.'

'Bud?'

'He doesn't think there's any more to this story, Alex. He said it was good riddance that Daley was dead, but he'd topped himself and that was that.'

'You pitched him the idea of raising awareness of these suicide forums? Told him it could be a campaign for the newspaper, could get more readers? Told him we – you – wanted to find a connection between Daley and Fleet?'

'Yep. All that and more. Phoned him this morning. Told him all that. He said it was merely a suicide. I said yes, but Daley was a big name. He said we would treat it as any other suicide story, but with an obituary for Daley. Then he said they needed an extra journalist in business and I was best placed to go. I couldn't argue with him. I need the job, and with all the uncertainty at the paper, well, you know. Bud doesn't let sentiment get in the way. Not that he thinks much of me anyway. We have to face it, he doesn't want to know, Alex.'

'Bloody hell, Heath.' Disappointment crashed over her. 'We've hardly started.'

'I know. I'm not sure I understand what's going on.'

'You thought it was worth going after, didn't you?'

'Yes.' The answer came back without any hesitation. 'Truly. It was interesting and in the public interest.'

'So help me? Please?'

There was a silence, then a sigh. 'I don't know. There's the job and Mimi—'

'Mimi?' What sort of a name was that?

'Mimi is the mother of my child.' He sounded weary.

'Oh yes, of course.'

'Alex, if you need help, I'll do it.'

'Thank you.'

'There's something else.'

There was a note in his voice that made her stand still, her heart thumping in her chest. 'Go on.'

'I heard something on the grapevine about your Malone.'

'He's not my Malone.'

'Alex, I'm trying to help you here.'

'Sorry, sorry.' Her hand was slippery on the phone.

'Okay, so I asked a couple of mates in the police, pretty high up mates and they wouldn't have been able to say anything—'

'Heath, please.' She hated the pleading in her voice.

'I'm trying to tell you – these mates of mine wouldn't have been able to say anything if he still worked for them.'

'"Worked for them"?'

'Undercover, you know.'

She thought back. Malone had been talking of leaving the force, telling them to stick their undercover jobs where, as he put it, 'the sun don't shine', but she had never thought he would go through with it – it was too much part of his life. So, she was surprised at what Heath had told her.

'You're trying to tell me he doesn't work undercover for the force any more?'

'Not undercover, not anything. He left, hung up his gun, his boots, whatever they do in that situation. But since then he's been under the radar. No one knows where he is.'

'No one?'

'Well—'

'What is it, Heath?' Alex sensed his reluctance.

'There is a rumour he was on the run from a child-trafficking gang whose boss he helped put away.'

Nothing about being on the run from his wife's family. It had been heartbreaking to find out that Malone was married, even if it was only one of convenience: a marriage forged to get close to a woman who had terrorist tendencies, whose whole family operated on the wrong side of the law. Despite knowing all this, Alex had trusted him with her life and heart. What a fool she had turned out to be.

'And?'

'They think he's abroad somewhere. Europe, most likely, but the trail is cold at the moment. I will keep digging, though, when I can.'

'Thank you.' She would think about all that later. 'Look, Heath, going back to the Broads, I still think this is a great story.' Something within her told her she shouldn't let it go, that there was more to the whole Broads deaths thing than met the eye. She could do it with or without Heath, though she would rather have him with her. 'I know you'll be busy and all that, but I will keep on it and I may run stuff past you, if you're not too involved with interest rates and the FTSE.'

'Fair enough. And Alex?'

'Yes?'

She heard him hesitate. 'Take care, won't you? There are some nasty people out there.'

He sounded genuinely concerned, thought Alex. He was all heart. But now what? She was at a dead end. What was the point in her going on with the story if Bud didn't want it? True, she could sell it elsewhere, but part of the fun, she had to admit to herself, had been the idea of working with Heath. So what now? She sat up straight. She could do it on her own, why not? What was stopping her? If she could put something together, she would find someone to buy it. She might even make a few calls later. She didn't need Heath Maitland or Bud Evans.

15

Cambridge 1976

After what I thought of as 'the incident' (it was the only way I could cope with the betrayal) with Willem and Rachel at the party, I threw myself into my work. I didn't want to talk to anybody. I hid in my room, emerging only to go to lectures or to forage for food. I ignored everybody as I nursed my hurt feelings. I tried to forget about both of them. On the days when I did venture out, I occasionally saw them around and about Cambridge: Rachel with another male student in tow; Willem with his arm flung around the shoulder of a girl one time, a boy another. I was civilized if our paths crossed, but any feelings I'd had for Rachel had gone as quickly as they had come.

Willem was a different matter. I did miss his wit and knowledge and I missed his sense of fun. I had worked out why he had done that to me, cheated on me, made Rachel cheat on me – he couldn't bear not being the main person in my life. I spent a few evenings and nights agonizing over whether Willem might actually fancy me, but then dismissed those thoughts. With Willem, it was all about him and what he wanted, and if you didn't go along with that, he didn't like it. He hadn't liked not being the centre of my

120

attention. But I was determined not to be caught in his web of control.

I went home for Christmas at the end of the Michaelmas term.

I spent Christmas Day with my family, enjoyed being with them even though I had to endure the usual 'is that a girl or a boy?' and 'are there any actual words to this song' remarks from Dad during *Top of the Pops*, which was followed by the Queen's speech. Dad still stood up for the national anthem.

I got together with old school friends, went to the local Chinese or to the pub, and to the squash club for New Year's Eve, managing to get off with Molly Perrin under the shrivelled mistletoe. Molly Perrin – what was I thinking? And when I ignored her for the rest of the holidays I knew I had turned into a heel. Not nice behaviour. I had to do better.

On the first day of Lent term I saw Stu at the porters' lodge. This was my chance to do better and to put the events of last term well and truly behind me.

'Hi,' I said, smiling at him. 'Did you have a good Christmas?'

He looked taken aback, as well he might considering I'd ignored him most of last term.

'Er, yes, thanks.' He pushed his glasses back up his nose. 'You?'

'Good, yes.' I nodded vigorously to underline the point. 'Want to come up for a coffee? Have you got time?'

'Yes. Great.'

I kept up a constant stream of chat as we went up the stairs and as I unlocked my room and flung my rucksack on the bed. I told him about my family and my parents' party and New Year. I even mentioned Molly Perrin.

'Gosh. I didn't think …' He blushed a pillar-box red.

'Didn't think what?'

He couldn't look at me. 'You know.'

I stared at him, and then the penny dropped. 'You thought I was—?'

He shrugged. 'Well, you were always hanging around with Willem Major.'

I laughed, though it sounded false to my ears. 'No. He was just a friend. Anyway, we're no longer such good mates. He let me down. Big time. Look, do you like films?' I didn't let him answer. 'Because there's a good one on at film club – *The Night Porter* – have you heard of it? It stars Dirk Bogarde and Charlotte Rampling. I think you'd like it.' How the hell did I know? I was merely trying to fill the air at this point, make him back into my friend, my ordinary from-the-Midlands friend. 'Shall we go and see it?' I finished.

He narrowed his eyes. 'You and me?'

I laughed. 'Yes. Don't worry, I'm not asking you out on a date. I thought it might be something to do, that's all.'

'Okay.' A smile spread across his face. 'That'd be great, thanks.'

'I've been told it's really good.' Willem had told me about it, weeks before, but I wasn't about to tell Stu that.

'Yeah, I can review it for the student rag too.'

After the film (which was a bit, you know, in parts), we began to knock about a bit together and I grew to like him more. He was a bit needy, unsure of himself. He didn't talk about family and didn't seem to have many friends, apart from me. I introduced him to a couple of people from my seminar group and we'd go to the bar together. Life went on.

Then I met Jen again.

I was on my own for once, sitting in a fuggy café in a back street of Cambridge after having pulled an essay all-nighter, condensation streaking the windows, a plate of fried egg, bacon, beans, hash browns and mushrooms on the Formica table in front of me. No black pudding, but a cup of tea the colour of mahogany and a pile of bread and marge. All I needed was a bowl of porridge with brown sugar and cream and it would feel like Saturday breakfast at home.

I was about to tuck in when there was a cold blast of air as the café door opened.

'Hi.' Jen sat down across the table from me. She looked at me with a slight smile. Her eyes were green, and her hair wasn't just black, it was jet black. She was wearing a green beaded necklace – each bead was the size of a pebble.

'Hi.' Last of the great communicators, me.

She didn't say anything else, merely sat and smoked as I ate my way through my breakfast.

Ten minutes later I was mopping up the remnants of the fried egg with my bread. I looked up to see Jen watching me, her lip curled in an amused smile, smoke from her cigarette curling up to the ceiling. 'What?'

'You. Cleaning your plate like that.'

I'd hardly heard her speak, but now I realized she had what Mum would call a 'plummy' accent. Posh. I stopped mopping and put my bread down.

'It's frightfully common.' She smiled and tapped some ash into the ashtray.

'Really?' I said, arching an eyebrow. Then I picked up the triangle of Mother's Pride and carried on. Was she flirting with me?

'Look …' For the first time her confidence seemed to have deserted her.

I looked up.

'I'm sorry about what Willem did. You know. With—'

'Rachel. My girlfriend. At the time.' I shrugged. 'It was a long time ago.' And it did feel like a long time ago. In the hothouse, fevered atmosphere of Cambridge, time telescoped in and out.

'Yeah. Rachel.' She tapped her ash into a saucer. 'So. I'm sorry. And Willem is too.'

I snorted. 'Is he? So why isn't he here?'

She gave a small smile. 'He's not very good at apologizing. He's a bastard, but when he likes you he's incredibly loyal.'

That made me laugh. 'Evidently he hates me, then. Shagging my girlfriend doesn't come very high on my loyalty table.'

'And I'd like to get to know you better.'

I narrowed my eyes as I looked at her. 'Really?'

'Really.' And she treated me to the full force of her smile. 'Come for supper tonight.'

'With you?' My heart began to thud.

'No, with the Queen of Sheba. Yes with me. And Derek and Roger. Willem possibly.'

'I'm supposed to be going to the flicks with Stu.'

'Oh.' She was silent for a minute. Then she smiled brightly. 'Bring him, too.'

Supper at Jen's house consisted of copious glasses of Cointreau on ice, weed, and chips, stodgy and doused with vinegar. I don't know what I was expecting, something more sophisticated perhaps, but I didn't get it, and we were soon all too drunk to care. Even Stu was letting go. His glasses were skew-whiff and there were beads of sweat along his forehead. He was also swaying to non-existent music and playing air guitar. Derek, who I gathered wanted to be a magazine editor some day, kept taking photographs and downing eye-watering amounts of the sticky orange-flavoured liqueur. His jokes became filthier and funnier the more he drank. Roger was a gentle soul. He didn't drink much or smoke anything but sat quietly reading a book, of all things. I sort of gathered he was what you might call sensitive. He was interesting to talk to. At least, I think he was; I could never remember what we actually spoke about. But we chilled out, breathing in the scents of fried food and pot, sweat and nicotine.

Through the haze I heard a knock on the door, then it was pushed open, hard. Willem filled the doorway, his arms stretched out wide, a huge smile on his face. His scarf was flung carelessly around his neck, his skin glowed and his blue eyes glittered, pupils dilated.

'Darlings, I have missed you so!' He frowned when he spied Stu draped along the sofa. 'Stuey, dear, hop along now. My friends and I have things to talk about.'

Stu stared at him, his mouth hanging open, drool at the corners.

'Stuey, did you hear what I said? Run along.' He gave a dismissive wave.

Stu glanced over at me. I smiled and shrugged. 'Sorry,' I mouthed.

He heaved himself off the cushions and weaved his way out through the door.

I was ashamed of myself.

Willem opened his arms to me. 'Come and hug.'

I looked at the others, at Derek and Roger. At Jen, who nodded to me encouragingly.

I hugged.

16

Margaret Winwood ushered Alex into the claustrophobic front room again. It was even gloomier than before – the afternoon sun didn't reach in.

'Thank you for coming,' she said, perching on the edge of an uncomfortable chair. 'I know you must be busy.' She looked past Alex and at the net-curtained window, wringing her hands, a worried look on her face.

'Mrs Winwood?'

Margaret Winwood turned her head towards her, eyes unseeing. 'Yes?'

'You wanted to see me?' Alex asked gently.

'Did I?'

'You called me this morning. You had my number from my business card. I came as soon as I could.'

Margaret Winwood seemed to mentally shake herself and stand taller. 'Of course. I hadn't forgotten.' It had been a stroke of luck that Mrs Winwood had called, as it saved her having to rack her brains to think of an excuse to visit Twickenham again.

'And?'

'Can I get you something to drink? Tea? Coffee? Something soft?'

Alex shook her head. 'I'm fine, really.'

The woman sat down heavily on one of the over-stuffed chairs. She was obviously troubled. 'I can't put it off any longer. It was that note, you see.' She fished around in her cardigan pocket.

'Note?'

'The police found it on the boat. Addressed to me. They let me see it, so I wrote down exactly what it said. I've looked at it so many times.' She thrust a creased and folded piece of paper towards Alex.

She opened it up.

Margaret.

If you have this it means I am gone. There is nothing else I can do – I have to take this path. I found my faith again in the end and prayed to the Lord Jesus Christ that I was doing the right thing, that He would forgive me as He knows why I am doing something as heinous as taking my own life. Please know it was not a decision taken lightly. I had to do it for you. I pray that one day you will forgive me.

All my love, Roger.

Alex looked up at Margaret Winwood. There were tears on the older woman's cheeks. She reached out and gently touched her hand.

'He obviously loved you, Mrs Winwood.'

'I wanted you to know what he'd written; that's why I called you.' She glared at Alex as though she should know what she meant.

Alex read it again. 'Do you know what he meant by "I had to do it for you"?'

'No idea,' she replied, helplessly. 'I really don't know why he would involve me in it at all. I find the whole thing so upsetting. I don't understand why he would take his own life. I knew, absolutely knew, he wouldn't do something like that. But there you are. People can surprise you, can't they? Well, more than surprise, really. Shock you. "All my love." I haven't heard him say anything affectionate to me in years. I know he wasn't the happiest of people. All that business after he left the college—' She stopped, probably realizing she had said too much.

'I went to the college. I saw the name of it on the back of the photo frame.' Alex indicated the frame that sat on the mantelpiece.

'You went to the college to pry.'

'I spoke to Father Paul Hayes – he's the principal there now – and he put me on to Father Vincent, who was at the college during your brother's time.'

'And?'

'He didn't want to say anything. He was very suspicious of the fact I was a journalist.'

'I don't blame him, do you? I hope you didn't go along there thinking you were going to get some sort of salacious story about my brother, some startling revelation, Miss Devlin?'

'No, of course not,' she lied.

'Good.'

'All I gathered was that Father Vincent wishes he and the college could have helped him more.'

'Yes, they should have done. He needed help and they abandoned him.'

'Why did he need help?' She knew something had happened at the college, not least because Margaret Winwood hadn't wanted to give her its name.

The older woman seemed to collapse in on herself. 'It happened after he left.'

'What did, Margaret? What happened?'

The woman let out a long sigh. 'Roger …' she paused and looked out of the window. 'Roger tried to take his own life a few weeks after he left Goldhay. When he was struggling with his faith. And his life. He got himself into a place where he didn't know what to do. It was more of a cry for help. Anyway, he managed to sort himself out somehow and then he abandoned his vows and his faith. That's the story really.'

'I see.' Alex sat back in her chair feeling vaguely disappointed. So Roger Fleet had a bit of history of trying to kill himself, and he had succeeded at last. Big time.

'Mrs Winwood – Margaret – why did you ask me here today? You could have easily told me what was in the letter over the phone.'

'I know. It wasn't just the note. The thing is you were so kind yesterday and so keen to help that I thought I would show you something.' She stood up and went over to a bookcase in the corner of the room, bringing out a large book covered in what looked like green leather. Not a book, a photograph album.

'I was looking through photographs of Roger yesterday, you know, just remembering what he was like when he seemed happy, and I found this.' She opened up the album. The photographs were pressed on stiff cream board between plastic covers. Better than today's storage, thought Alex. It wasn't the same scrolling through iPhoto or a computer, promising yourself that you would print out those photographs that were special to you and never getting round to doing it. Then losing half of them in some massive data crash.

'Look.' Margaret was talking to her. 'Here's Roger.'

It was a photograph of a group of young people taken in the mid- or late seventies, judging from the haircuts and fashion. There was a fresh-faced Roger, head thrown back, laughing. Flares. Cheesecloth shirt, if she wasn't much mistaken. There was no worry on his face, no cares etched in his features. A young man with his life in front of him. He was in a garden, a beer garden with picnic benches and drinks and empty glasses on the tables. Parasols. The glint of water. Early afternoon, maybe? There were a lot of people in the background and four people – students – in the foreground.

'It's a lovely photo of Roger, I can see why you like it.'

'Yes, yes, but look at who's with him. I didn't realize it at first, but then there have been so many pictures of him on the TV that I finally knew who it was.'

'Roger?' Alex was confused.

'No, no, that magazine man, Daley. The one Roger, well, you know, the one he was with when he died.'

Alex looked more closely. Margaret was right. It was a younger Derek Daley, with all his hair. He too looked carefree, starting out in life, the world at his feet. Derek Daley in a photograph with Roger Fleet. A connection, a real connection. Alex fought to contain her excitement.

'Do you know who the other two are?' she asked. One of them, a woman, was looking at Fleet and Daley, lifting her glass as if in a toast, and the third man – all blond hair and blue eyes – was smoking a cigarette in a cigarette holder, boldly looking straight at the camera and pointing at whoever was taking the picture. The young blond man's gaze was unsettling, and something nagged at the corner of Alex's mind about him. But she couldn't quite grasp it. She shook her head. It would come to her eventually.

Margaret looked again. 'No, I'm afraid not. I didn't know Roger's friends. I am, I was, that bit older than him and I'm afraid older sisters don't tend to involve themselves in the lives of their little brothers. Well, I didn't anyway. Water under the bridge now.'

Margaret looked more closely at the photograph, the ghost of a smile on her face. 'I expect the picture was taken somewhere in Cambridge. Roger was a student there. We were so proud of him when he got into university. He was the first in our family to go on to further education, never mind Cambridge. We were so proud. So proud. St Francis's College.' Her finger stroked the photograph. 'He was a lovely little boy, you know. Gentle and thoughtful, used to buy Mother little presents. He wasn't like those annoying brothers you hear about, fighting and such. Not particularly good-looking. He was happy in his own company.

Liked to read a lot. Clever at school. All of that.' Her smile was sad. 'You know, I should have been kinder to him these last years.' She wiped away a tear.

'He sounds lovely,' said Alex, quietly. 'A great brother to have.' She paused. 'My father was at Cambridge.'

'Really, dear? At which college?'

Alex smiled. 'I'm ashamed to say I don't know. He was only there for a short time – he became ill – and he doesn't like to talk about it. Probably regrets having to leave.'

Margaret Winwood nodded. 'For some, it was a privilege.' She looked at Alex. 'Thank you. It does help to talk. About him. And you've been the only one to take any interest. The police, well, they don't really care about Roger, not the real Roger. They just think he's a suicide and that's where it ends. Fair enough I suppose, they've got real crimes to see to, someone killing themselves will be low on their priorities.'

Alex did understand. She knew that families wanted to talk about their loved ones, wanted everyone to see them as people, not as a statistic or a victim or a headline. Journalists were often castigated for knocking on the doors of bereaved families, but very often they were the first person the families were able to talk to. However, she couldn't feel totally virtuous, after all she had gone there with an agenda, wanting to know more about Fleet and if there was any possible relationship with Daley. And she had found it.

She reached out and touched Margaret Winwood's arm. The woman's pain was palpable. 'I'm so sorry,' she said. 'Have you shown this photograph to the police?' Alex held her breath.

Margaret Winwood shook her head. 'No. As I said, they weren't interested in Roger the person, so I didn't feel inclined to.' She looked up. 'But I suppose I should?'

Alex struggled with her conscience, but knew she had to say yes. At least she was one step ahead of Berry at the moment. 'I think maybe you should. It shows there's more of a connection between the two of them than only meeting on the Internet.'

'It makes it a little better, somehow, that Roger was with someone he knew. At the end.'

They sat there for a minute, the older woman lost in her memories.

'Would you mind if I took a picture of the photo?' Alex asked eventually.

'No. But I don't know why you want to.'

Alex wasn't sure either, but she was becoming more and more certain there was more to this story than anyone had originally thought. She snapped it quickly.

'You never saw your brother with Derek Daley? Or heard him talk about him?'

'No, never.' She gave a sad smile. 'As I said, we didn't have much to do with each other, not really. This,' she gestured at the photograph, 'this is the first time I realized they knew each other. Strange, isn't it? That they should—' She stopped, unable to go on.

'And you've no idea who those other people are in the photo? Roger never mentioned any names?'

'No, I'm sorry. Is it important?'

Alex shook her head. 'No, not important.'

'At least,' said Margaret Winwood sadly, 'he's at peace now and we can bury him knowing that. Though ...'

'Yes?'

'It must have been something to make him get on a boat. He hated water.'

Exactly what Mrs Archer had said.

17

It was at that time of night, the time between dreaming and waking, when Alex remembered where she had seen the blond man in the picture before.

Willem Major. That's who it was. She sat bolt upright in bed. A much younger version, but you couldn't mistake the fine blond hair, the blue eyes and the thick eyebrows and eyelashes. And as an older man his face had been splashed across television, newspapers, and websites a few weeks before, accompanied by epithets such as 'tragic' and 'doomed'. He had been what? A businessman? A moneymaker? Something like that. That's right. He'd built up a successful chain of garden centres, which he sold after the tragedy.

Alex did what any self-respecting journalist did when first researching a story: she sat down at her computer and consulted Google.

There were plenty of hits on the name. She pulled up a newspaper article.

Willem Major ... successful businessman ... garden centres

Ah, she had been right.

133

family died in arson attack ... eldest daughter survived because she was at a friend's house ... arsonist or arsonists never found ... recluse.

Then the latest story from BBC News a month ago:

An investigation into a fire which killed three members of one family is proving 'difficult' and 'challenging' Cambridgeshire Police said.

Two months after Maria Major and two of her daughters, Katherine, aged 16, and 14-year-old Suzie died in the blaze at Owl Farm, Ely, the force has renewed its appeal for information.

Marie Major's husband Willem and eldest daughter Charlotte were the only survivors. The blaze, which experts say may have reached temperatures of 800 degrees centigrade, sent thick, choking smoke through the premises. Mr Major and Charlotte Major were not at home at the time of the fire.

An inquest heard that all the evidence pointed to arson, but firefighters could not rule out an accidental cause.

Cambridgeshire Police said it was 'desperate to find answers' and appealed to any members of the community to come forward with information.

She sat back in her chair. So, two men in the photograph had killed themselves; the third man – Willem Major – had lost practically his whole family. Had anything happened to the woman, or was it merely a string of horrible coincidences? And what of the person taking the photo? Were they important?

She thought about Willem Major. Almost his whole family wiped out. She knew how very hard it was to keep going when people close to you died in horrible circumstances. It was hard to put one foot in front of the other and hard not to blame someone, anyone, usually the person closest to you. She knew all this.

She searched again, trying to find any background on the man. There wasn't much; he had evidently avoided publicity throughout his life. There were a few financial and business articles about the garden centre empire he had built up, which included, she noted with surprise, the one just outside Yoxford, where she often went to buy the plants that she eventually killed. She noted the repeated words of 'ruthless', 'hard-headed', and 'lacking compassion'.

She looked at Major's picture on the news website and thought how unkind the last weeks had been to him.

She thought about the woman in the picture with Roger Fleet and the person who was taking the photograph. She thought how best to find out more. She had been so certain she could do it all on her own – and, to be fair, she could. But it would take her a lot longer. She could do with some help.

And, said a traitorous voice inside her head, she might hear something else about Malone.

She picked up her phone.

'Heath,' she said, when he answered, sounding as though he was half asleep. 'I—'

'Christ, Alex, do you realize what the time is?' Exasperation in his voice.

'What?' She looked at her watch. Six o'clock. Oh. Then she saw the soft light through the kitchen window. She became aware of the birds, the lack of traffic noise and that she needed coffee. 'Sorry, couldn't sleep.'

'Well I can. Goodbye.'

'Don't hang up, Heath,' she pleaded.

There was silence. A stifled yawn. Then: 'All right. I guess it's nearly time to get up. What do you want?' She heard the sound of bedclothes rustling.

'I've got a picture I want to send you.'

'A picture. Really? Not now, Alex. I've got to be at my desk in, what, about two hours looking as though I'm on top of things when someone shouts about bonds or futures at me. Or even the Dow Jones.' He sounded so gloomy that it made Alex smile.

'Listen, I might just save you from a lifetime of following the markets. I'm going to email you this picture—'

'Alex.'

'Listen to me, Heath. I could go alone on this, but I figured you could help me and we would both get something out of it. Like we agreed before.'

'Hmm.'

'There are four students. Three men and one woman. And another person, obviously, the person who took it. I want you to use your resources and that prizewinning journalistic acumen to find out who they are. I can give you a head start – one of them is Roger Fleet and another is Derek Daley. They were all at Cambridge University together in the late seventies. Roger Fleet was at St Francis's College.'

There was a silence for a moment. 'So they did know one another?'

'Roger Fleet and Derek Daley, yes. And another thing. The third person is Willem Major. Does that ring any bells?' She waited for the name to sink in.

Heath gave a low whistle. 'The garden centre guy? The one whose family was burnt to cinders in that fire?'

'The very same.'

'Interesting.'

'Wake up, Heath, it's more than "interesting". There's something going on here, and I want to find out what it is.'

'It's the girl you want me to find out about?'

'Yes,' she replied, impatiently.

'You could do that. You don't need me. You could sell the story to another newspaper.'

'I could.'

'So why don't you?'

136

Why didn't she? She pinched the bridge of her nose with her fingers. 'You said you thought it could be a good story, a good feature. You wanted to expose the truth about these forums as well. Surely you can't just drop it all like a stone? And you also thought you might be able to find out why Bud isn't interested in the story. I still can't understand why he isn't keen on the whole idea.'

'Look, I'll try and find out about the girl. Maybe use facial recognition software or something.' He paused. 'And I haven't forgotten.'

'Forgotten?'

'About Malone. I said I would help you there, and I will. Whatever happens about Daley and Fleet.'

Relief pooled in her stomach. 'Thank you.'

'Now let me go and look at the money markets.'

He sounded so bored at the prospect that Alex laughed. 'You see, helping me would be so much more exciting. And if I sell the story or Bud publishes it, I'll buy you dinner.'

'You could make me dinner. That would be better.'

'Don't push your luck, Heath.' She smiled as she cut the connection and pressed send on the email with the photograph attached.

'Who were you talking to?'

She looked up to see Sasha standing at the kitchen doorway in her dressing gown, eyes puffy with sleep.

'No one. A journalist. About a story.'

'At this time in the morning?'

She smiled. 'Early bird and all that. Come on, let's make some coffee.'

'What are you doing today?' Sasha yawned as she sat down at the kitchen table.

'I thought I might go to Lowdham.' In fact, until she said it, she hadn't thought about it, but it seemed the perfect time to go and see if she could find out anything about the woman who was seen arguing with Roger Fleet.

'Lowdham? The Broads? That's dull.'

'Maybe.' Alex busied herself with spooning coffee into the cafetière and putting the kettle on to boil.

'Whatever happened to Malone?'

'What?' Coffee cups. Milk. Why did she ask that? She kept her hands occupied so Sasha didn't see the effect his name had on her. 'Here you are.' She pushed a cup across to her sister.

'Malone. You were seeing him before I – well, you know.'

Before it all came out about her babies. Before she was sent away to Leacher's House to get well. That's what 'before' meant.

'Why are you asking now?'

Sasha shrugged. 'Don't know. His name popped into my head, that's all.'

'He went away. He came back. We were seeing each other for a while. Then he went away again.'

'Upped and fucked off. Same old story where men are concerned.'

'Stop it, Sasha.'

'True, isn't it?'

Her sister's words stung, but a knock on the door saved her from spitting out something she would later regret.

'Who's that at this time of the morning?' said Sasha, crossly. 'It's half past six, for Christ's sake.'

'Hallo, only me.' Lin peered round the door. 'I was out for an early morning walk and saw you were up, so wondered if you wanted to join me.' She waggled her fingers at Sasha. 'Hi Sasha.'

Hi Sasha? What was that? Alex looked from one to the other. 'I didn't know you two had met?'

'In the café on the high street.' Lin beamed at her. 'I knew it was your sister straight away.'

Was that before or after she had told Lin about Sasha? She felt uncomfortable. What would they have been talking about? And how could she have known that a woman sitting in a coffee shop was her sister – they didn't even look alike. She, Alex, was dark and small; Sasha was willowy with blonde hair.

She looked at Sasha. 'You never said?'

'You haven't given me a chance, have you?' Sasha was surly. 'You were in bed when I came in last night and you seemed in no mood to talk this morning. And anyway, do I have to tell you everything I do?'

'I was in no mood to talk?' Alex shook her head. 'I don't know what you mean.'

'Never mind.' Sasha stood. 'Nice to see you again, Lin. I'm off back to bed.' She picked up her cup and swept from the room.

Alex sighed. 'Sorry about that. She can sometimes be rather unforgivably rude.'

Lin put a hand on her arm. 'It really is okay. Like I said, I know what it's like. It's all up and down and treading on eggshells. Half the time you can't do right for doing wrong and the other half you're just wrong. It takes patience.'

'You can say that again. Anyway ...' Alex poured another coffee for Lin. 'When did you meet Sasha?'

Lin sat herself down at the table. 'I said, didn't I? Yesterday.'

After their conversation on the beach then.

'Now I'm here – and I am sorry it's so early, but as I said I did see that you were up and about, so shall we do something today? Apparently the weather is going to be gorgeous. We could go to Aldeburgh for a change if you like? Perhaps the lovely Gus can come with us? Though I suppose it's a bit early for someone of his age.'

Alex felt the worry start up again.

'What?' said Lin, smiling.

'It's just that, well, I haven't heard from him yet.'

Lin shrugged. 'So? He's young, probably having a wild party on Ibiza before he comes home. Or he's landed and gone to see some mates in London; you know what young people are like. Well, I don't but you do.'

'I'm not sure you're making me feel any better.' Alex sighed.

'You're probably right.' She looked at her phone again, hoping to see something from him, but there was nothing.

'I am right. Don't get too much in his face. Let him live his own life.'

'But ...' Alex stopped. She was getting tired of defending her parenting skills to people like her sister and even her friend. Perhaps Lin was right. Maybe he was enjoying a few days with his own friends and she would be a real interfering mother if she started to ring round to see where he was. He was old enough to take care of himself. Mentally, she shook herself. 'You make a good point,' she said.

'So, Aldeburgh, then,' Lin said.

Alex felt awkward. 'Actually, Lin, if you don't mind, there's something I've got to do, somewhere I need to be. It's to do with those deaths on the Broads.' She smiled apologetically. 'A couple of leads. So, work, you see?'

Lin lifted her eyebrows. 'I thought you were handing that over to someone else, that journalist guy.'

'I was. Heath Maitland. But, he can't put in the hours at the moment, so I'm sort of going it alone.'

'Ooo, sounds exciting.' She nudged Alex playfully. 'And he's quite good-looking, isn't he, this Heath Maitland?'

'Not especially.'

'And now you're blushing,' laughed Lin. 'I think I've struck a nerve.'

Alex swore under her breath. She hated that she blushed so very easily. 'He's a mate, that's all. Besides, he has a very pregnant girlfriend.'

'He says.'

'What do you mean?'

'Some men say that sort of thing to show their caring side, their softer side, don't they? Sometimes they pretend to have a dog. Or that they've rescued a cat. To make you feel sorry for them. Believe me, I know.'

'No, it's not like that at all. I've known Heath for a while and if he says he's got a pregnant girlfriend, then he's got a pregnant girlfriend.'

'If you say so.'

Alex looked sharply at her, but Lin's face was inscrutable.

'Anyway,' said Lin, suddenly smiling. 'Since you won't let me come along and hold your notebook for you I'll go home and drown my sorrows in a kale smoothie.'

'Really?'

She grinned. 'No. I just want you to be sorry for me.'

'Noted.' Alex followed her to the door. 'Thanks for calling in anyway. And for being so understanding about Sasha.'

'No worries. Call me when you get back. Fill me in on any grisly details. Where did you say you were going?'

'I didn't,' she smiled, 'but I'll tell you all about it later.'

She shut the door behind Lin and leaned against it, a bloom of worry in her chest.

Was it her imagination or was Lin just a little too keen to accompany her to Lowdham?

18

Lowdham shimmered under the blue sky as Alex parked her car on the road beside The King's Head. The outside of the ochre building was festooned with England flags, and a large banner declared the presence of an enormous flat-screen TV and the promise of plenty of football. A blackboard by the door advertised the pleasures of a Sunday carvery. No thanks. Too many memories of going out with her mum and dad to dreary pubs with lukewarm meat that had been cooked the night before and reheated, together with soggy vegetables and packet gravy. Though maybe she was being unfair and The King's Head put on a good spread.

Passing thatched cottages with outsides painted cream, pink or green, with white wrought-iron fences and Farrow & Ball woodwork, a florist, a greengrocer, and a hardware shop, she eventually reached the green with its shingle path by the water. Moorhens scuttled across the grass. Shiny boats were moored, stern on, some half-covered with tarpaulins waiting to begin their season of navigating the Broads, others were occupied – families, couples. People sat on boats, legs dangling into the water, reading, chatting, drinking tea. She saw a teenage boy, lolloping along the path, earbuds in, a net shopping bag dangling from his wrist.

'Don't forget the eggs,' his mother shouted from the doorway of one of the boats.

The words must have cut through whatever he was listening to because the boy lifted his hand in a half-wave without looking around. The scene reminded Alex of Gus when he was about fifteen – a teenager with too many hormones to know what to do with. Wanting to please (sometimes), but not wanting to show it.

Gus. In spite of what Lin had said earlier and her own brave stand of not wanting to interfere she still had a gnawing worry in her stomach. She looked at her watch. She could call Steve and see if he knew of any other plans their son had when he got to England, besides coming to stay with her. She scrolled through her contacts and found his number. Voicemail. 'Steve, it's me. Alex.' She swallowed. She wasn't used to talking to Steve – communication was mostly through Gus. She didn't know why she felt so awkward; after all these years she should be fine with it, but something always made her revert to the naive young woman she'd been on that press trip to Ibiza. 'Um. Sorry to bother you. I wanted to know if Gus was going to visit friends when he landed in England? Has he even left you yet? I haven't heard anything you see and …' She swallowed. 'Oh, call me when you get this. Thanks.'

'Hey, Alex, isn't it?' a voice shouted.

Alex looked up to see Mickey from Harper's Holidays finish tying up a boat to the moorings. He waved to her.

Her heart sank, but she waved back. He wandered over.

'Fancy seeing you here,' he said. 'Day out?'

'Something like that.'

'Nice.' He smiled widely at her. I'm testing out a boat.' He pointed to the water.

Alex looked. Firefly Queen. 'Right. Another of Colin Harper's.' She wondered what to say next. 'Would you like your own boat one day?'

'Nah. Like I said to you before, this job was a stroke of luck. A boat would be too much of a tie. Moorings and all that sort of stuff.'

'A houseboat would be fun to live on, I've often thought.'

'Good for the homeless you mean?'

'No, I didn't – I wasn't – I'm.' Alex felt stupid. She itched to get away.

Mickey laughed. 'I was only teasing. Wanted to make you blush. And I succeeded.'

He had. Alex could feel the heat from her breastbone upwards. She had to say something or she would carry on standing there looking like a plum tomato.

Her stomach rumbled, reminding her how early she had risen that morning and that she hadn't had anything to eat. Not good. She needed her food. 'Nice to have seen you again, Mickey, but I've got to find somewhere for breakfast.'

'Sure. I've got to get to the chandlery. Cheaper than the one on Lowdham Bridge. See you around.' He sauntered off, whistling.

Not if I see you first, she thought. There was something about Mickey – she couldn't quite put her finger on it – that he made her feel uneasy.

Alex walked in the opposite direction to Mickey until she came to a pretty building. The Waterfront Café, a thatched, half-timbered building with a pretty patio and picnic tables with brollies and a flint wall to one side and a sign that told her breakfast was on offer inside. Better still, it was right opposite the newsagent where Roger Fleet had been seen rowing with a young girl.

An old-fashioned bell announced her arrival, and a woman with a messy bun and a beaming smile greeted her.

'Hi,' said Alex. 'I was wondering about breakfast?'

'Of course – full Norfolk?'

Alex smiled. 'I presume that's like a full English?'

'Well now. It is and it isn't. It is because we've got egg, bacon, mushrooms, black pudding, toast and butter, and its special because all the ingredients come from Norfolk. Even the tea is blended in the county.'

'I'm impressed. It sounds good to me.'

'Why don't you sit outside – it's warm enough – and I'll bring it to you.'

Alex went outside and sat at one of the picnic tables. Apart from an old boy reading his paper at a round table, with a pot of tea in front of him, there was no one else there. The sun was climbing in the sky and the air was warm. Birds chirruped in the trees while skylarks sang and soared in the air. All was right with the world. If she didn't think of decomposing bodies or fatal fires, that is. Or Malone. Why couldn't she stop thinking about him? Why couldn't she 'move on', to use that horrible and cruel phrase. Certainly she'd been foolish asking Heath Maitland to find out what had happened to him – it was like peeling a plaster slowly off an unhealed cut. Not only that, but if Heath sensed a story in it, he would be in there like a pig in shit, whatever he said. Though pigs came out of it cleaner.

'Here we are my dear. You look as though you could do with a bit of something inside you.' The woman put a plate down in front of her. Alex's mouth watered. A beautifully cooked deep yellow fried egg, two rashers of crispy bacon, a large, fat pork sausage, a field mushroom, two slices of black pudding and two slices of toast. And it was proper butter in the little pot on the table, with small bottles of ketchup and brown sauce. And English mustard.

'Thank you, this looks fabulous.' She reached for the ketchup.

And it was fabulous. Fresh and not at all greasy. Alex couldn't remember when she'd last had a breakfast this good. She finished the last of the tea in the teapot, two teabags in there instead of the usual one you get in cafés. Altogether very satisfying.

'Are you done?' The café owner came out smiling. 'Can I get you anything else? Toast, perhaps?'

'No, that will set me up for the day nicely.'

The woman began to clear the plates.

'You're in a lovely position here,' said Alex, wanting to open a conversation. 'I mean you can see the boats, the marina, a lot of the village.'

The woman laughed. 'You can that. It's a great place to sit and people-watch.'

'Terrible thing that happened on the boat the other day.'

The woman nodded. 'Terrible. Hired it from Colin down at the bridge.'

'Yes, I was talking to him about it.'

The woman looked at her carefully. 'Ah. You're that journalist, aren't you? Colin told me about you.'

'Did he?'

The woman suddenly smiled. 'He's my other half. Not the better half, mind you,' she chuckled. 'I'm Dorothy.'

Alex grinned, relieved she didn't have to pussyfoot around Dorothy to ask her questions. 'Then you'll know I'm looking into their deaths?'

Dorothy nodded.

'I heard that one of the men who died was seen arguing with a woman just before they hired the boat? I wonder, did you see anything?'

Dorothy frowned. 'Which day would that be?'

'The Tuesday, probably?'

'I wasn't here then, my day off. I haven't heard anything. Hang on a minute.' She hurried back inside.

When she came back, she was followed by a young man dressed in chef's whites with Crocs on his feet. He looked about twenty-five, with spiky ginger hair.

'This is James,' said Dorothy. 'He's our cook most of the time; though when I'm on a day off he serves in the cafe.' She looked at the man. 'This lady—'

'Alex,' she said. 'And that breakfast was so good, thank you.'

James nodded.

'Alex wants to know if you saw anyone arguing somewhere round here last Tuesday.'

James thought for a minute. 'Can't say I did. Even if I had, I wouldn't have taken any notice, y'know? It's not like I don't have enough to do.'

'Ah,' said Dorothy. 'Was that the day you were in the kitchen as well?'

'Yep. That was the day. Juggling cooked breakfasts and scone dough. Not to mention carrot cake and chocolate gateaux.'

'As long as you didn't serve a fried egg with the carrot cake,' said Dorothy.

'Interesting combination, I should try that out some time,' James grinned.

Alex's heart sank. He hadn't seen anything. It had been a bit of a long shot.

'I saw them, love.' The old boy sitting at the round table spoke.

Alex sat up straighter. 'Really?'

The old boy folded up his newspaper and put it carefully back down on to the table. Alex could see a photo of the boat where Daley and Fleet were found across the front page. It was still news, then.

'Well, now, love, I couldn't rightly say if it's the couple you're looking for, but there was certainly a man arguing with a young lady just over there.' He pointed towards the moored boats. 'I see a lot of what's going on. Like to have my tea here, don't I, Dorothy? While I'm waiting for the pub to open.'

Alex took the picture of Roger Fleet and Derek Daley over to his table. She pointed to Fleet. 'Is this the man you saw?'

He peered with rheumy eyes, then shook his head. 'No, love, it wasn't him.'

'Are you sure?' Alex tasted the bitterness of disappointment.

'I may be old but I'm not losing my marbles yet, young lady. Of course I'm sure, I wouldn't have said otherwise, would I? I've been reading the paper same as everyone, haven't I?' He wagged his finger at her. 'And perhaps if you could let me finish?'

'Of course,' said Alex, trying not to smile. 'I'm sorry.'

'It wasn't that man.' He pointed to Roger Fleet. 'But it was him.' He pointed to the other picture.

Derek Daley.

'The woman – young lady – then came in here; don't you remember, James?'

James shook his head. 'Don't reckon so.'

'She was upset, crying. She had a pot of tea.'

He shrugged, as if a lot of women came into the café to cry and have tea. 'Can't say I noticed. I'm sorry. But I have seen the bloke around here before. Spoke to him a few weeks ago when he came in. Said he had a holiday home around here. Somewhere in the village.'

'Really?' Derek Daley with a holiday home in Norfolk. Roger Fleet not many miles away. Both at university together. Yet they meet on an Internet site and decide to get together that way. Why? Coincidence? Surely not?

'The young lady, did she say what they were arguing about?' she asked.

The old boy sniffed. 'No, just that her dad had upset her. Again. But she couldn't talk about it.'

Her dad. Derek Daley's daughter.

'Do you happen to know where the holiday home is?' she asked, holding her breath.

'That'll be the Butlers' old house,' said the old boy. 'My son helped with the garden. Landscaping they called it. Just pulled out some weeds and dug a few beds.'

'I bet it was more than that,' said James, grinning.

'Well, I call it old-fashioned gardening, nothing fancy. And they gutted the kitchen. Perfectly good it was.' He picked up his newspaper again.

'It needed gutting,' said James.

'Excuse me,' Alex interrupted, not wanting the conversation to go off at a complete tangent. 'Where is the Butlers' old house?'

The old boy peered over the top of his paper. 'Out of here, down the road a bit, turn right and you'll see the sign. Says Glory Farm. That's it. Back in my day it was a proper farm, now it's a second home. I don't know what the world's coming to, I really don't.'

'Thank you,' said Alex. 'You've been really helpful.'

She stood. No time like the present.

Down the road a bit and turn right wasn't exactly the most accurate of directions, but it was a beautiful morning and she'd had a good breakfast, so Alex wasn't too worried if she made a few wrong turns here and there.

But, as it happened, she found the sign that said Glory Farm easily. The pretty brick and flint house was set back off the road, with a path to the front door. There was a side driveway that led to what looked like a brand new cart lodge, big enough for at least two cars. The front garden did look new – the path was lined with box hedge that hadn't quite settled in; the lawn either side was lush and green – no sign at all of wear and tear. The trees looked as though they had been planted strategically. Her footsteps crunched on the pristine gravel. The house had an air of no one home; nevertheless she pulled on the bell-pull to the right of the front door. It echoed through the house.

Nothing.

She turned the handle. Locked. She went round to the back. The garden was long and beautiful. There was a pond, its surface brushed by the weeping branches of a willow tree. The grass was as green as the front lawn and there were beds full of plants, but it showed more life, more individuality than the front. There was a wooden climbing frame, swing, and slide. Must be for the grandchildren.

She knocked on the back door. Waited for a couple of minutes before trying the handle. It was locked. She looked around for a likely place for a spare key and— What the hell did she think she was doing? Was she really going to break into the house and have a snoop around? Snoop around and find out why a successful magazine editor would want to kill himself along with an old friend?

She was being ridiculous.

Hurrying round to the front of the house and down the gravel path, she closed the gate behind her, looking back over her shoulder waiting for someone to shout at her that she was trespassing.

At that moment a Land Rover came along the road at speed and indicated left. It swung into the driveway of Glory Farm, just missing the gateposts. Alex could see a woman at the wheel – probably mid-thirties – and an older woman sitting beside her. Daley's wife and daughter or daughter-in-law? And why were they in such a hurry?

She got her answer a couple of minutes later, when two trucks with satellite dishes on the top raced down the road and pulled up with a screech of brakes outside the house. The logos on the side of the vehicles were those of rival digital television companies.

A man and a woman jumped out of one of the trucks, smart suits, all of them. Another man, more dressed down – scruffy beard, ill-fitting jeans, open-necked shirt – clambered out of the second truck. Their heads swivelled as one towards her, hard gimlet eyes boring into her. Oh yes, she thought, the hard-nosed squad have arrived.

The woman waved her iPad at her. 'Hey, you,' she called. 'Is this where the Daleys come for their holidays?'

The first man strode towards her. 'Do you live round here? Is that their house?' He nodded towards Glory Farm. 'Do you know them?'

Whether it was because Alex sensed more of a story, or because of the arrogance of the journalists, treating her as though she was a village idiot – whatever it was – she shook her head, trying

150

to look gormless. If they thought she was an idiot then she would behave like one. She screwed her face up. 'No, it's not. Might have been.'

'What do you mean, "might have been"?' The woman from the truck asked.

Alex shrugged. 'It was sold last week. Just before – well, y'know. All that business and what-not.'

What-not? That was taking her acting skills a little too far.

'Before he was found on that boat?'

'Yeah. New people will be moving in soon. They're from Dorset, I believe. Wanted to come up here because their mum was—' She was enjoying this.

'All right, all right,' the woman said testily. 'I get your drift.' She turned to her companion. 'Duff info.'

'Why do you want them? The Daleys?' Alex asked, still trying to look dim and innocent at the same time.

The woman narrowed her eyes. 'What's it to you?'

'Just wondering, that's all.'

'You'll have to watch the news, then, won't you. Come on, Nigel, let's get out of here. Do some door knocking. Find some people who knew them. And we'll get some shots of where the boat was moored.'

The woman and Nigel jumped into their vehicle and it roared off. The second man watched it go before sighing and climbing wearily into his truck.

'Thanks love,' he called, before slamming the door shut.

'No problem.' Alex waved.

151

19

Alex watched the television vans with their reporters disappear down the street.

She looked at the house again, wondering what she should do. No, she knew what she should do – go and knock on the door and find out what was happening. But suddenly she didn't have the stomach for it. They had lost a husband and a father in horrible circumstances, she didn't want to make it worse for them.

A curtain twitched and a face appeared at the side of the window. It was the younger of the two women from the car. The daughter? She nodded to Alex, before disappearing again.

Alex walked down the road and found a bench to sit on before taking her phone out of her pocket.

Heath's number went straight to voicemail. Damn. She really needed to know why there was this sudden interest in the Daleys.

She sat thinking. Could she do it? And how should she approach it? Carefully, that's how. She punched in Bud Evans's number.

'Bud, it's Alex Devlin.'

'Alex. What do you want?' His voice was friendly, if a little cool.

She heard him shuffle papers on his desk, then: 'Damn, sod it, blast', as a pile of them fell onto the floor.

'I'm in Lowdham—'

'Alex, could you be quick. I'm busy. News and all that.'

And thank you for dropping everything and going to Dillingham Broad to play lackey for one of our other reporters. Ungrateful man.

'I hope my copy was okay for you. About Derek Daley and Roger Fleet.'

'Yes, thank you for that. Was there something else?'

There was the sound of more papers rustling, emails pinging into his computer. A phone began to ring. She drew a deep breath. 'Derek Daley had a holiday home in Lowdham and a load of reporters have just turned up. I was hoping—'

'Wait one minute, Alex. What do you mean? You're in Lowdham at Derek Daley's holiday home?'

The phone was still ringing forlornly.

'I ... look, I'll come clean. I thought the story about Daley and Fleet's deaths on the Broads was worth a bit more. I was interested in the suicide forum angle.'

'Heath told me. And, if I remember correctly, I said I wasn't interested.'

'I know, but—'

'You've been doing a bit of investigating?'

She nodded, then realized Bud couldn't see her. 'Yes.'

'Bit of a waste of your time, isn't it?' His voice was cool.

'I thought if you weren't interested, someone else might be.' Sometimes the threat of a possible story going to a rival paper was enough to get a news editor interested at least.

'Don't be too hasty, Alex.' She heard him puffing on his e-cigarette – Bud had taken up vaping big time. 'I'd be interested in a feature on Internet suicide, so don't go touting it anywhere else. But Daley and Fleet killed themselves. End of story.'

'They knew each other before, though.'

There was a silence. She heard Bud breathing. 'Really? Could be interesting. More likely a coincidence. I'll have someone look into it.'

'But I—'

'You stick to the Internet suicide line, give me something on that.'

Alex gritted her teeth. 'Okay. The reporters—'

'What reporters?'

'The ones who turned up here a few minutes ago. They wouldn't tell me why. I thought maybe—'

'That I might know? Why?'

'Daley was a colleague of yours.' This was like pulling teeth.

'I wouldn't say that. He was in the same business as me, but our paths didn't cross often. I never liked the man.' Bud sighed. 'Okay. I'll give you this. He was about to be arrested for kiddie porn. Before he died. That's presumably why he killed himself.' The phone, which had gone silent, began to ring again. 'I've got to go. Keep me up to date with what you're doing.' He ended the call.

Alex wanted to throw her phone onto the grass in frustration. Bud had given her a half-hearted go-ahead for the Internet forum feature, but was not too interested in the fact that Daley and Fleet had known each other before. But if they had known each other before, then why bother with the Internet forum? And now this new development. What was she supposed to think about that? Children. Pornography.

She leaned back on the bench and closed her eyes.

Alex sensed someone near her and opened her eyes to see a woman with lank hair standing by the bench. She looked as though she had been crying for a week. Her complexion was grey and there was a cold sore at the corner of her mouth. The woman gripped the back of the bench.

'I saw you as we turned into the drive,' the woman started. 'And you were talking to those revolting people, sending them

154

away. I don't know what you said to them but, whatever it was, thank you.' The woman looked as though she was about to cry.

Alex smiled at her. 'No problem. And you must be—?'

'Laurie. Laurie Cooke. I'm Derek Daley's daughter, but I guess you knew that already. And I know who you are.' She gave a wan smile. 'I used to love your articles in *The Post*. I recognize you from your byline picture. I guess you know why the TV people were so keen to get hold of us.'

'I've just heard—' Alex held out her phone. 'From my, er, news editor.'

Laurie nodded. 'Right. So you know he was going to be investigated for child pornography. Child porn.' She shook her head. 'I can't believe it. Still. The police have taken away his computer, so I expect they'll find something on that. Well, I wanted to say thank you and I have.' She made to go.

'I'm so sorry about your father.' Alex wanted Laurie to stay and talk some more.

Laurie looked into the distance. 'Are you? I don't know what to think. Mum's in the house at the moment, tearing open boxes Dad put in the attic when we bought the farmhouse. She's crying, and her nails are getting ruined, but she's convinced she's going to find horrible photos. She wants to see for herself, she says.'

'Did … did your mother know? About the—'

'Paedophilia? That's what it was, wasn't it?' Laurie said, the bitterness evident in her voice. 'Persuading children to take off their clothes and pose for him. So here's a question.' She turned and looked at Alex. 'They say that wives, family, should have known something when this sort of thing happens, and I'm trying to think, to remember. But, from Mum's reaction, I'd say no, she didn't have a clue. What do you think? She seems genuinely shocked and has aged about twenty years. All the Botox and fillers in the world aren't helping her now.' She shrugged helplessly. 'What do I know? Maybe I'm wrong. Maybe she did know.'

Maybe. Alex had been in court often enough looking at men

155

or women found guilty of assault, abuse, rape, murder and had glanced over at their families, wondering if they really hadn't suspected anything, if in their hearts they had known. After all, if you are that close to someone, how could you not be aware of a large chunk of their lives? It beat her.

'And my memories of a loving father and happy childhood are completely tarnished. More than that. Smashed to smithereens. How can I think of happy times with Dad without wondering what was going on in his head at the time? A beach holiday – was he looking at the kids and wanting to photograph them without their clothes? He always had a camera with him. It was a part of him, even when he became really successful. Now we know why. And those times he took me to the theme park? Or the zoo? Or just the local park? Was he really only looking for subjects for his nasty hobby?' She buried her face in her hands. 'I'll never know.'

'Laurie,' began Alex, hesitating, not wanting to add to the other woman's distress, 'do you think your father killed himself because he'd been found out?'

Laurie lifted her head out of her hands and looked at her with haunted eyes. 'I killed him,' she said, simply. 'I killed him because I found out about all his so-called models.' She looked drained.

Alex patted the bench beside her. 'Sit down. You didn't kill him, Laurie. He took his own life.'

'But I might have been able to stop him if I'd only talked to him properly. Instead I lost my temper and threw all the accusations at him, told him he was an ugly, evil old man.'

'How did you find out about—?' Alex asked.

'The modelling stuff? His secret life?' She shook her head. 'Christ. It was a letter through the post. A letter, can you believe it? In this day and age. Pictures. Testimonies. Evidence.'

'And who was the letter from?'

Laurie shrugged. 'No idea. One of his victims, I guess. There was nothing in the envelope to suggest who it might have been.

156

The pictures were horrible, horrible.' She dashed away more tears. 'Their faces were full of hope to start with. But then Dad – Derek –' she spat out his name, 'made them do more and more lewd stuff and you could see the hope dying in their eyes. And he'd documented it all. What sort of sicko does that? I expect he threatened to tell their families about the photos if they tried to object.' She plucked at her sleeves. 'How could a man like that be my father? I can't believe it. Not really.'

'Was your dad in the pictures?'

'No. You just see a hand or a foot.'

'When you lost your temper with him it was what? A few days before he died?'

She smiled grimly. 'Yes. It was near the boats, by the water. Obviously.' She gave a hiccuping laugh. 'I wanted him to go to the police, give himself up. But you know what? He denied it all, everything. Said he hadn't taken the photographs. He'd been set up, he said.'

'Set up?'

'Yes. He said the pictures weren't his; any proof had been fabricated; he knew who had sent them, blah, blah, blah. They always say that, though, don't they? And so I said, tell the police it wasn't you. Tell them who it really was. But he looked at me, tears in his eyes and said he couldn't. That's when I realized I didn't believe him.' She gulped down more tears. 'I told him … that day … I said I wished he'd die.' She clenched her fists. 'And then he did. When I saw him on the day we argued he said he had to do it for me. I didn't understand what he meant then; I didn't know he was going to kill himself. And then he did.'

He had to do it for me. The same sort of phrase Roger Fleet used in his letter to his sister. A shiver went down her spine.

Alex put her hand on top of Laurie's. Her skin was cold like ice. 'Were those his exact words?'

Laurie nodded. 'As far as I can remember, yes.'

157

'And did he give any reason why he had to "do it for you" as he said?'

Laurie shook her head. 'Not really. I suppose he thought he had let us down.'

'And you went to the police.'

'The day his body was found,' she whispered, 'I'd been up all night wondering what to do. But then I kept thinking of all those little faces and I knew I couldn't – I didn't know it was him on that boat. Not then. I didn't know.'

'So,' said Alex, 'had you told him you were going to go to the police?'

'You mean, could that have pushed him over the edge?' She gave a twisted sort of smile. 'No, of course I didn't tell him. If I had he would have got rid of all the evidence, wouldn't he? What I wanted was for him to go to the police himself. Then I began hoping there had been some sort of horrible mistake.' Her shoulders drooped. 'Though I knew there hadn't been, otherwise why wouldn't he have tried to clear his name? Then I became so angry, so angry.' Her whole body had gone rigid and she was clenching her fists. 'So angry. And now he's dead.'

'It's not your fault,' Alex said softly.

'It is. If I had been more understanding, I could have persuaded him to give himself up. I'm sure of it. But ...' She chewed her bottom lip. 'Oh, I don't know any more. I don't know what to think. In one way, he's got away with it, hasn't he? Left me and Mum and our family to deal with the fallout.'

Alex tried to think clearly. Derek Daley was well down the path to suicide before his daughter turned up at Lowdham – the boat had been booked weeks before – so it wasn't the threat of being exposed that pushed him over the edge. Unless there was someone else who was threatening or even blackmailing him. And what could she say to Laurie? That there were dark days ahead but that she would come through it? Sounded so glib, but it was her experience.

'Laurie, did the police tell you about the Internet forum?'

She nodded.

'So you see,' said Alex, 'it looked as though he and Roger Fleet had been planning it for a while.'

'I suppose so. Then why——?'

'What I'm saying is that it wasn't the accusation that was the last straw; it wasn't you. He was going to do it anyway. The question is why. One other thing – did you know that he and Roger Fleet knew each other? In the past, I mean?'

'No. What do you mean?'

'They were at Cambridge together.'

Laurie looked bewildered. 'I had no idea. Now I really don't know what to think.' Her shoulders slumped with exhaustion. 'Anyway, I'd better get back to Mum before she does something stupid. And how I'm going to explain it to the kids, I don't know. I mean, they're so young. I can't tell them about that … that … filth.'

Alex put her hand over Laurie's. 'Maybe not. But their grandfather loved them, and they'll remember that.'

Laurie stared at her for a moment. 'But I'll always wonder, won't I?' And with that, she turned and ran back to the house.

Alex leaned back on the bench feeling wrung out. She could feel nothing but sympathy for Laurie caught in a maelstrom that would die down in the public forum, but never in her life. And the reporters would be back. Soon Laurie was going to wonder if her own children had been safe from her father. She knew only too well how the actions of others could profoundly affect those closest to you. It was easy enough to see in her own family. How Sasha's actions had affected Gus.

Talking of Gus, where the hell was he?

She took out her phone see if there was anything from him. Nothing. She hesitated for a moment, then found the number she wanted and pressed the call button.

'Steve?' she said. 'It's Alex. Didn't you get my message?'

There was hesitation before he spoke. 'Sorry. I've been meaning to ring, it's just that …' His voice trailed off. Alex waited for him to speak again. 'Anyway, it's good to hear from you. How are things? I trust Gus arrived safely; he was supposed to text me when he got to your place, but I guess he had better things to do.'

Her stomach contracted. 'That's why I'm ringing, Steve. I've heard nothing from him. I don't even know when he was supposed to be arriving.'

She realized at that moment that she was worried, very worried. Her Gus would let her know what he was doing. She knew she was a bit clingy, but he understood that, understood how the whole thing with Sasha and the twins had affected her. It wasn't that she wanted to know what he was doing every hour of every day – God knows that hadn't been possible during his time in Ibiza – but she did like him to keep in touch, and he knew that.

'Look, Alex, he's twenty. Cut him a bit of slack. He'll turn up. Probably nursing an almighty hangover.' Steve laughed, and Alex tried not to feel irritated. But she was also cross with herself for worrying. Honestly, when she was younger she'd imagined Gus would be away and off her hands at eighteen and she wouldn't have to give him too much thought. But it didn't work like that, not like that at all. Worrying about her son and worrying about her parents. The sandwich generation, that's what she was.

'Is there anyone I can ring, just to check? Any friends you know of?' Alex tried not to sound like an overprotective mother. Even more, she hated having to admit that Steve might know more about his friends than she did.

There was silence for a few moments. 'I know he was fooling about on various Internet forums, like they do, and there was a girl he seemed pretty friendly with.'

'How do you know? Did he tell you?'

Now the silence felt uncomfortable. 'Not exactly,' said Steve, in what sounded like a careful voice. 'I went into his room when he was out—'

'You did what?' Alex felt the anger bubbling up inside.

'Look, I know he's been painting a picture of sunshine and laughter out here, but it's been hard for all of us, you know?' There was the trace of a whine in Steve's voice.

'No, I don't know. Tell me.' The bubbling anger threatened to expand, and her jaw ached with tension.

'I think he was feeling a bit lonely, missing home, so he went online a lot. We were getting a bit worried because at first he loved playing with the kids but then he began to withdraw into himself. But he seemed happier after he'd met this girl online.' He sighed. 'Look, he told us about her, right? Her name was Martha. They clicked apparently. That's all I know.'

'My son was unhappy and you didn't think to tell me?' Alex could not believe Steve hadn't told her about Gus straight away. No question.

'Our son,' he said, pointedly. 'And I had hoped to be able to deal with it. When he said he wanted to go home to you I was relieved.'

I bet you were, she thought. Relieved of the responsibility more like.

'So, do you have any contact details for this girl?'

'No.'

There was something in his voice. 'But? What aren't you telling me?'

'I think she was going to meet him at Stansted and drive up to you. That's what it seemed to say.'

'What do you mean?'

There was silence. Then: 'I took a look at the forum – there was no password protect on it and it was easy to go through his history. I saw the latest messages.'

Alex wasn't sure how she felt about that. If Gus had been fifteen then she would have been perfectly happy for his father to snoop through his Internet history. But he wasn't a teenager any more. On the other hand, he was still her son. And he still hadn't got in touch with her. 'Bloody hell, Steve, couldn't you have told me this earlier?'

She could almost feel him shrug. 'He's a lad, Alex. Don't get all aerated about it.'

'Okay. I won't.' She didn't bother to say goodbye.

Now what? Should she report him missing? The trouble was, he wasn't a child, he wasn't a vulnerable adult. He was a normal young man. All the police would say is leave it, he'll come home. Like Steve, and Lin for that matter, they would probably think he had gone on the lash somewhere and would come home when he was good and ready. But this was Gus. She knew he wouldn't leave her in limbo wondering where he was. Would he?

And what if he had been lonely and unable to find his place in the world? What then? She knew only too well that suicide was the biggest cause of death of men under forty-five – she didn't want Gus to be a statistic. And although she had buried the thought deep, there was that worry he might have inherited some of her sister's mental instability.

God, that was one way of putting it.

He would be in touch. She knew it. She had to trust him.

A shadow fell over her. 'Well, wherever we go, you seem to be there first.'

Alex looked up. 'Detective Inspector Berry, how lovely to see you. And you, Detective Sergeant Logan.' She smiled sweetly at them. DI Berry's smile stretched his mouth across his face. More of a grimace, Alex thought. Idly, she wondered if he was married. She glanced down. Yes. A wedding ring. Takes all sorts.

'May I?' He pointed at the bench.

'Of course.'

DS Logan remained standing, poised as if she were on watch. DI Berry put his hands on his knees and cleared his throat. 'Can I ask what you are doing here?'

Alex endeavoured to appear surprised. 'Having a look around. Enjoying the sunshine. You?'

Berry grimaced again. A tractor and trailer trundled by. A black cat wandered over and started curling around Alex's legs. She reached down to stroke it.

'We saw you talking to Laurie Cooke.'

'Yes.' Alex continued stroking the cat.

'We would rather you left any sleuthing to us.'

Alex wanted to smile at the word 'sleuthing'. 'Laurie came out to talk to me. She's devastated about her father. It's all so fresh and raw.' She stopped stroking the cat and looked at Berry. 'Do you think he was a paedophile?'

Berry's face was impassive. 'We are looking into it.'

'But he was on the suicide forum way before he died. The paedophile accusation didn't come until later.'

'I am aware of that.'

'Don't you think it strange?'

DI Berry stood. 'Miss Devlin, please don't interfere with police work, will you? It wouldn't go down well. Not well at all.'

'DI Berry, I'm not interfering, I only want to know why Derek Daley and Roger Fleet killed themselves. You do know they knew one another? Before meeting on the Internet?'

She could see Berry working his jaw. 'We are looking into every angle.'

'Which means you didn't.' Alex stood. 'They were at Cambridge together. In the 1970s.' She sighed and sat down again. 'I don't want to be seen as trying to get one over on you. I want to write about suicide forums, but I keep coming up against the fact they knew each other before. And I am asking myself what was the point of going on the forum? Surely not a coincidence?'

He gave a thin smile. 'We're looking into everything.'

That was one man with a very large chip on his shoulder, thought Alex, as she watched him and Logan walk up the farm-house drive. She wondered which journalist had hurt him and how. And so much for trying to help. She would have told them about the photograph Margaret Winwood had shown her if they'd given her half a chance. Still, they would probably get there soon enough.

Willem Major. She wanted to find him. She tried Heath's number again. Nothing. Where was he when she needed him?

She sat, staring over the road and to the fields beyond, then she stirred herself and punched in some numbers on the phone from memory, imagining it ringing one of several phones in an airless house in Streatham, the light kept out by blankets over the windows.

The phone was answered. 'Alex?'

'Honey, I need some help.'

'Yeah?' Honey's voice was not betraying any emotion.

Honey was a computer hacker who operated outside the law. Alex had helped her to avoid jail once, and Honey was forever grateful, helping Alex out when she needed information from under the radar.

'Can you find someone for me? He's gone off the grid, so I can't track him down by any conventional means, and I also don't want to draw attention to the fact I want to find him—'

'Yeah, yeah, no worries. Send me his name. Just one thing, though …'

For the first time ever Alex heard a trace of hesitation in Honey's voice.

'Tell me?'

'I've gotta lie low for a while. Disappear, y'know?'

'Honey, what's going on?'

A brittle laugh. 'You don't want to know, you really don't. But there's no need to worry; if I keep out of sight, offline, do nothing for a while it'll be okay. So—'

'So, don't ask for any more favours. I get it.' How Honey would be able to keep offline was anybody's guess.

'Yeah.'

'Honey?'

'Yeah?'

She almost did it. Almost asked Honey if she could hack into the CCTV at Stansted Airport to see if Gus was on it anywhere. But it was a stupid idea. An overreaction. Besides, there would be hours to trawl through. She must have more faith in Gus. 'Take care of yourself, won't you?'

'Yeah.'

The line went dead.

Alex pulled up the burn app on her phone to send a text message that immediately deleted itself from the receiver's and the sender's phone once it was read.

'Find Willem Major. Businessman. Family killed in a fire. Please.'

There. At least she was doing something.

20

Cambridge 1976

Life was brighter, more adrenaline-fuelled with Willem back centre stage. He never apologized about the sex with Rachel, never explained; he acted as though the rift had never happened. I was happy with that; I didn't want to re-open old wounds, especially as they had healed over. I did take a stand on one thing, however – Stu.

'He's coming with us,' I said when a trip to the pub was decided upon.

'Darling, he's dreary, so provincial,' said Willem, dismissively.

'No, he's not, he's been a good friend to me. When you weren't.' I looked Willem straight in the eye, determined to stand my ground and claw back some of the self-respect I had lost over the Rachel affair.

Willem shrugged. 'A dull Barnardo's Boy, that's all he is. Dull, dull, dull.'

'Still.'

'Don't blame me if he leeches the fun out of everything.'

I had won the battle. And I had learned that Stu was an orphan, which went some way to explaining his neediness.

Willem's mischievousness knew no bounds. Somehow he managed to persuade some of the students from the mountaineering club to put cones on all four spires of King's College chapel – they had to be taken down by steeplejacks at great expense. At his instigation, a Robin Reliant was punted down the river; it was he who organized a streak around Cambridge, taking in the Round Church and Jesus Green Lock, ending with a naked punt along the River Cam. He himself didn't take part, but such was his charisma he was able to persuade others. Including us five. Including Roger, who'd had a phobia of water since his father had thrown him in the deep end of a swimming pool. And Stu, often the butt of Willem's cruel jokes – Stu took part as well.

I remember standing shivering on the corner of Adams Road and Wilberforce Road just as the sun was rising, fervently hoping that no one would see my white goosebumped flesh. We all avoided each other's eyes, yet we did it.

'One, two, three, go!' shouted Willem. 'Remember it's for charity.'

Was it? I don't remember, but we ran naked down that track, down pavements, across roads, not looking at one another, wanting it to end, but wanting Willem to be proud of us and reward us with his good humour.

I think Stu stuck around out of sheer bloody-mindedness. He knew Willem didn't like him, but he was damned if he was going to give him the satisfaction of going away, however many times Willem told him to 'fuck off, darling'.

Then came the evening we went to the church.

'An event,' Willem exclaimed one evening as he burst into my room without so much as a knock on the door. 'I want you to come.' He flung his arms around me. I wriggled. I wasn't too keen on these physical displays of affection, particularly when Stu was around, as he was that evening.

'Gerroff ... I'm trying to come to terms with Kant.'

'Aren't we all? Oh, I'm sure he's a jolly good fellow, but put him away and come with me.'

I looked up at him. 'An event? What sort of an event? And on a Tuesday night?'

'Yes. A Tuesday night. Monday, Friday, Sunday, why not? The week is so dreary, so endless otherwise. The others are waiting. Come, come.'

'And Stu,' I said pointedly.

Willem opened his mouth to object. I stared him down. He shrugged, but a sly expression flashed across his face and for a moment I wondered if we were all going to regret this evening.

Squashed into a battered Hillman Imp Willem had borrowed from someone, or perhaps stolen, I left Immanuel Kant and his morality theory behind and drove out of Cambridge and into the countryside. Derek, Roger, Jen, and Stu were in the back, practically sitting on each other's laps. As the lights of the city faded behind us, the fog grew thicker and the roads dark and narrow, overgrown hedges to one side, trees with bare branches twisting up to the fog on the other. Willem, hunched over the steering wheel, could hardly see where he was going. I spied one signpost.

Devil's Ditch.

'Here.'

We turned off the road and parked up on a grass verge.

'Come on,' said Willem, putting on the steering wheel lock so no one could steal the heap of junk that called itself a car. 'Let's go and see what's happening.'

We piled out and walked up to the wrought-iron gate.

'It's a church,' I said, rather unnecessarily. It was built, as far as I could make out, from brick and flint. There was no tower only a stump of bricks where that should have been – it looked as though it had collapsed in times past. The leaded arched windows were lit from inside: candles, I guessed from the muted quality of the light. Either side of the overgrown pebble path to the door were tombstones – some standing, others listing perilously to one side. I saw a smashed angel on the ground. The fog swirled, making my skin and hair damp. I heard singing. No, not singing but chanting that was vaguely hypnotic. It all made me uneasy. Jen slipped her hand in mine. Both our hands were sweaty.

'What is this place?' she whispered.

'I told you,' said Willem. 'A church.' He rubbed his hands together, whether from the cold or with glee I wasn't sure.

'You didn't tell us we were going to a church. You know I'm not religious and nor are you. Anyhow, I want to go back.' Jen tossed her hair behind her shoulder.

'Here,' he said, handing round some white pills. 'Take these.'

Jen hesitated, then took one, swallowing it obediently, her earlier half-hearted defiance dissolved. Roger and Derek swallowed theirs without a murmur. Stu hesitated. The look on Willem's face dared him to take it. He did. I didn't like Willem's smile.

'What are they?' I asked.

'Something to help you enjoy the party more. Heighten the experience.' He grinned at my discomfort. 'Don't be so parochial.'

I frowned. 'You know I don't—'

'Oh, stop arguing and get on with it.' This from Derek. 'We're here now; it's only one little pill and quite honestly I need something to get me in the mood.'

My friends were behaving oddly. It was as if the fog and the chanting and the flickering lights had got to them. I swallowed the pill.

Willem led us to the doorway and into the church porch, with its stone seating on either side and the noticeboard with pieces of paper still stapled to it. I tried to peer at what they said. I could pick up something about church service times and a flower festival, but the notices were faded and torn.

Willem put a hand on Derek's arm. 'No pictures, okay?' He nodded at Derek's rucksack that he took everywhere with him. 'Leave that here.'

'I can't, man,' he said. 'I've got expensive gear in here.'

'Then you should have left it in the car. I told you earlier, no pictures.' He looked coolly at him.

Derek dropped his gaze first. 'Okay.' He bundled his rucksack underneath the stone bench.

Willem nodded with satisfaction, then pushed open the heavy wooden doors, putting his finger to his lips as he did so.

The church was indeed lit by candles, hundreds and hundreds of black candles. I could see people in the nave – I don't know, maybe forty of them – dressed in black robes with black hoods. A fire that emitted an odd, bitter smell was burning, and I wondered if they had used any of the old wooden chairs lying discarded around the church as fuel. In the dim light that spiked across the walls, I could see the plaster was blown, marked with damp and streaked brown where the rain had found its way in. At the end of the chancel was a magnificent stained-glass window. There were no statues or holy pictures. Definitely an abandoned church, then. Or something more sinister.

The chanting was becoming louder and louder but I couldn't make out the words. I started to laugh. 'What is this?' I asked in a stage whisper. 'Are we on a film set?' Because that was what it felt like to me. It was as though I was looking at it all from outside of myself.

Willem frowned and shook his head, holding out a restraining hand. 'Ssh,' he said. 'We're not supposed to be here.'

'What is it?' hissed Roger.

Instead of answering, Willem crept into the church, his shoes making little noise on the flagstones. We followed behind.

The people in the robes were chanting so hard they didn't notice us. We crouched behind the cracked and mildewed baptismal font. There was a makeshift altar in front of one of the old dirty windows. A goat was tethered to it. A goat? This was like something out of the Dennis Wheatley novels I used to read and be terrified by as a teenager. What was the goat for? A sacrifice? Come on.

Yet there were prickles of unease across my scalp.

Then, out of the blue, my heart felt as though it was speeding up and I felt alert and ready for anything. I wanted to tell Willem how much I loved him. I wanted to tell Jen I loved her. Christ – inappropriate word in this setting – I wanted to hug Roger and Derek and tell Derek to live his life as he wanted, and I wanted to tell Roger to relax. I wanted to say to Stu that he was my friend even though he was a bit nerdy. The chanting filled my head. The bitter smoke from the fire wreathed around our heads, until I could smell nothing else but its bitterness with an undertone of sweetness. I was euphoric.

I could distinguish the words of the chant now:

Do what thou wilt
Do what thou wilt
Do what thou wilt

I found myself mouthing the words, and I heard the others chanting also – Willem's deep voice, Roger's quiet voice getting louder, Derek almost shouting, and Jen determined. And Stu. Stu was swaying from side to side, his eyes bright and unfocused. He was chanting the loudest of all of us while the candlelight danced and writhed across the walls, became spiders, locusts, snakes, yellow, green, red, so much red. I saw faces on the walls, faces with contorted mouths and black holes for eyes. Bodies, blackened by fire, twisting and turning. My head, my limbs, my brain were filled with the chanting.

I stood up and danced my way towards the nave.

171

21

It was odd, mused Alex as she walked up the track to her parents' home, you didn't think of your mum and dad as having a life before you. As a teenager she could remember being totally self-absorbed, looking up only when she had to deal with Sasha. Her parents hardly came into the equation at all, except to provide meals and a taxi service. She had taken their love for granted.

Something made her stop – a sound, perhaps? The hairs on the back of her neck were standing up. She was being watched. She turned quickly, hoping to catch whoever it was off guard.

Nothing.

She scanned the trees and hedges around her. Could someone be hiding? Perhaps in the field beyond, but tracking her steps? She hadn't heard a car or been aware of one following her, and surely she would have noticed something as she drove down the narrow country lanes to her parents' house?

Was that a shadow behind the tree?

She stood absolutely still. 'Hello? Is there anybody there?'

There was nothing but the singing of the birds in the trees and the distant sound of an aeroplane, high in the sky. There was no strange noise, she was alone, and with too much imagination.

'Alex!'

Her mother looked surprised to see her when she answered the door. And no wonder – she didn't usually visit more than once a month, and now here she was, for the second time in less than a week; but it had been nagging at her, the thought that her father had been at Cambridge at the same time as Fleet and Daley, and she wanted to find out if he had come across them. A long shot, given the state of his memory; though, often he remembered things from the distant past as though it were yesterday.

'Mum. I thought—'

Her mother held the door open wider. 'Come in, come in. It is the day we normally go shopping, have a bit of lunch, that sort of thing, but your father, well, he didn't feel up to it.' Her mother smiled; it didn't reach her eyes.

Alex hesitated. 'Are you sure?' Her mother appeared anxious, careworn. Hair was escaping from her normally tidy bun, and her cardigan was buttoned up the wrong way.

'Of course, of course. I haven't tidied up yet—'

'Don't worry about that,' said Alex, leaning in to hug her mother. 'As if that matters. It's only me.'

But she wasn't prepared for just how untidy and dirty the place was.

There was a musty smell and an air of neglect in the usually immaculate kitchen. The sink was piled high with greasy plates and dirty glasses. The usually clear worktops had open packets of rice and pasta and sugar spilling out their contents. A blackened saucepan sat on top of the cooker with what looked like mouse droppings in the bottom, but were hopefully only burnt baked beans.

'As I said, I haven't had a chance to—' Her mother was hovering behind her as Alex looked around with dismay. 'It's been a difficult couple of days.'

'It's all right, Mum,' she said, pity twisting in her heart. She opened the fridge to see if there was enough food, and found a packet of soap powder, a roll of bin bags and an old copy of *Good Housekeeping* in there instead. 'Mum—'

Her mother reached around her, shutting the fridge door, and then stood with her back against it. 'I'll get them out later. Your father – he likes to tidy up, but he doesn't always remember where to put things, and I told you, we usually go shopping on a Tuesday but today we haven't. Too busy.'

'You said Dad wasn't up to it.' Her father was deteriorating faster than she'd thought.

'Too busy,' her mother said, defiantly.

Alex looked at her mother and was shocked all over again at how much she had aged in the last few months. Her hair was thinning, her skin was grey and her wrinkles cut deeper grooves down her face. She was not eating enough, that was certain. Why hadn't she noticed it before? Had she been so desperate to get away that she hadn't bothered to look at her mother properly?

'Mum—'

Her mother moved away from the fridge, took a ragged cloth from beside the sink and began to wipe the worktops, folding the tops of the food packets down and shoving them in cupboards. 'Why are you here? I mean, it's lovely to see you …' The rest of the sentence, the 'but you usually only come when you absolutely have to' was left unspoken.

Something like shame filled her. It was true that she had found it much more difficult to visit her parents since her dad had become ill. She could hardly bear to see him deteriorate. A selfish emotion – especially as her mother had it far worse.

'I—' Why was she here? Because something had been nagging at her that she wanted to find out about, but she also genuinely wanted to see how her parents were coping.

'Who's there?'

Her father's voice came from upstairs.

'It's me,' called Alex, going to the foot of the stairs.

'Who's me?' He was in the bedroom.

'Alex.'

'Alex who?'

Alex looked at her mother who gave her a tremulous smile. 'Your daughter Alex.'

'Oh.'

She tried again. 'Are you coming down?'

'Of course not. I'm in bed.' Querulous. 'And I'm busy.'

Her mother's shoulders sagged. 'Do you want a cup of tea?'

Alex smiled. 'That would be lovely.'

'At least it'll be made a bit quicker,' her mother said lightly, busying around the kitchen.

'Have you actually got milk in that fridge?'

Her mother laughed. 'Oh yes. And when I get the milk out I can take my magazine out too. Saves walking into the sitting room to get it.'

They smiled at one another, united by circumstance.

'Mum, you're not eating properly, are you?'

'We're managing fine, thank you. You don't need to worry about us. It's time you stopped taking all the cares of this family – especially Sasha – on your shoulders.' Her mother poured the tea, and pushed a mug across to Alex. 'And talking of Sasha, how is she?' There was sadness in her mother's eyes.

'She's, well, she's, you know, Sasha.'

'I'm glad she's with you.'

'Are you? I'm not sure I am.' There. She'd said it.

Her mother took her hand. 'We would have had her here, gladly, but she wanted to be with you. And that gives me some comfort. I know how ... up and down she can be. And don't ever think we didn't know how much Sasha relied on you growing up. How much we relied on you. It was too much for a child, and I'm sorry for that.'

Alex stared at her mother, more aware than ever she was responsible for her parents now, they weren't responsible for her anymore. Yet the child in her wanted to tell her mum about all the times she would lie awake at night worrying about Sasha. How she had protected her against the bullies. Washed her sister's arms when she cut into her flesh trying to control one thing in her life. Tried not to mind when Sasha walked off with *her* boyfriend. And then married him.

She drained her mug. 'Here,' she said. She went over to the sink and filled it with hot water, putting in a squirt of washing-up liquid, 'let me.'

'I couldn't possibly—'

'Mum,' she said. 'Let me.' They were a family who didn't talk easily to one another about the serious things in life, but she could do the washing-up for her mum. She began to scrub away at the dried-on food.

Her mother sat down heavily on a kitchen chair that creaked as it took her slight weight. 'Alex, I …'

Alex looked over to her mother and saw the tears rolling down her face. She put down the saucepan she was trying to rescue, dried her hands and bent over to give her a hug.

'Two hugs in almost as many days, that must be a record,' her mum said with a smile. She traced a pattern on the pine table. 'On his good days, his lucid days – and he still has a fair few of those – your dad says his illness is a punishment.'

'"A punishment"? What on earth does he mean by that?'

Her mum closed her eyes for a moment, as if gathering herself. 'We were young when we met. We were on the same accountancy course. Boring, I know, but there we are. He never liked talking about his past, used to say what was done was done and he wanted to lead a good life. Though he could never define what a good life was.'

'Mum, you have led a good life.'

Her mother laughed mirthlessly. 'As long as you don't count Sasha. A difficult child who grew up into a difficult adult.'

'I'd say that was just Sasha. You brought us both up the same.'

'Did we?'

'Look, we don't want to have a debate about nature versus nurture, do we?'

176

'I suppose not. But we must have done something awful for this to happen to us.'

'Mum, you must stop punishing yourself. What's done is done, and whatever happens to Dad was going to happen.'

'But he's not some ninety-year-old. He's only in his sixties.' Her voice shook. 'And I'm so frightened.' These last words came out in a whisper.

Alex swallowed hard. 'I know, Mum. I'll help you.'

'Oh, you've got enough to do, what with your job and looking after Gus.'

'Gus is old enough to look after himself, on the whole.' Where was he?

'He's a good lad, your Gus,' said her mother before taking a sip of the tea. 'You've done a good job there; and I've never told you this, but I'm really proud of the way you've coped all these years. Really proud.' She put her cup down and rubbed her face as if trying to wake herself up. 'Now, Alex,' her voice was stronger, 'you didn't come here to dish out tea and sympathy, did you?'

'No, not really. I actually want to talk to Dad.'

'Join the queue.'

They both smiled at her mother's grim humour.

'Was it about something in particular?' Her mother looked at her over the rim of her mug.

Alex nodded.

'Go on.'

'He was at Cambridge in the mid-seventies, wasn't he?'

Her mother blinked slowly. 'He was, but it wasn't an easy time for him. He doesn't like talking about it. It's what I was saying earlier, he wanted a quiet life. A good life. He said Cambridge was not going to give him that.'

There was something her mother wasn't saying.

'I didn't think you were that interested in family history?' her mother continued. 'Too much harping on about the past, you used to say.'

Alex put her hands around her mug. 'You're right. I wasn't that interested before. I think it's probably only as you get older you realize what you don't know about your family and what you'd like to know. Find your roots if you like. Perhaps it's when it dawns on you no one lives forever and one day we won't be able to hear their stories however much we want to.' She frowned. 'And part of me thinks that it's almost too late to know more about Dad. I mean, he's always been that, just Dad. But he is more than that, isn't he? More than just Dad, just a dad?' She knew then that she thought exactly that. Although she had come to see her parents for a particular reason, and a reason to do with the deaths on the Broads, she knew that she was feeling the gradual loss of her father and the regret that she never really knew him as a person and now probably never would.

'There's something else, isn't there?' Her mother looked at her shrewdly.

Alex nodded. 'I'm doing a background feature on a couple of people who were found dead on the Broads.'

'Drowned?'

'No.' Of course, her mum would be too busy with her dad to see any reports on television, and they'd stopped having a news-paper when Sasha's children first disappeared. 'They were found on their boat. It's thought they killed themselves.'

Her mother put her hand to her throat. 'How awful.'

'I know.' Alex grimaced. 'They were in their sixties too.'

'Oh?'

'It seems they knew each other. In fact, they were at university together.' She paused. 'Cambridge. Their names were Derek Daley and Roger Fleet.'

Her mother got up and poured what was left of her tea down the sink.

'I wondered …' Alex went on. God, this was hard. 'I wondered if Dad would have known them?'

'Why should he have done?' The question came quickly, defensively. Her mother began to wash her mug.

'Because he would have been at Cambridge at about the same time as them.'

'So what? It doesn't necessarily mean they would have been friends.' She took up the scrubbing of the saucepan. 'It's a big place, Cambridge. Colleges and all that. You didn't meet everybody. And your dad was only there for a year.'

'Which college was he in?'

'Why does it matter?' Still her mother had her back to her.

'Mum, what's wrong?'

'Nothing.'

Alex frowned. It was, she thought, a perfectly ordinary question to ask. After all, she knew very little about her father's time at university; it was something he never talked about and she had learned never to ask about. 'The men who died were in St Francis's College.'

Her mother's back stiffened, and her hands were stilled.

'That was Dad's college, wasn't it?' she asked, with a flash of intuition.

'Yes, yes it was. But it doesn't necessarily mean he knew those men.'

Alex pressed on. 'But he might have done. Has he ever mentioned the names to you? Roger Fleet and Derek Daley?'

'Derek Daley?' Her father's voice came from the doorway. 'Why are you talking about Derek?'

Alex jumped up and led her father to a chair. He shuffled rather than walked. His jumper was on back to front.

'You knew Derek Daley, Dad?'

'Yes, of course I did.'

'And what about a man called Roger Fleet?'

Her father nodded. 'Roger. Yes. He was a gentle soul. Wasn't cut out for ...'

'For what, Dad?'

179

Her father looked guarded. 'Nothing. Why are you talking about them?'

'I've got some bad news, Dad. About Derek Daley and Roger Fleet.'

Her mother was looking at her, her face pale, grim. 'No, Alex. Not now. He won't understand.'

'Mum—'

Her father peered at her.

'Who are you?' he asked irritably.

'I'm Alex,' she said. 'Your daughter. Alex.'

He waved his hand. 'I know that. How are you?'

'I'm okay, Dad.'

He smiled, and she saw her father of old behind his eyes. 'Why were you talking about Derek?'

'You were at university with them, weren't you, Dad? At Cambridge?'

'Cambridge?' He looked at her mother. 'I don't like talking about Cambridge.' He flexed the fingers on both hands. In. Out. In. Out. 'I was ill. I had to leave.'

'I know, Dad,' said Alex, stroking his arm soothingly. 'I'm sorry. What about—?'

'Alex,' said her mother, warningly.

'It's important, Mum, really. What about Derek and Roger? How well did you know them?'

Her father's face suddenly cleared, and his hands stilled. 'Derek and Roger. I haven't heard those names in a while. I wonder how they are?' He turned to his wife. 'Do you know how they are?'

She shook her head.

'So you knew them?' asked Alex, eagerly.

Her father frowned. 'Who?'

'Derek Daley and Roger Fleet.'

'Derek and Roger. I haven't heard those names in a while. I wonder how they are? Who are you?'

Alex sighed.

Her father frowned, his face cleared, then he hauled himself out of the chair. 'Wait a minute.'

He shuffled over to the sideboard, bringing out an envelope. 'Here,' he said, tearing it open and shaking out the contents. 'Cambridge. I hated it.'

Photographs lay jumbled on the table. Alex picked up the top one. It showed a group of people she had never seen before, posing, arms around one another.

'Alex,' her mother said, voice sharp. 'I don't think your father would really want you to look through these.'

'Why not?' she said, rifling through the photos, knowing she probably had limited time. Cheesecloth shirts. Girls with scrubbed faces. Boys with long hair. CND tee shirts. Everybody smoking. Two girls sitting on a bed, raising their drinks. A boy – man – with curtains of hair sitting on top of a statue in a well-tended garden, waving a glass. At one of the colleges, she presumed. More photographs of young people with varying lengths of hair, baggy jeans and tee shirts. Someone strumming a guitar. Seven or eight people around a table in a restaurant, cheering. What if she found one of Derek Daley or Roger Fleet? What would that prove? Nothing. Just that her father knew one of them because he had been studying at the same college.

'I used to like taking photos.'

Alex looked up at her father. 'I know you did, Dad,' she said. 'I remember all those times we had to pose for hours while you got the perfect background for the perfect shot. Do you remember that?'

Her father frowned. 'What are you talking about?'

She smiled gently. 'It doesn't matter.' She carried on looking through the photos.

Then, there. She held her breath. A young Willem Major, cocky smile as though he owned the world, hands in his pockets, staring at the camera. Staring at her. 'You knew Willem Major as well?' She asked the question casually.

'As well as what?'

'As well as Derek and Roger?'

'Derek and Roger. Whatever happened to them? Hmm? Whatever happened to them? I haven't heard those names in so long. And Willem.' A tear dripped down his cheek. 'Well I never.' All at once he smiled; it was like a watery shaft of sunshine after the rain, the tears forgotten. 'And Jen? What about her?'

Jen. Alex got the picture she had taken at Margaret Winwood's house up on her phone. The four students captured in a moment of time. Forever young.

'Dad? Is this Jen?' She pointed to the girl.

Her father nodded. 'She was – I liked ... I ...' He fell silent.

'There,' her mother said, briskly gathering up the old photographs before Alex could look at any more. 'That's enough. Put that away. You're upsetting your father.'

'But—'

'What ever happened to them all?'

'Dad—'

'No. Alex does not know what happened to them, do you, Alex?'

She looked at the stern, implacable face of her mother, and the wobbling cheeks of her father and wondered what the agenda was. She let go of her breath. 'No, I don't.'

Her mother bowed her head. 'Thank you,' she whispered.

'Who are you?' Her father asked.

'I'm Alex. Your daughter.' Sudden tears threatened. For God's sake, stop it, she told herself.

'I'm tired, Alex. Can I go up to bed please?'

'I'll take you,' said her mother, grabbing his elbow.

Alex kissed her father's stubbly cheek. 'Bye, Dad.'

'Bye, love,' he said, his eyes clear. He grasped her hand. 'That photograph?'

'Yes?'

'I thought they were my friends.'

22

Alex loved sitting on the shoreline near her home in Sole Bay. She loved listening to the endless tug of the sea on the beach, smelling the salt in the air, watching the tankers far out on the horizon, the sailing boats closer to shore, the windsurfers that skimmed effortlessly across the waves. She liked to imagine the people on those far-off tankers – mostly men, she presumed though not necessarily – working to transfer oil from one hulking ship to the next. She liked to imagine what sort of lives they had – girlfriends, boyfriends, wives, husbands. Children, perhaps, who didn't see their daddies for weeks at a time, but who would write to them, sending pictures carefully coloured in with wax crayons. Actually, she thought, as she scooped up a handful of sand and pebbles, they more likely drew pictures on their iPads and sent their daddies emails. Or Skyped them. Or didn't miss them at all. She let the sand drain through her fingers. But the very fact of people getting on with their lives, busying themselves, made her feel safe. She liked the normality of it. It was the nearest she came to feeling really happy.

That was not quite true. She had felt happy for those few short weeks with Malone. He had – what was the word? She looked up into the sky, at the few fluffy clouds that drifted along like dancers. Completed her. That was it. She had found someone who completed her.

Then he'd fucked off.

What was so wrong with her that would have made him leave her like that?

She scooped up another handful of sand and pebbles. Stop it, she told herself firmly. It is done with. And there's nothing so unattractive as self-pity. What's more, she wasn't likely to hear any more about him as Heath seemed to have disappeared off the face of the earth. She had tried to ring him, text him, left messages for him. Nothing. Not a thing. What was that all about? She had spoken to one his colleagues at the business unit who said they hadn't seen him and maybe he was off sick, but that didn't explain why he wasn't getting in touch with her.

Should she be worried about him? She took her phone out of her bag and dialled his number for what felt like the fiftieth time. Voicemail. She left another curt message. 'Call me.' Soon his voicemail box would be full, unless he was listening to the messages and ignoring them before deleting them.

She thought about Derek Daley and Roger Fleet, wondered about their last hours on the boat. Did they lie down in their beds and wait for the drugs and the fumes to do their thing? Or had they chatted for a while, caught up on their lives? She gave a hollow laugh. If you know you're about to die you're not going to engage in idle chit-chat, are you? How are you? What have you been doing with yourself? Family all well? Feeling sleepy yet? It was hardly likely. So what had made them go meekly to their deaths?

She looked at the phone and the photograph that seemed to be in the middle of this mess. So Fleet and Daley were dead. Willem Major had gone to ground after that fatal, horrible fire. What about the woman in the picture? What had her father called her? Jen, that was it. And who had taken the photograph? Who was behind the camera? Was it possible that whatever had happened in Cambridge all those years ago had some bearing on what was happening today? And if so, why had it taken nearly forty years to happen?

This had become personal. These people had been friends of her father's, and she had learned more about her mum and dad in the last twenty-four hours than she had ever known before.

She needed to find this Jen woman; perhaps she would have some answers. Though how easy that was going to be with just a first name she wasn't sure, and she couldn't ask Honey to help.

Reluctantly she stood up, brushing the sand off the back of her jeans. She wasn't going to find anyone or get any further forward by sitting on her backside on the beach, however therapeutic that was. Perhaps it was time to visit Cambridge, see the college where her father spent time as a student. It was only some forty years ago – maybe there would be someone there who would remember them?

Cambridge was a beautiful city, with ancient colleges at its heart, their grounds rolling down to the winding River Cam, and leafy green meadows that encircled the city. The spring light gave the old stone a mellow hue, thought Alex as she walked along St Francis's Road towards her father's old college, dodging cyclists along the way. Now she had a dim memory of her mum pointing it out to her many years ago when they had a rare family day trip to the city, but neither she nor Sasha had been remotely interested – too wrapped up in themselves and their teenage spots and tantrums. And she didn't want to think about the last time she was here, a few short months ago with Malone.

There it was, one of the entrances to the college. A large archway made of red brick the colour of blood, topped by a magnificent oriel window. The wicket door, a small door that could be opened separately from the large gates, was ajar. A noticeboard at the entrance told Alex that a tour of the college had just begun. If she could find it she could join its tail and then maybe peel off to do some exploring of her own. Perfect. She slipped through the gate and into the courtyard and was in luck. Ahead of her were a group of people clustered around a stocky, short-haired and capable-looking woman with an umbrella.

' … in the First Court …' the woman was saying. 'St Francis's College was founded in 1347 and is one of a small number founded by a woman.'

There was a murmur of approval from the group, who appeared to hail from all corners of the world.

Alex looked around. It was magnificent. The hurly-burly of the city seemed miles away, there was a tranquility in the air. Even the smell was different. Clean, freshly mown grass. There were large stone urns overflowing with early summer flowers. A shingle pathway went all the way round the courtyard, and cobble-stones were laid at intervals next to the buildings.

'If you look over there,' the guide pointed to her left, 'you will see the original chapel that has a magnificent plaster ceiling. To your right is New Court, where first year undergraduates live. If you look carefully, you can see entrances to staircases marked with the letters of the alphabet—'

Which staircase had been her father's? She tried to imagine how he must have felt, coming to a place as grand as this when he was still a teenager. How intimidating it must have been. How he must have wondered whether he would fit in.

'The Master's Lodge is behind you. As I'm sure you know, the Master is the head of the college here in Cambridge, a sort of Chief Executive, if you like.' She gave a brief smile. 'Across the way you can see the dining hall, a fine example of—'

Alex tuned out. Much as she was enjoying learning about the college, she wasn't here for the guided tour.

She walked confidently across the quad and through another archway. If she looked as though she was supposed to be doing what she was doing, then no one would question her.

No one did.

She found herself in another well-manicured area – like a

private garden, she thought. There was a magnificent fountain in the centre of the lawn, with angelic cherubs spouting water. Privet hedges and topiary trees did, indeed, suggest she was in a private area – perhaps it was the Master's garden? She spied yet another stone archway and hurried on through.

'Can I help you, miss?' A portly man in his late sixties was in the inner courtyard. He was wearing a smart coat and carrying several bunches of keys. The porter, she guessed. She hurried towards him, her best smile on her face.

'Are you the porter here, at St Francis's?'

'I am,' he said gravely. 'May I ask what you're doing in the Inner Court? And I saw you come out of the Master's garden. The tours don't generally take in that area. It's not done.'

'I'm sorry—'

'I can escort you back to the tour guide and group. It's no trouble. This way.' He took her elbow to steer her towards the tour group she could see in the distance.

'I wonder if you could help me. The thing is, my father was a student here many years ago. About forty, in fact. I don't suppose you were the porter here then?'

He stopped. 'You suppose wrong. I was a porter, but very junior. Normally they prefer older, family men, like I am now, but then they made an exception for me for reasons I don't want to go into. So, I've been here more than forty years. I can't hardly believe it. And I've seen some students come and go, I can tell you.'

'Just imagine, you might have known my dad.' Alex crossed her fingers. Could she be in luck?

'Name?'

'My dad's name?'

'Well, you can tell me yours for good measure if you like.' He smiled, and suddenly he looked like a favourite uncle and Alex relaxed a little.

'I'm Alex, Alex Devlin.'

'And my name is Arthur Street. You can call me Mr Street.'

Alex suppressed a grin. 'My father's name was Anthony,' she said.

The porter frowned. 'Anthony Devlin, let me think. Would he have been called Anthony or Tony?'

'Oh. I don't know. He left after a year. Look.' She got a picture of him up on her phone. 'This is him about five years ago, but can you—'

'Hmm.' The porter shook his head. 'Can't say I recognize him. If he was one of those who kept his head down and gave us porters no trouble then I probably wouldn't. Sorry, love.'

Alex smiled. 'I don't think he was the type to give you trouble. It must be a difficult job trying to keep the students in line?'

'You're not wrong there, love. You have to be really firm sometimes, make sure they're not coming to any harm.' His face darkened. 'It's awful when that happens, and you're always wondering if there was something you could have done. But then there's the good times when the students include you in their lives. I still get cards at Christmas from some.'

'There was another student. A girl.' This time Alex showed Mr Street the photograph on her phone she had taken at Mrs Winwood's. 'I only know her first name is Jen.'

Mr Street peered at the picture. 'Oh yes, I recognize her all right.' He smiled. 'She was always sweet and polite. Asked after me and the family. Sends me a Christmas card every year, she does. From America. Jen Tamsett was her name. Lovely girl. Never married.'

'What about Willem Major? Here.' She pointed to him.

At that name Arthur Street's face darkened. 'Now he was a bad lot, he was. Always playing practical jokes, made us porters' lives a misery, trying to get one over on us. Sneaking in and out of various colleges. And he was rude to me the whole time, as if I wasn't worth anything. Oh yes, I remember him as if it was yesterday.' He sniffed and jiggled his keys. 'But I did read about what happened to his family. Nobody deserves that. Nobody. Losing his missus and everyone like that.'

'He finished his degree, didn't he?'

'As far as I can remember, yes. Did quite well too, I think. And he made a good living for himself afterwards, didn't he? But he was one of those who came from a privileged background and that opened a few doors for him. There was something that was hushed up, but I never knew what it was. That was something, I can tell you, if us porters never knew about it.' He frowned. 'Hang on, Tony Devlin. Let me have another look at that photo you've got of your dad.'

Alex showed him.

'Yes, yes, he was always hanging around with Major. There was gossip too.'

'Gossip?'

Arthur Street scratched his nose. 'You know. Talk. Gay stuff.' His face cleared. 'Just talk.'

Gay? Her father? That would be a lot to take in.

The porter jangled his keys again. 'I don't know if I've been much help to you—'

'Oh you have, thank you, Mr Street. It's been good to see where Dad was at university, if only for a year.'

'Did he do well, your dad, afterwards?'

Alex nodded. 'Yes, he did well. He's lived an ordinary life, but he's been a great dad.'

'You can't ask for more than that,' said Mr Street, nodding.

'No,' said Alex. 'You can't.'

23

Alex sat in her study wasting time on social media, watching videos of dogs eating bowls of spaghetti and cats wearing pirate costumes and acrobats auditioning for talent shows. She was trying to distract herself, occupy her mind with trivia so she wouldn't start thinking about her father and her childhood. It wasn't working.

If she examined her memory really hard, she could find things she and her dad had done together, that they'd all done together, as a family. A holiday on the Grand Union Canal. A week in the Lake District. A visit to a theme park – she couldn't remember which one, but she could remember sitting in the car of a roll-ercoaster and feeling safe because her dad's arm was around her, the heat of his body next to hers. Her mum and Sasha were waiting outside the ride for them.

There'd been a row on that day because they'd forgotten Sasha's favourite ginger nut biscuits for the picnic. Sasha had flounced off. Mum had refused to let Dad go after her, so Dad spent the whole of the picnic looking miserable and worried. Her mother had sat there with pursed lips in between telling Alex to eat something, but it all turned to cardboard in her mouth. On the way home, after a search found Sasha talking to Teddy the Bear

190

in the so-called Bear Hut and generally having an enjoyable time, she didn't know who to be more angry with.

Sasha. She didn't want to think about Sasha. When she'd got home earlier there had been no sign of her. The kitchen was neat and tidy, not the trail of crumbs and butter and dirty knives and plates her sister normally left behind. No, everywhere was clean, with the washing-up cloth folded neatly by the sink and the drying-up cloths hung up where they should be. There had been a note on the table.

Gone to see friends.

Great.

Alex looked out of the window onto the patchy grass that passed for a lawn. She picked up a pen and began to doodle. It wasn't until she had been forced to be the parent to her parents that she had even begun to think about what they might have been like as people. How she wished there was someone she could talk to about it, someone who would listen without judgement. In her heart she knew who that was, but he wasn't around; he had chosen not to be around. And anyway, the chances of her finding out any more about him were slim now Heath had gone walkabout.

She looked at her doodles. Boxes within boxes, circles within squares. Had to be something significant in those. Feeling boxed in. Nowhere to go. She threw the pen down and put her head in her hands. She should be making notes, drafting her backgrounder for *The Post*. But she couldn't concentrate. Her father had known Daley and Fleet. And Willem Major and Jen Tamsett. They'd been at the same college together, and he seemed to have known them well. They were his friends, he said. Merely one big coincidence, or something more? She didn't believe in coincidences.

There was a ping as an email from something or someone called 'The Secret Policeman' came in. More bloody spam. She was about to delete it when, with a flash of insight, she realized who it was from: who would have the temerity to call himself 'The Secret Policeman', for fuck's sake?

To: Alex Devlin
From: The Secret Policeman
Subject: None

Alex. I'm sorry for everything – you have no idea how sorry. The reason I had to leave you without saying goodbye that day was because you were in danger.

Oh yeah, heard that one before. What the fuck was this anyway? Months without any sort of communication then he emails out of the blue and talks about being sorry and about danger? Her shoulders were up round her ears, and her throat was scratchy.

I can see you saying that you've heard that one before

Sure have, matey. Her finger hovered over the delete button.

and I know you're about to delete this email

Bloody man.

but hear me out. You've been trying to find me. Don't. As I said, you're in danger. The only way is to forget all about me. Don't think about me, don't look for me. But, watch out for yourself, don't trust anyone. M.

Great. That was it. No endearments, no wasted words, straight-talking, that was all. And no details. Not even his name, just 'M'. As if that would fool anybody who was really looking for him. Though he was nearly as good as Honey when it came to covering his digital tracks. What was she supposed to do? Spend the rest of

192

her life looking around, worrying that someone was going to hit her on the head because of Malone? Was that the sort of danger he meant? How the hell was she supposed to know? But why was she in danger? And who could be threatening her anyway? And that bollocks about not trusting anyone – who exactly did he mean? Bloody, bloody Malone. Fucking with her life as bloody usual.

She prodded the delete button. Hard.

For God's sake. Time to get down to work. Find Jen Tamsett on social media. She opened Facebook, knowing it was a long shot. She scanned the search results. One Jenna Tamest and two Jennifer Tamsetts. One of the Jennifers was a teenager, the other a woman in her thirties, as far as she could tell from the pictures. Nothing on Twitter. Nothing on LinkedIn. A complete blank.

Okay. She put Jen's name into Google and hit the News tab. And there it was.

A story from two months ago.

Manhunt After Woman Killed in Hit-and-run
   The body of renowned academic, Jennifer Tamsett (63), was found by the side of a country road in Hampshire ...

That was the right age.

Alex learned that Jennifer Tamsett had been well regarded in her field of economics, she had been unmarried and had been educated at Cambridge University in the mid-seventies before leaving for Harvard. She'd lived in America for many years, and had come back to the UK three months earlier. There was a picture attached to the story, and there was no doubt the dead Jennifer Tamsett was an older version of the young Jen of her father's time at Cambridge. Her death was described as 'random' by police. No one had been arrested – she scrolled through Google news – or had been since the story was written. There were no living relatives. No one to care. And Alex was willing to bet that no one ever would be held accountable for her death.

A police spokesman said the investigation was 'ongoing'.

Alex's skin tingled. Another student from the photograph gone. Dead, killed by a hit-and-run. Murdered? And she had come back to the UK around the time of the fire at Willem Major's home. Coincidence? And was it a coincidence that three of the students from the photograph had died recently? Was it all connected? And if she was right and it was more than a coincidence that her father knew them, could he be in danger too?

Or was she being too fanciful?

Her mother answered the phone on its third ring. 'Mum—' God, she hadn't thought this through. What was she going to say? 'Mum, is everything all right at home?'

'Yes. As all right as it can be. Your father is watching a David Attenborough documentary for about the fifteenth time and keeps calling me to go and watch it with him. I'm trying to clean up while I can, put the washing on and … Sorry, darling, I didn't mean to go on at you like that, but it's good to talk to someone else sometimes, particularly when you've been asked the same question about meerkats over and over again. Why are you asking?'

'Would you and Dad like to come and stay here? With me?' The words came out in a rush.

'What on earth for?'

Should she come clean? 'Because I'm worried that Dad might be in danger.'

'Danger? What are you talking about?'

'That photograph I showed Dad, well, Derek Daley and Roger Fleet are dead.'

'I know, you said. And thank you for not saying anything to your dad, because he would have been upset and then forgotten and then been upset all over again if you told him again.'

'I understand, Mum, I really do. But listen. They're dead. Willem Major, you know, remember, the other person in the picture? His family were virtually wiped out in an arson attack.

And the girl, Jen Tamsett, was killed in a hit-and-run. Recently, too.'

'What's this got to do with your dad? Those two men, Derek Daley and Roger—'

'Fleet,' supplied Alex.

'Fleet, that's it. It was suicide, wasn't it?'

'It looks that way, but I'm not totally convinced.'

A thought struck her. Yes, that was certainly a possibility. She bit her bottom lip. She had to ask. 'Mum, could Dad have taken the photograph?'

'What?'

'Could he have taken the photo I showed you?'

'It's possible I suppose,' her mother said, slowly.

'That's why he isn't in it, because he took it.' Of course. Or was it too big a leap to think that? 'Look, Mum, I'm really worried how safe he is.'

'What are you talking about?' Her mother sounded truly bewildered.

'I'm not sure, Mum. But people Dad knew are dead or have been badly hurt.'

'Is this a so-called journalistic hunch?'

Was it? Was it no more than a hunch? She sighed. 'Maybe. Even if it is only a hunch, can't you come here for a few days?'

'Of course I can't, Alex.' Her mother sounded more business-like now. 'Your father needs to know where he is. He needs routine, not change.' There was a large crash in the background. 'Oh Lord, he's knocked something over, I'm going to have to go.'

'Mum, will you think about it, please?' But she was talking to thin air.

Damn. That didn't go as she had hoped. She had to find Willem Major, see what he had to say. And hope she was being over-cautious about wanting her parents to stay with her.

She tried to ring Heath to tell him she had found out about Jen Tamsett and he could stop using his facial recognition software or, more likely, scouring the electoral register, but there was no answer. Oh, for God's sake.

She sat thinking. Suicide forums. Something she should have done before.

The first entry on the search engine was for the Samaritans. She looked down the list. Several sites devoted to mental health and how to cope with suicidal thoughts. Then *The Suicide Place*. Alex clicked.

I'm 22 and I don't wanna to keep living
Anyone know a lethal combination of prescription pills?
Anyone want to drive with me to anywhere and go buy H2S pls email
Want to die but don't want them to know I chose death
... what do I do?

The hopelessness and alienation pressed down on Alex. These websites ought to come with warnings on them, particularly for young people, otherwise you might as well give some poor kid a gun and pull the trigger. She went at first hot and then cold as she remembered what Steve had said – that Gus had been lonely and had been – how had he put it? – 'Fooling about' on the Internet and on forums. He'd been a bit depressed, Steve said. Oh God, what if he'd been looking at something like this? What if he'd seen this sort of stuff and thought there might be a way out for him and had got in touch with someone, maybe even the person who was looking to drive anywhere and use H2S (whatever that was), and he had flown to the UK and met up with this person and was even now lying dead in a car on a deserted road and ... She took a deep breath. Stop. Just. Stop. There was no point in frightening herself in this way. Gus would not do that to her. (Are you sure? a little voice murmured in her ear.) No, Gus would not do that to her. There was a reason why Gus hadn't phoned her since telling her he was getting a flight the next day, a reason and a perfectly reasonable explanation.

She slowed her breathing down. The panic subsided.

Had Daley and Fleet really posted on this sort of forum? Would two men in their sixties – one solvent and highly successful – really look to something like this? And if they did, how much of a coincidence was it that they had known one another before?

There was a ping as another email came in. From Honey, this time, telling her that Willem Major was staying in Cley in north Norfolk, and giving her the coordinates of his house. Alex quickly wrote them down, knowing she should really memorize them. And eat the piece of paper. She pulled up the software that would completely wipe Honey's emails and attachments from her computer. She knew there was no way they could be traced from Honey to her or vice versa as they would have been routed on servers from Russia to Kazakhstan to Outer Mongolia, round the houses and back again.

That done, she stared out of the window once more, thinking that if she didn't look at her phone, Gus would call her.

Her phone suddenly rang out its tune. Bud. Maybe he'd changed his mind about the campaign on suicide forums.

'Heath Maitland. Where is he?' said Bud without any preamble.

Alex wanted to stick out her tongue at the phone. He was so rude sometimes. 'What do you mean? You pulled him back to the business unit.'

'I know. He's only been there five minutes and he's fucked off,' Bud said testily. 'Dickhead. Thought he might be with you.'

'He's not, Bud.'

'What's he doing then?'

'I don't know.' How the hell would she know? She'd been trying to get hold of him too. Something made her hold back from telling Bud that.

'He should be here. Now.'

'Well I'm really sorry, I don't know where he is.

197

'For someone who was desperate to keep his job, he's going the wrong bloody way about it.'

The sound of him slamming the phone down reverberated in her ear.

The light was beginning to fade. A single magpie landed on what passed for her lawn. She counted from ten down to one. She thought about Malone, wondering where he was now and what he was doing. And what she would do if Heath got back in touch. She frowned. Heath. Bloody man. Like all the men she came across. Bloody, bloody man. The trouble was, she so wanted him to carry on his digging, business unit or no business unit. Come on, she was wasting her time thinking about Heath.

She stretched. Time for a cup of something, or a glass of something stronger. She was about to walk out of her study when she heard a noise. The smallest of noises followed by a creak in the sitting room below. There was another creak and a thud, followed by the sibilance of a voice. She stood stock still, listening hard.

Footsteps.

As usual she had left the front door unlocked.

Someone was in the house.

She looked around. If she were in a crime novel there would be a handy baseball bat or two propped up in the corner. She had nothing like that. A heavy edition of the Oxford dictionary. That would have to do.

Having negotiated the stairs without standing on the noisy treads, she crept along the hall. Daylight was fading fast. There was a light in the sitting room – torchlight, she thought.

She opened the door.

It all happened in a matter of seconds: a figure clad in black with their back to her. The anger building at the thought of someone in her home, invading her space. An enormous shout from deep within her chest. The figure turning around. A balaclava covering the face. The thud as she slammed the dictionary at the side of the intruder's face. Missed. Caught the arm instead. A grunt of pain. Something sharp, stinging in her nostrils. A smell with a whisper of familiarity. The pain exploding in her head as a fist caught her temple. Flashes of light behind her eyes. Falling. The shock of the back of her head hitting the ground. Then nothing.

24

It took me three days to recover from the experience in the abandoned church. Three days of sweating in my bed, leaving it only to run and throw up in the tiny shared bathroom. God only knew what the other inhabitants of Staircase C must have thought. Eventually I was able to get out of my grimy, smelly bed and look for something to eat. But there was only cornflakes, dry and straight out of the packet.

What had gone on that night? And, more importantly, what was in those pills Willem had given us? They seemed more than the normal uppers. My memory was shrouded in mists and darkness. I couldn't tell what was a real memory and what was an hallucination. Were there naked men and women writhing on the floor? Did I see a man (woman?) in a black robe and mask bring a knife down onto the goat? Did I hear its death squeal? And the chanting, oh, that chanting. I couldn't get it out of my head.

Nor the screaming.

Stu.

Now I remembered his face that night. Contorted. Crying.

200

Horrified. Eyes popping out of his head. A bad trip. What had been in those fucking pills? I remember him grabbing onto me, not letting me go, gibbering like a baby, telling me flies were bursting from his mouth, maggots undulating under his skin. He had torn at his clothes, had scratched his skin until he bled. I closed my eyes, trying to remember more.

I think we carried him out of the church, stuffed him in the car. Did we? I told Willem to drive, to get us out of there. Willem had looked affronted, as if we had spoiled his fun. As if Stu had spoiled his fun. I suppose we had. What happened when we arrived back in Cambridge? I think I took Stu to his room, rolled him into bed. Then it was a blank.

God.

With legs that were still weak, I made my way to Stu's room and knocked on the door. There was no reply. I pushed the door, hoping he had left it on the latch for a quick route to the toilet. I was in luck.

The room was in darkness and smelled of sweat and vomit. Stu was lying prone on the bed, with a stinky bucket by his side. He wasn't alone. Jen was there, gently wiping his face with a wet flannel.

'Jen,' I said.

She looked up. 'I couldn't leave him on his own,' she said, tearfully. 'He was having a bad trip and now—' She pointed at him.

Stu's skin was mottled. I mean, a really horrible mottled red. 'Jen, what was it all about?'

'Whatever Willem gave him it was fucking strong. Stronger than whatever we had. Or he didn't have as much tolerance as us.'

What she meant was that we had become used to popping the pills Willem fed us. I felt something akin to shame flood my body. What was I doing? This was madness.

She bit her bottom lip. 'I think he might need to go to hospital.'

She looked so vulnerable, I wanted to go over and hug her. 'Bloody Willem.'

I sought Willem out.

'What did you think you were doing?' I said, my voice sounding loud and shrill.

'Experience, darling.' His eyes shone. 'Didn't you enjoy it?'

'Enjoy it? I can barely remember anything except coming down. It was bad, Willem, really bad. And Stu's in a terrible state.'

Willem's lip curled, actually curled. 'He shouldn't play with the big boys. Jumped-up little oik.' He rubbed his hands together. 'What did you think?'

'Think?'

'Of the church?'

'Willem, I can barely remember it.' Not quite true. But my memories were nightmares of flickering shadows, grotesque silhouettes, discordant noises.

He laughed. 'It was the good people of the Aleister Crowley Society.'

I thought for a minute. 'Aleister Crowley. He was some sort of occultist, wasn't he?' My childhood Dennis Wheatley obsession was coming in useful.

Willem nodded. 'Clever boy.'

'Can you be a little more patronizing?'

'He was a student at Trinity at the end of the nineteenth century.' Willem carried on as if he hadn't heard me. 'Believed in doing what you wanted to satisfy yourself. Ordinary morality is only for ordinary people. Those of similar mind follow his teaching.'

'Do what thou wilt,' I said, remembering the words, tasting them in my mouth. 'Oh, for Christ's sake.' Remembering that as I chanted I felt all-powerful, as if I could do whatever I wanted and there would be no consequences. I could do whatever I wanted and nothing and no one could stop me. I shivered. 'Life isn't like that,' I said. 'Are you part of the society?'

'Me?' Willem laughed. 'No chance, darling. All too woo-woo and flat-sandaled for me. Roger didn't like it either, poor boy. He's got old-time religion as it is. Goes to church every week, wouldn't want to bat for the Devil. Derek was angry because he couldn't take any pictures. Jen is angry with me because Jen always is, but Stu? Well.' Willem looked at me, a smile curving his lips. 'He really joined in. Discarded his clothes and got, well, stuck in, to use the vernacular.'

'I'll ask you again, Willem. What did you give Stu?'

He opened his eyes wide, trying to look innocent. 'Merely something to help him enjoy the evening.'

I banged the table. 'It was too bloody strong. Jen is about to cart him off to hospital. You could have killed him.'

'He would have died smiling.'

Willem had no boundaries.

'Willem—'

He held his hands up in surrender. 'I'm sorry, okay? Don't be angry with me. I was only trying to help.'

'I'd hate to see you if you were hindering.'

Suddenly, shockingly, he leaned forward and kissed me on the lips. I fought the urge to wipe it away with the back of my hand.

For once, Willem looked embarrassed. 'I've been wanting to do that for a long time. Oh, I know you are not my way inclined, but still. If I didn't do it, I would regret it all my life.'

'I—'

'Please,' said Willem. 'Don't say anything.'

'I won't. About Stu—'

'Oh, never mind Stu. He'll never amount to anything.'

I eyed Willem. 'You're wicked.'

He grinned. 'I know.'

25

'Alex? Alex? Are you all right?' The panicky voice came from the bottom of a lift shaft.

Alex tried to lift her head and open her eyes and immediately wished she hadn't, as waves of pain crashed over her. She heard someone groaning and wished they would stop. Then she realized it was her.

'Take it easy.'

Was that who she thought it was?

She opened her eyes again. The pain was marginally less this time.

'Are you okay?'

It *was* who she thought it was.

'What the fuck are you doing here?'

Heath's face swam into focus. She sat up carefully, holding her head, her tongue probing her teeth, one at a time. They all felt as though they were loose. She hoped she was imagining that. The pickaxes in her head had slowed down; it was now more of an intermittent banging.

'Never mind me, what's happened to you?' Heath, crouching down in front of her, eyed her anxiously.

She thought rolling her eyes might be a bad idea. 'Having a little rest.'

'What?'

'Someone was here, they hit me with – I don't know what. Knocked me out. It bloody hurts.'

The pickaxes started up again, big time. She closed her eyes for a moment to allow them to slow down. She opened them again. Nausea rose in her throat. 'What are you doing here is more to the point.' A thought came into her head. 'Please tell me you're not the one who attacked me?'

'I'd hardly have stuck around if I had been,' he said indignantly.

'You might. To allay suspicion.'

'Allay – for goodness' sake, Alex you're talking nonsense. You must be concussed. I was coming to your gate when someone came out of your house, running like Usain Bolt. I was worried about you, especially when I saw the front door had been left wide open. So, I came in, and there you were on the floor. God, I thought you were dead at first.'

'That would have been inconvenient. Or a good story. First on the scene and all that.' She touched the back of her head and flinched. Her fingers came away sticky with blood. 'I must have been out for a few minutes then.'

'Right.' Heath stood. 'That's it. I'm taking you to A&E.'

'No, you're not, I'm fine.'

'Alex.'

'I am fine. I'll go in the morning if I still have a headache. But I haven't got double vision, I don't feel sick, at least not to the point where I want to throw up. I'm not going. It's a waste of time.'

'Bloody hell, you can be stubborn.'

'I know.' She grinned. But that hurt, so she frowned instead. 'Did you see who it was who ran out?'

He shook his head. 'No. They were wearing a balaclava. I thought they'd stopped making those things years ago. I didn't run after them because I was worried about you. Is anything missing?'

Alex looked around. 'I don't know.' It felt like too much of an effort to get up and make an inventory. There was nothing valuable in the house – she didn't own anything valuable. The television and her computer were the only things worth stealing, but her computer was upstairs and the television was still in the corner. 'I don't think so.' She looked at Heath. 'Come on, you haven't told me what—' Then it was as if she had just realized who was standing in her living room. 'Bloody hell, Heath. Where have you been? I've been so worried about you. I thought you were chained to that business desk, but every time I try to get hold of you, you're not there. And I must have phoned you a dozen times. Texted you. I've needed to tell you things. Where the fuck have you been?'

Heath held up his hands as if to defend himself. 'Okay, okay, I'm sorry.' He groaned and sat down in an armchair. 'Don't make me feel any worse. I couldn't talk to you. And I didn't get any of your texts.'

'Don't worry about me, I'll get up off the floor without your help.' Alex hauled herself slowly up and settled in the other armchair next to him. Leaning her head back, she closed her eyes, trying not to think about the blood that would be seeping into the back of the chair. 'So what have you been doing? And have you been ignoring the heavily pregnant Mimi as well? Does she even exist?'

'All these questions, Alex. Have you got a drink?'

'Kettle's in the kitchen.'

'Not that sort of drink.' He peered at her. 'And maybe you ought to have a brandy or something, you're as white as Bud's legs.'

'How do you know about Bud's legs? When did you see those? That would be a thing, wouldn't it? Just imagine the office gossip about the pair of you.'

'Alex, you're rambling. It was on a newspaper away day. That I saw his legs. In the swimming pool. Oh, never mind.'

Despite her exhaustion Alex managed to smile at Heath tying himself up in knots.

'That's better,' said Heath. 'You had me worried for a minute.'

'Tell me, Heath.'

She heard Heath shift on the chair, then a sigh. 'Yes, of course Mimi does. Exist, I mean.' Heath was indignant. 'But she's not my girlfriend.'

Alex opened her eyes. 'Ah. Someone you happened to get pregnant? Well done.'

'It isn't like that—' He stopped when he saw Alex's face. 'Maybe it is. I'm sorry. But I do need the steady dosh the job brings. For the moment anyway.'

'How did you expect to get away with the hearts and flowers story for nine months? How would you have faced me and told me how happy the three of you were as a family?'

He shook his head. 'Don't, Alex. And anyway, there probably won't be a job in nine months the way things are going.'

'What are you doing here, Heath? Why did you even agree to help me? Or was that a lie too?' God, she needed to sleep.

He heaved himself out of his chair and went to the kitchen. Alex heard him opening and shutting the kitchen cupboards. He came back brandishing a bottle of brandy and two glasses. 'Here we are,' he said, pouring it into the glasses with a flourish and handing one to her. 'That'll get the colour back into your cheeks. And no, it wasn't a lie.' He hesitated.

Suddenly her pulse was racing. 'Yes?'

'Malone. He's been in Greece. On an island – Ithaka.'

For a wild moment thoughts of flights and hotels and hiring a car chased away the pounding in her brain.

'But he's not there any more.' Heath's voice broke into her skittering thoughts. 'Disappeared at the same time as the Albanian child-trafficker who was looking for him.'

The pounding returned. 'Does that mean—?'

'Alex.' Heath's voice was gentle, which made her bite her lip even more to stop easy tears threatening. 'It just means he's off the grid at the moment. It doesn't necessarily mean anything has happened to him.'

'But it might have.'

'Perhaps. But my contact said it was most likely he's gone to ground.'

'But ...' Her world was suddenly out of sync. 'I might never find out if anything happens to him. No one will tell me. No one even really knows about him and me.' She was grateful for Heath's silence. 'So you don't know where he is now?' The question came out of her mouth before she had time to think. The blow to her head had sent her stupid.

He sipped the brandy and grimaced. 'Bit rough, this. The last I heard was that he could be travelling back to the UK.'

'Right.' Then she heard the words again in her head. 'The last you heard? From your contact?'

'Yes. I did keep that end of the bargain. Though Malone's a dangerous man, Alex. But I expect you know that.'

Alex reached across to him. 'Thank you.'

Then she saw him properly for the first time. He was looking into the distance, his skin appeared grey, and there were deep grooves at the corners of his mouth. He took a silver cigarette case out of his jeans. 'Do you mind?'

Alex shook her head. 'Where have you been, Heath? I even had Bud haranguing me on the phone.' She sipped her drink cautiously.

He turned and looked at her. 'Bud?'

'Yes. Don't worry, I couldn't tell him anything because I didn't know where you were.'

'You didn't say anything about me doing some digging for you? Helping you?'

'No. Why?'

He shrugged. 'Nothing. Don't want him on my back, that's all.'

'Where have you been?'

208

He shrugged again. 'You don't need to know, but I had to leave the desk for a couple of days. I wanted to follow up a lead.'

'A lead?'

'Yup.' He took out a cigarette paper, and shook tobacco out of a pouch, lining it up along the paper. He reached inside his pocket again, hesitated, took his hand away. Then he rolled the cigarette before lighting it and drawing deeply on it. 'Working on the business unit, I found out a couple of things.'

'What?'

He shook his head. 'I can't tell you. Not just at the moment. It could be something or nothing. But equally—'

'Stop being so bloody mysterious, Heath, I'm not buying it.'

'Suit yourself.'

'Why are you here?'

'I was just passing.' He grinned, weakly.

'Heath, tell me the truth. What am I missing?'

He leaned his head back, blew smoke out of his mouth in a steady stream. 'I wanted to make sure you were okay.'

'You could have answered your phone and done that,' she replied, tartly.

'Okay. I also had some things to find out.'

'What things?'

He didn't say anything, merely shook his head.

'Here, in Sole Bay?'

'Maybe.'

God, the man was infuriating. 'Why on earth have you antagonized Bud, leaving the desk like that? You could lose your job: exactly what you didn't want. For God's sake, Heath, you're a good journalist. Maybe one day you could be a great one—'

'Come off it, Alex. It's not going anywhere, is it, these days? Journalism, hmm? Papers closing, staff laid off, bloody so-called citizen journalists.'

'Don't be so defeatist. Fight it. Write good stories. Uncover corruption. All of that.' She waved her hand at him. Why was she having this conversation now?

'Don't be naive, Alex. Corruption is everywhere. Too much of it.'

'Tell me what you found.'

'No.' His face turned ugly. 'Maybe I want to keep it to myself. Maybe I want to have a scoop, write a good story, be a hero. Maybe that's exactly what I'm doing, Alex, but you're so wrapped up in yourself and how everything affects you that you can't see it.'

'That's unfair,' she said quietly.

'Is it?'

Alex looked at his handsome if tired face, the casual way he had draped himself in her chair. She thought of all the times in the newsroom he had made her laugh. How he had flirted with her and with others, sometimes made a grey day brighter. How she had once – briefly – entertained the idea that they might get together and what fun that would be, and she couldn't be angry with him. All she wanted now was to be left alone. She couldn't deal with Heath on his high horse. Particularly when he'd hit a nerve.

'Go, Heath,' she said, wearily.

He nodded, and stood. 'One more thing. I think you should call the police, tell them about the break-in.'

'There's not much point, really. Nothing was taken, not that I can think of, anyway. I'd left the front door unlocked as usual.'

'But—'

'I'll think about it.'

He gave her a sad smile. 'That'll have to do then. Please believe me that I'm only trying to help, to get to the bottom of this. Roger Fleet, Derek Daley, Willem Major.'

'And Jen Tamsett,'

'The girl in the photograph? You found her?'

'Yes. Google. She's dead too.'

210

'Do you know who took the photograph?'

Alex shook her head. 'No. Not yet.'

He hesitated. 'Alex, I think I might have—'

She'd had enough. 'I don't want to know, Heath. Go.'

Heath nodded, then pinched the end of his roll-up and put it in his pocket. 'Take care, Alex, won't you?' He drained his brandy glass. 'Don't trust anyone. Anyone at all.'

So mysterious. 'Not even you?'

He gave a brief smile. 'Not even me. See you around.'

Alex nodded. 'See you around.'

She sat in the chair, her legs tucked up underneath her. She finished her brandy. She had lied to Heath. Her hunch was that her father had taken that photograph. And she had lied because there had been so many questions Heath had avoided.

26

'What are you doing, sitting here in the dark?'

The light snapped on, and Alex blinked slowly, her eyes adjusting to the glare. She had been sitting in the living room, not moving, since Heath had left. Not moving because her head was really throbbing now, and she didn't have the energy to even go and find herself some pills.

Sasha marched over to her chair, and picked the brandy bottle up off the floor. 'What's this? It's practically empty, Alex. What have you been doing?'

Alex opened her eyes wide. 'Drinking it, I expect.'

'What's going on here?' It was Lin's voice from the doorway.

'Where have you been?' Alex ignored Lin and gazed at the two Sashas in front of her instead, aware her voice sounded belligerent.

'You're drunk?' Her sister raised her eyebrows.

Alex shook her head. Bad mistake. Again. She kept making mistakes though, didn't she? Fucking everything up.

'Look, I'll make some coffee.' That came from Lin.

'I reckon we'll need it,' said Sasha. 'Why the booze?'

Alex hung her head, which was woolly and full of muddled thoughts – of her dad, of Willem Major, of Heath, Gus, even bloody Malone.

'Alex? Alex, what on earth has been happening? What's that on your shirt? Blood?'

She felt cool hands parting her hair, then a sharp intake of breath. 'You've got a really nasty gash on the back of your head. What have you been doing?'

'I was … there was …'

'What?'

She steadied herself. 'Someone in the house. They hit me. I fell down. Was out of it for a few minutes.'

Two audible gasps. 'Oh my God, oh my God, are you all right? Do you need to go to hospital?'

Despite the fuddle in her head Alex heard the concern in Sasha's voice. She tried to clear her mind. She definitely needed that coffee. 'No, I'm fine. Heath Maitland was here just after it happened. He looked after me. Sort of. We came to the conclusion that I'll live.'

'Heath Maitland?' asked Sasha.

'Reporter.'

'The one you're doing the Broads story with?'

Alex grimaced. 'Sort of.'

Lin put a cup of coffee in her hand. 'The guy who wanted you to do all the work and he'd get all the praise.'

'I don't want to go into that again, Lin, not now.'

'I'll go and get some water and TCP for that cut,' said Sasha. It looks nasty.' She disappeared to the kitchen.

Alex gritted her teeth as a wave of pain crashed through her head. The brandy was wearing off.

'What did you and Sasha get up to tonight?' Alex wanted to talk to keep her mind off the pain.

'Here, let me clean that up.' Her sister appeared with a bowl and some cotton wool and began bathing the gash on the back of Alex's head. Despite her cool and gentle hands, Alex winced.

'Sorry,' said Sasha.

'No, I'm being a wimp.'

213

Lin crouched in front of her. 'Sorry, love. I know Heath Maitland is an off-limits subject, but he's like a bad penny, turning up just when you don't need him.'

'But I did need him this time,' Alex protested. 'He helped me. He chased the intruder away.'

'Did he?' said Lin. 'Really? How do you know? Didn't I hear you say that you were unconscious for a few minutes? So how do you know he "just turned up"? And what was he doing near your house in the first place?'

'Lin's got a point,' said Sasha, wrinkling her brow. 'Maybe it was him who broke in and then he came back and acted all concerned to put you off the scent?'

'"Off the scent"?' Alex wanted to laugh. 'What are you talking about?'

'Okay,' said Lin, rubbing Alex's forearms. 'Perhaps not. But it does seem a real coincidence that he turns up just in time to rescue you. What was he doing round here anyway? I thought he was back in London.'

'You have to admit, it does sound a bit odd,' said Sasha.

Did it? Alex didn't know any more. And how did Lin know he'd gone back to London? Had she told Lin that?

'Has anything been taken?' That was Lin being practical again.

'No,' said Alex, to avoid any more questions.

'So what did they want?' Lin was nothing if not persistent. 'I mean, they could have killed you. They must have been looking for something. If it was Heath—'

'It wasn't,' said Alex, but with a little less conviction. She didn't know what to think.

Lin ignored her. 'But what was he looking for?'

Alex stilled one of Lin's hands. 'It doesn't matter. I'm okay.'

'And that's what matters, that's all that matters,' said Sasha, relief on her face. 'Who would help me redecorate my flat if you weren't here, eh, Alex? I've got boxes of books to go through and everything.'

'I told you,' said Lin, 'I can help you with that.'

'I know.' Sasha didn't take her eyes off Alex. 'And it's really kind of you. But—'

'I want to do it with you,' said Alex. She looked at Lin. 'It would draw a line under everything. You know.'

Lin nodded. 'Of course. I totally understand. Me and my big feet crashing in where they're not wanted.'

'No, no, you mustn't think that. It's just that, well …'

'You're sisters. Family. You pull together.' Her eyes were misty. 'I wish I had family like you. That my brother wasn't—'

Despite her exhaustion, Alex gripped her hand. 'I know. I'm here for you, though.'

'Thank you. Now,' Lin stood up, 'I'd better be off. Work to do and all that. Convert some of my photographs into beautiful works of art.'

Alex smiled. 'I'll come and see them some time, if I may?'

'Of course,' said Lin. 'Anyway, I'll leave you two to it.'

After she'd gone, the sisters sat in silence for a few minutes.

'Bastard,' said Sasha. 'Whoever broke in. And what for? Nothing. Were they in here?'

'Yes.' Alex sat up straight, her mind clear for the first time since being hit on the head. That's right, she'd heard the sound of drawers being opened and shut quietly. Drawers. Her grandmother's old desk. 'Bloody hell, whoever they were, they were rooting about in my desk.' She got up quickly out of the chair, steadying herself as a wave of nausea made her dizzy.

'What's in there?'

'Old bills. Stuff from my accountant. Some spare cash.'

She opened the top drawer. The documents had been disturbed, she could tell that. She prised the lid off the old mustard tin at the back of the drawer. The money was gone. She slid open the bottom drawer. There was only one folder in it. She looked inside and gave an intake of breath. All the papers, all her memories, were all gone.

'Alex, what is it?'

'I don't understand. Why would anybody—?'

'What is it? Tell me.'

'It's silly, really, but in this folder I had kept things that meant something to me. Mementoes from gigs I've been to. Old theatre tickets. Press cuttings of mine. Printouts of a couple of emails. But they've all gone.' She looked at Sasha. 'Why would anyone want stuff like that?'

'Beats me.'

Could it have been something to do with Malone, she thought, frowning? It seemed a bit far-fetched, but quite a lot of the stuff in the folder had to do with Malone. She kept bits and pieces from their time together – nothing valuable, only things like menus or guides to art exhibitions. The odd card he had given her. Why would anyone take those? Why take her memories? She would probably never know.

'Come back and sit down, Lexi, you look really pale.'

Alex did as her sister asked. It was true – she even felt pale, if that was possible.

'I went to Dad's college today,' said Alex into the silence.

'Really? In Cambridge?'

'Yes. I spoke to someone who remembered him. Hinted he might have had a fling with a gay man.'

'Dad?' Sasha laughed. 'Not our dad, surely?'

'I've been thinking a lot about the past lately. About how we only see our parents as, well, parents and not as people. We forget they were like us once, young—'

'Ish,' said Sasha.

'Ish,' conceded Alex, chuckling. 'And wanting to have their own lives. But we never talk to our parents as friends, do we? Not really.'

'And would it matter to you if he had been in a relationship like that?'

Alex frowned. 'No, I don't think so. If he turned out to be gay,

216

then I think that would be massive. But it sounded if anything like it was a bit of, you know, experimenting.'

'I never knew which college he went to. Why did you go anyway?'

'It was St Francis's College and it's to do with that story I'm looking into, you know, the deaths on the Broads. I think Dad might be involved somehow.' There. She'd said it.

'Dad? Bloody hell, this is getting stranger by the minute. Tell me.'

Alex hesitated.

'Tell me,' Sasha said with more urgency. 'We've kept enough from each other over the years. I've given you a tough time; even now I'm out of hospital I haven't been fair on you. Staying out. Not telling you where I was. What I was doing. Look, a lot of what I've been doing is thinking. Sitting up near the harbour, chatting to the fishermen and thinking. I've never done so much bloody thinking in my life.' She gave a brittle laugh. 'But I know that in order to get on with my life I've got to take back control.'

'Now there's a familiar phrase.' Alex smiled wryly.

It was wonderful to see Sasha grin. 'Yes, true. But I mean it, Alex. I want to be a better sister to you,' she said. 'And seeing you like this it's, well, it's heartbreaking. I could have lost you if whoever attacked you had a knife or something.'

Did her vulnerable sister mean it? Could she really have come through the traumas of the last few years?

There was a more confident air around Sasha – something she, Alex, wasn't used to seeing and couldn't remember ever seeing before. And how badly she wanted to share things with her. Have Sasha be her equal instead of always having to shield her from things. She might as well start now.

And so Alex told Sasha about the photograph at Margaret Winwood's house, about talking to her father, how Roger Fleet, Derek Daley, Jen Tamsett and Willem Major and their father were all friends at Cambridge. She told her that she thought Heath was hiding something, but she couldn't work out what and finally she told her sister how she thought it was all connected by something in the past, but again she didn't know what, except she thought her father was involved and now suspected he could have been the one behind the camera.

'Look,' said Sasha, frowning, 'this stuff about the past and the present being connected somehow. I mean, that must be one of the first things to sort out? Once that's done, it might all fall into place?'

Alex nodded. 'Probably. I've got Willem Major's address and I plan to go tomorrow. But what about Dad? I'm worried about him, Sasha.'

'Maybe he's not involved at all. After all, you can't be sure he took that picture.'

'Not sure, no.'

'But your gut journalistic instinct tells you there's no smoke without fire? God, I hate clichés, but there you are. You're a good journalist, Alex, I know it. I trust your judgement.' She paused. 'I could go and stay with them. I'll ring Mum first thing and suggest it. That way you won't have to worry.'

Alex shook her head, smiling. 'Sasha, where have you been hiding?'

'Leacher's House,' she said, eyebrows raised. 'Seriously, though, Lexi, I know I can be shitty and contrary—'

'And obstinate and mercurial.'

'All of that. But underneath it all I do love you. And I'm sorry. For everything I've put you through over the years. I know sorry's not adequate—'

'It is.' Alex reached out and linked her fingers with Sasha's.

'Do you ever feel lonely, Lexi?'

'Yes. Especially now Gus—'

'Has got his own life?'

Alex punched her sister playfully on an arm. 'Stop reading my mind, you.'

Sasha laughed.

'It's good to be back,' she said.

'Good to have you back,' replied Alex, meaning it.

They sat in a comfortable silence, and Alex felt her headache easing. 'So, tell me, what did you get up to with Lin today?'

'Lin?'

'Yes. You left a note saying you were with friends. I presumed when you came in with her that you and she had been together. I know you get on. I don't mind, you know. She's a nice woman.'

'I know she's nice, but she's your friend. I hardly know her really.'

'Oh. I got the impression – guess I was wrong. Though she does always seem to turn up at crucial times, doesn't she?'

'What are you saying, Alex?'

Alex closed her eyes, exhausted. 'I don't know. I don't know what I'm saying.'

But the thought kept going round and round in her head: Malone had told her to trust no one.

27

Another beautiful day, thought Alex, as she gazed out of the window, the remnants of yesterday's events still behind her eyes in the form of a headache.

She loved late May – the promise of spring beginning to bear fruit in the early summer. If she looked hard enough she could just about see blades of grass pushing through the soil. At least, she might have done if she'd bothered to buy any seed and spread it on the earth. Still, she had some bedding plants in pots ready to go out. This year she would be more careful and wait until she was certain there would be no more frost. She didn't want to have to buy two lots of plants again.

Who had knocked her out? They could have killed her. A sobering thought. And she couldn't believe it was Heath. Why not, though? Was she letting sentiment get in the way? The whole episode had made her feel uneasy, not safe in her own home. As she had gone to the shop down the road to replenish the milk and bread stocks she'd felt as though someone was watching her. She'd sensed it a few times lately. A figure seen out of the corner of her eye, a shadow behind her. Was this what Malone was warning her about?

At least one good thing had come out of it all so far – a new and comfortable relationship with Sasha. She smiled as she thought about her sister ringing their mum early this morning and not taking no for an answer. She was going to stay at their house for a couple of nights, whether they liked it or not. Alex would bet their mother was thrilled. And it gave her peace of mind.

Opening up a file on her computer, she flexed her fingers. Today was the day when she would begin to map out the backgrounder on the deaths on the Broads. She would sketch out some ideas, try to come up with an opener, then she was going to track down Willem Major.

She began to write down what she knew. Roger Fleet. Left the priesthood, lost his faith. Lived on a smallholding in Suffolk. Found his faith again. Told sister he was doing it for her. What? Killing himself for her? Derek Daley. He was doing it too. Killing himself for who? For his family? Was going to be outed as a paedophile. Blackmail? She underlined the word three times. Jen Tamsett. Killed by a speeding driver. No family. No one to miss her. Willem Major. His family decimated in a fire, him in hiding. Sold his business, opted out of the world. Her father. Where did Anthony Devlin fit in? Had he some sort of past relationship with Willem Major? Was it important? Could she accept her parents had a life before her and Sasha – and what business was it of hers anyway? Did any of this have anything to do with all these deaths?

She heard a dog barking in the distance, someone shouting. Hooves on the tarmac as the horse-drawn dray took barrels of local beer to the town's pubs.

Lin. Who was she? Where had she said her brother was? Craighill, that was it. Had she ever given her brother a name? She thought hard.

Bobby. So, it would be Bobby Meadows.

She turned to Google and found the number of the Craighill mental health unit. She rang the number for reception.

'I'd like to book a visit with one of your patients, please. My name is Alex Devlin.'

'And who is it that you're hoping to visit?' the friendly voice on the other end of the phone asked.

'Bobby Meadows.'

'Bobby Meadows. Just one moment.'

There was a pause. Alex's heart beat faster.

'Hello? Ms Devlin? Are you sure you have the right place? We don't have a Bobby Meadows here.'

'Could he have been discharged recently?'

'There doesn't seem to have been anyone with that name here at Craighill in the recent past anyway. Could you have got the wrong mental health unit?'

So. No Bobby Meadows at Craighill. Had Lin got the name of the place wrong? Or was she lying to her? But Lin was her friend, wasn't she? Someone she had confided in. They'd shared gossip and laughter and secrets ...

An email pinged into her inbox. It was from Father Paul at Goldhay College.

Dear Alex

I know you will appreciate that because of data protection I can't give you any private details about Roger Fleet. What I can say is that I have spoken to two or three people who knew him while he was here. They all said he was a gentle soul but obviously had a troubled mind and heart. They surmised that something had happened in his past that weighed heavily on him. He was, by all accounts, a very dedicated and learned teacher. If you do write about him, please let your readers know that.

God bless.

With best wishes

Father Paul

At least Father Paul had done what he said he would do, even if it didn't take her much further.

Alex jumped as the sound of a loud knock on the door reverberated through the house.

She went downstairs, for once thinking to put the safety chain on before she opened the door.

'Hello.' Laurie Cooke looked at Alex, tension in her hunched shoulders and in her eyes that darted here and there.

'Laurie.' Alex was surprised to see Derek's daughter.

'Sorry … I … sorry …' she trailed off, swallowing nervously. She looked thinner and more grey than she had when Alex had seen her last.

'No, it's no problem. Come inside. Please.' She took the safety chain off.

Alex led Laurie through to the kitchen. 'Sit down. Can I get you anything?'

Laurie shook her head. Then nodded. 'Coffee would be nice, and I hope I'm not disturbing you but I felt I had to—'

'Hey, hey, it's okay,' said Alex, while she spooned coffee into the cafetière. 'I've got plenty of time.'

'I had to get out of the house. Those four walls. And Mum was driving me mad. Crying and beating her breast, metaphorically speaking.' She managed a weak smile. 'And all she can do is talk about Dad and how he's betrayed her and how is she going to face her bridge club and the book club. As if they mattered.' She took a deep breath. 'And I'm thinking what am I going to tell the children about their grandfather and his liking for kids not much older than them, and then there are the letters and emails I found. Nasty, vicious emails and—'

Alex put her hand on Laurie's shoulder. 'It's okay. Slow down.' She put a cup of coffee in front of Laurie. 'Tell me why you're here.'

'Of course. I'm sorry.'

She sat, motionless. Alex let her gather her thoughts.

'I found an old iPad of his.' She looked embarrassed. 'I used to spy on him when I was little, and I knew he used to hide things and where he used to hide them. He had a secret drawer in his desk. And the desk came with us to Glory Farm. Anyway, I found it. And some letters.' Her voice was steady. She didn't look at Alex. 'On the iPad were three emails saying basically the same thing.'

'Which was?' Alex prompted.

'Do as I say. If you love your family. The subject line said "Do it".'

'That's it?'

'Yes. Those said the same thing.'

'And the sender?'

'The address was a string of letters and numbers. That's all. I'm frightened, Alex. What does it all mean?'

'You said there were letters?'

'Yes. Again, they all said the same thing. "Do as I say".'

'Hmm. "Do as I say". What had the writer said? What could they have told your dad to do?'

'I've no idea. I asked Mum if there had been any funny phone calls for Dad in the last few weeks, but she didn't know. I can't say I'm surprised, I think Dad had about three mobile phones. I couldn't find any of them.'

'Could the police have taken them?'

'Very possibly.'

'You said "those said the same thing" – the emails on the iPad. Was there another email?'

'One. From the same sender. It said he – or she – had sent some encouragement.'

Alex thought for a moment. 'Could that "encouragement" have been the photos and the accusation of paedophilia, do you think? Did the person send them to you and tell the police to make your dad do whatever it was he was supposed to do?'

'It's possible, I suppose.' She screwed up her face. 'I'm trying to remember the dates. I think that last message came about a week before he died.'

'Hmm.' Alex thought for a minute. 'But he and Roger Fleet had already booked the boat. Maybe he was having second thoughts about killing himself, so whoever is behind all this sent the photos to make him do it.'

'What do you mean "whoever's behind all this"?' Laurie looked bewildered.

'I think there's more to your father's and Roger Fleet's deaths than simple suicides.'

Laurie looked up towards the ceiling – Alex knew that tactic, it helped stop the tears. She crouched down in front of Laurie. 'Look, I am not going to stop until I find out the truth.'

'Really?'

'Really.' Oh, it was a rash promise to make, and she didn't know where it was going to lead her, but for her own sanity, she needed to get to the bottom of what was going on.

Laurie picked up her bag. 'I'd better get back to Mum.'

'Try to remember your father as he was, before all these accusations. Before he died. Look for the good memories and hug them to yourself.'

'How can I?' said Laurie as she went out of the door.

28

Poor Laurie Cooke, thought Alex, as she drove along the road towards Lapford and Roger Fleet's home, the misery surrounding her father had only just begun. The tabloids were bound to dissect his life with a scalpel. That was why she had to find out what had been happening so she could try and protect her own family somehow. They would all need shielding if her father was caught up with the deaths in any way. At the very least, all the stuff with Sasha would be dragged up. She could see the headlines: 'Father of child-killer involved in death of well-known magazine editor'. And that would be one of the kinder ones.

When would it hit the papers, though? How many days' grace did she have? Not too many; they'd want to get it out there as soon as anything – any little thing – was verified by the police.

She pulled up by the five-bar gate that led to Roger Fleet's smallholding. She had set off for the village without thinking through what she was going to do. Late morning, so there could be someone around, but it was unlikely, surely? She couldn't smell the pigs or hear the clucking of chickens, so livestock must have been taken away.

There was no police tape across the front door anymore. Good. Walking round to the back of the bungalow she found upturned buckets on the ground, with the remnants of feed spilling out. The whole place had an abandoned air. So soon, she thought. It didn't take long before the life went out of a place. It was as if the very bricks and mortar sensed there was no one coming back. Even the birdsong was muted.

All at once there was a flurry of barking, and a chocolate Labrador came hurtling around the corner, skidding to a halt just in front of Alex. A pair of soft brown eyes looked up at her, a pink tongue lolling out of the dog's mouth. It looked as though it was smiling.

Alex bent down to stroke it. 'Are you Bramble or Cotton?' she asked it.

'That there's Bramble,' said Mrs Archer, as she came panting around the corner. 'And I don't know what business it is of – oh it's you. The journalist.'

Alex straightened up. 'That's right. Mrs Archer, isn't it?' Same muddy skirt. Same tee shirt. Same flowery cardigan.

'Aye, that's right.' Her eyes narrowed. 'And what is it you wanted?'

'Are you looking after the dogs now, Mrs Archer? And I see all the animals have gone.'

'Yes. They went to market. I expect the chickens will be plucked and trussed and eaten b'now. She wanted to put the dogs down, you know. The sister. Said she couldn't keep them.' She sniffed. 'Didn't want no reminders of her poor brother, more like.'

Alex smiled down at Bramble, who was now sniffing at the ground around her feet. 'I suppose grief can take us in different ways. Did she go into the house?'

'Oh yes. And took most of the nice stuff, I shouldn't wonder. I know there was a lovely grandfather clock and some other bits and pieces. Couldn't wait to get her hands on it. He's not even buried yet. Anyway, you should know. Being a journalist and all that. Did he really kill himself? I mean, I know that's what the papers say. They say he did it with a famous magazine editor or summat. Can't say I'd ever heard of him. Don't have time to read magazines anyway. But why would Roger choose him to go to the Lord with?'

'Mrs Archer, did Mr Fleet ever talk about Derek Daley?'

'That the magazine editor? No, never talked about him. He came here once, though.'

Alex's ears pricked up. 'Here? To the smallholding?'

'Yes. Funny little man. I was here helping Roger with the animals – one of the pigs was farrowing – and he di'n't say a word to me. Not one word. And then Roger and him went inside. Roger was as meek as a lamb he was. Meek as a lamb.'

'Have you told the police this?'

'They didn't ask, did they? Just told me he'd topped himself and that was that.'

'Mrs Archer,' Alex began carefully.

'You want to go and look inside the house, don't you?'

'Well—'

Mrs Archer nodded with satisfaction. 'I've seen it on the telly. That's what happens in crime programmes and the like.' She took a rusty key out of her skirt pocket. 'Here. It's the spare one from the flowerpot.'

She pressed it into Alex's palm.

Roger Fleet's bungalow smelt musty and damp. There was an overtone of animal, too. Alex thought it must have been built in the sixties, and hadn't been changed much. Stained Formica worktops in the kitchen, woodchip wallpaper in what Alex took to be the dining room, which also had a coal fire at one end, the ash grey and dismal. There were brighter squares on the wall, presumably where pictures had hung for years but were now gone. A long hallway. Could have been where the grandfather clock had stood. Three doors. She opened the first one. A junk room. Nothing but boxes and old chairs. An ironing board. A couple of framed pictures. A filing cabinet. Was it worth a look? Maybe.

The second door opened onto Roger Fleet's bedroom. The curtains were drawn, but were so thin that plenty of light came through. There was a single bed with a grey quilt. A picture of Madonna with Christ above the bed. A table at the side of the bed with a rosary, a glass of water, and a book face down. Alex went over to have a look. *The Imitation of Christ.* Blimey, he really was getting his faith back. Against one wall was a dressing table covered with a fine layer of dust, a brush and comb on its top. That was it. It was all very austere.

She opened one of the dressing table drawers. There were socks, neatly rolled into balls. She tried to push the drawer back in, but something was caught at the back. She pulled it right out and peered into the gap. A piece of paper. She scrabbled about and eventually it came out into her hand. She read it.

Remember Zoe, Roger. Do as I say.

Zoe? She frowned. Who the hell was she?

There was something else caught too. A blurry photo of Margaret Winwood in a supermarket with her head blacked out by felt-tip pen. The threat was obvious. Do as he was told or your sister gets it.

How must he have felt when he got this?

A car door slammed.

Alex froze. She had been so intent on creeping round Roger Fleet's bungalow, she hadn't been listening out for possible visitors.

'Mrs Winwood, isn't it?' She heard Mrs Archer call out in a particularly loud voice.

'Mrs—'

'Archer. I've been trying to keep Roger's veg going, but it's a losing battle.'

Alex smiled as she wondered what Margaret Winwood thought of Mrs Archer's shouting. More immediately, what the hell was she going to do? She looked around.

'Well I wouldn't worry yourself, Mrs Archer. I'm putting the bungalow and the land up for sale.'

'Really? It would be a shame if developers got hold of it. Throw up a whole lot of boxy houses.'

'Has to be done, I'm afraid. Now, if you'll excuse me, I want to go in and check there's nothing valuable that I've left. The estate agent will be around tomorrow.'

Roger's sister certainly wasn't hanging around.

'Are you going through the front door or the patio door? In the sitting room?'

Bless you, Mrs Archer, thought Alex, as she stuffed the bit of paper and the photo into her pocket and made her way as fast and as silently as she could to the sitting room and the patio door.

Thank God, the key was in the lock.

She slipped out of the door and went to the corner of the bungalow, carefully peering round, hoping her loudly beating heart wouldn't give her away. Margaret Winwood was on the front step, frowning. Alex guessed she was wondering why the door was unlocked. There was nothing she could do about that now.

As soon as Margaret Winwood had stepped inside, Alex hurried down the drive, hoping the woman wouldn't look out of a window and see her. She waved to Mrs Archer, who gave her a thumbs up in reply.

Alex got into her car and breathed a sigh of relief.

She'd made it.

29

Was she in the right place? Standing by her car in the lay-by, Alex squinted at the piece of paper in her hand on which she had written Willem Major's address.

'He didn't want to be found,' Honey had told her when she rang to thank the hacker for her help. 'That's for sure. And he has the money to cover his tracks. It was a bit of a task, I can tell you – harder than I thought it would be. I think he must have had professional help along the way.'

'From someone like you?'

'From someone like me.' Alex heard the rare smile in Honey's voice. 'I guess after that tragedy – losing his family and all – he wanted to be somewhere where nobody knew him. Now, like I said, no more contact, right?'

Not only where no one knew him, but also in a place where no one would visit by accident. On the north Norfolk coast, down a long track through the marshes and reed beds, across the sand and on a spit of land that stretched out into the sluggish grey sea, was a solid brick house. She squinted through her binoculars. Four windows, a door, and a chimney, like a children's drawing. All it lacked was smoke curling into the air. Could he really be there? There was no movement and no sign of a car. And there was no way she was going to be able to approach the house without being seen.

Gulls cried and wheeled in the blue sky. At least it was reasonably warm: the east wind wasn't knifing through her and in the distance she could see walkers in shirtsleeves with rucksacks on their backs. She squinted through the binoculars at the house again. There was nothing else for it, she was going to have to go up there and see if he was in.

She drove the car onto a narrow sandy track running across the marsh and between its myriad of water inlets, trying to avoid the worst of the ruts and potholes.

The track ended at the house. The sea was only a few metres away, behind a sandbank, and as she got out of the car, she could hear it pulling and sucking on the shore, the only sound on the air. Even the gulls were too far away to hear. She stood still to test how she was feeling, what she was feeling. Somehow she knew that Willem Major had a pivotal part to play in all of this. He was connected to Derek Daley and Roger Fleet. And Jen Tamsett. He was connected to her father. Her father had known him at Cambridge – and not merely as a passing acquaintance – there was more to it than that. Something had happened all those years ago.

And then there was the mysterious Zoe, who Roger was supposed to remember.

The front door was blocked by a stone trough of dead and dying pansies, so Alex made her way around to the back. She could detect no movement, nor hear any human noise. There was, however, a motorbike parked on the shingle that had been out of sight when she'd scoped the house with her binoculars.

She lifted her hand to knock at the door when it was flung open.

A man stood there, thick white-blond hair framing his face and curling over his collar. His face was tanned and weathered, with several days of greying stubble. He had a patrician's nose and an air of arrogance. His blue eyes, sharp and piercing, were full of pain. And he held a baseball bat in his raised hand.

Alex acted instinctively. She smiled and held out her hand. 'Willem Major? I've been looking for you.'

'So have a lot of people for a long time.' He looked at the bat in his hand then back at Alex. He smiled wryly. 'Not needed?'

'Not needed,' Alex agreed.

He ran a hand through his hair. 'You'd better come in. I've been expecting you.' He put the bat down in the corner by the door and led Alex into the little kitchen.

If the Fablon-topped units and small teak table under the window were anything to go by, the house hadn't been updated since the sixties. It smelt of the sea and of mould and cooking fat. It was dark and dingy, not a place she particularly wanted to spend time in. As her eyes got used to the gloom, she saw dirty plates on the side by the sink. A window looked out over the sand dunes. A woodburner full of grey ash was set into a wall recess, the tiled hearth dirty and stained.

Willem Major had obviously seen the expression on her face, because he took an old Barbour jacket off a chair and motioned back towards the door. 'Let's go out. It's too depressing in here. Your car?'

Alex drove back down the rutted track she had driven up minutes before.

'I didn't think you would want to leave the house.'

'Sometimes I like to live dangerously.'

'I know a nice café near here,' she ventured.

Willem Major grunted. She took that as an okay.

She reached the main road again and after about half a mile she stopped by a wooden building standing on its own with tables and benches outside. A couple of families were sitting enjoying the warmth of the sun. 'The bird café,' she said.

'Bird café?' He pointed at the sign above the door. 'It says "Traveller's Rest".'

Alex smiled and opened the car door. 'I'll always know it as the bird café. Let's have a coffee.'

She got out of the car and looked around, breathing in the sea-salt air. She hadn't been here since she was small. Her dad had brought her and Sasha one day when a bird from Africa had landed on the marsh and all the twitchers came to peer at it through their telescopes. It was where the birdwatchers had all come to for fuelling up with tea and more tea and to compare notes. In those days there was even a book on the counter in which they could list their sightings. She remembered the café as quaint with rickety tables inside, blue and white checked cloths and tea in white china teapots and white china cups and saucers. She thought they'd eaten doorstep cheese sandwiches and that the day had been grey and drizzly.

Her and Sasha and her dad.

What could she remember about her dad that day? Had he been chatty? Loving? Jokey? No, probably not that. He'd been – Dad. Just Dad.

'I came here with my father,' she told Willem Major. 'You knew him as Anthony Devlin.'

She looked at him, waiting for a reaction.

Willem Major nodded and sighed. He stared at the wide East Anglian sky that dipped to meet the horizon. 'I didn't have him down as a birdwatcher.'

'Is that all you've got to say?'

'What else is there?'

She thought hard. 'He used to like going to the pub with the newspaper and having a pint.' How funny, she'd forgotten that until now. Somehow it seemed important to tell Willem Major about her father, what he was like – had been like. 'He loved white bread toasted with butter and golden syrup. We used to have that on a Friday evening when Mum had gone to bed. It was a bit of a ritual. You know, toast the bread until it was just the right side of brown. Tate & Lyle from the cupboard. And

234

thickly spread Lurpak butter. Then we'd watch the late-night film.'
She stopped, the memories jammed in her throat. Often, she only
remembered the bad times. The silences. The rows. The banging
of the door as Sasha flounced off. Again. But it was all the little
things that made up a life. The good and the bad memories. How
odd, she thought, that we edit our memories so that we see them
as they are now, not as they actually were in the past. In the past
it was just the thing that happened on a Friday night. Now it was
a precious memory to hold on to. A memory all of her own.

Willem Major nodded. 'That's good,' he said.

Alex gazed over the marshes before going inside the café and
ordering them both tea and cake. There were still blue and white
checked cloths on the tables.

The pot of tea – white china – and two slices of carrot cake
arrived. Alex licked the frosting. 'I love that,' she said, savouring
the creamy sweetness. 'So, you were expecting me?'

Willem Major nodded. 'Not exactly expecting you, but I wasn't
surprised to see you either. Ever since I heard about Roger and
Derek. But first there was Jen. A speeding driver, they said.' His
face was impassive.

'"*They said*"? So, you don't believe it?'

He shook his head.

'I've followed you, you know. Your work, I mean. I came to
see your father once, many years ago. You were about ten. He
was so proud of you.'

All at once a memory flickered across her mind, like a ripple
across a pool. 'You gave me some money.'

'Did I?' Surprise in his voice. 'Not the sort of thing I usually
do.'

'Yes. I remember you visiting, I think. But I definitely remember
the money. I decided then I liked you.' She laughed.

'And now?' His hands that had been playing with a sugar packet
were still. His eyes bored into hers. 'You're lucky. He loves you. I
could see that when I came.' He smiled briefly. 'Anyway, how did

you find me? I thought I'd covered all bases. I didn't want to be tracked by the media, or ghouls or …' He hesitated. 'Or anyone else.'

'A friend who knows how to look.'

'Ah.' He nodded. 'Someone to hack into the systems. Clever of you.'

Alex brushed the compliment aside. 'What was your relationship with my father?'

Major stretched his legs out. Alex noticed his eyes kept flicking over to the door. He ignored her question.

'And now I'm going to have to move on. Who knows, someone may have recognized me already.'

Alex gazed around the café. There was only one other table occupied – a family, with mum, dad and two children, sitting having tea and juice.

'I am sorry.' Was she really sorry that she'd disrupted this man's life again? Probably; but her need to know more about her father and his involvement with Willem Major was greater. 'My father. Your relationship with him,' she prompted.

'Relationship. That's a difficult one.'

Alex waited for him to elaborate.

'Does this place sell booze?' He said, suddenly alert.

'No.' She pointed to his coffee. 'Just tea and coffee and soft drinks.' She wriggled with impatience. She needed to hear about her dad from him, from Willem Major.

'Right.' He slumped in his seat.

'So, you haven't been out much, then?' Alex was beginning to get a bit irritated with him.

'What?'

'You haven't been here before? I mean, this café's pretty close to your cottage.'

His mouth twisted. 'Until I was forced out of my house, I hadn't been to the cottage for years. And no one knows it belongs to me. Try and trace the owners and you end up at a shell company.

236

Your hacker was good, getting through the walls. Anyway, it's been a refuge but, as I said, I guess I'm going to have to move on now. If you can find me then …'

For a moment, Alex felt ashamed. In her desire to solve the puzzle of the deaths on the Broads and the enigma that was her father, she had almost forgotten this man had suffered a tragedy of unimaginable proportions. She put her hand out, then took it back. He didn't seem the type of man to want that sort of gesture. 'I'm really sorry about the fire. About the loss of your family.'

'Yeah. Well. Charlotte survived, but she won't talk to me now. The one thing I can do for her is to make sure she's safe. As soon as I hear that …' He shrugged. His expression was hard, but the pain in his eyes was still there.

'I'm sorry,' she said. 'The words are inadequate, I know, but I mean them.'

His face softened. Slightly. 'I know you've suffered too.' Those eyes looked into her again. She could feel their intense magnetic quality.

'Thank you. And I'm sorry if you feel you're going to have to leave here. If it's any consolation, I won't give it away. Where you're living.'

'It's not any consolation.' His eyes flashed dangerously.

'And now you want me to talk about the relationship I had with Tony.' He took a gulp of his coffee and grimaced. 'You know I felt something for him. I think he did for me. A little bit. But for him it was more about discovery. Exploring his feelings, if you want to get hippy-dippy about it. Cambridge was an eye-opener for him; he'd come from a sheltered background. I would have liked it if …' He stopped, rolled his shoulders. 'But it was not going to happen. I wasn't very nice to him once. More than once. I think it's up to you to ask him about it.'

'That's going to be a bit difficult.' Alex cut a piece of cake with her fork. 'He's got dementia. Oh, it hasn't completely taken him

237

over, but it's getting there. He has lucid days and not so lucid days.'

'Ah, that's crap.' He rubbed his hand over his face. 'Dementia. Tony. How we all grow old.' He looked at her, and she saw what an attractive man he must have been. And the charisma that she doubted would ever fade, a charisma that probably made people do whatever he wanted them to do.

She had to know. She leaned forward, jabbing her fork at him. 'So you see, there is only you to tell me about those Cambridge days, and why my father left so suddenly. And why Roger Fleet was a mess. And about this photograph.' Alex showed him the photo of the four student friends on her phone. 'Taken by my dad, I guess.'

'Well I'm damned,' Willem said, taking the phone from her and looking at the picture from all angles. 'There we all are. We look so ... hopeful. Well, drunk and stoned really, I think.' He grinned. 'There was a lot of that in those days. Not like today when it's oh-so-serious and everybody's got to get a good degree to then go and do fuck-all.'

'Did the partying get out of hand, then?'

'You might say that, yeah.' He smiled as though he was remembering good times. 'After that was taken ...' He was still smiling, but there was a flash of cruelty behind it that made Alex shiver.

'After that was taken, what?'

'Nothing.'

'Look.' She sat up straight. 'I feel there's a connection between this photograph and the deaths of Roger Fleet and Derek Daley. And most likely Jen Tamsett. And you're connected, too, somehow. So tell me, was the photo taken by my dad?'

Willem Major nodded. 'It was a lovely afternoon: the beginning of the end.'

'What do you mean?'

He shrugged. Infuriating.

'And you're holed up here because you're frightened that

whoever set the fire originally is going to come back for you.'

Willem Major's face closed down. 'I don't want to talk about it. I can't talk about it. I told you. Not until Charlotte is safe.'

The back of her neck prickled. She could understand that he didn't want to talk about it, how painful it must be for him, but she had to know. 'I read about it. It was deliberate, and the police are still looking for whoever did it. Willem, you've got to talk to me. Everyone in that photo has had something awful happen to them. Dad could be next. You have to tell me what went on.'

'Let's go.' He threw some money onto the table and strode out of the café.

Alex found she had to walk very quickly to keep up with Willem. They marched along the road, until he made an abrupt turn down a track that led to the sea.

'The fire was set as a punishment,' he said eventually, as they made their way onto a shingle path by the shoreline. She could see his cottage in the distance.

'"Punishment"?' Alex tried not to pant. God, she was unfit. Time to get a personal trainer. Stop it, concentrate, she told herself.

'Apparently, because I would not cooperate.' He bit out the words. 'And because I would not cooperate, my family died.'

Alex stopped dead. 'What do you mean?'

'Exactly that. I would not do as I was asked and so they killed my family. And now I have had to hide.'

'What did this person want you to do? And, more importantly, why?'

Willem Major stopped and looked up into the sky. He filled his lungs with the sea air. 'Why?' His mouth twisted in a parody of a smile. 'Because I was involved in the death of a girl when I was at university, and this person wanted me to kill myself. In retribution. That's what they said. "Retribution". Oh, and "atonement". Bit dramatic, I think. When I refused, they killed my family. So, they took my life away from me anyway.' He looked at her.

'Wonderful words, don't you think? Retribution. Atonement. Biblical. Of course it's all bollocks.'

It all clicked into place. Roger Fleet and Derek Daley were blackmailed into killing themselves. Probably by threats to their families. That's what those words meant. *I did it for you.* So why the accusations of child porn? Most likely, as she'd surmised, Daley was having second thoughts. Refusing to go through with it. And if he rebelled, 'they' might have lost their hold over Fleet, hence the child porn stuff. Jen Tamsett had no family – maybe she'd been blackmailed, maybe not – but she'd been killed by a car and the driver had never been found. Willem Major had lost most of his family. Only her father was left.

'And the girl, the one who died, was it Zoe?'

Willem Major looked around. 'It's beautiful here, isn't it? I've never really noticed. Too busy watching for someone to come and finally finish the job. At least I can see them coming. Got a great view from the house.' He chuckled mirthlessly. 'Perhaps I won't bother moving on. I'm tired of looking over my shoulder all the time.'

'Tell me, was it Zoe who died? And who was she?'

'Zoe was a nobody. Nothing.' There was no emotion in his voice. 'Really. Nobody. She had no family. Nobody would have missed her. Nobody did miss her.' His hands chopped the air, his voice fierce.

'Why did she die? Did you murder her? Was my father involved?' Alex whispered.

Willem laughed. 'It was an accident; I didn't kill her. Nobody killed her. At least I don't think so. Yes, your father was there. So were Roger and Derek. Jen too. Stu. And we buried her.'

'Where?'

Willem smiled. 'In a churchyard.'

'Where?' Her heart was thudding.

'I don't remember.'

'And I don't believe you.'

He sighed. 'It was a long time ago. We were high. Drunk. Out of it. Whatever. I don't remember where we drove to. I only remember it was a church somewhere in the Fens.'

'And someone close to her wants revenge; is that what this is all about?'

'Have you got a cigarette?'

Alex took her emergency packet out of her bag and offered him a cigarette. He held it loosely between his fingers.

'He said he was Zoe's long-lost son.'

'And do you believe him?'

He laughed harshly. 'No. Who knows? Maybe he's an opportunist who found out about what happened and is making some sort of sick capital out of it. To be honest, for once in my life, I think it's Stu.' He laughed without mirth.

'Stu.' She frowned. 'You mentioned him just now. I haven't heard his name before.'

Willem shook his head. 'Stu was a miserable little worm. Weak. Not part of our set. Wanted to be like us so badly. A light?' He cupped his hands around the flame before drawing on the cigarette. 'Besides, he went off into oblivion after university. Never heard from him again.'

'What was his last name?'

'Stu?' He smiled. 'Eliot. He was a Barnardo's Boy.'

Excitement began to fizz in Alex's stomach. 'But don't you see? He must be involved.'

'Maybe. Maybe not. Why has he waited all this time if it is? I don't care any more, I just want out.'

As quickly as the fizz had come, it subsided. Nevertheless, she filed Stu Eliot's name away.

'Didn't you care, when Zoe died?' She was curious about his detachment.

'Not particularly. Why should I have done?'

Why had her father been friends with this man? 'Because you're a human being?'

'I've paid for it though,' he went on. 'Paid for the accidental death of some girl I—'

'You what?'

'Nothing.' He looked sideways at her. 'Look after your dad, won't you? He was a good person.'

'He still is.' Alex's heart began beating furiously. She was suddenly very afraid for her father. 'I must go and see him. Now.'

Willem Major nodded, a sudden breeze ruffling his hair, making him look slightly mad. Which he probably was, thought Alex. If he wasn't mad before, the loss of his family because of a shocking act forty years ago would be enough to send any sane man crazy.

She began to run, back towards her car.

'Your father was quite special, you know,' he called out after her.

Alex stopped running.

'I know,' she shouted. 'I've always known.'

But the wind whipped her words away.

30

Cambridge 1976

Stu reported Willem to the university authorities and the police. Willem spent an uncomfortable twenty-four hours at the police station, but I gathered, due to his father's influence and the greasing of palms with cash, he got off with a warning. He was humiliated though, and anger flashed in his eyes when I asked him about it.

'I don't want to talk about it,' he spat. 'Dad gave him a fat cheque, and I had to apologize to the little shit and that was bad enough without having to think about it any more.'

I left the subject alone.

Gradually, the memories of the night we spent at the abandoned church receded, became even more dreamlike, almost to the point where I wondered if I had actually dreamed it. By a silent mutual consent, none of us talked to each other about it either and soon it didn't cross my mind for days at a time. I saw Jen, Derek, and Roger when I was able. They were good friends, and I enjoyed their company, more so now that we seemed to be out of Willem's orbit. We would go to the cinema, to the bar, maybe a concert, but work was becoming more demanding and exams would soon be looming such that I found myself in my room on my own more often than not. Jen seemed to see me as a friend only, much to my disappointment. Willem did still occasionally flit in and out of our lives – he was usually high on something, often manic.

One day, while walking on Midsummer Common trying to breathe in the air and lower my stress levels after a particularly bruising and punishing session with my tutor, I saw Stu for the first time since that night. Stu with a girl. Proper arms-wrapped-around-each-other Stu with a girl. It was time to make things right.

They didn't see me until it was too late for him to avoid me.

'Hi, Stu,' I said pleasantly. 'How are things?'

He stiffened, and I willed him to be cool, not to get angry, not to start sweating, not to show himself up in front of this freckled, nice-looking girl.

'Hi,' he said, before starting to walk away.

'Stu, it is good to see you. Really.'

There must have been something in my voice, I don't know, sincerity or pleading, but he stopped. 'Really?'

I nodded, smiling. 'I'm really sorry about – you know.'

He glanced over at his companion and then back to me. 'S'okay.'

'Perhaps we could get together sometime? Have a beer. Both of you, I mean. You and …?'

'Zoe,' said the girl. 'I'm Zoe.'

'Which college are you in?' I asked.

'Zoe isn't in college,' said Stu, quickly. 'She works in the city.'

'I see.'

'I think it would be lovely,' said Zoe. 'I haven't met many of Stu's friends.' She smiled, and it lit up her face. She was pretty, with milky skin under the freckles and a turned-up nose. I wondered what she saw in Stu, then told myself not to be so uncharitable.

'Anyway,' said Stu. 'Thanks. Maybe. A beer, I mean.'

The year drifted on. I never did meet up with Stu and Zoe, though I did see him around a few times and exchanged pleasantries. He and Zoe were still an item and yes, he would say every time, we must have that beer. Easter Term came and I tried to work hard. I took my philosophy exams in a state of nervous tension and wished I had started to revise earlier. But what was done was done and I would have to wait.

I was lying on my bed, rehearsing what I would say to Jen when I eventually plucked up courage to ask her to St Francis's May Ball – I had bought the tickets, I only needed the right girl – when Willem walked in, unannounced.

'Lovely boy, how are you?' he declaimed.

I closed my eyes. 'Fine.' I was hot. Sticky. The room was airless. The temperature had been unseasonably high for days. I was not in the mood for Willem.

I felt the bed sag as he sat on the end. 'Come on, you can do better than that.' He rubbed my leg. 'We haven't all been together in weeks.'

'No.'

'Don't sound as though you're glad.'

I opened my eyes. 'Willem, what do you want?'

'I want us to go and have a celebratory drink. You, me, Roger, Derek and Jen. To welcome in May Week. To say "sod exams". To celebrate life. Come on, what do you say?'

I wanted to tell him to fuck off, but then I thought about Jen and that perhaps a few drinks in she might say yes to coming with me to the May Ball.

'All right then.'

Did I imagine it, or did a look of triumph flash across his face?

I decided I imagined it.

Mistake.

The Freemason's Arms was one of those cosy, whitewashed pubs with dim lighting that served real ale. It was also famed for its meals of huge T-bone steaks and chips, and I had managed not to finish more than one meal here. The garden, consisting chiefly of grass and a few picnic tables, stretched down to the River Cam, and on any warm day at lunchtime it was packed out. At this time of year and in this heat it was heaving. The air was filled with the noise of people chatting and the sound of glasses clinking. The smell of yeast mingled with the stench of rotting vegetation from the river.

Derek, Jen, and Roger were sitting at a table close to the water. They were downing pints and sharing a couple of bags of cheese and onion crisps. Jen in particular appeared delighted when I sat down with Willem. I dared to hope she did have some feelings for me.

Willem produced a bottle of champagne and glasses like a magician producing a rabbit out of a hat. 'There,' he said, pouring it into the glasses, 'let's have a toast.'

We clinked glasses.

'A picture, Derek, let's have a picture,' said Willem.

'No, I'll take it,' I said, jumping up. 'Derek's always doing them. We'll have one with him in it this time.'

Derek handed me his camera and the others made silly faces. 'Come on, smile,' I said. They smiled. Roger laughed. Willem pointed at me. I took the picture.

'More drink,' said Willem, taking another bottle of champagne out of his bag.

As I raised my glass, I looked around and saw Stu sitting behind us at a table with a couple of other students from college. 'Come over,' I called.

Willem looked. 'Ah, dear Stu. Where's the girlfriend?' He waved. 'Yes, come on.'

'Willem?' I said.

He smiled. 'Can't hold a grudge forever.'

Stu shook his head, and turned back to his friends.

Willem went over to him and put out his hand. 'Stu. I am

truly sorry for what happened. Please come and join us so we can let bygones be bygones.'

What was he doing? I'd never, ever known him to apologize. Stu looked Willem up and down, hesitated, then took his hand.

'Excellent,' said Willem. 'Now come and join us.'

And so the afternoon passed. When the champagne ran out, Willem bought us more drinks. He produced pills, which me and Stu refused, Stu saying he hoped he was meeting Zoe later and he didn't want to be off his head. Mercifully Willem merely shrugged and swallowed his. Swans swam majestically on the river. A rowing boat glided by. I was feeling pleasantly relaxed. Even Stu had unbent and was laughing at Willem's jokes. In fact, Willem was being particularly charming towards Stu, I thought.

'Come on,' said Willem, jumping up, 'let's go.'

I propped myself up by my elbows. 'What are you talking about?'

'Look, I've got a whole lot of food and plenty of booze at my folks' house. We could make a night of it.'

'Come off it, Willem.'

'No,' said Jen, putting her hand on my arm sending a tingling feeling up and down my skin, 'it could be fun. What about it Roger? Derek? Stu?'

'But I'm supposed to be meeting Zoe later and—'

'Come on, Stu,' said Willem. 'Live a little, eh? I can get you back to see your lady love later.' He winked.

Willem never winked.

'Okay,' said Stu. 'If everyone else is going.'

I was outnumbered.

But two hours in Willem's latest motor – a metallic green Ford Capri – and everyone was complaining.

'Hang on, hang on, we're just about there,' he said, pulling off the road and onto a track across flat land. Marshland, I guessed. Birds – gulls? Marsh harriers? I didn't know – wheeled and turned and cried above us. We bumped along the track towards a solid brick-built house with four windows and a door. It took ten minutes to reach it on the spit of land that stretched out into the sea.

We drew up in front of the house and tumbled out of the car. The salty air hit my sun-burned skin with a sting. The air should have been fresher here on the coast, but it was still muggy. Clouds were building. Perhaps the hot weather would break and we would finally have some rain. I heard the sea around the back of the house.

'What's this?' I asked, looking up at the blank windows, the cold brick, the darkening sky.

'My parents' holiday cottage. It's their bolthole, where they like to get back to nature, or some such shit. A bit of a tax dodge, probably. Remote, isn't it?' He grinned.

I looked around. The grass was scrub really, and there were several piles of gravel and rubble. 'To fill in the potholes,' said Willem when he saw me looking. 'Entrance is round the back.'

We all trooped into a kitchen that had seen better days. It was pretty basic, with that Fablon stuff on the kitchen tops and cupboards along one wall. A brick floor. A woodburner was set back in a recess of another wall, with a tiled surround.

'A bit old-fashioned. But the parents like it.'

'Is that you, Billy?' A voice came from another room, and there was the sound of footsteps before the door opened.

Willem smiled.

Zoe, Stu's Zoe stood on the threshold, in nothing but a silk dressing gown, one I had seen Willem wearing many times.

The air held its breath.

Nobody spoke.

Then: 'What the fuck is this?' Stu stared at Zoe, bewildered. 'What are you doing here, Zoe? Is this some sort of silly surprise or what?'

'Stu, I ...' Her face was contorted with anguish. Her lip trembled.

'Oh?' Willem appeared surprised. 'Zoe, angel, I thought you'd said something to Stuey.'

'Said what, Willem? What was she supposed to have said?' Stu looked at Willem, then Zoe. Then at me. 'Do you know what this is about? It's a surprise, right?' He gave a tentative smile. I didn't smile back.

We were all waiting. It was a strange tableau – me, Jen, Derek and Roger frozen to the spot. Zoe, crying. Stu, not understanding anything. Willem, languid, a small smile on his face.

Willem moved. He took Zoe in his arms and kissed her, full on the mouth. She fitted into the curve of his body. As if she belonged.

It was so bloody hot.

31

Cambridge 1976

I felt the sweat trickling down my back.

'Zoe? What are you doing with him?' Stu nodded his head towards Willem, without taking his eyes off Zoe.

Willem pushed her away from him. 'Enough.'

Zoe looked at Stu, tears luminous in her eyes. 'I'm really sorry, Stu. But—' She looked up at Willem. 'We're together now, aren't we, Willem?'

Willem patted her bottom. 'Not really, sweetie.' He looked across at Stu. 'My dear boy,' drawled Willem, 'you can have her if you like.'

I think it was Willem's smile that was Stu's undoing.

'You bastard.'

With a roar Stu leapt forward, fists raised. Before any of us could move, he had punched Willem in the face and was poised for a second go.

I grasped Stu's wrists. Blood streamed from Willem's nose. Stu tried to shake me off but he was like a man possessed by the Devil. He was determined to get at Willem. I had never seen him this angry, never imagined he could become like this. 'Stu, leave it.'

'Get the fuck off me,' he gasped, twisting his body away from me.

Then Roger and Jen were by my side, pulling at Stu. I tasted sweat and fear.

Zoe grabbed at him. 'Stop it, Stu, stop it. Please stop it.' She caught hold of one of his flailing hands. Stu pushed her away. She stumbled. Tripped. Fell against Willem. Roger's hands on her. Jen's hands. I tried to catch her. Failed.

She fell with a crack against the hearth.

Silence.

32

'We're not going anywhere,' her mother said when Alex tried again to persuade her to come and stay with her in Sole Bay. 'Your father needs to be somewhere familiar. It upsets him when he goes to places he doesn't know. And Sasha's here. She'll look after us.'

Alex sat down at the table and watched as her mother went about making her the inevitable cup of tea, putting the kettle on to boil. She noticed how slowly her mother moved, the droop of her shoulders, the swellings in her knuckles. Old before her time. Looking after her father was taking its toll on her.

'Sasha,' she said to her sister. 'Make her see.'

Sasha took the mugs out of the cupboard, then went over to the fridge for the milk. 'I can't tell Mum anything, can I Mum?'

Alex was astonished to see Sasha rub their mother's back with real affection. That hadn't happened in a long time. This new Sasha was a revelation.

'Though,' Sasha continued, 'it might be a good idea.'

'But why? What am I running from? What are *we* running from?'

'That's the trouble,' said Alex. 'I don't know.' She looked straight at her mother. 'Did you know about Zoe?'

Her mother turned away, but Alex saw her shoulders stiffen.

'Mum?'

Her mother faced her and looked, if anything, even older than she had five minutes earlier. Her face was drained of colour. 'What did you say?' Her attempt at appearing casual was laughable.

'Zoe. Did you know about her? From Dad's time at Cambridge. She died.'

Her mother sat down. 'Where did you get that name from? How did you find out about her?'

'Is it true? Did Dad help to hide her death?'

'How did you find out?' her mother asked again.

'I spoke to Willem Major.'

'Him.' Her mother spat the word out.

The kettle boiled, its whistle cutting through the air. The noise went on and on, until Alex took it off the heat and poured the water into the teapot. She didn't have time to dance around the subject.

'I saw Willem Major and he told me that someone had threatened his family. They said he had to kill himself or his family would suffer.' Alex was amazed at how matter-of-fact she sounded.

'He had to do what?' The surprise in her mother's voice was genuine.

Her mother didn't believe her, she could tell. 'I know it seems fantastical, but it's true.'

'That's what that man told you, is it?' Her mother's lip curled.

'It is. And I have no reason not to believe him. Look, it all fits. I think the same threat was made against Roger Fleet and Derek Daley, but they chose to kill themselves.'

'Mum,' said Sasha, urgency in her voice. 'Listen to Alex, please. She's been working on this story, and she knows what she's talking about.' She flashed a grin at Alex. 'At least, I think she does.'

'Typical that Willem Major couldn't sacrifice himself for his family.' Her mother sniffed.

'That's why you've got to leave, I really think you and Dad could be in danger. Look, I must talk to Dad.'

'But—'

Alex sat down. 'I know, I know he might not remember Zoe, he probably won't even remember who I am, but I've got to try, Mum.'

'He does remember who you are. He knows you. And me. And Sasha. Oh, he's really enjoyed having Sasha around. Do you know, they even had toast and golden syrup last night, didn't you love?'

'Yes. But we had to watch a David Attenborough documentary instead of a film. Very dull.'

'At least that was the first time you've had to sit through it. Wait until you've seen it nineteen times, then you can complain. But yesterday was one of his good days. Anyway, love, he's not here.'

'What do you mean, "he's not here"?' Alex was alarmed.

'It's his day for the centre. He's only been going for a couple of weeks, but he really enjoys it.' She grabbed her daughter's hand. 'And it helps me, too.'

A centre. Old people. Knitting. Basket weaving. Max Bygraves on an old turntable. Alex felt more of her childhood slip out of her grasp. She let out a breath, and stroked the back of her mother's hand, feeling her soft skin, the bird-like bones beneath. 'It's hard for you, Mum. I realize that. Please, tell me what you know.'

Then her phone rang. It was Heath. Not now, she thought. She let it go to voicemail.

'Please, Mum.'

Her mother looked into the distance. 'All right.' She swallowed. 'When your father went off to Cambridge, he wanted to be someone different, to lead an exciting life – he wanted adventure and he saw that possibility in Willem Major. Willem was glamorous, amoral, exciting. Flouted authority. Totally different to your father. However, Willem was also manipulative and liked to control people. By the time your father realized that, it was too late, he was already in too deep.'

'He was flattered by Willem Major's attention,' said Alex, thinking back to how she had felt the charisma flow around the man that morning like some sort of aura.

'Yes,' said her mother. 'He was.'

Alex poured the tea, trying to keep her hand steady.

'And Zoe? Where did she fit in?'

Her mother swallowed. 'Zoe was the girlfriend of someone from his college, someone who was on the outside of their circle, who'd had a run-in with Willem.'

'Stu Eliot. The Barnardo's Boy.'

Her mother nodded. 'That's right. He had been friends with your dad, studied Philosophy like he did. Apparently there was some sort of fight – I don't know, your father gets so upset when he talks about it – it was at Willem's family seaside cottage near Cley and ended up with Zoe dead.'

The house at Cley. Willem's house. Where it had happened.

Her mother looked at her oddly. 'What is it?'

Alex shook her head. 'Nothing. Go on.'

Her mother stared at her hands curved around her mug. 'There's nothing more to say. According to your father it was an accident. A stupid, unnecessary accident. But it affected your father very badly.'

'And then they buried her as if she was nothing.'

Her mother hung her head.

'Why?' Alex couldn't understand it. What had they been thinking? 'If it was an accident, why not tell the police or the university or anybody?'

Her mother was twisting her hands together. 'Willem Major persuaded them it would ruin their lives if they did that. Zoe was a nobody, he said. No one would miss her. She wasn't a student; she was working, doing odd jobs in Cambridge.' She leaned across the table and took Alex's hands in hers. 'But you've got to know that your father left Cambridge after the accident because he didn't want to live in what he had come to see as somewhere poisonous. He regretted what happened so very much and regretted never going to the police. He needed to remove himself from Willem's orbit. And he did.' Her eyes were bright with unshed tears. 'You know we met on that boring course. All very ordinary. And that's who your father was then, after university, a man who wanted to live a very ordinary life. A blameless life. To sort of, I don't know, atone for what had happened. He wanted to fit in, have a family, lead a good life. And he has.'

Alex nodded. 'I know.'

'I persuaded him to leave it in the past,' said her mother.

Alex looked at her mother who had lived with her father's secret all these years. But, she thought, what's done is done. 'I think Dad's in danger. Has he had any emails? Letters?'

Her mother smiled sadly. 'If he's had any emails, he wouldn't have read them. He uses the computer sometimes, but mostly he doesn't know what he's doing. I used to read any he received out to him, but that's about it.'

'Did he put any letters anywhere?'

'Like the washing machine, do you mean?' Her mother laughed drily then shook her head. 'I collect the post. See to it all. I really can't trust him with any of it.'

'Can I – may I have a look at the computer? And also perhaps where he kept any letters before he became ill?' She was aware it was a big ask. What parent wanted their child to rifle through their private lives?

'I don't know.' Her mother's forehead creased. 'I don't think your father would like it.'

'In case there's something there. It might help solve the mystery.'

Her mother pushed the hair away from her forehead. 'Come on then.'

The smell of her parent's room transported Alex back twenty years. That mix of her mother's perfume, books and clean clothes. The room was decently furnished, like the rest of the cottage. A king-size bed, two chests of drawers and a white wicker chair under the window.

'This was the one he used for bits and pieces,' said her mother, sliding the top drawer of the chest open.

A faux-leather passport holder. A cufflinks box with a pair of gold cufflinks nestling inside it. 'I bought those for him for our wedding,' said her mother. A photograph in a frame perpetuating the lives of two chickens they had once owned. Alex remembered her and Sasha giving it to their father one Christmas. Sadness washed over her. A couple of scribbled notes. 'Return library books.' 'Do not forget birthday'. Three odd socks. Old credit card bills. Old credit cards.

'Nothing mysterious, is there?' said her mother. 'No note saying "kill yourself or I'll have your family".'

Alex looked at her mother. 'You don't sound convinced?'

'I'm not, my love. I believe you think something's going on, but I don't. I can't see how your poor father is in any danger. And I've told you I don't trust that Willem Major any further than I could throw him. Oh, I know I've never met him, but I've heard enough about him to know what I think. What happened to him was a terrible, ghastly accident. I know I should feel sorry for him, but I don't. I can't.'

Maybe now was the time. 'He said he came here once. When I was little.'

'Did he indeed? Not when I was here. I would have thrown him out.' She sighed. 'Though I expect that was the point. He wouldn't come when I was here. Your father – well, Willem always cast a spell over him.'

They went back downstairs and Alex turned on the computer that sat like a plump bug in the corner of the living room. There was no password, and Alex opened up her father's email account. Nothing. Adverts for *The Times* and *The Economist*: magazines he wouldn't read now with any degree of enjoyment. Offers for cheap rooms at Premier Inn. Nothing that could remotely be seen as threatening.

So, what did that mean? Alex wondered as she scrolled further back in her father's emails. Could it be that whoever was behind the deaths of Fleet, Daley, and Jen Tamsett and the deaths of Willem Major's family didn't know her father was involved? That didn't seem likely, when she considered all the trouble the killer had gone to.

Then she saw it. From three months ago. An email from an account whose name was a string of letters and numbers, with the subject 'Zoe'. Just as Laurie Cooke had said was on her father's computer.

She opened it.

You did nothing.

That was all. A different message to the one Derek Daley had received, but a message from the killer nonetheless, of that she was certain.

She scrolled backwards and forwards, but there was nothing else. No other email.

'Did you know he had this?'

Her mother shook her head. 'No. I don't suppose he's even seen it. And if he had he probably wouldn't have known what it meant. Though—' she frowned.

'What?'

'Long-term memory is often the last to go, so I suppose the name Zoe could have sparked something. It's hard to know. If it had at the time, he would have forgotten by now.'

'Okay.' Alex was frustrated. She wasn't getting anywhere. There were so many threads to sew together and she didn't have the needle.

'What happens now?' her mother asked.

'I don't know.' And not for the first time, she really, really wished Malone was around so she could bounce some ideas off him. He was always so good at cutting through the crap and seeing a way out.

But he wasn't here. And not likely to be either. All he was good for was putting her in danger. Which, according to him, was all around her. Well, thanks very much for that, Malone. Nice of you to tell me. Something else to worry about.

'Are you all right, Alex? You look anxious.'

Alex deliberately relaxed her face. 'I'm fine. Don't worry.'

Her phone rang in her pocket. An 0845 number. A scam or PPI or a wonderful holiday she had won. Sod that. She rejected the call, then noticed the red blob that indicated she had voice-mail. Of course, that would be Heath.

'Mum – do you mind if—?' She held up her phone.

'You go ahead. I'll make you a sandwich.'

She listened to the message. Heath was whispering, and it sounded as though he had his hand curved around his mouth. There was a tremor in his voice. 'I know you don't want to hear from me, but you've got to listen. I think I know who's behind this. I know.' There was a pause. Alex listened carefully. What could she hear in the background? Another voice? She concentrated hard but couldn't be sure. Then Heath spoke again, desperation in his voice. 'Ring me as soon as you get this.'

The voicemail ended.

Bloody Heath, he always enjoyed being mysterious. She was tempted to leave it, but something in his voice nagged at her. She pressed 'call'.

The call connected, but there was silence on the other end.

'Heath? Are you there?'

Nothing.

'For goodness' sake, Heath, answer me.'

'Alex.' His voice was flat and low.

'You asked me to call.'

'Your dad.'

Alex looked at the phone. 'My Dad? What are you talking about?'

'Your father is here, with me.'

Alex was confused. 'He can't be. He's at his day care place.'

'No. I promise you, Alex. He's here.'

'What are you talking about, Heath? Where are you?'

'It doesn't matter. But I'm to tell you that we'll be at St

259

Sebastian's Abbey later tonight, and you're to come if you want to see your father again.'

She laughed. 'Stop being so melodramatic. Who's we? What do you mean about my father? I told you, today's the day Mum has a break.'

'You've got to listen to me. Please.' His voice was urgent. 'Your father's life depends on it. Come to the Abbey tonight, after dark. No police.'

The line went dead.

'Alex?' Her mother put the sandwich down in front of her. 'You're frowning. Is everything all right?'

Alex looked at the phone in her hand, then up at her mother. 'That was Heath – my friend from the paper. He says I've got to go to St Sebastian's Abbey later tonight and that Dad's life depends on it.'

'That's nonsense. He's at his day care centre,' her mother said briskly.

'Mum. Ring the centre, make sure Dad's there.'

'That's ridiculous, Alex.'

'Please. For me. To set my mind at rest.'

Her mother sighed, but picked up the phone.

Two minutes later, she put it down, placing it carefully on the table. 'He's not there, Alex. They said a member of his family had picked him up. It was a new volunteer who let him go without asking any questions. They've been rushed off their feet, apparently. But he's gone. Someone's taken him. Alex, what are we going to do?'

'I've got to call the police.'

'No,' Alex shook her head. 'No, Mum. Heath said no police. I think it's better if we don't call them just yet. I'll go to the Abbey.'

Her mother's skin was grey. 'But Alex—'

'I'll get him back, Mum.'

260

33

There were only two ways to get to St Sebastian's Abbey – by boat along the river or walking through farmland and marsh. Since Alex had no intention of trying to navigate a boat along a river at any time, never mind in the middle of the night, walking was the only option.

She left her car in the nearby pub car park, and began to follow the signs to the Abbey. She had been there only once before. It was a ruin, having originally been built in the ninth century and stood in the middle of a field not too far from the river. There wasn't much to see – a gatehouse and a wind pump that was later built onto it, with grassy mounds surrounding it.

The air was still warm, and a thin mist curled up off the ground. She knew the killer wouldn't bring Heath and her dad to the Abbey until later, but she wanted to get there first. She had to be one step ahead.

At first it was easy. By the light of her pen torch, which she'd put in her pocket before she left the house, she made her way down a narrow road, past a couple of farms, two or three bungalows and Alf's shed that was open every day and sold the freshest produce on the whole of the Broads, according to the dozen notices nailed about the place.

She turned off the road and onto a rutted track. An owl glided and swooped by the light of the moon.

After some twenty minutes of walking she came to a five-bar gate with a roll of barbed wire along the top. More barbed wire made up the fence on either side. There was a large notice on a wooden pole. Alex shone her torch at it.

NO ENTRY it shouted.

She reached through and undid the gate. All the barbed wire in the world was of no use if no one put a padlock on the bloody thing.

The path went straight through fields and marshland. The sky was an inky black, the stars pinpricks of light, the moon still reassuringly above her. Alex stood still for a moment, listening. There was absolute silence, save for the rustling of grass nearby as some creature – a fox, perhaps – made use of the night. A hoot from the owl. The one she had seen earlier? It was reassuring, somehow. She shivered. It might be early summer, but the evenings could chill. And she was getting closer to the water, she could smell that faint muddiness. She took a deep breath, feeling she was the only person for miles around. Loneliness threatened to overwhelm her.

She shook herself. This was not about her.

Clouds scuttled across the sky and obscured the moon. The path was overgrown, rough grass brushed her ankles. Alex used the torch to light her way to avoid nettles and brambles.

'Fuck,' she whispered, as she stumbled over large stones in the middle of the path.

A bark in the distance made her jump. She stopped and listened. There it was again, an ethereal sound on the air. Not a dog's bark, but that of a muntjac deer marking out its territory. Her heartbeat returned to almost normal.

At last she saw it. The moon came out from behind the cloud and the Abbey gatehouse and mill top were etched against the sky. She switched off her torch.

She walked the last hundred metres wondering if she had been seen by whoever had her father and Heath.

She stood, looking at the ruins, listening. Nothing. Not even the sound of insects or birds or water. She took a deep breath and stepped into the ruins of the gatehouse and through to the old mill. She pushed open a heavy wooden door, and the walls closed in on her. Looking up, she saw a slice of starlit sky through the round open mill top. She shone her torch around. Graffiti was scratched into the stone, an empty crisp packet and a couple of beer cans on the earth floor. There was another hoot from the owl, muffled this time by the thick brick walls. Alex's heart was racing, almost as if she had palpitations. It smelt musty in here, and something else, something almost tangy.

There. There, against the round mill wall was a bundle of clothes. She was rooted to the spot. A body. Dad. It was her dad.

She gave a cry and hurried over to the bundle, her mouth dry. A leather bomber jacket. Mulberry scarf. Jeans. She dropped her torch and put her hand on his shoulder. Sticky. Gently, she pulled him over, dreading what she might see.

It was not her father at all.

Heath. His eyes flickering, blood oozing from some sort of wound in his shoulder, a bruise beginning to flower around his jaw. Blood stained the corner of his mouth. He groaned.

'Heath, Heath, wake up,' she whispered.

Nothing.

'Heath, please.' She felt the tears rising in her throat.

He opened his eyes slowly and blinked a few times. He was not seeing her – his eyes were unfocused. She stroked his cheek. 'Heath, tell me what happened. Please.'

His eyes cleared, and he opened his mouth to speak, but only another groan came out.

She took off her jacket and then her cardigan, folding it up and pressing it against the wound. She had to stop the bleeding.

'Heath.' She picked up his other hand, tried to make him press it on the folded-up cardigan. 'Keep your hand there, Heath. Stop the bleeding. I'll go and get help.' But she kept her hand on his, reluctant to leave him. Why was he involved at all?

'Alex.' His eyes were open, clearer. 'It's not as bad as it looks. I don't think he hit anything vital.'

'Still—'

'Alex.' His voice was urgent. 'You need to know—'

'A lovely scene,' came a voice from behind her. 'How very touching. But he is good-looking. And I'm sorry I ruined his jacket.'

Alex whirled round.

She had to shield her eyes against the bright white head torch he was wearing.

Mickey Grainger.

What was he doing here? Then she saw the knife in his hand and understood. Homeless Mickey. Lucky to get a job Mickey. Friendly Mickey. But now who was he?

'Why did you have to hurt him?' She felt heavy, her bones, her organs, her skin, heavy with sadness.

Mickey shrugged. 'He tried to run. I didn't want that.' He sighed. 'It was a gamble, really, involving him, but I thought it was better he should phone you, given your dad's a nutter. Talks bollocks most of the time. I thought pretty boy would convince you to come.' He grinned. 'It worked, didn't it?' He waved the large wicked-looking knife in the air. 'I'm not even sure he saw it coming. He might have heard the swish of the blade, of course.' He ran his thumb along the steel. 'Hmm.' He sucked his finger. 'It went straight through. It may have missed an artery. It certainly missed the bone. It could have got some muscles—'

'Enough,' said Alex, swallowing the bile in her throat.

Mickey shook his head. 'Sorry. I'm upsetting you. Not what I meant to do at all. But you see, once he had lured you here – I like that word, lured, don't you? – I was going to finish him off, but he ran and I didn't get him where I wanted.' He shrugged. 'You win some, you lose some. But, there are no second chances.' 'He stepped forward, knife raised to head height.

'No!' Alex shouted.

Heath had slumped forward. Was he feigning it? It was hard to tell.

Mickey shrugged and lowered the knife. 'He'll probably die of blood loss before morning anyway. And I've got you and your dad.'

Alex struggled to keep her composure, but she had to, she absolutely had to. She balled her hands into fists and kept them rigidly by her sides.

'Where is my dad?'

Mickey cocked his head to one side and pouted. He pointed the knife at her. 'Not far away. He's daft though, isn't he? Not quite all there.' He tapped the side of his head. 'What's wrong with him? Has he always been like that?'

'He's got dementia. Early-onset,' Alex said through gritted teeth. 'If you've hurt him ...'

'Tut, tut, that's a bit unfortunate. So, he'll be as daft as a brush in no time. Still, gotta do it.'

'Got to do what?' Though she knew what he meant. 'I'll ask you again: where is he? What have you done with him?'

'Do you know what?' said Mickey, leaning back against the brick wall and folding his arms, knife still prominent. 'I wanted to do something really special with him. Your dad.' His voice was a sneer. 'Put him in quicksand and watch him go slowly or bury him in the marshes and wait for the tide to roll over him.' He smiled. 'I like being inventive. But then I realized there is no quicksand here, and burying him in the marshes would be too much like hard work.' He rolled his eyes. 'You see the sort of decisions I have to make? Like Jen Tamsett. Actually, that was a bit boring, bit obvious, being hit by a car; but then you do things in different ways and no one connects them, see? Boring, but not

265

as much fun. But then she was boring, wasn't she? Economics. I mean, who cares? Now, what *was* fun was telling Fleet and Daley I would kill members of their families if they didn't top themselves. I enjoyed watching them realize I meant it. Enjoyed the tussle they had with their consciences. Fleet was right on in there, happy to do it. Daley took a bit more persuasion. But then he got cold feet.' He raised his eyes to the sky. 'Fucking idiot.'

'So, you concocted those pictures, the child porn.'

'Sort of.' He pushed himself away from the wall. 'Come on, I haven't got all night.' He waved the knife in the direction of the exit.

'What about Willem?' Keep him talking.

'Ah, he was less pliable.' Mickey's eyes clouded over. 'And I haven't got him yet. Though I will. Now I know where he lives. Thanks to you.'

Dread crawled across her skin. 'You were following me.'

'Yep. Now, where were we? Oh yes, where is Dad?' Again that hateful smile. 'He's on my boat, actually. Do you want to come?'

How could he sound so normal when he was talking about killing people?

Mickey looked up at the sky through the open top of the windmill, just as she had done. 'Nice and dark now, not that it matters. There's no one to hear you scream.' He thought for a moment. 'Hmm, I think that was a line in a film, wasn't it?'

For a wild moment Alex wondered whether she could rush at him, surprise him, wrestle the knife from him.

He fixed her with his eyes. 'Don't even think about it.'

Alex stared at him, keeping her fists clenched, determined not to be intimidated. 'Just take me to Dad.'

'Please.'

She gritted her teeth. 'Please.'

'Your phone.'

Alex's heart sank. It had been too much to hope that Mickey wouldn't think of that.

'Take it out of your pocket and throw it over here. Slowly. Now.'

She did as she was told. Mickey picked it up and put it in his jeans. 'Follow me.'

'Wait. What about Heath?' She looked across at him. He was still slumped against the wall, eyes closed. Was it her imagination, or was his breathing a little shallower, his skin a little more grey? Had he lost too much blood already?

Mickey shrugged. 'Leave him.'

'But—'

'I said leave him. I'll think about it. For now, you come with me.' He grabbed her arm and pulled her through the wooden door, which he pushed shut behind him. 'Here.' He tossed something at Alex. A chain and padlock. 'Fix that to the handle. We don't want Mr Maitland to get a sudden burst of strength and manage to stumble out of there, do we?'

'But he'll die if you leave him there.'

'So?'

'But—'

'Get on with it. The longer you fuck about, the longer your dad is on his own. And my, is he miserable.'

With trembling hands, Alex fixed the chain and padlock to the handle, thinking of Heath alone and cold and losing blood.

Mickey pushed Alex in front of him, along the footpath to the river. She felt the prick of the knife at her neck. Any hint of a breeze had gone, it was as still as the grave. Now she could hear the gentle lapping of the water against the bank. Her palms were sweaty, and her neck was rigid with tension. She tasted fear in her mouth.

'Here we are. Ladies first.'

A solitary boat was moored by the bank.

Mickey saw her looking up and down the river. He chuckled. 'No one else here. No one to rescue you. No one at all.'

'My mother will call the police when I don't come home.' She would, wouldn't she?

'No, she won't. She's too frightened for herself and your daft Dad to do that. She's going to hang on for as long as possible before she does anything at all. It's taken forty years for them to talk about Zoe, so they've got form for procrastinating.' Another grin. 'Enough of this chitter chatter.' He bowed and indicated she should step on board the boat.

Firefly Sister.

He reached past her and unlocked the door.

'After you, milady.'

Alex stepped onboard, wondering if she would ever leave.

34

The boat was as she remembered it, seats either side of the steering wheel, through to a small seating area and compact all-you-need kitchen. A single, dirty plate, with a knife and fork neatly placed side by side, was on the draining board and two open tins on the work surface. She knew further on was the minuscule bathroom and then the bedrooms. Two? A part of her knew she was doing this inventory to keep her mind off what was happening. Another part screeched: what the fuck are you doing? Get out, get out.

Her feet wouldn't move.

She turned.

Mickey was blocking the doorway. 'Sit down, make yourself comfortable. You do remember how comfortable the boat is, after the little guided tour I gave you? That was very amusing.'

She sat and said nothing.

'Now then.' He locked the door of the boat and put the key in his pocket. 'Dad,' he shouted. 'Dad, come on out.'

Her father came out of one of the bedrooms, and walked – not shuffled, Alex noted – towards them. 'I'm here.'

His voice was strong, his eyes sharp. He appeared to be in a window of lucidity. He came towards Alex. 'I'd love to hold you

269

darling, but—' He nodded towards his wrists that were bound in front of him by plastic cable ties.

Alex willed away the tears that had sprung to her eyes.

'Sit down, Anthony,' said Mickey. 'That's your name, isn't it? Anthony? Actually, I think I'll call you Tony. More matey, don't you think? Friendly like.'

'I don't know,' her father said quietly.

'You too.' Mickey waved the knife in Alex's direction.

She perched on the end of the covered bench, her father next to her.

'All right, Tony? Now then,' said Mickey, 'what are we going to do with you two?' He clicked his fingers. 'I know, we'll play a little game, it's called—'

'Mickey,' said Alex, desperately, 'you have been so clever, haven't you?' She tried to smile and felt her mouth obeying her. 'I mean, getting Derek Daley and Roger Fleet to get on that boat, and then kill themselves. Such a great idea. It'll go down in history.'

He chuckled. 'It was clever, wasn't it? And how clever you've been, running around after this story, chasing your tail but eventually figuring things out. So we're all fucking clever around here.'

'I haven't figured everything out. And I don't understand what it's all about. Why you wanted all these people dead.'

'Why?' Mickey sat down opposite. He put the knife carefully down on the table. 'A good question.'

'Who are you?' Her father asked.

'I told you, my name is Mickey.'

Her father turned to Alex. 'You're Alex.' Confusion was back in his eyes.

She gripped his hand, willing him to stay with her. 'Yes, Dad. Your daughter. And I love you. You have to hold on if we're going to get out of here.'

'I'm sure you'll get out of here,' said Mickey, grinning. 'One way or another.'

'You're Alex,' her dad said again. He began tapping his foot,

270

jiggling his leg. 'You're Alex.' It was as if he was trying to fix it in his mind.

She put her hands on top of his. His legs stilled. 'Yes, Dad. I'm Alex. Everything's going to be all right.' She ignored the snort from Mickey. 'As I said, Mickey.' Alex tried to keep the desperation out of her voice. She had to keep him talking, make him see they were people, not objects. She couldn't let him just kill them, not without a fight. Flatter him. 'It was such a clever idea. What made you think of that, I really want to know?'

'Well, now.' Mickey smiled. 'Here's the thing. You think I'm some flaky dude out to murder you for one reason or another.' He cocked his head to one side. 'And you think if you flatter me I'll let you go. Oh no.' He put the knife to his lips as if to kiss it. 'You know what it's all about, don't you? It's all about the woman, Zoe.'

Zoe. Had she been his sister? Much older sister? His mother, aunt, family friend? What did Mickey have to do with Zoe?

'And now you're thinking what did I have to do with Zoe? The girl who died some forty years ago?' He shook his head. 'Nothing. Sweet F.A. Zilch, that's what.'

Alex's heart sank as she realized the implications of what he was saying. 'You're a hired hand,' she said, dully.

He looked annoyed. 'No, not a "hired hand"; I'm much more talented than that. No one "hires" me for anything. Look, I owed someone a favour, so I am putting my talents to good use. That's how loyal I am – if I owe, I pay. And, vice versa, of course.'

'Of course,' said Alex. 'So, let me get this right. Someone asked you to kill Jen Tamsett, Roger Fleet, Derek Daley, Willem Major and my dad.'

Mickey clapped his hands, still keeping hold of the knife. 'Well done. That was easy, wasn't it?'

'And they wanted it done so the deaths wouldn't be connected.'

'Bravo!'

'Who was it, Mickey? Was it Zoe's family?'

271

Mickey waggled his finger. 'No, no, no, you don't get me that easily. You think you can get me to confess all and then escape like they do the films. It ain't gonna happen lady.' He clapped his hand over his mouth. 'See what I did there? An American accent. I should be in films.'

'It's Stu, isn't it? He's behind this.' The Stu who had been at university with them; the man Willem said had disappeared after he left.

Mickey shrugged, though his eyes danced.

'Why did you want me here?'

Mickey grinned. She was beginning to really hate that grin. 'Too interfering. Digging around too much, trying to make connections that weren't there, poking your nose in where it shouldn't go. Like that Heath Maitland.' He leaned towards her, waggled the knife in her face. 'You should have left well alone, then you wouldn't be in this mess. It would be just me and Tony here, wouldn't it, Tone?'

'I ...' Her dad looked so confused she wanted to cry. She bit the inside of her cheek. That wasn't going to happen.

'What are you going to do?'

A laugh from Mickey that grated on her nerves. 'Another couple of deaths on the Broads. Carbon monoxide poisoning from a faulty gas heater this time, I think. Or maybe something's wrong with the engine.' He grinned. 'That sounds good, doesn't it? Has happened a few times. And I know how to make it happen, being an employee of Harper's Holidays. Easy.'

'But it will look suspicious, won't it? More carbon monoxide poisoning and on a Harper's Holidays boat again?' Alex knew she was grasping at straws.

Mickey shrugged. 'Not really. It'll seem that Harper's Holidays don't maintain their boats properly. Besides, that fucker Colin Harper has it coming. Might close his business down with a bit of luck. Or at the very least he'll have Health and Safety crawling all over it. Lord-fucking-bountiful. Gave me a job out of the goodness of his heart? Tight bugger more like. Paid me peanuts because I told him I'd been homeless and that. Honestly, I treat my dogs better than he treated me. And there's a thing – I'll be glad to get back to my dogs. I'm not sure the dog-sitter's up to the job.' He grinned. 'Still, you don't have to worry about that.'

'Why not give us drugs, like you did Daley and Fleet?'

Mickey blew air through his lips. 'Well, their deaths needed to look like suicide, didn't they?' he explained with exaggerated patience. 'And I'm a kind man; I wanted to make it easy for them, that's why they had a nice drug-laced drink. Then I put the barbecue inside the boat for good measure. Belt and braces is the phrase, I believe. Didn't want to have another cock-up.'

'Willem Major, you mean?'

'Like I said, I will get him. But as for you ...' he pointed the knife at Alex. 'I don't have to make it look as though you killed yourselves. I like to mix it up a bit. And the plods might get suspicious if you were full of drugs, might start doing some real detective work. So, for you, an accident will do.'

'But even so, poisoning us with carbon monoxide, the police could put it all together. Know it was connected somehow,' she said, hating the desperation in her voice.

'Maybe we'll have a fire. Destroy all the evidence.' His eyes glittered. 'Yeah, I like that idea.'

Dear God, he was mad. A sadist.

'I don't understand.' Her father's voice was thin, reedy. A bewildered look in his eyes.

'He's going to kill us, Dad. He got Roger Fleet and Derek Daley to kill themselves to save their families.'

'Roger and Derek are dead?'

'Yes.'

'What about Jen and Willem?'

'Jen's dead – a hit-and-run – Willem's alive,' Alex said.

'Roger and Derek dead? And Jen? But I only saw them last week. And who are you?'

273

'I'm Alex. Your daughter,' she said, stroking his hand again.

'Who? I don't have any daughters.'

'Yes, you do, it's Alex here, for fuck's sake.' Mickey was growing impatient. 'Your bloody daughter.'

Her father shook his head. 'But, I don't know her.' He pointed at Alex. 'I don't care if she's alive or dead. Why should I?'

'Because – oh, fuck this.' He stood, put his hands on the table and shouted in her father's face. 'Because she's your daughter, you stupid old man.' Spittle landed on their cheeks.

Her father frowned, bafflement on his features. 'I've just told you: I don't have a daughter.'

Alex could only marvel at her father's calm.

'I've got to go and make a phone call. You—' he gestured at Alex. 'Stand up in the galley.' He picked up the knife. 'Now.'

Alex did as she was told, wondering again if she could rush him. But the space was so confined, anybody could get hurt.

'Turn around, put your hands behind your back, wrists together.'

She felt her wrists being pulled tight, plastic digging into the soft flesh.

'Kneel on the bench.'

Her ankles received the same treatment.

'Now, get over to the steering wheel and sit.'

'I don't want—'

Mickey punched the side of her head. She stumbled across to the steering wheel and sat down, swallowing the vomit in her throat. The boat seemed to rock under her feet. For a moment there were two Mickeys.

Mickey took a roll of duct tape out of his pocket and lashed Alex's wrists to the wheel. She wondered woozily whether his pockets were like Dr Who's Tardis – such a lot seemed to come out of them.

She watched as Mickey tied her father's legs with a plastic tie. 'Don't move, Tone.'

274

Her father shook his head. 'I won't.'

Mickey came over to Alex once again. 'There's no one around to hear you. No boats, no walkers. It's the middle of the night.' He looked at her, thoughtfully. 'But I don't trust you.' His hand shot out and he punched her again.

Her world went black.

35

'Alex, Alex, wake up. Please wake up.'

The voice was piercing her brain. Alex wanted to tell it to go away and to leave her to sleep. That was all she wanted to do, to drift back down into a deep and dreamless state.

'Alex. Darling.'

Darling. Who was that? She opened her eyes one at a time. Her head hurt. She groaned. Deja vu. When she got out of this – if she got out of this – she was definitely going to take self-defence classes.

She lifted her head up to see her father staring at her, tears on his face. She remembered. Mickey Grainger.

She bowed her throbbing head. She felt nauseous. 'Dad.' She wanted to cry.

'It's all right, Alex. Really, it's all right. I do know who you are. I was only pretending. I hoped if he thought I didn't know you he might let you go. But it doesn't work like that, does it?'

'Oh, Dad.' Sadness filled her whole being.

'He's gone outside somewhere. Before he went he blocked up the … the …' He shook his head in frustration. 'I don't know what and then he was fiddling about with the boat's … the boat's …'

'Dad.' Alex knew she had to stay calm. 'Think. The boat's what?'

'The thing that makes it go,' he shouted. 'The thing that makes it go.'

'The engine?'

'Yes, that's right.' He nodded vigorously. 'The engine. Yes.' He slumped back on the bench. 'My head hurts. And I feel sick.' He began to whimper.

'Don't worry, Dad. We'll get out of here.' Though how?

The cabin was spinning around, slowly. Her tongue was thick in her mouth. The effects of carbon monoxide poisoning. Of course he meant to kill both of them. Blearily she wondered if the drugs had got Fleet and Daley before the fumes. Or if – stop it. Think. She shook her head, trying to clear it. Think.

She twisted as much as her taped hands would allow and looked her father in the eye. 'Listen to me, Dad. Hold your hands up high in the air. As high as you can.'

He did as he was told. 'I can't see you properly, Alex. I don't feel well.' He blinked hard.

'I know you don't, but hold on, Dad, try and do as I say. That's it,' she said, encouragingly. How long had she been unconscious? How much time did they have before Mickey came back? 'Now, bring your arms down fast, jerking your hands and elbows apart. Go on, do it now.'

Her father made a feeble attempt at it. Nothing happened. 'That hurt,' he said.

Alex gritted her teeth. How much time did they have?

'I know. But you've got to try again, Dad. Arms up, then down, fast and hard. Fast down and pull apart. Now.'

Her father looked at her, then brought his arms down fast, pulling his hands and elbows apart as she'd instructed.

He cried out in pain.

The cable ties snapped.

Alex breathed a sigh of relief.

'That hurt again. A lot,' said her father. Then he smiled. 'But it worked. Clever girl. Where did you learn that?'

She smiled weakly. 'The *Daily Mail*, for my sins.' And a few practice sessions with Malone, which ended up with them laughing until they cried, but he had wanted her to be able to break free of cable ties 'just in case'. She turned her attention back to her father. 'Now, we haven't got much time. Go and see if there's a sharp knife in one of the drawers.'

'My legs are tied.'

'Hobble across, Dad.'

Her father stood up and lurched around the edge of the table, before launching himself towards the drawers. He held on to the work top and swayed. 'Now my head hurts.'

'I know, Dad. Concentrate. A knife, scissors, anything sharp in the drawer.'

The room had stopped spinning, but the feeling of nausea was almost overwhelming.

Agonizingly slowly it seemed to Alex, her father inched open the drawer. 'Here,' he said, brandishing a pair of scissors, 'cutting things.'

'Well done, Dad. Cutting things.' She laughed, though there were tears on her cheeks. 'Now cut the tie round your ankles then come to me.'

He looked down at his feet. 'Tie?'

'Around your ankles. At the bottom of your feet.'

'Feet?' That bewildered look.

Alex wanted to scream at him. The dizziness was getting worse. 'Come on, Dad, concentrate. Your feet, Dad, your feet.'

He smiled. 'I can't reach my feet.' He stopped smiling. 'I think I'm going to be sick.'

'Cut the ties, Dad. Sit on the seat, bend down and use the scissors.'

At last her father did as she asked.

'Now come here and cut my hands free.'

He went over to Alex and used the scissors to saw through the duct tape binding her hands to the steering wheel. She wanted to scream at him to hurry, hurry, but she knew if she did her dad would probably stop or cry. She had to keep calm. At last her hands were free.

'Snippety snap,' he said, before vomiting on the floor.

'Snippety snap, Dad,' she said wearily, taking the scissors out of his hands and freeing her ankles, the sour smell of vomit wafting around her.

She stood up and immediately the cabin began to spin again. She put the scissors on the table. She couldn't think, she couldn't order her thoughts.

'Alex. Should we leave?' Her father stood in front of her.

'Yes, Dad, we should.'

They put their arms around each other and stumbled towards the sliding door. Locked. Alex lifted her foot and smashed the wood as hard as she could. The door flew open.

They fell out of the boat together.

36

Alex and her father gulped down the fresh air to the sound of a slow handclap.

Mickey. Holding a gun in his hand this time. No way they could rush him as he was bound to fire off one shot at least, and he was so close he wouldn't miss. Alex couldn't take that chance.

She sank to her knees. The fresh air was helping to clear her head, but no new ideas were coming to her. She wanted to curl up on the ground and sleep.

'Well done,' Mickey said with a smile. 'Managed to escape. I admire that. Daddy's still got it then? A parent's instinct?'

'He's still got it.' She tried to ignore the headache, the vertigo, the nausea. 'Is that the problem? Your parents didn't care about you?'

'Psychologist are we now?' he sneered.

'No. I wondered why, that was all.'

'Oh, you don't need to try and analyse me. I'm an ordinary boy from an ordinary family. I turned bad, that's my story. So you worked out what it's all about yet?' He leered at her. 'I told you, I owed a favour. And there was cash involved. Tut, tut, what are we going to do with you both now?'

'I'll go back,' her father said on his knees. 'Onboard the boat. Stay there. But you have to let her go.'

'Really? That is good news, sort of.'

'Dad, don't—'

'Be quiet, Alex,' her father glared at her. 'I have to do something right in this life of mine. I must do it.'

'But—'

'Alex, please. Let me do this one thing for you, for my family.' He looked at Mickey. 'But you will have to let her go.'

'Of course I will,' smiled Mickey. 'How could I not after that lovely little speech? Let's jump back onto the boat and we'll let the little girl run, shall we?' He grinned at Alex.

She knew, as he did, there was no way she was going to run. She had to help her father. Besides, where would she run to? And she was so weak, her legs were like jelly.

'Come on, old man.' Mickey gestured to her father. 'Let's move.'

Her father smiled bravely at Alex, then turned.

'No, Dad.' She put out her hand to stop him.

'Alex. It's all right. Please.'

She looked into his face. So familiar, yet so unknown.

Mickey stood behind him. Her father stumbled. Mickey put out his free hand to steady him, the gun pointing up in the air. In that split second her father whirled round and jabbed Mickey in the stomach. Once. Twice. Three times.

Her father stepped back, panting. There was blood over the front of his shirt and on his hands. There was blood on Mickey too. What had he done?

Mickey looked down at the blood spreading across his stomach with astonishment.

He staggered, before dropping the gun and sinking to his knees.

'You left the cutting things on the table. I picked them up. Did I do the right thing?'

She looked at Mickey, at the scissors sticking out of him.

'Yes,' said Alex. 'You did absolutely the right thing.'

Around her, the sky was getting lighter and the dawn chorus was beginning. Alex and her father sat on the damp ground, arms around each other.

37

Alex reached out her hand. Her father was asleep, or unconscious. She needed to stretch her back, her arms, her legs. Her head was still throbbing, her clothes sopping wet from the dew. The sun was casting an orange light in the sky, and she could hear the gentle slap of the water against the river bank and the tuneful call of birds. She wished she knew what they were.

How long had she been out of it? Not too long, she judged.

She crawled over to Mickey and felt inside his pocket for her phone, trying to ignore his dead eyes and the odd early morning insect that was beginning to investigate the body. Then she sat back on her heels, thinking for a moment before making herself curl her hand around the handles of the scissors.

She shook her father awake.

He sat up and looked around. 'Where are we? What am I doing here? Why are my clothes wet?' He started to cry.

Alex put her arms back around him. 'Sssh, Dad, it's okay. We're safe now.'

He pushed her away, his face, creased from sleep, contorted with fear. 'Who are you? I don't know you.' He was shivering. 'I don't know you at all.'

'I'm Alex.'

'Alex, I don't know an Alex. Where's Sarah? I want my Sarah.'

Alex grabbed his hand, and didn't let it go when he tried to pull it away. 'Dad, it's all right.'

'Who's he?' His shaking finger pointed at Mickey on the ground, his eyes staring up at the sky, blood congealed on his abdomen, the stainless steel handles of the scissors glinting in the light.

'Nobody. He's nobody.' She stood, trying to ignore the aching in her body, and held her hand out to her father. 'We have to get up and start walking, Dad.'

'Don't call me Dad. I'm not your dad.' He folded his arms and looked away from her.

An unbearable feeling of loss swept over Alex. For a few short hours she'd had her father back, now he had retreated into the lace-like holes in his mind.

'Alex, Alex, are you okay?' She heard shouts from not far away. She looked up and blinked slowly. Was she really seeing ...?

Sasha and Lin were running towards them, panting, their faces red with exertion. They came to a stop.

'Are you okay? Alex? Dad? Oh my God, there's blood on your clothes.' Sasha began to dab at her shirt.

Alex looked down at herself and saw the dried blood. Mickey's? Or Heath's? Heath, how could she have forgotten him? 'It doesn't matter,' she said, gently removing Sasha's hand. 'It's not mine or Dad's. It's probably Heath's.'

'The journalist?' Lin wanted to know.

'Yes. He's back there, in the Abbey. He's hurt.' She started to run.

'Wait,' called Sasha, 'I'm coming with you.'

'No,' said Lin, her hand on Sasha's shoulder. 'You stay with your dad. I'll go.' She handed Sasha her phone. 'Call the air ambulance. Now. Do it.'

When they got to the ruin, Alex looked around for a large rock so she could smash the padlock. She hit it once, twice. It didn't budge. How hard could it be? It always worked in the movies.

'Here.' Lin pushed her out of the way. 'Let me.'

Lin attacked the padlock as though she had done it many times before. It gave way, and Alex rushed into the ruin.

Heath was in the corner where she had left him. He hadn't moved. His skin was cold and waxy, and his breathing laboured, but she could feel the small flutter of a pulse on his neck and there was no more fresh blood. 'Thank God. Thank God. Stay with me, Heath. Don't let me down now.' Tears tracked down her cheeks.

'Alex. Alex.'

She became aware of Lin behind her, speaking to her.

'We'd better get him out of here. It's too cold and damp. Can you help me lift him?'

Alex nodded. 'Yes.'

Lin began to talk. 'Heath, Heath. Wake up. We need to move you, but you have to help.'

Heath groaned and opened his eyes. He began to shiver. 'Alex,' he whispered.

'Sssh, keep your strength,' said Alex. 'We must get you out of here. The air ambulance is on its way.'

'Alex—'

'Not another word.'

Somehow they managed to get Heath out of the ruins and into the open air. They laid him gently on the ground. The sun was fully risen now, and was beginning to warm the earth. Overhead, a skein of geese flew across the sky.

'I'll go and get a blanket from the boat,' said Lin.

Sasha came over to her, leading their father by the hand. Coaxing him along, like a mother to a child. Sasha put her free arm around Alex, and Alex laid her head on her sister's shoulder.

'How is he?' asked Sasha, looking at Heath.

'I don't know.'

Heath had lost consciousness again and, if anything, his skin was even more grey as if the life was draining out of him.

'Who is he?' Sasha pointed a shaking finger at the boat where Mickey's body lay.

Alex sighed. 'He was Mickey Grainger. He worked for Harper's Holidays, but it was a cover so he could get to Derek Daley and Roger Fleet.'

Sasha's mouth dropped open. 'He killed them?'

'Yep. And Jen Tamsett. And Willem Major's family.'

'And now he's dead.'

'Yes. Now he's dead.'

'So, Dad is safe?'

'I hope so, Sash, I really hope so.' She didn't want to voice her fear to Sasha that, though Mickey was the killer and the brains behind the methods of killing, there was someone else involved. Mickey had said he was the hired hand, so who had hired him?

'Did you—?'

'I stabbed him,' said Alex. 'And I would do it again.'

'It's easy when you're threatened,' said Sasha.

Alex watched Lin as she came back from a boat which was moored behind Firefly Sister.

'Here. This'll help.' Lin covered Heath with a blanket. 'And you, Alex? How are you?'

'Fine.' She gazed at Lin. 'Fine. Where did you get the boat from? Too early to hire one.'

'The boat?' She glanced back over her shoulder. 'Oh, that. It belongs to a friend. An old friend. He lets me use it when he's abroad. He works abroad. And in return I keep an eye on it.'

'You never told me.'

'It never came up. Here, I brought some tea for you. Hot and sweet.' She undid the top of a thermos, poured out the liquid and handed it to Alex. 'And one for your dad.'

'Sit down, Dad,' said Sasha gently.

'I want to go home,' he said.

'We will. Soon,' said Alex, pushing away the thought that Lin had over-explained about the boat. 'We have to wait for the police. They'll be here any moment. And they'll take us back.'

Her father sat down. Sasha sat next to him, her arm still around him.

'I probably won't hang around,' said Lin. 'You know.' She glanced around. Was she nervous?

Why did Lin want to disappear so quickly?

You are my enemy, she thought suddenly.

It was the smell that had alerted her. Being beside Lin in the Abbey, helping carry Heath, she'd caught a whiff of something acrid and sharp. It had tugged at her memory.

It came to her now, the thought slamming into her chest. The intruder. They had smelled of something acrid and sharp, and she didn't think it was Chanel. It was the smell of paint cleaner. Turps? White spirit? Something an artist would use.

'How did you find us, Lin?' Alex nursed her tea. She moved away from Sasha and her father, kept her voice low.

'Sasha phoned me in the early hours. Your mum was worried about you because she hadn't heard anything. Sasha insisted on calling me, and thank Christ she did.'

'But steering a boat at night when you're not supposed to even be on the Broads, you must be quite experienced. Were you asleep when Sasha called?'

'Luckily I wasn't. I was finishing off a painting.'

A beat. 'Who are you, Lin?'

'What on earth do you mean?' Lin watched her with a guarded smile.

Alex tried to think what to say. She wanted to get it right, but her head was muddy with fatigue. 'It seems to me,' she began, 'that you're altogether too calm and collected. You came here to rescue us as if you're quite used to that sort of thing. And you broke into my house. Why?'

'Too calm and collected?' She raised her eyebrows. 'Not inside,

Alex. I'm trying to be brave for you and your dad and for Sasha. That poor girl was scared shitless that something might have happened to you. So if I'm not giving off the right signals, then I'm very sorry.'

It sounded so plausible, but Alex was convinced Lin had been her intruder.

'But you did break into my house.'

'What on earth do you mean?' But her smile wasn't quite so certain now.

'Drop the pretence, Lin. Tell me who you really are. What are you doing, befriending me and my family? Are you a journalist who wants a scoop? Is it Sasha you're really after?'

'Sasha? No. No.'

'Then what?'

Lin pushed her hands into her pockets and blew out air through pursed lips. 'Ah, fuck. I told him you wouldn't fall for it.'

'Who? For what?'

'Malone.'

'*Malone?*' She couldn't speak, couldn't think. What was this? 'Who are you really? And don't give me any more bullshit.'

'It really doesn't matter who I am.'

Alex searched Lin's closed face. 'Tell me about Malone, then.'

'He asked me to keep an eye on you.'

'*An eye on me.*' She closed her eyes. So weary, oh so weary.

'Malone saw pictures on the BBC online news. It was of all the people standing on the staithe waiting for the boat with the bodies to be brought back to shore. Do you remember?'

'Of course I do,' she snapped. 'Dillingham Broad. It wasn't that long ago.'

'He saw a member of his wife's family in that picture.'

'Gillian's family?'

'Correct. Her family are—'

'Gangsters, terrorists.' If Alex had felt weary before, she now felt dead on her feet.

288

'Yes. One of them was watching you, and Malone was worried you could get hurt.'

'And Malone could see all this from an image on an online story, could he?' Could she believe her?

'Yes.'

'So, he sent you to babysit.'

'In a manner of speaking.'

'But you were in Sole Bay way before that.'

'Malone wanted to keep you safe. He knew someone from his ex-wife's family would try to get to you, to put pressure on you, so asked me to get to know you. Be a bit of protection for you.'

'I did sometimes feel that someone was following me,' said Alex, slowly.

'That'll be it.'

'But why did you break into my house?'

Lin blushed. 'Ah. You won't like it.'

'Go on.'

'Malone asked me to make sure that there was nothing in your house that could lead anybody to him. Any papers, notes, anything you'd printed out about him. Maybe phone numbers you had.'

Alex was so angry she could hardly speak. 'He wanted to eradicate any sign of a relationship with me.'

'I wouldn't say that.'

'Then what would you say?'

'I would say he wanted to protect you. And if I could break into your house, then his enemies could too, again, and find stuff about him that could lead them to him.'

Did she believe Lin? Perhaps she had no option.

'How did you know it was me?' Lin asked.

'You smelt of turps or something similar. And just now too.'

'Ah.' She winced. 'Mistake. Getting too comfortable with you, that was the trouble.'

'It was all a lie, wasn't it? Your friendship with me? I already

289

know you don't have a brother in Craighill. You made that up to get close to me.'

'Maybe.' For the first time, Lin couldn't meet her eyes.

Who was this woman?

'Malone doesn't trust me on my own.'

'He cares about you.' Lin looked out over the water. 'You're lucky.' There was a wistful note to her voice.

'And what happened to whoever was supposed to be watching me?' She knew she sounded sarcastic, but she couldn't help it.

'Let's just say he won't be bothering you again. Ever.'

'Right.'

'Look, I must go. Before—'

'The police arrive?'

Lin gave a small smile. 'Something like that.'

'If you speak to Malone …' she hesitated.

'Yes?'

'Tell him …' Tell him what? Was there anything left to say? 'Nothing. Tell him nothing.'

Lin squeezed her arm. 'Probably for the best.'

Alex's stomach churned as she watched Lin hurry to her boat. Somehow, it all seemed very final.

She went over to check on Heath. He was still breathing. She looked up into the sky. Where was that helicopter?

'Everything all right, Alex?' Her sister spoke quietly so as not to disturb their dozing father.

Alex smiled grimly. 'I hope so, Sasha, I really do.'

She took her phone out of her pocket. Mickey had switched it off. She pressed the 'on' button.

As it powered up, the screen became full of text messages. She scrolled through them. Gus. They were all from Gus. And one from Heath. All at once she remembered that Heath had said he'd sent her a text, but she'd never got it. There must have been something wrong with her phone – the last message she'd had was from Gus saying he was going to let her know when he was coming home. Always turn it off and back on again if you think something's wrong, that's what her son always told her. And she hadn't done that. But Gus had been in touch with her. Relief swelled in her chest as she scrolled through some of the messages.

Been delayed. Will be home on Friday. Will let you know.

Friday. Today. She was weak with relief. Gus hadn't let her down. She'd always known he wouldn't. She must learn to trust him more, not to try and keep him so close.

Definitely Friday. Early morning. Friend picking me up and we'll drive up to Sole Bay.

You okay Mum?

Message me

Signal weak here. Will phone when I land

Looking forward to seeing you

She was about to dial 999 when she heard the helicopter in the sky, and the gentle chug chug of a boat on the water. The cavalry were coming.

Then her phone rang out in the clear air.

'Hi Ma, I've just landed.'

'Gus.' She smiled, shaky with relief.

'I kept sending you messages, but you didn't reply. Is everything okay?' He sounded worried.

'Everything's fine. It was a – um – glitch on my phone. Nothing to worry about.'

'Good. I've got a lot to tell you. About Ibiza. About Martha.'

'Martha?'

'She's great, Mum. So grounded. I'm dying for you to meet her. She wants to meet you too. I know you'll love her as much as I do.'

'So, she's bringing you to Sole Bay?'

'Yeah. We might stop off for some breakfast. Is that okay?'

'Of course,' she said, keeping her voice buoyant. 'Aunty Sasha is looking forward to seeing you.'

'Aunty Sasha?' He sounded surprised. 'She's home? Great.

Anything else been happening? Besides Aunty Sasha coming home?'

'"Anything else"?' Alex smiled into the phone. 'No, not really.' Then she remembered how she hated that her parents had kept so much from her over the years. 'As a matter of fact, Gus, quite a lot has been happening, but I'll tell you all about it when I see you.'

'Okay, Ma.' There was laughter in the background, and Alex could tell Gus was only half listening to her.

'See you soon, love.'

'Yeah. See ya, Ma.'

Maybe she would tell him later she had been talking to him with a dead body and a badly wounded man nearby.

The noise of the helicopter was much louder now. Thank goodness Heath would be getting the help he needed.

A police cruiser swung in behind Firefly Sister.

Sasha and her father were fully awake as the helicopter landed in a field about fifty metres away. A doctor and a paramedic climbed out.

Two police officers stepped gingerly off the cruiser.

DI Berry and DS Logan. Didn't they ever sleep?

38

Cambridge 1976

All I could hear was the thumping of my heart, my ragged breathing. Then a keening. Jen, her mouth open, snot and tears streaking her cheeks. Roger, standing there, just standing, shaking. Stu, slumped against the wall, his hands hiding his face. Derek, shock on his face. His fingers on his ever-present camera. Not now, I thought. Please.

And Willem, impassive, holding a once-white handkerchief to his bleeding nose.

I made myself look at Zoe. She lay on the corner of the tiled hearth, motionless. Blood, more black than red, seeping from the back of her head, forming a pool around her.

Sweat trickled down my back.

No one spoke.

Willem was the first to move. 'She's dead,' he said, his voice nasal.

We all looked at him. All of us hoping he had an answer, any answer, as to what we should do.

But I knew what we should do. 'We must call the police,' I said. 'Leave everything here as it is and go and find a phone box.

293

Unless there's a phone here?' I looked around, not really seeing anything.

'And then Dixon of Dock Green will come and pat your shoulder and say "there, there, don't you worry, lad." Yeah. Of course. Good call,' said Willem, tipping his head back, trying to staunch the bleeding.

'Well, what else?' I was defiant, but wanting to cry at the same time.

Willem waved the bloodied hanky. 'What land are you living in? Cloud cuckoo or what?'

Stu was sobbing. Messy tears. He sank to his knees and cradled her head in his arms.

'Who was she? What was she doing here anyway?' whispered Roger, who was as pale as snow.

'Her name was Zoe. She was Stu's girlfriend.' My mind flashed back to the Michaelmas term and Willem screwing Rachel. 'You did it deliberately, didn't you, Willem? You knew Stu had a girlfriend and you flattered her and seduced her. What did you do then? Spin her a story to get her out here and wait for you? Then you brought Stu here. Why?'

But I knew why. Nausea rose in my throat. He hadn't forgiven Stu for reporting him to the authorities, for getting one over on him, for having a good-looking girlfriend. He had known Stu would be in the pub. Jealousy and revenge. Again, he had manipulated all of us. I held my hands by my sides, fingers stiff and straight to stop myself from shaking. 'You shit.'

Willem looked at me. 'The question now is what are we going to do?'

'I said, we must call the police.' Why was no one listening to me?

'And ruin all our lives? I don't think so.'

'What do you mean?' My head had started to ache.

'What's going to happen when PC Plod gets here? He'll arrest us all. That's it. Careers over. Life over.'

'We were trying to stop her falling.' Jen's voice was small and faint.

'The police won't see it that way,' Willem said, dabbing at his nose. The bleeding had almost stopped. 'Think of the publicity. The shame. We have been complicit in a girl's death.'

'It was an accident,' I said.

'Really? Are you sure about that?'

I rubbed my forehead. What was he trying to say?

'Look.' Willem at his most reasonable. 'Zoe came from Scotland. She had no family as far as I'm aware – like Barnardo's Boy there.' He nodded at Stu. 'She worked hand to mouth – a bar job here, waitressing there.'

'What's your point?'

'No one's going to miss her. That's my point.'

'"No one's going to miss her"?' I echoed.

'Exactly. So, we bury her.'

'"Bury her"?'

'Stop sounding like a parrot. Yes, we bury her and that's it. All done with. We can get on with our lives. Trust me, it's the best thing. She's dead. Let's not ruin all our lives over some chit of a girl.'

'Willem's right,' Derek piped up. 'My parents will cut off my allowance.'

'I want to study in America,' said Jen, biting her lip. 'I've wanted to do that all my life.'

'Even you, Jen,' I said, a big stone lodging in my stomach. 'Roger?'

He blanched. 'I don't know.'

'And you,' said Willem to me. 'You. What are your parents going to say, going to think, when their golden boy is arrested for murder? The press camped out on their doorstep. Pictures in the paper. No one giving you a job because you'll be tainted. Can you put them through that? Make them pariahs in that parochial place you call home? Can you?'

I knew I should walk out of there, call the police, do the right thing. I couldn't be sure what had happened. Zoe had fallen. But had one of us pushed her by accident in our attempts to stop Stu from hitting Willem? Was Willem covering himself? It was all muddled in my head. I knew Willem wanted to be in control, to make us waltz to his tune. I knew all that. But his words about my parents had hit home.

'And so we do it and then we don't talk about it ever again. Never. We don't talk to each other. We go our separate ways. Can you do that?'

Do it. Bury a girl like she was nothing.

I nodded my head and said okay and consigned myself to feeling guilty for the rest of my life. A guilt that would soon overwhelm me.

I hadn't realized how hard it was to bury a human being. How slippery the plastic sheeting would become as the rain that had been threatening finally fell while we tried to carry it – her – to the car. How heavy a bag of gravel was. How difficult it would be to manoeuvre the body into the car in the darkness. The limbs. The torso. Her head. How physical and tiring it was to dig a hole deep enough in the old abandoned churchyard we found.

We all took turns to shovel the soil over her body. I was the first.

39

The sun shone through the window and dust motes danced in its beams. The room was hot, the air heavy. She had to work to catch her breath.

'So,' said Alex, addressing Heath, 'I'm pleading self-defence over Mickey's killing, and my lawyer says I've got a watertight case. Even Logan and Berry seemed impressed – apparently the Met has been trying to get him on all sorts for years: kidnapping, corruption, protection rackets, people smuggling, the lot. And it only took a pair of scissors to get him.' She wiped away tears that seemed to have sprung from nowhere. 'Actually, I think the cops are pissed off because he's dead. No grandstanding trial. And he had absolutely nothing to do with Zoe.' She leaned in close to him. 'Can I tell you a secret?' she breathed in his ear. 'I didn't kill him. But don't tell anyone.'

She drew back and looked at him. How peaceful he seemed, lying there on the hospital bed, his face smooth and untroubled. But then there were the wires, the monitors, the bleeps. The tube down his throat, the antiseptic smell, the curtains around the bed, the quiet chat of nurses and doctors.

She sat back down in the chair and took hold of his hand. Although the wound in his shoulder had not been serious, he had lost a great deal of blood. And then the infections had set in. In the wound. In his chest. His lungs. It had been touch and go for a while, but the doctors said he was over the worst.

But he hadn't woken up. Not yet.

'You were trying to tell me something when you were in the Abbey, weren't you? When I think back, I could see it in your eyes. What was it? Had you found out something? Was that why you disappeared? And why were you there anyway?' She sighed. 'Oh, Heath, I wish you could talk to me.'

The monitors bleeped in reply.

'Willem Major's dead. Swept out to sea, apparently. It could have been suicide. Or not. They couldn't tell. He died of head injuries.' She took a couple of the grapes she had brought and popped them in her mouth. 'You don't mind, do you? Only, you're not eating them and I don't want them to spoil—' Her throat closed up again. 'Sorry, sorry. I promised myself I wouldn't cry. I'm trying to be normal.' She swallowed. Hard. 'Anyway, I gather his daughter's now doing voluntary work somewhere in Africa, so she's safe. If it was suicide, I think he was waiting for that.'

There. A twitch. Had she imagined it? She looked at Heath's hand held in hers. Had he squeezed her fingers slightly? She held her breath, but nothing. She had probably imagined it.

She sighed. 'I wish I knew what was going on in that head of yours.' She got up and walked over to the window. The view was over an inner courtyard garden. There were two people sitting on a bench, both hooked up to IV drips. One of them was a young man who didn't look any older than her son.

She sat down, and stroked the back of his hand again, avoiding the wires and the tubes going into his body. 'You'll be glad to know I wrote the feature for Bud. Sent it to him this morning.'

She frowned. 'A student called Stu was also there the day Zoe died. But I don't know much more about him. He disappeared not long after leaving university. Willem said he hadn't been part of their "set". That sounds awful, doesn't it? Like schoolboys. Though I suppose they weren't much more than that at the time, were they?' She began to chew the skin at the side of her thumb. 'I don't know, Heath. Willem thought Stu might have been behind it all, but I can't find him anywhere. I ran my theory past Bud, but he seemed to agree with the police. That Mickey was some sort of crazed killer with a grudge against Derek and Roger. And Willem. They have found evidence that he had been responsible for the arson at Willem's house. So, the cops are trying to find out what the grudge might have been. By the way, Bud's very keen to hear how you're doing, so perhaps he'll forgive you for going AWOL. May even get your job back.' She grinned. 'That would be good, wouldn't it?'

Heath's eyes were open, looking straight at her. She gasped.

At that moment the curtains around Heath's bed were snatched back and Mimi, Heath's pregnant girlfriend tottered in.

'He opened his eyes,' Alex said, excited, but her heart was sinking slightly at the same time. She and Mimi hadn't hit it off at all since meeting in the relatives waiting room at the hospital after Heath had been brought in. Mimi blamed Alex for everything that had happened to him.

'What are you doing here?' she hissed now. 'I thought I told you I didn't want you here?' She put the pile of magazines she'd been carrying down on the locker by the bed. *Men's Health. GQ. Wallpaper.* Very sophisticated.

'I know,' said Alex. 'I had to talk to him. But he opened his eyes. That's progress, don't you think?'

'Well they're closed now.'

'But—'

'Thank you. I'll let the doctor know. They said this might happen and it would be a good sign. But he's not out of the woods yet. Thanks to you.'

'Mimi, I've told you how sorry I am, but it was Heath's choice to help me with the story.'

'I don't want to know. Now. If you don't mind?' She tapped her foot impatiently, cradling her bump.

'Of course, of course.' Alex jumped out of the chair. 'You sit down. I was about to go anyway.'

'Good. Heath doesn't need you. He's got me.'

And she was going to eat him alive, thought Alex, as she hurried down the corridors of the hospital and out into the sun and fresh air. If he got better, that was. Please, let him get better.

Her phone rang.

'Is that Alex Devlin? It's Laurie here. Laurie Cooke. I don't know if you remember me—?'

'Of course I do,' said Alex, walking across the car park to her car. 'How are things?'

'Oh, you know.'

And she did know. When the tabloids, and even some of the broadsheets, got hold of a story with any whiff of paedophilia it drained every last drop out of it, and then some.

'Alex, the reason I phoned is because I found something among Dad's papers here at the farmhouse that, well, could you come and have a look? I don't really want to talk on the phone. You know?'

She did know. Despite all the phone hacking scandals and inquiries there were still some unscrupulous journalists around. 'I'll be there as soon as I can.'

'So, what have we got?'

Alex was sitting at the table in the large kitchen of Derek Daley's holiday home, papers spread out in front of her.

'Look,' said Laurie, pushing a sheaf of papers towards her. 'I found these. They go back years.'

Alex picked up the first sheet. Bank statements. 'I don't want to pry—'

'No, no,' said Laurie, impatiently. 'It's okay. It's an account that neither Mum nor I knew about. I don't expect you to go through

300

them all, but if you look, at least a thousand pounds a month has been deposited in it in the last few years, sometimes a lot more. It was less before that. It's been going on for years.'

Alex took a closer look.

'Can you see?' said Laurie. 'I looked it up, and those deposits are from a bank based in the Cayman Islands.'

An offshore bank account – perfect for keeping secrets.

Another entry caught her eye. A hefty sum from Worldwide Listening. She thought for a minute. The Irish radio station that had been bought out a few years earlier by The Lewes Press Group that owned *The Post*. Was that right? She would have to check. Could be innocuous: Daley could have done some work for them. A hell of a lot of work, which seemed strange as Bud and Daley were not exactly friends. Her interest was growing with the tingling in her fingers. 'Your mum doesn't know anything about this?'

'No, she left all the finances to Dad. Stupid, isn't it, in this day and age? And then there was this.' She pushed another piece of paper over to Alex. 'I found it in his email sent items from a couple of months ago on that hidden iPad I told you about. I printed it out to show you.'

To: Middlemarch
From: Double Dee
Subject: Upping the ante
I hear things are moving. Terms are changing.

'And that's it?'

Laurie nodded. 'Nothing else. No reply. That was the last of the messages.'

'And this was sent before your dad was booked onto the boat?'

'Yes,' said Laurie, 'I thought it was strange because the police told me that this Mickey character had been responsible for Dad's death. Then I found these emails. What do you think it means?'

Alex frowned. 'It certainly looks like your dad was blackmailing this Middlemarch somehow.' She frowned. 'I wonder what that was all about?'

'So, could Middlemarch have been Mickey, and he was taking his revenge?'

Alex shook her head. 'He said he was working for someone else, and I believe him.'

'So, it's the someone else who is Middlemarch?'

'Maybe.'

'Perhaps,' said Laurie, 'they're not connected?'

'Perhaps not. But then again—'

What was she missing? She picked up her bag. 'I'm going to go home and dig around a bit. See if I can find anything. In the meantime, you ought to give that stuff to the police.' She got to the door. 'One other thing – did your dad ever mention anyone called Stu Eliot?'

Laurie thought for a minute, her brow furrowed. 'I don't think so, no.'

Alex left.

40

It proved surprisingly easy to find out about Derek Daley's business affairs on the web. She learned that as well as the magazine he had owned and edited, Daley had owned three others. And they were barely keeping afloat, yet Daley hadn't given up his lavish lifestyle. He was getting cash from somewhere.

Blackmail money.

But who was he blackmailing? Who was Middlemarch? And why him – if it was a him – in particular?

She delved further, thinking about the company that was on the bank statements Laurie had shown her.

As she had thought, Worldwide Listening was a media group based in Ireland. It was the owner of several Irish local radio stations and had been bought out a few years ago by The Lewes Press Group that included titles such as *The World This Week*, the *Buckinghamshire Times* and *The Post*. Right. So where did that take her? The Lewes Press Group was owned by Bud. But she hadn't realized quite how much he'd acquired.

What was she missing? She thought about Heath and how he had taken himself off when he was with the business unit. Perhaps he had been doing some digging and had come across something significant. Had he been trying to tell her something that night he rescued her from Lin? She closed her eyes, remembering his reluctance to talk to her, his tired and worried demeanour. Would he have told her more if she had asked the right questions?

'Hey, Lexi, got time for a bit of decorating?' Sasha leaned on the doorjamb of Alex's study.

Alex rubbed her eyes. She'd had too much of looking at computers lately, but she did want to delve a bit further into Derek Daley's affairs. And quite possibly those of Bud. 'Sasha, I've—' She waved a hand at the screen.

'Come on, Lexi, you did say you would, and I've sort of screwed up the courage now to clear it out. Gently put away the memories.'

Alex looked up at her sister and saw the pleading and vulnerability on her face. This was important. Daley could wait.

At first, taking the old photographs of Sasha's twins off the wall had been heartbreaking and painful, but Sasha was determined. 'I want to remember them with love,' she said, 'not sadness. I know it was all down to me—'

'You were ill,' said Alex quietly. 'You didn't know what you were doing.'

Sasha nodded. 'I know. I've learned to accept that. You know, I can't remember anything about that night, the night they drowned.'

'Sash.'

'No, I want to talk about them. I want to see them in my head again. I've spent far too many years thinking I could forget, but I know I can't and I don't want to.'

For the next few hours Alex and Sasha worked side by side, clearing and cleaning the room, while talking about her children and reliving some of the happy memories.

'We'll get some new frames and put the best pictures of the twins in them, Sasha. Happy pictures. And one or two of you with them.'

'I'd like that.'

'Look,' said Alex, pulling a box from behind one of Sasha's old chairs, 'here are some of your books.'

Sasha opened up the flaps and peered inside. 'Ha. These are from one of my self-improvement phases, you know, reading some of the classics. Trying to gloss over the fact I did nothing with my life.' She pulled one out. '*The Call of the Wild* by Jack London.'

Alex snatched it from her hand. 'I wondered where that had got to. Did you steal it from my bookcase?'

'Maybe,' said Sasha, colouring.

'What else of mine have you got in here?' Alex began to root through the box.

'Nothing. I don't think.' She grinned, pushed her hair out of her eyes.

'Bet you have. Let me see. Hmm. *Thérèse Raquin. Nana. Germinal.*'

'Yeah, well, I was going through a French phase.'

'*War and Peace.* Dostoyevsky. Your Russian phase.'

'Yep.'

'*Wuthering Heights. Jane Eyre. Middlemarch—*'

'My English phase. Did you know that Charlotte Brontë first published under the pen name Currer Bell?'

'Yes, yes,' said Alex. 'And George Eliot was really Mary Anne Evans and—' She stopped. Could that be it? Could that be bloody well it?

'Alex? Are you all right? You've gone a funny colour.'

Alex scrambled up from the floor. 'I'll be back later,' she said. 'I promise. I've got to go and look something up.'

Her head was buzzing as her fingers flew over the keyboard.

Bud Evans. Stu Eliot. Mary Anne Evans. George Eliot. Surely it was too far-fetched, and she was putting two and two together and making considerably more than four? But Bud blowing hot and cold over the story about Daley and Fleet's deaths. Wanting to know what was going on, then demanding she drop the story.

His odd treatment of Heath. Then Heath on the business unit and disappearing. Business. Money. Bud.

Okay. So Bud had begun his career on the *Falmouth Packet*. Went to the *Birmingham Post*. Then the *Daily Mail*. Yes, yes, she knew all that. No family. No siblings, no wife, no children. In interviews he joked he was married to whichever newspaper he was working on. And not just in interviews, at all social occasions too. What had Willem called Stu Eliot? The Barnardo's Boy, that was it.

Back to Bud. Joined *The Post* in the mid-eighties. Climbed to the top, buying the paper from its owners when it was threatened with closure. Turned its fortunes around. Acquired a local weekly. A Midlands radio group. Bought Worldwide Listening in Ireland. Nothing new there.

But how many people had he trodden on while on the way up? No one – or very few people – get to be as successful as that without rattling more than a few cages.

But Bud? Really?

Come on, come on, there must be something, surely. Or maybe she was massively wrong. Think. What about the rumours, the very strong rumours, that there were going to be big changes at *The Post*, that jobs were threatened, that there was a sale in the offing?

And then, bingo.

It was a paragraph in the middle of a dry and dusty business article. The Lewes Press Group was about to be sold to a giant Australian media corporation for a whole load of cash. A life-changing amount of cash. Her eyes could hardly take in the sums of money the article writer was quoting. The sale had been gone over by the media regulators and given a clean bill of health.

She thought about what someone might do if they thought that sort of money could be taken away from them.

She thought about what someone might do if they were threatened about a particularly nasty secret from the past.

She thought about the photograph that seemed to be at the heart of all that had been going on.

Alex had only ever looked at it on her phone, but now she transferred it to the big screen of her computer. As ever, it made her sad to see the hope on the faces of the students and to think of the tragedy that was to come. It had been a lovely day when it was taken in that pub garden by the river. There were plenty of people in the background, all enjoying the sunshine: families, couples, students.

She looked closely.

There was one young man, a student, she guessed, sitting at a picnic bench behind Roger, Derek, Willem, and Jen, staring at them. Malevolence shone out of the photo. She enlarged the picture as far as she could without it becoming grainy.

She sat back in her chair.

Bud Evans, also known as Stu Eliot.

'This is all very cloak-and-dagger, Alex,' said Bud, as he lowered himself onto the bench in Riverside Walk Gardens. He took a handkerchief out of his pocket and wiped his forehead. 'Nice day for it, though. Watching the Thames.' He looked around. 'Can't say I've ever sat here.'

'Millbank Prison used to stand here. Convicts were deported to Australia from it.'

'Cheerful.'

Boats travelled with purpose up and down the great river; they didn't meander like on the Broads. Everything about London was urgent, busy, stifling. She was longing to get back to the wide skies of East Anglia. The gentler pace, the space to breathe. But she had wanted to meet Bud here, out in the open. Somewhere safe.

'Well?' he asked.

It was strange to see Bud out of the office. She only ever thought of him behind a desk piled high with papers and barking at hapless members of the editorial team. He had been her friend, her mentor over the years. He had pulled her up when she was at rock bottom. She sipped her coffee. Her stomach was tense. 'Are you Stu Eliot?'

'What are you talking about?' He spoke evenly, without surprise.

'Were you at Cambridge with my dad? And Roger Fleet, Derek Daley, Jen Tamsett and Willem Major?'

'Alex.' He sounded pained.

'Were you?'

Two children began to run up and down the steps near their bench. Their harassed mother called out to them. 'Alfie, Nicky, come on. Please. Now.' A woman posed in front of Henry Moore's *Locking Piece* while her partner took a photo.

'There's only you and me here, Bud.'

'I'm a journalist, remember?'

Alex shrugged. 'I know. But I want to learn the truth. That's all. You were there when Zoe died.'

He blew air out through pursed lips. 'How did you find out about me?'

She was right. '*Middlemarch*.'

'Really?'

'Derek Daley was blackmailing you. Your name was Middlemarch, his was – rather less imaginatively, Double Dee. You were Stu Eliot, then Bud Evans. George Eliot. Mary Anne Evans.' She felt tired now. 'Even your company – The Lewes Press Group – is part of the puzzle. Nothing to do with the town, but called after Mary Anne Evans's lover, George Lewes. A philosopher.'

'Ah. The name was a bit of vanity.' He pulled his e-cigarette out of his pocket. 'However. Not as clever as I thought I was.'

'What I don't understand is that Daley was there the day she died, so he was all part of it too.'

Bud vaped. 'Yes. But he could prove I was involved. He took a picture of me wrapping Zoe's body in my jacket. He was always carrying that damn camera around. And it was only me and Zoe in that picture. There were also other things I did at university that I'm not proud of but that would harm me very badly if they came out. Derek has been a thorn in my side for years. Years. I generally keep out of the limelight, but he saw me somewhere – I don't know where, a dinner I think. I thought I'd changed enough.' He shrugged. 'Obviously I hadn't.'

'So, he began to blackmail you.'

'Threatened to tell the world who I really was. Yes. At first it was nothing very much; no more than I could handle. "To tide me over", he'd say. Of course, blackmailers never stop.'

'And then he found out about the sale of The Lewes Press Group.'

Bud smiled. 'That sale is going to net me a lot of money. Derek wanted more and more. He got too greedy. And I realized that when I sold the company, there could be a lot of publicity and my cover might be blown. More people might recognize me. If Derek wanted more money, what about Roger Fleet? He might not have wanted the cash, but he might have worried about his soul. And Jen? She could have tried something. You see, I reinvented myself after Cambridge. Buried Stu, and Bud was born. It was easy in those days. Probably wouldn't be able to do it now. I'd done some work for the student mag – reviews mostly, but I carried on writing when I left and found I loved it, and I was good at it.' He vaped hard. A helicopter thudded overhead. 'I became a journalist and clambered up the greasy pole. I did well, Alex. I wasn't going to have all that taken away. I knew any one of those people who'd been there when Zoe died could blow the whistle on me.'

'But my father couldn't harm you.'

'I didn't know that. You never told me your father had dementia.'

'Did you know who I was when you gave me my first job?'

Bud turned to her and smiled. 'Of course I did. It amused me to have Tony's daughter in my debt. Mind you, Tony was one of the good guys. His death I would have been sad about.'

'And what about Willem's family?'

'Mickey enjoyed the job a little too much sometimes.'

'You wanted me dead too, Bud.'

'I didn't, not really.' He sounded almost sad. 'But then you wouldn't stop, would you, Alex? I tried to stifle the story and still you carried on.' For the first time he became angry. 'Asking questions. Digging. Ferreting around. Like Heath. Always bloody ferreting.'

'That's what you taught us.'

Bud laughed, anger having subsided. 'Touché. But I couldn't see my life's work blown to bits. I'd worked really hard to build up my company. I started with nothing. Well, not exactly nothing. Willem's father gave me a good wedge to keep me quiet about the dirty drugs underworld Willem Major was involved in. But I built The Lewes Press Group from the bottom up. It's worth a hell of a lot of money now, and I've got a buyer. I can finally lead the life I want to, the life I'm entitled to. There's only you in my way, Alex. But you've got no proof, have you?' Another smile. Smug.

'What secrets might your computer give up?'

'Have you ever heard of the onion router, Alex?' His voice was bored now. 'The dark web? You're not the only one that can use a hacker to help.'

'No,' she said. 'True. Who was Mickey?'

'A man who owed me a favour. You come across all sorts in this game, as you know.' He vaped some more. 'There is no line from Mickey to me. I can be outed as Stu Eliot, but I can't be tied to any of the deaths. The picture of me with Zoe died with Derek. I didn't kill anybody.'

'Except Zoe.'

'It was an accident.'

'If they find her body—'

'They won't. No one knows where it's buried. So no getting DNA to match to mine, even if any has survived.'

'They got DNA from Richard III.'

Bud stood. 'They have to find the body first, Alex.'

He walked away from her towards Tate Britain, then was brought to a stop by a woman and a man. Good old Logan and Berry. At last they'd come in useful. Maybe Bud couldn't be prosecuted for instigating the murders, but taking him in for questioning and perhaps raking up some dirt on him might mean his business deal would fall through. Logan and Berry would do their best.

She got up off the bench. The London air smelled of diesel, hamburgers and sweat. Litter churned lazily at her feet. Traffic came at her from all directions, horns blared, sirens screeched, the sun shone through low cloud. People hurried past her, heads down, peering down at phone screens or at the pavement. Her stomach churned. It had been so hard to confront Bud like that. This was the man who had mentored her, shaped her career, who she almost looked upon as a father figure, who'd helped her when she was at rock bottom. Who had betrayed her trust in him. She was unbearably sad.

It was time to go home now. To Sole Bay and her family.

As she began to walk towards Vauxhall Bridge, something made her look across the road. A man was standing there. Tall, dark-haired, loose-limbed. Even from a distance she could see a smile on his face. He raised his hand.

Malone.

For a moment, time was suspended.

Then she walked on.

41

One Month Later

Alex drew the sharp, briny air into her lungs and leaned against the railings separating the prom from the road. It was a beautiful day with not a cloud in the sky. In another month the beach would be crowded with families coming for their holidays, enjoying the sand and the cold North Sea, but now there were only a few couples, some with babies and toddlers.

'Hey.' Heath's voice.

'Hey yourself.' She smiled as he stood beside her. 'How did you know to find me here?'

'I didn't. I called at your house and you weren't there, so I thought I would have a stroll by the beach just in case.' He tapped his nose. 'Journalist's instinct.'

'Of course. I'd think nothing less.'

'You haven't answered any of my calls. Or texts. For all you knew I could have had a relapse.'

Alex laughed. 'I somehow think you would have told me in one of your numerous messages. Anyway, I did answer some of them.'

'A couple, maybe. With one word like "fine". What does "fine" mean when I ask you how you are?'

'Exactly that.' Alex turned away and gazed out over the sea again. 'There's something about the sea, the way it comes in and goes out. The waves, pulling at the shoreline. It never stops. It's always there.'

'It's called the tide.'

'Very amusing. What I mean is, it's reliable. Whatever else happens, the tide comes in and the tide goes out.'

'Philosophical.'

'I thought Bud would always be there for me. I thought he was one of the good guys.' She sighed. 'I can't get used to calling him Stu. And he was right, you know, what he said to me. The police can't find any tie-up between him and Mickey.'

'No. But they got him on company fraud, insider trading and other financial stuff, so he will go away for a long time.'

'Not long enough.'

'No, but it's better than nothing.'

Alex sighed. 'You never told me why you came back to Sole Bay that night, when you rescued me from my intruder – from Lin?'

'No, I never did.'

'Well?'

'I was getting close to finding out about Bud and who he really was. And my friend had told me that there was someone in Sole Bay connected to Malone. I wanted to make sure you were safe, that's all.' He grinned. 'Maybe take you out for dinner, but the events of the evening put paid to that idea.'

She laughed, then grew sombre. 'Thanks, Heath. But I don't think Mimi would approve.'

'"Mimi"?'

'*Mimi*. The mother of your child. Your partner.'

He raised his eyebrows. 'What makes you think we're an item?'

'Are you kidding me? She was pretty possessive when she came to visit you in hospital.'

'That's just Mimi.'

You have no idea, thought Alex.

'We've agreed on the co-parenting diary.'

'The what?'

'Co-parenting. It's what couples do when they're not together. So Mimi says.'

'Right.'

And ...' She sensed him hesitating. 'Malone? Have you heard anything. My source has come to a complete dead end.'

She gave a wry smile. 'Malone? No. Nothing. I don't expect I will again.'

'So—' He put his hand over hers.

'Not now.' She gently took her hand away.

'You don't know what I was going to say.' His tone was light.

'I think I do.'

He shook his head. 'I was going to say that I've bought *The Post*.'

She looked at him, trying to decide if he was kidding or not. 'You've what?'

'Bought the paper. After all the scandals the group got broken up, and the paper was going pretty cheap. I mean, it was only a minor player at the best of times.' He blushed. 'My mother helped.'

Alex burst out laughing. 'How old are you, Heath? Still relying on the bank of Mum?'

'Not entirely. I've got to pay her back. In time.'

'Okay.' She shook her head, still chuckling.

'I might install myself as news editor.'

'Stop it, Heath. You're making me laugh too much.'

He looked affronted, then became serious. 'There's always a job for you. Staff or freelance.'

She grew sombre. 'I don't know, Heath. What with Gus, and Mum and Dad—'

'Think about it, won't you?'

'I'll think about it.'

He nodded and looked at his watch. 'I'd better get back. You know, being as how I'm an important entrepreneur and all that.'

'Of course.'

He leaned across and kissed her cheek. 'Be seeing you, Alex. By the way …'

'Yes?'

'I know you didn't kill Mickey.' He grinned, then walked away.

'Heath?' she called.

'Yes?'

'I'll be in touch.'

He waved.

***

From the **Peterborough Mail**

An investigation has begun into the mystery of an unmarked grave discovered recently in a 13th century churchyard in Cambridgeshire. The human remains were confirmed by forensic officers after a walker's dog dug up a femur in the graveyard of the abandoned Church of St John, near Wisbech. Detectives descended on the churchyard after the grave was found on Tuesday. Cambridgeshire Police believe it had been dug in the last fifty years. The makeshift grave was concealed by a layer of gravel, which helped protect its contents.

Chief Inspector Ian Childs said: 'At this stage we are trying to find out what's happened. It might be ancient, it might be new, although it's definitely not very new. It's hard to say anything for certain at the moment.

'The grave is situated on the edge of the churchyard, and there are no graves directly next to it. We are appealing for anyone who has information that might help us in our enquiry to contact us.'

Acknowledgements

I want to thank my agent, Teresa Chris, whose support and belief in me knows no bounds. Thanks also to my editor Sarah Hodgson for her insightfulness and enthusiasm for my stories and characters. And I must mention all the team at Killer Reads/Harper Collins who helped push the book out into the world – and Janette Currie who covers up all my punctuation mistakes.

To Jenny Knight, who deserves more bottles of Prosecco than I have given her for her reading of the manuscript and coming up with excellent ideas, and to her family – Jamie, Felix and Max – whose names and expertise I have shamefully borrowed throughout the Alex Devlin series.

Sarah Bower, Susan Rae and Julia Champion, thank you for your support.

And to Melanie McCarthy I just say thank you for everything.

To the book bloggers who do a fantastic job of spreading the #booklove, and especially to you, the readers, who wanted Alex Devlin to live another day.

And to Kim, Edward, Peter and Esme (and their long-suffering partners Emily, Jenni and Nick), love and thanks. I couldn't have done any of this without you.

KILLER READS

DISCOVER THE BEST
IN CRIME AND THRILLER

Follow us on social media to get to know the team behind the books, enter exclusive giveaways, learn about the latest competitions, hear from our authors, and lots more:

 /KillerReads    /KillerReads